774

1st ed

Fd

THE LOST REBELLION

THE LOST

A NOVEL BY

 TRIDENT PRESS

REBELLION

JAMES WYLIE

Beginning to think is beginning to be undermined. Society has but little connection with such beginnings. The worm is in man's heart. That is where it must be sought.

ALBERT CAMUS

And tell me who sews the ribbons all over the general's chest? who carves the capon for the usurer? who proudly dangles an Iron Cross from his rumbling navel? who rakes in the tip, the thirty pieces of silver, the hush money? listen: there are plenty of victims, very few thieves; who's the first to applaud them, who pins on the merit badge, who's crazy for lies?

HANS MAGNUS ENZENBURGER

THE LOST REBELLION

CHAPTER ONE

THE TINY ROOM behind the stage was crowded when James got there. All five men in the protection detail were loading their pistols from a box of copper-jacketed .38 cartridges on the table. In one corner Brother Nicholas sat on a folding chair studying the introduction he had written out on a yellow legal pad. As James entered everyone nodded politely. No one said much. They rarely did in the minutes before Brother Miles delivered his Sunday lecture to the faithful. James double-checked the bodyguards and dispatched them to their posts. Then he went up on stage and supervised the lowering of a grand but faded red curtain.

"I want some pink lights on that curtain," he snapped.

"Yes, sir, Brother James," came a quick answer out of the wings.

He checked his watch. Ten minutes to go and Miles had not arrived yet. He was always late—partly for the sake of drama and partly from innate caution, an involuntary waywardness he had taken on during his years as a street hustler.

Out in front the orchestra was filling up rapidly. Groups of black people came in past the guards and looked around with something like relief, as if they had reached some destination

9

in their lives that was very important to them. A few people appeared in the balcony seats. From the stage they seemed demure and very still. James had counted five white people when Brother Nicholas came out and said Miles wanted to see him.

As he crossed the stage, James nervously ran through the list of details under his authority. Everything checked perfectly and he was pleased because Miles hated small mistakes in the program. More than once in the past he'd gone into a rage over the failure of a spotlight or a microphone, but since James took charge, all of these blunders had disappeared. James was very efficient and he knew it. A ridiculous, almost petty sense of pride touched him as he went into the backstage room and saw Miles break off his conversation with another Brother and come up to him.

For the briefest of moments Miles said nothing. He hadn't seen James for three days and he wanted to examine him, for Miles always marveled at how far this man had come. Brother James Fitzgerald, despite his studied and morose earnestness, was brilliantly dependable and precise. He possessed a pride in what the Brotherhood was doing. He conveyed its infallibility and its stoutness, and for this Miles valued and trusted him a bit more than most men. But he had good reasons for this. He had found James wandering the downward spiral into insanity and carried him up on his back. With an undeniable accuracy Miles sensed the prize was worth the burden. The two men shook hands warmly and easily. Their eyes showed something like affection.

"How does it look out there?" Miles asked briskly.

"Its looking pretty good," James replied.

"Fine, tell Brother Nicholas to put the African student on first."

"Yes, sir," James said earnestly.

On stage a huge white-and-crimson satin banner proclaiming the New Brotherhood of Islam had been tacked to the main curtain. Seven small wooden folding chairs stood in a line beneath it. At each end a vigilant bodyguard sat uneasily and scanned the audience. To everyone's surprise, there was a white man up there too, a woefully nervous, lanky gentleman from the state of Oregon who was a long-time Communist and said he knew how to dismantle the capitalist system without chaos. An Arab wearing a fez, one of the two student guests, languidly went over his notes, while a young man from Ghana surveyed the large and now voluble audience with unconcealed delight, imagining it to be a crowd in some dusty African market town awaiting his royal absolution; a feeling of expectation, almost tangible in its presence, permeated the decrepit old movie theater. Only the television people working over their cameras and lights in the rear were untouched by it all.

At last the African student, confidently aware of a tape recorder sitting on the stage a few feet away, began his speech. It did not go as well as he had hoped. Slowly he rambled through a list of Africa's problems and came up with a few pompous and rhetorical conclusions. "In closing may I say that what is working in Africa today can and should work here. It requires teamwork, nothing more." The applause was steady and polite, then quite suddenly it spilled over into an obsessive torrent of hand clapping. Without turning around the student accepted with a nobility he did not possess; he had turned to sit down again when finally he caught sight of the imposing and gracious figure of Brother Miles hovering in the doorway leading onstage, hovering between a kind of shyness and an allure that grew bolder and more pronounced as he plunged through the atmosphere of exhilaration and strode to the rostrum. The introduction was forgotten. The television crew went to work as dazzling lights materialized and threw over Miles an aura of overwhelming magnetism and stardust.

"Brothers and Sisters, *Salaam Aleikum,*" he cried.

"*Aleikum Salaam,*" they roared in a voice heightened nearly to frenzy.

"We have come together this evening to discuss our fate as a people," Miles shouted.

There was an enormously heavy groan, but it was whimsical and did not express any real disappointment. Miles grinned softly into the microphone. The audience, knowing its secret was out, responded with lighthearted laughter. A splash of respectful clapping applauded Miles's perspicacity, but arrogantly he waved it off and allowed a still moment to pass so expectation could enter the scene. Only then did Miles begin to talk. His voice was loud, guttural, slightly urgent, but not unpleasant once the ear portrayed its rhythms. It held only a little of the effervescence often found in black voices and that was compressed into the acute, slashing phrases that fired animosity and pride, hatred and euphoria so spectacularly in the minds of his listeners that it was not unusual to hear him eagerly quoted for weeks after he had spoken on a particular subject. And as he stood there before them, stark and powerful, with all the mysterious solemnity of a primitive statue on a far mountaintop, the enraptured black throng jammed into the old movie house once more perceived that Miles was attempting to inculcate in it the eternal wisdom of vanished ancestors they'd never been allowed to know. No objections were raised. No one challenged the commanding voice filling up Brotherhood Hall, for Miles possessed the glitter and allure, the quintessential arrogant glamour of a mythical leader. All that was known of him, his arduous life, his flare for fame, his angry style, his scathing shibboleths, all these facts had been absorbed by his audience as thoroughly as if they were radioactive emissions. And artfully, with a touch of snobbish ease Miles assured them he alone embodied all their perceptions and yearnings.

As he spoke, in the hard, even rise and fall of his powerful voice, the audience felt his strength. This was the force they had come to be near; for everything Miles dealt with sounded so irrefutable, so mythic that the swarm of reverential and anxious people extending out from the rostrum in neat packed rows believed it had been said a hundred thousand times before. Intuitively they were sure the phrasing came out of the antiquity of their race, that the very words quite possibly were carved on a stone now sitting in the dank basement of some prestigious museum, undeciphered and scorned. In a spasm of pique forgotten black kings and deposed emperors must have spoken this way. There was nothing to disprove it. The language was hypnotic, ceremonial, and infused with the driving ritualistic fervor of a sacrifice around the bonfire. The clever patterning of words was more symbolic than literal or specific, more rhetorical than enlightening. And all of it had the magical righteousness always employed by true leaders, the weighty pride likely to be heard again on occasions in future epochs when a distant star cluster was about to be annexed by our planet. Then abruptly, in the middle of the inaudible but wild ardor he loved so completely, Miles subtly altered the tone of his remarks. He became brisk and a little impatient. Two or three vernacular expressions came through the microphone. The audience knew its initial fun was over.

"Calm down," he demanded, "we have important things to discuss this afternoon. All you people out there who scrub floors during the week, I'm talking to you. You people who sit in the park all day minding rich babies, turn your ear to what I say," Miles cried suddenly. "You have been cheated all your lives! You've been sold cheap. Those miles of floors you've mopped probably stretch from here to the moon, but if you mop for the rest of your days, all you'll ever see when you're through is the reflection of something bunchy and fat bent over next to a pail just like a cow would be. That's you! That's what this country thinks of you or any man it can't tip its hat to. Mark my words when I tell you that you have more in common with our Brothers sitting right here"—he gestured to the students behind him—"than you'll ever have with that spoiled kid they pay you slave wages to play momma to."

A great spontaneous cheer leapt up from the orchestra. One small group of women in African turbans jumped up and down gleefully, doing a little shimmying dance. Behind the oak rostrum Miles mopped his brow elegantly. He was just beginning.

A bit of warm zest, a suggestion of something intimately passionate crept into the voice now controlling everything within its range. Yet there was a trace of admonition in his

13

tone as Miles prepared to repeat again what he believed was the great elusive theme of his movement and his life: the merciless necessity in all men, and especially in the exhausted and sometimes feckless black man, to rise up and combat life; the drastic need in all human beings to be more than they essentially were. The permutations of this thesis were familiar and imposing to most of the audience. Some people sat with displeasure, their arms folded, preferring for the moment to betray no emotion. But secretly even the anxious Brothers and Sisters peering up respectfully at Miles speaking behind the massive rostrum knew he asked too much. They did not comprehend what was meant by discovering the meaning of one's life. The struggle for individuality sounded like something out of a library book. Self-exploration held terrifying possibilities. And they understood more keenly than Miles that battling the worst things in yourself was an idealist's silly fantasy. Miles was again asking more than he had any right to, but he did it beautifully. Everyone noticed that now and then a terrible poignancy suffused his face, a stricken rapt expression, which aroused curiosity and wariness. For in this strange agony it was clear Miles wanted the pure fulfillment of his will over the complexities of life. Reverently all wished him well, especially if he could bring back some luck for them. And as Miles finished his message there was something like an extended silence throughout the hall. It was not a cold break in communication, just a wordless, deeply thankful expression of approval and respect for the speaker.

"Brothers and Sisters in Islam, I want to issue a warning now. Do not ever let yourselves be fooled. Only the man who is on guard can really see what he's up against and not form the wrong alliances," Miles said slowly, casting a full range of baleful and threatening glances at the handful of white people in the audience.

"Remember, our friends in the world grow stronger each day. Six months ago I attended the Afro-Asian Peoples Conference in Djakarta, Indonesia. I talked with many heads of state in your behalf. These people recognized me as your formal representative at the conference. They sent you their greetings and, let me tell you, I firmly believe that in the end they are our only real allies. Remember that!" Now he spoke in a loud voice tremulous with outrage. "Remember what I've told you today. It's the only way, the only possible way to put an end to our sickness and our terrible affliction."

People began to clap sporadically as Miles went into his finale. Slowly and deliberately he brought his clenched fists to his breast and began a lengthy, righteous diatribe whose agonized language came not from the Muslim God Allah or his disciples, but from the spirit of hardened Puritans begging warily for divine justice. The ambiguous haughty phrases, the exalted rectitude being shouted by Miles recalled from forgotten histories all the stiffness and boiling frustration and frontier morality of a hard-faced Puritan congregation in some bitter, little New England settlement now a century passed into dust. And beyond the dazzling words whose roots and nuances could never quite express enough emotion, Miles knew everything he said this day was an embittered demand for recompense from America, a demand bound to go unheard, a futile cry, but a peculiar one, for it came out of a world where genuine retribution had never really been possible. A squalid, exotic place where humiliation was never cheated, where no one could be trusted or untainted enough to warrant personal involvement on such a grand, transcendental issue. Only Miles could even make it believable. He was the only living person strong enough to do it and he held this power by the grace of one unshakable virtue: Miles was innocence. He was the repentant whimper of the stumblebum in the gutter that touched even the most callous men and made them shudder. He was the hope in the eyes of a porter gone off to the racetrack for a long day of degradation. Miles was the man at the door selling a twenty-four volume set of books about the world. The magic in his art sustained the unlucky lives of numbers runners, junkies, queers, white-collar thieves, alcoholic housewives; his was the voice forever crying out that pitiful phrase: please, don't make me do it!

15

The audience got to its feet as his address reached its climax. People began to shriek and scream uncontrollably in a rising tribute of noisemaking and emotion welling up out of a thousand suddenly awakened souls just barely in control. It was a horrible noise, a maddened and violent sound that threatened to carry the whole meeting away, and for a few tense minutes Miles feared he had finally lost control of them. Frantically he waved his arms for quiet. Ushers ran up and down the aisles testily demanding silence, but the demonstration went on with a violently heedless unanimity, which refused to abate and died down very reluctantly ten minutes later when the audience realized somehow that Miles was furious with it.

The highly amplified voice, tense and angry, seemed to surround them with heavenly recrimination. "How many times, Brothers and Sisters, have I asked you never to do that? How many times," Miles pleaded, "have I told you not to bring those revival church manners in here? We are a religion dedicated to decorum and progress. I've said that too I think. So please try to be different. Try to act out what you want to be. I hope I can count on you for at least that much after all our years together."

He enunciated these last words very harshly, and quickly shuffled some papers on the rostrum. The audience, sensing his mood, silenced completely. Then Miles spoke again. His tone was informative, and businesslike.

"Now next week we will discuss some of the political and economic aspects of our struggle. But now I want you to listen to these Brothers sitting up here behind me. Then we will have a question period."

James opened the stage door and watched Miles walk toward him. He looked graceful and exultant like a great athlete coming in off the field.

"I think you ought to rest it for a few minutes, Miles. You've got a TV panel show tonight."

Miles allowed himself a tight little smile. Never had he let fame conceal from him the vast and tenuous complexity of his relationship with the American people. He knew television had made him a star of sorts; and he wondered if this night would not mark the inevitable moment when Americans felt, quite subtly, that he'd exceeded their imaginations and stomped their sensibilities just once too many times. He lay an affectionate hand on his lieutenant's shoulder. "I haven't forgotten the show, Brother James."

"Never mind that. I want you to rest," James said a little helplessly.

"Yes, sir, Brother James," Miles said as he stretched out on a folding cot. "I promise not to collapse until you have all been saved," he intoned playfully in the full, rich voice of the classic black preacher. "Call me after the last speaker."

Almost immediately Miles was asleep, pulled deep down into an even slumber by the nervousness, suspicion, and impossible aspirations of all his days and half his nights. As the muffled noise from the auditorium receded, Miles roamed the plains of Abyssinia and the African savanna, stalking through the virginal silence to find and destroy his enemies, real or mythological, wherever they appeared. James did not leave the room. He sat down at the table with some papers and busied himself with the tedious work he'd taken refuge in. He felt protected, and in a prideful way, rather important. Deep down he knew Miles had pushed him hard to achieve this little conceit, and James was very grateful.

Not long after midnight James arrived home. He noticed something in his mailbox and took out a large picture postcard of downtown New York with the United Nations complex standing prominently in the foreground. It was from someone who said she was an old girl friend, but he had great difficulty placing her, and besides he wondered why mail had been delivered on Sunday.

CHAPTER TWO

IT WAS SHORTLY after ten in the morning when James left his apartment, one of the two he maintained, and set out for the United Nations. The harsh, late winter sun fell on the upper stories of the tenements across the street and made weird patterns as it broke and angled down through the fire escapes and stretched crazy designs across the weathered brick faces of all the buildings leading up the hill to Broadway. At the top of the hill he surveyed the little groups of men standing around speaking Spanish in tones of half-tragic despair.

These were his neighbors, a host of Puerto Ricans and dark-skinned Cubans who knew only the empty despair of jobless-ness and the small, sweet pleasures of cheap cold beer, furi-ously intimate conversation, and sidewalk games of dominoes, which seemed never to end. This morning James envied their idleness, but he could not say why because the whole rigid, controlled structure of his emotions wavered badly under a premonition too vague for him to define. Sometime during the night the meaning of that innocent postcard in the mailbox had come to him and destroyed his composure. Now squinting against the morning glare, he looked around once more and attempted to ward off his fears. For a clear moment he understood he should not be going out this particular morning; yet he knew the courage to do anything else had seeped out of him as soon as he realized a summons was in his hands.

He took the subway. It was a boring ride all the way downtown from 137th Street to Times Square but he experienced a touch of ominous excitement as the shuttle train came into Grand Central and he mingled with the quick, huge, flowing crowds. Swiftly he made his way to the street and began walking eastward toward the river. Between First and Second avenues the block seemed empty, even lonely, and James was tempted to turn back. But then he reached the corner and saw the great United Nations Secretariat Building presiding over a small, mathematically conceived plaza with the General Assembly Hall sloping off to one side. It's all very noble, he thought to himself seriously.

At the gate a guard wanted to know which office he was going to.

"Economic Committee on Asia and the Far East," he said.

"Fine, you may obtain a pass at the desk."

"Thank you."

He walked across the plaza with its enormous circular fountain and went into the building. A dark-haired girl at the desk, who answered her telephone in three languages, called upstairs and then politely wrote out a pass. The elevator noiselessly deposited him on the twentieth floor, where he was met by a pretty blonde secretary who was perhaps a Dane.

"Mr. Fitzgerald?"

She had a very sunny smile, but James deliberately looked away before replying. Very good-looking women made him nervous. He never knew what they wanted.

"This way, please," she said pleasantly.

In the corridor an international group passed them looking peculiar, otherworldly, and affected as if they really didn't belong together and were not. James was led into an outer office, the secretary announced him, and he was ushered in. As the large mahogany door closed softly behind him, a little Pakistani gentleman came around from behind his big desk. He was small, James thought, terribly small.

"James," he said with some delight.

"Sir," James replied tentatively, not sure of what emotion to show with a man he'd never seen before.

"I'm glad to know we could still get in touch with you," the little man said warmly. They shook hands very formally. It was quiet in the room. A low hum emanated from somewhere beyond the walls. "Look," the Pakistani suddenly announced in a voice sounding very English, "why don't we go to the lounge and talk. No one will be there at this hour. Everyone is at an important debate in the Security Council."

The Delegates Lounge was cool and rarified. Steel-and-leather Mies van der Rohe furniture sat elegantly on vast thick green carpets resembling very old and fine English lawns. A large picture window looked out upon the roof of the General Assembly Building which, together with the hard blue sky and the East River beyond, formed an abstract, architectural vista, beautiful and completely deserted. They settled down into leather armchairs as a waiter who had watched them enter came up with two glasses of Scotch and a small ice bucket.

"I don't drink," James said apologetically. "My religion forbids it."

"Not at all?" the Pakistani asked with a touch of merriment in his tone. "Well then," he said to the waiter mischievously, "bring us an orange squash or something."

James eyed him coolly. Dr. George Mahanti was well dressed in a heavy dark-blue suit of British cut. His dainty shoes were Italian and quite expensive. The tie he wore had the emblem of Trinity College, Cambridge, woven into it. James wondered why they had sent such a peculiar little man.

"You know," Mahanti said in a professorial way, "with us it is the rule to be casual. It is the Russians who are insanely clandestine. Why it would not be possible to sit here with a member of the NKVD, or the KGB, or whatever they call themselves this year, and indulge in a civilized discussion. The backs of their necks would be bright pink. They never leave the atmosphere of Russia behind. The American informers around here know this of course. It is a trait they count on."

To James it was apparent a smile was expected of him, but he refused. A trace of suspicion ran through his mind. The morning had made him edgy and now a surge of anger was building up on the slight fatigue he'd been unable to shake. He listened to his host irritably. And suddenly he heard his voice speaking out very softly, trying to screen away its little strains of indignation.

"Why did you send for me?" he asked.

There was in this question a tightness and hostility that surprised Mahanti, but he did not show it. He merely switched to a more formal level of conversation. "I wanted to see you. I wanted to see what you looked like. It would have been easy for me to just send you a message, but you see, I've very special orders for you," Mahanti said evenly. "It occurred to me only a highly capable person could execute them."

James sighed heavily to relieve the tension that had now spread to every muscle. He knew Mahanti was staring at him so he glanced out of the window and spied a tugboat moving slowly over the placid surface of the East River. He wanted to bolt the lounge and run from the building; he wanted to disappear, but a saturating oppression, inseparable from his weariness, forced James to remain where he was, and this fed his anger. His mind struggled to account for his surroundings. He was sure after four whole years he'd been forgotten, overlooked, or dismissed. A touch of despair and self-pity wormed through him and ignited his ire. He turned to Mahanti again.

"Do me a favor," he said harshly, "and put down that drink."

The other man smiled back at James tolerantly, as if he could read his confused thoughts. He continued to sip from the glass. James glared at him. A rage was gradually taking control of him. Without warning he leaned across the small white table between them and whispered savagely, "If you were half the limey you think you are, you'd know a real gentleman doesn't start drinking before noon."

Mahanti's eyes narrowed. A look of genuine discomfort passed over his thin, haughty face. Obstinately he drained his glass before putting it down.

The two men slowly made their way across the plaza to the main gate. Mahanti had an apartment in a hotel on East 44th Street and James demanded they go there. Not a word passed between them until Mahanti opened his front door. "This is it. A little bit of home," he said happily.

It was rather beautiful. The product of a lush and frivolous hand. In style everything was Chippendale except a magnificent Regency sideboard against one wall. On top of it, crowded off to one side were half a dozen oversized cut-glass decanters of liquor. Nothing one could see was from Pakistan.

Mahanti turned on a table lamp to dispel the late morning gloom slanting through the apartment. He sat down carefully and tried to remember the most pertinent details from the file of the black man standing before him. Fitzgerald was a war hero, he recalled that clearly; but not a major chestful-of-ribbons-and-medals hero. No, Fitzgerald had been a minor combat star, a murderous, implacable destroyer—the kind of man every squad must have to be effective. And it showed in the sloping of those strong shoulders into a pose that was sullen and adolescent and obscurely dangerous. He motioned for him to sit down, but James petulantly shifted his weight from one foot to the other and stood leaning on the back of a chair.

Mahanti gave a contemptuous little snort. "You're a very unfinished young man," he said with clipped distaste as his eyes roved over the face opposite him noting a tiny, fretful network of lines that bracketed a peevish mouth ready to spit obscenities.

"This is a rough country," James answered irritably.

"Yes," Mahanti said, looking around the elegant room.

James sensed the insult in this and pounced. "What the hell do you know about it?" he asked with a snarl.

Mahanti looked straight back at him, attempting through

concentration to conceal his delighted surprise at the agitation and worry in everything Fitzgerald said. Like an upper-class English actor a studied expression of extreme forbearance creased his face. He did not know James had already seen the depths of lingering amazement in his dark eyes. "Look, do not misunderstand me," he said just a bit too quickly. "We are in the same movement. Surely you must appreciate the fact that my sympathies are entirely with your people. In Pakistan, in the entire Third World, the scale of daily suffering and personal anguish is unimaginable. Isn't that why we are here together? Isn't that what we are struggling to correct?"

"We're not struggling to correct anything," James said fiercely. He was attempting to offend and goad Mahanti in the vague hope of being dismissed as unreliable. "We are at war." He sounded a little like Miles now, and this lifted his confidence.

But Mahanti sensed he had an edge here. "Not exactly," he snapped. "Remember what you were taught. Our goal is the spread of controlled chaos. We want to establish the idea of rebellion, to turn disorder on and off. We are a band of insurgents, not an army. When you speak of war, it sounds very rash to me."

"It is war," James insisted, knowing he'd faltered a bit and been drawn into an argument he didn't want. Anger and irritation were betraying him but he felt an urge to continue talking and humiliate Mahanti. "How else can you get freedom?" he asked more reasonably.

The bare suggestion of a smile touched Mahanti's face. The discussion was turning his way. He liked being asked questions.

"You might have started by working for it sooner," he replied testily.

"We've been working at it for generations," James said, abruptly raising his voice. He wanted to shout, to rage, to push Mahanti away, for working within him was a knowledge that his force had slackened and this, in some terrible way, meant

23

far more than just losing an argument. "Revolts are nothing new in this country," he continued, fighting off the deepening sensation that Mahanti had very accurately insinuated his protests were childish or worse, irresponsible.

"Of course," Mahanti came back smoothly, "they gave a class on that sort of thing, in Switzerland I believe. But ah . . . Brother James is it now?" The smile was sardonic, rather wicked. James felt an involuntary little shudder creep up his back. He nodded obediently.

"Brother James, it seems to me that in your haste to defend your people you neglect to deal with the question of political organization. You have had leaders, as you say. However, they all seem to perish before any real organization gets underway. Why is that?"

James felt trapped. He would begin making excuses now, advancing the very arguments he hated. Mahanti was too clever for him. A fear and loathing of the man was taking possession of him. "It's always been difficult," he began tentatively. "Leaders have been bought off, killed. We have been raised in an environment that precludes genuine leadership." He sounded hollow and knew it. Mahanti's keen eyes followed him closely, egging him onward. "We are a minority, don't you see?" he said with a plea in his voice which turned quickly to a desperate, harsh anger. "We are not the Chinese or the Pakistanis living on each other's backs."

"And that is why you need China I suppose."

"Go to hell," James shouted.

"You sound American. That is your mistake. You accept the American system while the system does nothing for you." Mahanti was half out of his chair, speaking rapidly, articulately, and jabbing his finger at James. "To be frank, from what I see of you now, I'm afraid you think your feelings and your half-witted ideas are more important than what you were sent here to do. That is what you think, isn't it?"

Mahanti observed James shrewdly until he saw a look of bewildered defeat flee across his adversary's face.

A full minute went by, then James spoke again, this time in

a voice full of dutiful self-reproach. "I believe the pure Marxist-Leninist system adhered to by Mao Tse-tung must be set up in America for blacks to have any freedom at all. Anything and anyone must be sacrificed to bring this about, including me."

Mahanti was visibly pleased. "Now you sound a bit more intelligent," he said smugly. "Peking is counting on you to make black Americans see their destiny."

James said nothing. He sat down quietly. The chair he took was much too small for his large frame and this discomfort only increased the stinging humiliation he experienced at having his loyalty questioned by a sniveling minor functionary. But there was no one more powerful he could appeal to and he burned for revenge. For whole seconds his anger became unbearable and he thought of knocking Mahanti to the floor and watching him writhe there like a crippled, quivering bird about to die. Vaguely through his fury James could hear the little man babbling on. "The colored peoples of this earth are the future, James, and I know you want your people to be part of the future."

Finally he broke into the empty monologue. His voice was bitter and fiery, but Mahanti was already accustomed to all this. "You weren't sent here to deliver a major address! Where the hell are my orders?" he demanded.

"In a minute, sir," Mahanti said in a condescending tone. Abruptly he got up and left James. Walking away with a surprising quickness, he disappeared into the bedroom; almost immediately he returned with a long brown envelope closed with a wax seal. "The embassy in Bern has asked me to tell you that Peking considers this the most important operation we have yet undertaken in the United States."

James rose from his chair slightly bewildered. "Thank you," he said slowly and politely. Then he went to the door and let himself out.

Mahanti sat down in one of his Chippendale chairs. Soon he was due back at the building. In half an hour a delegation from the Kobe Steel Works in Japan would arrive at his office, and after that he had scheduled an informal talk with students from the Malagasy Republic. He hoped he had succeeded in making James angry enough to do an exceptional job. And with that he went over to the sideboard and poured himself a drink. He felt he deserved it.

CHAPTER THREE

WHEN JAMES FINALLY got home it was late afternoon. A long, meandering walk had taken him over half of Manhattan, from the United Nations over to Fifth Avenue, then in and out of the dormant wilderness of Central Park several times, and eventually over to the West Side. There he made his stolid way across the gigantic mock heroic campus of Columbia University before heading up Broadway under the enormous steel arches of the El trestle to the noisy and suppurating Puerto Rican neighborhood where he lived. Not once did he forget the envelope in his pocket.

Slowly he went through his small apartment into a dingy kitchen where he poured a glass of cold soda, although what he really wanted was the pleasantly searing trickle of whiskey gulped from a shot glass. After a few minutes he sat down heavily at the kitchen table without taking off his overcoat and withdrew the envelope from his pocket in an absent and reluctant way, imagining he watched his movements from a secret vantage point within the room. It was an ordinary number ten envelope he held in his hand. If it weren't for the bright red wax seal he might have guessed it was a bill. Inside an easily deciphered message (he was astonished at how fluently his mind picked through the rows of numbers and symbols), typed on cheap onionskin paper, said tersely that he was to arrange, as soon as possible, for the assassination of the black American leader Miles King and then wait for a postal signal. That was all. There was no word of greeting, no suggestion of personal inquiry, just an order that seemed oddly ridiculous and removed from his life. For moments at a time he struggled to comprehend the simple message before him with all the vividly reluctant clarity of someone reading a death notice. He even tried to laugh when he realized how far the message had come. But suddenly a feeling of immense and bitter loneliness spread over him. Quickly and violently he fought it down, as he did almost any emotion that threatened to overcome his senses and propel him madly beyond the strictures of reason. It was not too difficult. For years he had grappled with panic and won.

As afternoon blackened into night outside his windows, James meditated on the petty and amateur way the system worked, recalling without effort a whole string of pathetic little scandals that had made the ministry a joke in embassy drawing rooms around the world. In Bern they explained these failures by claiming the system was not yet perfected. At every lecture the instructors, who remained nameless, assured them patiently that when things functioned at peak efficiency the West would shudder with internal dissension. Most agents in training believed this, and the remarkable run of success in Africa kept morale fairly high. In keeping with the Chinese tradition, they were as enthralled and captured with the beauty of what the ministry was doing as they had been on the day of recruitment.

For him it all began during the Korean War. One afternoon while on furlough, he went sightseeing alone at Tokyo University. He marveled at the serenity of the place and felt uncomfortably tough and conspicuous in his American army uniform, but he wanted to try out a little of his phrase-book Japanese and find a pretty Japanese girl to be nice to. That first excursion was a failure. No one even noticed him and he went back to his hotel worried about the descent into the frenetic world of the guys on leave, into the world of filthy over-crowded bars, back alley brawls, and the defeated whores who wore long American skirts and possessed flat, ravenous eyes that forever haunted every man who dealt with them.

On his fourth visit to the university he struck up a friend-ship. A group of students, who noticed the lonely black Ameri-can soldier with his camera always in the case, began a conver-sation with him as he sat disconsolately on a bench. They spoke careful English and almost immediately wanted to know all about the war. James didn't know what to say. He knew he vaguely opposed the war. It seemed to him a political mistake, a squalid miniature conflict wrapped up in the rhetoric of vi-sionary politics. He was completely unprepared for their vio-lent denunciation of it as a deliberately provoked imperialist-racist attack. But he was very lonely and a little curious about their beliefs.

Every evening for the remainder of his furlough was spent at the Free Students Union Club, where they discussed politics endlessly, wore foppish Billy Eckstine collars, and did the lindy hop. The club, everyone told him, was a place of protest against the timidity and mass conformity the older generation wallowed in, and Professor Siato, the club's faculty adviser, took great care in explaining to James just what the sins of the elders were.

Siato was a short, pipe-smoking, very handsome Japanese with vaguely Western features and impeccable Eastern man-ners. He showed James all of Tokyo: the heaped, rotting prole-tarian enclaves where people stared at visitors in mute unctu-ous fear, and the smooth elegance of famous restaurants James had never heard of. Once he suggested an auto trip to Hiro-shima, but James refused to go. In a way Siato was the perfect Communist intellectual, an utterly smooth dialectician, clever, engaging, a brilliant talker who opened areas of historical understanding without all the dreary reasoning. There was nothing of the doomsday attitude in anything he said. For Siato communism was a vibrant part of life, almost as prac-ticed and familiar as the tea ceremony or the art of arranging flowers. After a while James began to see a certain order in it too.

When James returned on his next furlough Siato went to work on him again. He loved to discuss the progress of the Korean War, and sensing that James wasn't sure what he was fighting for, he began in a roundabout way to play upon this uncertainty. One afternoon as they strolled through the campus, Siato told James that he was struck by his individuality. "You are quite remarkable," he said admiringly. "A soldier who keeps his identity. In the Japanese army no one could do that. It was impossible. We trotted around"—he mimicked their movements—"and took orders with humble fervor. And of course we lost the war," he added humorously. "You Americans burned down our cities and made us a nation of beggars for a while."

"When you say Americans, don't include me in that. I thought dropping the bomb was awful."

"I know. I'm not blaming you, or even America necessarily. In her position we might have done the same thing. It merely points out how one's historical philosophy can force decisions the people are not always ready to face. Take this detestable war in Korea, James. One of the reasons it continues, I believe, is that the Chinese, even though their legitimate regime is but four years old, are being forced to fight by their belief that America and the West can be successfully confronted and turned back in this part of the world. In Peking they see many dividends in this fight. They think this effort should be made to show other countries, notably the Indochinese states and Malaya, what properly motivated Asians can accomplish. Nations always abide by their concept of what events mean even if they're plainly mistaken. In nineteen forty-five having the bomb meant to Americans that it had to be dropped. They believed it was the magical instrument that could knock out Japan forever and make the Russians cherish the idea of peace. Now China believes that same power can be confronted on land and overwhelmed. As a fighting soldier, you must know this philosophy is being proven out every day. Your position is not that good." And then in a smooth cheerful voice, "America claims this war is a police action. China says it advances a theory of history."

James didn't reply and they walked on in silence for a few minutes before Siato asked, "What do you believe, my friend?"

Whenever someone asked this question, James was inwardly startled. He didn't possess a well-formulated view of life like Siato. He had never thought of himself as holding any philosophical or political beliefs. As one of half a dozen black students at a tiny New England college, he'd simply contented himself with a pleasant manner and excellent grades. Generally he felt isolated and the enforced communal life of the army had done little to relieve his solitude. In a vaguely American way he believed in individual liberty and freedom, whatever that was. It was only later on in Bern where his instructors told him that all the values he had accepted—his education, conventional morality, hard work, freedom—were all part of the infrastructure of capitalism, a pernicious system of irrelevant, platitudinous associations exerting an invisible force that kept him in check, a submissive and, from the standpoint of history, an uninteresting human being. At that juncture the logic of what they said could not have been more apparent.

With his friendly and unending round of questions, Siato began to draw James closer to him. They were very good friends now and on every leave James faithfully returned to the university. Imperceptibly his life divided itself into two parts. One was the fantastic world of the front in Korea where men died shrieking horribly and lay mutilated along the mountain roads, eyes transfixed with that air of suspended disbelief all dead people have. The other was Siato's world of casual communism, the university, Friday night dances spoiled by lingering disgust and guilt.

Almost effortlessly Siato burdened James with guilt for the war. For weeks on end, especially when he saw James wanted to discuss it, he would ignore the subject and shrug off leading questions. Then he would ask how the war was going with a great show of enthusiasm before retreating into silence again.

31

James began to feel their friendship was failing. He could not understand why Siato seemed a little reserved, even slightly put out when they met. It disturbed him tremendously. He blamed himself and questioned his role as a soldier. He searched the motives of the officers and the other men and found them brutal, mindless, riddled with petty hatreds, and as he moved through this maze of associations a great loathing and self-contempt grew inside of him.

His guilt ballooned, but still his mind mapped out certain reservations. If he looked at things Siato's way, he was merely a despicable pawn. But Siato was an intellectual encumbered by theories. In Korea there were no intellectuals. Discursive thinking of any kind faded into eternity, leaving only the pure and deeply thrilling experience of combat. James loved combat. He cherished the moment of concentrated fear and emotion everyone felt before an attack. In battle he fought wildly, manfully throwing himself into the act of obliteration with a fierce virtuosity that almost frightened the hardened soldiers around him. Three times he won medals for stunning accomplishments of bravery. In a small way he was a legend and everyone respected him, but he had no friends. There was in his manner something above the ordinary limits of jocularity and warmth found in army comradeships. No one ever dared suggest to him what it was, but around the card tables and honky-tonk joints in Seoul he was known as a lone and possibly crazed killer, an animal who went on silent feet to the ritual of murder and returned soaked and fouled by the enemy's blood. It never occurred to anyone that because of his prowess James Fitzgerald was becoming a lost and drifting personality ready to divide against himself. Here Professor Siato stepped in as a friend once more.

They no longer talked about the war. Siato knew he had a potential agent on his hands. Carefully he studied and probed James for personal information. He inquired into his background, friends, education. Did he always have feelings of isolation? Was he secretive as a child? What did he want from life? Gradually the portrait of an intelligent, amazingly ambivalent, fearful, and overly righteous man emerged. There was also a hidden fierceness, a great well of enormous latent anger which appealed to Siato. As a man who depended on his inner resources of strength, James at that stage of his life was a horrendous failure. Siato, in his insidious way, made all of this absolutely clear, knowing the pain it caused his friend would open him up for what was coming next. Then he began his real task.

One day when they were walking in a remote part of the campus Siato asked, "You are a Negro and a brave man. Why are you fighting other colored peoples in a war that troubles you?"

For a while James said nothing. Automatically he tried to fall back on something plausible, something sane, but it was no longer there. "Because I'm being used," he replied with stunned resignation.

After that Siato found it easier. He looked for the signs of change and found them. James was edgier, not in any particular way, just in general. He talked more freely and recklessly. He hated discrimination violently. Siato inquired if it existed in the army, and James told him bitter tales about Toyko bars where Negroes were never invited in, and thrown out to a chorus of whooping and cursing if somehow they strayed in by mistake.

"Don't these people have a point? I mean in America your Constitution guarantees the individual the right to associate with whom he pleases."

"Yes it does, and I hate the whole rotten system."

"Do you?" Siato asked cautiously.

"Why not, what the hell has it done to protect my feelings?"

It went on that way. Siato built up a level of anger and righteousness in James, then began giving him tidbits of information about Chinese communism and its objectives. He never made it sound too easy, but it was rich in hope. "Dare to think and dare to do," Chairman Mao had said. And so Siato spoke of a land where back-splitting labor was an everyday demand, which by night still left millions numb and spare, sucking in starvation with every breath. But in all of this suffering, there was a new difference. The partly broken cycle of youth-in-death promised a new hope completely unknown to the classical serenity of the Confucian landscape in which no one moved or even lived unless it was ordained. Mao, the plump and cruel dictator, had slain the landlords and chased the moneylenders from his temple, not for personal power, but for the people. He made a religion of hard work as the Calvinists had, and then called it the powerful expression of Chinese destiny. Armed thus with destiny, China began to move slowly, very slowly, but under a new sign for sure, not the Confucian sign of fixed order and manners, English manners, French manners, but the bright, constant, workable sign, the sign of the Red Star.

The war had to be seen under this sign, for in Korea the Chinese had clearly turned back an American challenge. The war had to end soon and surely on terms unfavorable to the American military men. Perhaps it meant nothing to him now, but someday it might. Now James wanted to know more. Desperately he nearly demanded to know more. He ached to know what it all might have to do with him, but Siato would not tell him. He liked James, he said, their relationship had been fruitful, but he thought perhaps it would be best if James reached his personal understanding of the world alone, after he had forgotten about Japan and the war. "I won't forget this place. It's been a great release just to talk to a man like you." Siato noted in this remark a certain pathos, which seemed to creep up on James now and again and, oddly enough, immobilize his anger even while he talked. This demonstration of compulsive sadness fascinated Siato and he wondered if it would ever be of any use in intelligence work.

At the time neither man knew it would be their last real meeting. The Army Counter-Intelligence Corps had opened a file on James. His commanding officer had been notified, and in outrage was about to send for him when at last the news everyone had been waiting for finally came through. An armistice had been signed with the untrustworthy Chinese. The war was over. It had petered out with both sides energetically claiming victory. James was in an outfit scheduled to leave Japan in the first troop convoy, and after quickly making preparations he barely had time to taxi out to the university and say good-bye.

Siato greeted him with perfunctory friendliness, as if he could not spare a moment from something vastly more important. There was a vaguely conspiratorial atmosphere in the room as Siato explained that he knew James might have difficulties when he got home. Wars did strange things to men and it was not always possible to return to a former way of life. It was good to have insurance, he added hastily, and because they were good friends (James wished he had said brothers), he wanted James to know he could always find a job with a relative in Bern, Switzerland, who ran an import-export business. Fumbling in his wallet a minute, he took out a card and handed it to James, who was about to cry. For a few minutes they talked about old times: the Free Students meeting place, the good solid discussions. The air of conspiracy dissipated and melancholy replaced it; neither man spoke now, they just sat together isolated by what each imagined to be a feeling of immense sadness. Finally James got up. He had to go, he announced in a faraway, cracked voice. Siato rose too and told him if he needed money for air fare, he could go and see a Pakistani diplomat at the United Nations whose name was written on the back of the card. They shook hands a little formally, as if it weren't really necessary. Then James left. He never saw Siato again.

James was discharged on the West Coast and took a train to New York. His first few weeks were spent at home, trying to get over the hypocritical lectures given to all army personnel about to reenter civilian life. Before the war he dated a pretty girl he thought he cared for, but he shortly found that their temperaments were abrasive and he had never actually known her. Then the money he'd accumulated during his tour of duty began to run low and he faced the inevitable task of job hunting. To his surprise a degree from his college was worth something and one of the large banks, after great and obscure deliberation, took him into a training program.

From the start it went badly. It was boring, tedious work; the mock committees, impassioned debate around the table, the whole self-conscious blend of seriousness and conformity bored him to death. He remembered when they fired him. The section manager, speaking very earnestly, took him aside and said he would have to do a hell of a lot better if he wanted to set a good example. But James didn't care about examples, although, on his next application for another training job in one of the larger corporations, he said it mattered to him greatly. Personnel managers liked that sort of honest, chipper statement, and when he said, at the last interview, that he was getting up a second wind, they took it as evidence of a new personal discipline and hired him; but he was a horrible failure, as perhaps he intended to be. The word around was that he was lazy. He denied it, and when the whispering continued, he charged discrimination. From then on the atmosphere of work was seeded with hostility, and the company had already decided to get rid of him before his fierce anger and self-righteousness burst out of control and he got into a terrible fight in the washroom and inflicted wounds on another man's head that took fifty stitches to close.

As a first offender James was given a short suspended sentence, and embittered he drifted in the city. His excessive pride melted into ostentatious hatred for his country. In bars he denounced all of its workings to anyone near him. He dallied with whores he despised, fondling their banged-up bodies as if they were the sacred forms of madonnas. For a time he drank insanely and ran with a pack of vicious pimps, then tried to hide behind the shame. The idea of going to Switzerland and starting again had an appeal, but only intermittently, only now and then. Yet it stayed with him and eventually, almost a year and a half after leaving Korea, seeing it was his only way to escape disintegration, James made contact with the Pakistani diplomat, who was a part-time courier in the system, and obtained a one-way air ticket to Switzerland along with a hundred dollars for expenses.

Once in Bern he was cleverly merged into the system. The charming Japanese at the Eastern Star Import-Export Company graciously told him they had no jobs currently open, but recommended him to another Oriental gentleman, a cultural attaché in the Chinese Embassy, who often helped foreigners in distress. This attaché, a tall, amazingly handsome and brilliant man in his middle thirties, met James for dinner several times. In precise, almost academic English he explained China's interest in all the dark peoples of the world. Frequently he delineated their future, drawing his examples from the Indochinese and Algerian wars. But he never rushed his thesis. Nimbly he brought James along, knowing that the other man's money was nearly exhausted and he would soon feel the bite of real desperation. Then after each meeting, he'd return to his office and read long sections of Professor Siato's preliminary report on the subdued and fidgety Negro he'd just dined with. For a long time he could not decide if James had enough potential for intelligence work. Somewhere in his brain a speck of knowledge told him James was not trustworthy. So like a scientist piecing together an involved concept, he matched his impressions against work already done, correlating Siato's incisive details with every nuance he could recall James passing over to him until he had enough interesting material for his superiors to read. Once his report was handed in, he took James to dinner and again quietly but deftly probed his allegiance to the United States. When the meal was over, he loaned James twenty-five dollars and promised to call in two weeks. One month later a final evaluation on James came down from plans section: he was not a counteragent. His possibilities were encouraging. He was to be offered a job. That night at dinner James was informed rather coolly that the Chinese Embassy had decided to give him some training in international relations, which would lead eventually, the attaché said, to an excellent job in the European offices of the Bank of

China. Greedily he accepted, and five hundred dollars was handed across the table for his use in settling debts. Then an odd thing happened. With a cold hostility flashing in his eyes, the attaché rose from his chair, executed a stiffly courteous little bow, and ordered James to report to the embassy at seven in the morning. As he left the restaurant alone that night, James was absorbed in a swirl of trepidation and puzzlement. He didn't really know what the Chinese thought of him.

When he reported to the embassy, James almost immediately discovered that behind the facade of a legitimate diplomatic enterprise the Chinese ran a huge, clandestine intelligence apparatus. The first two floors of the embassy conducted the open business of the Peoples Republic of China and the remaining six were divided into secret hermetic compartments where various sections of experts carried out and directed their country's effort in the strategic war against the Western nations. The entire operation was under the Ministry of Foreign Affairs.

For the first week he was allowed to wander around the building with a small nervous guide, and observe what went on. But in the middle of his second week James returned from a good Swiss lunch to find a note on his desk sent down from one of the upper floors. The broad looping scrawl on the paper directed him to appear at a certain room on the same floor later that afternoon. When he arrived, a short husky Chinese man in a neat, gray double-breasted suit motioned him to a chair. What he said did not surprise James in any way, for proudly he already understood the embassy considered him too important for ordinary bank work. He expected to be offered an assignment as an intelligence officer for the Ministry of Foreign Affairs. The Chinese, who did not divulge his name, appreciated all of this and left out any appeals to gratitude or racial anger. Instead he calmly drove right into the center of James's vanity. Slyly and with an obvious hint of relish he said, "Our operatives in their reports assure me you are quite a unique and brilliant man. They say you are very brave. We need men like you and so do your people in America. Together we may be able to aid their struggle. Will you consent to join us?" He spoke quietly, masking the suggestion of a plea in his voice. Awed and humbled, James said he would. He promised to do anything. Like a righteous young seminarian he was almost stupidly thankful to be in the service of the Chinese. And only later in his hotel room, after he had taken tea with his host in the cafeteria dominated by a portrait of Mao and been told this man headed plans section, only then did it come to James that his life might have ended on that very day if his answer had been anything but yes.

When he began his formal duties as an apprentice, James found that the third floor of the embassy had been given to the intelligence section. There thin, studious-looking men greeted each other respectfully and browsed in the stacks of a private library. These men were intellectuals—economists, mathematicians, an occasional scientist or engineer on leave from duties at home; they all knew several languages and analyzed daily all the open material—books, newspapers, specialized journals —coming from every Western country. It was their task to fit all of it together and get out lengthy reports on the long-range political, economic, and social ills of the West. Later James realized that all of the manuals he read on American Negroes had been the work of this section.

The next floor belonged to research. Only a few men worked there, but the embassy considered them the most important personnel in the building. They slept in dormitory rooms and never left the premises without authorization and passes stamped with a time limit. Even then they were followed, for the Chinese could not afford to let these men defect or be abducted. They represented an important segment of China's trained scientific manpower. Some had worked with the Russians on early stages of the atomic bomb, and every one of them knew a great deal about the nuclear weaponry and military computer systems used in NATO countries. It was their responsibility to assess scientific data and predict what advances were likely to come and how soon. During the week James began his training their section head, who had been investigating the problem for months, announced to his delighted colleagues that Russia would be first to launch an earth satellite.

Directly above research, support section had its offices. All day twenty male secretaries typed out requisitions while supply officers kept track of the matériel needs for special operations all over the world. The Chinese were burdened by a lack of transport planes so friendly nations had to be approached through diplomatic channels and asked to supply aircraft and loading personnel. The logistical problems alone were astounding. It cost thirty thousand dollars a day to support three hundred rebels in the Eastern Congo. Each country along the route demanded a fee for the overflight to be paid into a Swiss bank in advance, and even then there were the usual problems with overloaded, inadequate aircraft, second-rate pilots, and sabotage; yet most operations were well supplied, and if they failed, support always had its perfect records to fall back on and rarely, if ever, took the blame.

In addition to logistics, support section devised and ultimately deciphered every code in use. As in research, security was extra tight. Certain clerks worked only on code systems and never had any idea of where or how the codes would be used. Other clerks, with top-level clearance, deciphered codes and sent the messages immediately to plans section. The ministry did not want even a stray scrap of paper on the floors, and each of the clerks, hidden from the others behind a soundproof partition, had his wastebasket emptied every half hour by an armed guard. Anyone leaving the floor without a pass from the section chief was to be shot, out of hand.

On the floor above, the plans section had its headquarters. Plans, as James got to know it, was the most fascinating section of all. From this section every covert operation in the West received direction. Plans sent out highly trained spies and agents provocateurs to any country worth penetrating and overcame the obstacles in mounting a genuinely potent espionage system in the West.

The lack of diplomatic relations between the Peoples Republic and the West hampered it seriously at first. Without recognition it was impossible to enjoy the diplomatic cover the Russians had; then too recruiting Western-born agents was difficult. Foreigners could not easily travel in China and the visibility factor made it hard to make unnoticed contacts in the West. Also the overseas Chinese were watched by the Western intelligence services, and excellent internal surveillance, especially in the United States, made putting in illegal agents virtually unthinkable.

To establish themselves, the Chinese fell back on a system of political indoctrination and highly specialized intelligence training for selected foreign nationals. In the group James started out with, he found Africans from Rhodesia, Mozambique, Angola, and South Africa. These men trained in Bern for only one year and then went back to hidden training camps in their countries to work, along with Chinese officers, at readying liberation armies and national liberation fronts. The South Americans, mainly Brazilians with a few men from Venezuela, followed almost the same pattern but spent more time on politics and economics. James envied them all, because eventually they would free continents, while his role in America, still undesignated, had to be mainly sacrificial.

After getting into the routine, James discovered more of the business of plans section. The traffic in usable information from untrained peddlers was handled by the New China News Agency whose men trained in Peking and ran operations in countries where they were stationed ostensibly as reporters. Cultural, economic, and trade delegations going out from Peking traveled with huge sums of money and took care of certain industrial spying, but the most significant effort was put into the training of foreigners.

In the first year they learned standard intelligence techniques—high-speed radio transmission, weapons, self-defense, surveillance, signals, and codes. After this initial phase the original group of twenty diminished to six men who studied the methods of operation used by the Western intelligence services, and finally went out on operational problems. They were carefully watched. Once a week each man met with his adviser to speak out about any personal problems he had; only one man, a diminutive and brash Jamaican, failed to satisfy the section chief. Later James heard he had been dismissed, for medical reasons.

Toward the end of training, political indoctrination was stepped up. Twice a day the group went upstairs to the political section for a brief but intense lecture. Generally the practice was to let them linger for half an hour in the library next to their classroom to read the magazines and books assembled there in many languages by the Foreign Language Publishing House in Peking. This was done to remind them of the ministry's efficiency and total foresight.

Their lecturer, who never gave his name, was an alert, bouncy little man wearing rimless glasses and possessing a remarkably brisk cheerfulness. Like a professor, he employed a long pointer to help explain the terms written on the blackboard. His lectures all contained similar themes—freedom was an imperialist abstraction, salvation an exercise in self-delusion, and individualism simply a means of isolating the most dangerous elements in something called Western society, a decadent and outmoded way of life with no concept of loyalty to a supreme doctrine, and riddled with utter contempt for Afro-Asian culture. All of it was very neat, and yet in James it stirred a certain restlessness, perhaps a yearning for home, or a long suppressed dislike for the peremptory joyfulness of the lecturer who was, James thought, too spruce, too sure and puritanical in his subtle demands for intellectual surrender. However, as with almost everything in the embassy, this seemingly invisible manifestation of ambivalence did not escape his section chief, and it was noted, along with other observations, in his final fitness report to be weighed as a factor in determining the mission James was now ordered to undertake.

CHAPTER FOUR

FOR THE NEXT WEEK James Fitzgerald went about his duties as Brotherhood secretary alternating between a clutching, feverish turmoil and an amorphous sensation verging on swooning disbelief. Intermittently and without warning, traces of pure terror stole through his belly and nipped at his nerves like a cold vindictive wind racing through an empty room. As usual he counterattacked, using extreme self-control (a legacy of his strict and pretentious middle-class childhood, he assumed) to nullify the charge and bite of anxiety within him. But it was never quite enough. Always he remembered what the ministry had ordered him to do. There was no way for him to be alone with himself, to think dispassionately and without the grasp of sudden fear as he had done almost habitually before the ministry contact. Over and over he returned to the horrible scene in his shabby kitchen where, bent double on a creaking chair, he gazed in bemused astonishment at the flimsy piece of typing paper, which seemed now to have channeled his life into darkness and unutterable confusion.

And right away he made an important decision. Out of repugnance, chilled horror, inchoate fears of madness, and a dozen other forebodings he couldn't articulate, James determined never in his life would he lift one hand to harm Miles King. Childishly he swore it to himself. In a weak private voice he promised himself somehow this would be so. For whole days he believed it fervently, then at a stray moment in his busy schedule the illusion would disappear completely and leave him isolated and terrified.

Yet James always recovered. In the drawn-out, spectacularly nervous and icy tension he lived under, James invariably pulled himself together. He never relinquished his tenuous faith in the idea that he would not kill Miles, but strangely this seemed irrelevant. A premonition, a secret fear told James his resolve didn't matter. Desperately he tried to shut this information out of his mind, but all the while he knew it was true. He had no real strength of will, just an accomplished ability to keep from going insane, a magnificent but superficial self-control. Other people were always able to shape his will and make him compliant. Siato did it beautifully and Miles had artfully made him an administrative genius. Still he understood bitterly that in an ultimate way this left him with nothing. In and of himself he amounted to very little because he'd never been able to master his peculiar drives and bring together the disparate angles of his ambiguities. James lived in a perpetual state of concealed helplessness.

He blamed part of his inadequacy on the war. When the army first called him, he was not unhappy because he maintained the naïve assumption that military service would, through a stringently undefined process, make him a complete man. He even welcomed going to Korea to steel himself in the cruelty of war. But with the bleak, silent front before him, James changed by slow degrees. He began to think he'd be killed before it was possible for him to grasp the maturity and manly confidence he now perceived slipping away. And very quickly his response turned to hysteria. In battle he began to kill, lustfully and well. Yet the more enemy soldiers he killed, the more inadequate he felt until it came to him at the long end of another interminable patrol that all the deaths to his credit had come too easily. In war killing was the perfect solution to everything except personal sensitivities. And with his polished skills and foolish courage he was solving all the military problems while crazily propelling himself into the restrained charity of a mental ward. Suddenly he saw how completely the army had fooled him. He began to despise himself because he'd enjoyed the slaughter. But his self-loathing didn't subvert the immense guilt overtaking him, and on leaving Korea he couldn't escape the malignant fear that his life would be shortened and tormented. Then abruptly his fear of the ministry was in the room again, circling him angrily like an old enemy. Somehow he had thought the ministry would never contact him. It had been so long ago.

In the days that followed James determinedly struggled to forget the ministry and its impossible demand. During the daylight hours it was easy. With the arrival of dawn he was always strengthened, for the cool scent of fear wandering through his mind lifted like a mist and he enjoyed the superficialities of a normal life while handling the Brotherhood's business flawlessly. At night everything was different. As evening lengthened he had the sickening feeling he would not make it to the morning. A horrible melodramatic dread played over his senses; James was afraid to sleep. Only complete nervous exhaustion released him from his ordeal, and then just temporarily. Often he dreamed of the embassy in Bern, imagining his presence traveling the long, polished corridors, nodding to the extra-polite Chinese gentlemen passing by; it was all so very far away but still vividly real, remote yet distinctly tangible, encircling, inescapable, like the motif of the Red Star, which seemed to be in every room, in every lapel, on every document to signify belief in the great secular religion as the cross of God had symbolized Christianity in the Middle Ages and so separated the barbarians from the just.

But he could not return to the ministry. And he could not bring the ministry close enough to his present life for it to have any meaning. James could only be trapped into the deep fears and shifting doubts silently ripping at him. Wisely he refused to consider the question of final allegiance. Instead his mind dwelt on ways to escape the ministry order. Briefly he considered putting himself under psychiatric care to establish his unreliability. Suicide zipped through his mind and disappeared, only to quietly return and sit on the periphery of his consciousness like an alert, patient, dead-eyed vulture. Half a dozen schemes devoured his evenings, yet through all of his frantic agonies a familiar ambiguous tension saved him from collapse. Almost whimsically he knew it was hopeless for the ministry to think he would plot to kill Miles. No longer was he the totally baffled young man they'd assessed and trained and pampered. Much of his brutality had subsided, although he still possessed a quick, vicious temper. And any thought of the mayhem he achieved in Korea filled him with a thick mournful repentance. But in spite of time and change, there was still an inexplicable order from the Ministry of Foreign Affairs, which demanded a response. And at the end of all his precarious deliberations, James could only decide to do nothing at all. His nerves told him to delay everything, to wait tensely for the day Mahanti would summon him once again.

As secretary of the Brotherhood, James managed Miles's engagements in the tough argumentive way the newspaper and television people hostilely accepted only because they had no other choice; for by dexterous manipulation and clever grooming, James had been made the one reliable link to Brother Miles King, a man now acknowledged as one of the few real grass-roots personalities of the century.

Before his knowledgeable audiences, Miles needed only to state the bare and dramatic circumstances of his formative years: out of school at twelve and into the fetid streets of South Philadelphia to rob and then pimp until the age of sixteen, all of this followed by a bizarre supermarket robbery (a cash drawer bolted closed and smashed his hand) for which he paid with five years out of his young life. Most of his twenties were spent hiding from detectives in several states (extortion in Trenton and Newark, a little prostitution in Cleveland, narcotics in East Saint Louis and Chicago, a complicated blackmail plot involving a prominent congressman). During his early thirties he was continuously on parole. Then he drifted to the Black Belt of the Deep South, back to the hopeless farm life his father had fled. He cropped on shares, cut pine in the mills, and eventually followed the trail of winter crops to California, where he was beaten savagely for instigating a wildcat strike in the tomato fields.

On his way back to Philadelphia by bus, he discovered the religion of Islam in a thirty-five-cent paperback he'd bought because when he was young his father told him the Islamic Arabs were a dark people who'd once been great. Reading late into the night and missing half the words because he had no dictionary, Miles became enchanted with the Arabs and Islam. He understood enough to see that a powerful beauty and harsh mysticism pervaded this strange faith. With the excitement drawn from this discovery he slowly began to think of himself as someone exotic and perhaps even special because he was a dark man like the Islam worshipers.

In Philadelphia he was stifled and alone. Most people who remembered him at all just wanted news about old friends in prison. Many of his childhood buddies were dead. No one wanted to hear about the thousand little discoveries of life he'd secretly cataloged. In the bars and barbershops everyone irritably accused him of turning philosopher. People shrank from him. They said he was a bit strange now. Miles sank into odd jobs and his new preoccupation, the lonesome study of Islam.

Clumsily and with great slowness, he mounted timid forays into the complicated terrain of African anthropology and Islamic history. After a time he dared to think there was an important message for the American black man in the mystical unity of the faraway Islamic peoples. But he could never be certain what the message was. Still he always returned to the notion of Islam as a spiritual force because the whole idea comforted him more than anything he'd ever known before. In the simplicity of Islam, pleasingly free of involved concepts and the constant portent of sin, he felt completely relaxed. He even began to pray in secret, in the dark, prostrating himself

47

on the cold dusty floorboards in his room, mumbling quietly, hoping no one would hear him or abruptly open the door, and by the light of the naked bulb in the hall, see his long muscular frame obscenely stretched out before their astonished eyes. But even as he immersed himself in Islam, Miles knew he did not really perceive or appreciate all of it. And so, despite many strong fears of humiliation and belittlement, he left Philadelphia for the last time and came to Harlem to begin free classes in Islamic history at the Middle East Institute, a school they had told him about at the neighborhood library.

At first he was frightened and intimidated by everything around him. The well-dressed, elegantly groomed people sitting in the classes seemed so indescribably poised and educated beside his ordinary shabbiness. But not long after, when the first test papers were handed back, Miles heard a slow ripple of amazement spread over the room as it was discovered that the diffident and intense American black man had emerged near the top of the class. Miles was emboldened by his academic success. Studying almost twenty hours a week after laboring all day as a floor sweeper in a dark, filthy slaughterhouse, he found himself daring to believe an inchoate but simple intelligence was squirming to develop in his untutored brain. He noticed his observations were abruptly quicker and ran in a true line to the cogent arguments he wanted to reveal. In class he spoke up readily. And in the cutting sharpness of his perceptions, Miles came upon a new quality in himself—a stinging, lacerating shaft of wit coming partly from his immense feelings of residual inadequacy.

None of this went unnoticed. After classes Miles discovered more and more respectful, openly admiring glances floating over to where he stood. Soon polite little discussion groups eddied about him. Passionate questioning eyes met his for the first time, and Miles was fascinated and stirred. At the beginning of the second term, Miles found his life veering subtly into a kind of annoying veneration. He was seldom alone. His new Arab friends, along with their inquisitive and idle acquaintances, consumed most of the time he'd set aside for his studies. They badgered him with tedious questions ("Do they kill pigs in the place where you work?"), but he responded with grace and good cheer. On the streets he now affected a woolen skullcap, and his daily prayers to Allah were offered up from the luxurious International Mosque located in an office building fifty stories above Manhattan.

Almost without the fact registering in his brain, Miles was formally converted to Islam (henceforth his Arabic name was Ismail Kebir, Ismail the Great). And after a while his conversion was very gaudy. He was given a good job by a Moroccan importer, and soon casually acquired two mistresses. The routine of his life was clustered into stultifying hours spent in Islamic-Christian friendship groups and a wearying round of receptions and parties at Arab embassies where all the African and Asian diplomats were anxious to see the black American Muslim. ("In my mind he'd have to be a cross between King Kong and Sitting Bull," he once overheard someone say.) But in a vain childish way Miles tolerated all of it for a while, even as he saw how shallow his life had become, for Islam had given him the cloak of an identity when before he was naked.

He knew the dazzling personalities around him did not need religion to enhance their splendor. Their accouterments— crimson tapestries woven with polished gold thread, precious vases colored pale blue instead of white with the aging of time, massive tables lacquered to the bottomless depths of fine mirrors, magically beautiful rugs, intricate chandeliers, and suites of rooms opening upon each other with the rushing excitement of Versailles—all of these things left him wary and sullen. In spite of the chauffered cars and the delicious perfumed smell of rich young women that was beginning to palpitate like a narcotic in his nostrils, Miles never forgot that in the Arab lands money flowed only to those already glutted.

Inadvertently an air of faint disgust and deprecation began to show in his manner. Often he found himself interrupting and quarreling with the people around him. An old strain of malicious candor and honest perversity in his character would not remain dormant. Suddenly the Arabs were markedly

49

cooler toward him, more suavely circumspect and elusive, as they had been when he first encountered them at the institute. Then one night, at an enormous dinner party for a sheikh whose harem was gossiped about even more than his fabulous wealth, Miles was confronted with the terms of his future. A friend, Saad Al Abdulah, a thoughtful and mystical Hashimite, brought his face very close and said slowly, almost hissingly, as his great, wet brown eyes dwelt upon Miles, "We understand your hesitancy, all of us. You are not Muhammadan by birth. It is an acquired belief, but you must open your soul and give yourself to it completely. In time you must become the leader, the pasha, the chieftan to your people. Then you will know Allah best. Only then can he know you. And if I may say so, my friend, you show promise of being one of his most favored subjects."

Shortly after, Miles vanished from the polished aristocratic circle of Arabs in New York. In the mannered and hermetic world he'd left behind, people remembered him with an unsatisfying mixture of pity and keen curiosity. They did not know he had retreated to Harlem, where in his bare cramped room he attempted to dissect the future. They did not know Miles was already fearfully committed to the religion of Islam. He was fascinated and appalled by the power this extraordinary following, with its excitable, dark babbling peoples, asserted over his thoughts. But secretly he loved the idea of being a pasha or a chieftan. In these lush arrogant words he found a suggestion of mystical authority that exhilarated him.

Six months contorted by indecision and timidity rolled ominously away before Miles opened his first mosque. It was a forty-five-dollar-a-month storefront freshly painted and available for morning and evening prayers only. During the day Miles worked in a factory turning out plastic mop handles. At night, after the last prayers he often chatted about the glories of Islam with a handful of curious and reverent people left behind. Those first sessions were both overdramatic and endlessly dull. Many converts dropped out less than a week after giving their allegiance to Allah, wandering bitterly out into the streets, perhaps sensing the ridiculous disparity between their helpless lives and the magical fulfillment of Islam.

Still Miles kept on. Legally he changed his name from Booth to King, and directed emphasis away from the ethereal presence of Allah. Employing a frenetic imagination and practical verve that at first surprised him, Miles altered traditional Islam to suit his needs and audience. In place of its complex exaltation he placed his own bold and uncertain motif—a boisterous, colloquial melodramatic interpretation soon to be noticed across the entire country. Pork and alcohol were still forbidden, but discreetly circumcision was never mentioned. He chose a simple name, the New Brotherhood of Islam, which he believed interpreted the spirit of his enterprise. But Miles never ceased inculcating the idea of arduous lifelong struggle in his converts. Each night to swelling audiences he expounded on how difficult it was to gain personal fulfillment, especially if you were black. In every speech he hounded the inadequacies revealed in the startled anguished looks people flashed up at him. He raged against lassitude and indifference. He pleaded with his followers to battle the worst things in themselves. Always he made war on the conformity of American life that held down the spontaneity of everyone, even the comfortable white people beyond the ghettos. Rather coolly, but not without a touch of stern righteousness, Miles demanded everyone in his Brotherhood read about the predicament of the nonwhite races. At every meeting he extracted a fighting cheering commitment to defend the sanctity of the Brotherhood, although he knew it was quite meaningless. And beyond all these things Miles pledged himself to try to direct the destiny of black people. Never once did this amazing promise fail to start a mysterious and reverential clapping of hands.

But success left Miles apprehensive. He feared someday his audiences would suspect he needed the urgings shouted through the storefront more than anyone else. Frequently he felt distended and moody after his speeches. Fits of worry often took away his vitality when he was alone. With alarm he dwelt on the disquieting phenomenon that brought more worshipers to him as he continued to violently demand only struggle and sacrifice. He suspected his Islam was still too tepid and mystical. (Once a famous woman journalist asked," Don't you yourself find it terribly naïve?") Still Miles clung to the Brotherhood because it was the only thing he'd ever created.

A year later Miles presided over a small satrapy of eight ghetto mosques in New York and became the center of a strident local cult. In another six months the membership doubled and two additional mosques were opened in abandoned supermarkets. Wildly the Brotherhood sped through a dozen vivid stages of maturation like a simple organism evolving into something larger and infinitely more sinister. In two quick years there were mosques in ten big cities. To many black people the rise of Miles King was a metaphor for everything that was possible.

The pace of his life was exhausting. In other days, in the stifling heat on the roads and in the fields he had rarely been tired. Now he was drained. He made extensive ghetto tours three times a week and almost every day a foreign visitor came to see him for lunch or a chat. Even the Russian Embassy dispatched a pudgy and cheerful vice-consul to investigate the Brotherhood. Out of all this frenzy Miles detected a certain mature assurance coalescing in him. But he could never be positive. More than once he'd been jerked from the depths of his sleep in withering terror, not knowing what he was. A suspicion that his life had taken the wrong turn dogged him. Yet as the Brotherhood went into its fifth year he outwardly became bolder and more indomitable. He moved about the Brotherhood's territories with something approaching aristocratic familiarity. Once a week he even played basketball with his bodyguards, nicknamed the Fung after a dynasty of temple-building, war-loving black Muhammadans whose civilization flourished for a time on the banks of the Upper Nile.

In the middle of its sixth year of existence, claiming five hundred thousand names on its secret membership lists and mosques in every niche of the country, the Brotherhood developed Miles into a figure of national consequence. To religious wisdom Miles had added a muted but arresting touch of militancy and white people listened to him now, but merely with delighted tolerance. Quite suddenly the country claimed him as a fascinating but controllable menace, a tortured, perhaps nihilistic black man with a brilliant mind not quite his own. When he appeared on television the ratings showed a compulsively high interest. One national magazine sold out two days after coming out with a long picture essay on Miles's pilgrimage to Mecca, the traditional hajj or journey every convert to Allah must make at least once in his life. Advertising agencies approached Miles for product endorsements. ("We think you have marvelous potential in certain well-chosen markets.") And at the same time he began to make enemies.

Bales of confused letters protesting his very existence were sent to every member of Congress. Angrily Miles was denounced for advocating black sedition and anarchy. Conservative orators warned that he harbored Marxist ideals. His trips to Islamic nations were interpreted as signs of a developing international conspiracy. Soon a group of ambitious senators subpoenaed Miles to appear before their investigating subcommittee. On the appointed day he materialized in Washington with the regal and indifferent air of a sheikh who is amused to somehow find himself beyond the boundaries of his kingdom. To the rancorous questions hurled at him, Miles presented straightforward and innocently convincing answers. He stated what he believed and was subtly reproached. But rather calmly he turned back each venal thrust and corrosive insinuation. ("Is there something Communistic in calling yourselves Brothers and Sisters? People in my state write me that there is." Patiently and with a hint of condescension the answer came across the polished table. "My followers believe they are related in their allegiance to Allah.") By noon it was all over and several dozen reporters drifted into the high-ceilinged hearing room, cutting through the strong shafts of camera lights somewhat reluctantly, as if they were quite wary of Miles and the seductive mystery crouching in the turns of his life.

*　　*　　*

Two weeks after his first meeting with Mahanti, filled with an insatiable turmoil he could never entirely subdue into stillness, James arrived at Brotherhood Hall early one morning and found Miles going through his files. Halfway down the hall he'd seen his office door was open, and involuntarily his step softened and an almost pleasing tension arched his body forward slightly. Without Miles ever hearing him, James stood full in the door. A gaze blurred with slightly humorous contempt and tinged with outrage played down upon the tall man gracefully bent over the bottom drawer of a file cabinet. Instantaneously it occurred to James that it would not be too hard to kick Miles over backward and stomp him senseless before he could react. But he didn't move. And in the next instant, while another stray vision of mayhem flashed through his brain, Miles turned elegantly on the soles of his polished black shoes and looked up amiably, with just a whisper of surprise in his face, for it was only James who'd arrived.

Quickly, sensing anger in the way James stood there, Miles got to his feet. His lean hardened body straightened up over James and he looked down now, a little apologetically, and said he was sorry to rummage around without permission but he'd needed some information fast. James murmured something irritably, to hint at his displeasure. Miles was not supposed to violate his little domain. He knew that. He knew access to the secretary's files had to be in writing to make sure nothing was stolen or copied.

Sullenly James went to his desk, but not without noticing something taut and preoccupied hung about Miles this morning. As he sat down Miles came up and leaned across the uncluttered surface between them. His face revealed frustration and muted rage, as it always did when he had not slept. Rather absently he explained he'd been working in the files half the night. He said he was planning an urgent new membership drive on the West Coast using the Brotherhood's contacts in black radio stations.

"We've got to have some new strength in California," he said in a sudden burst of poignant distress, which startled James. "There's a lot of unrest out there. Everyone blames us —the governor, the newspapers, everyone. The police are beating hell out of our people," he exclaimed passionately. "Beating living hell out of them. They called me from L.A. last night," he went on with a suggestion of worried pride. "They want me to come out. Even those who aren't in the Brotherhood are begging for me. You don't see them running to politicians anymore. Believe me, that's a good sign, Brother," Miles said, staring fervently into the emotionless face behind the well-ordered desk. "A couple of hours ago I sent Brother Charles out there to clear the way for me."

In his chair James stiffened with hostility and outrage. Brother Charles was Charles De Young, sometimes called Brother D. He was an insidious favorite throughout the Brotherhood. Between them nothing existed but malicious disrespect. James was about to ask out loud why he was not sent.

"I know you're wondering why I didn't call and have you go right out to California," Miles said, trying to suppress a whimsical smile. "I don't want to hurt your feelings or downgrade you," he added warmly, "but I need you here. Two national magazines are doing cover stories on me this month and I want you by my side to keep these reporters in line. When I can't afford to offend them, you'll have to yell and scream for me."

From behind his desk James smiled wanly, with just a touch of gritty malevolence. Miles reached out and put a firm reassuring hand on his shoulder. He was sure James looked forward to the excitement of meeting the national press and had already forgotten his brief intrusion.

Later the same day, at the beginning of a lull he knew would stretch for several hours, James returned to his office. Quietly he closed the door and flopped down on a leather sofa he kept for nights when sleeping over was necessary. With the crude absorbed languor of a bather just emerging from the sea, he allowed his accumulated weariness to drain from him. And then abruptly his thoughts drifted through the hours to what had happened that morning. Again he experienced a surge of hostility as the sight of Miles industriously picking through the files focused in his mind. He tried to settle himself, to arrogantly dismiss the episode, but the whole thing exacted from him a convoluted uneasiness that was totally new—a nauseating sensation of danger, suspicion, and betrayal Miles only temporarily suspended with his sincere explanations.

Not that he was afraid of Miles. They had always been very close friends in a perverse, oblique sort of way, almost as if each of them understood tacitly that the other man ultimately wished to be alone in the world by deliberate design and the recesses of temperament. This strangeness brought them together. They respected each other's singularity as some kind of near-religious sign. Curiously James had first seen Miles on television and not in person. As the bluish electronic image fluttered through the unkempt apartment he still occupied, a strange fascination moved him. About this famous, haughty, and odd personality he sensed an exciting implacability. At the next weekly meeting in Brotherhood Hall, which turned out to be an old movie house, James was there packed into the mob, shouting with it, resonating when it did. On the following weekend he was back, enticed into the hall again especially to hear Miles lecture on the principle of struggle and self-discovery in life. During that same week he joined the Brotherhood, mesmerized by the existence of a black American male who had developed a driving personal philosophy and then lived by it.

In those days he'd badly needed something to believe in, because once again his life had run dry. He was certain the ministry had abandoned him. Whether it was deliberate or somehow accidental, he could never be sure. But he knew he was lost again, just as he had been when Korea was over and the army released him completely to his uncertainties. This time the awareness of withering deprivation came on him more quickly and awesomely, for he had departed from Bern reluctantly and almost in tears, convinced he was leaving the shrine of a stern yet beautiful faith. His final instructions (he'd sailed from Le

Havre to help conceal the record of his passage) were to acquire a respectable job and await a signal from the ministry. They promised the signal would come within six months, but two years came and went as James waited and gradually merged into the trivial routine of his job as a clerk in a brokerage house.

Miles had rescued him though; with his terrible excitement and the compelling theme of self-discovery Miles had torn him away from his morbid absorption with the permutations of misery. Years after, when he'd become nicely ensconced in the hierarchy of the Brotherhood, James glanced back upon that bleak period knowing cryptically that by minute degrees he'd been going insane. A doctor he'd consulted called his distress an acute but temporary psychological depression. Cheerfully he advised his nervous patient to request a vacation, get out more, mingle, take charge of a woman or two. But James saw the depraved hand of confusion in every move he made, in the slowly receding tableau of everyday life. And one Sunday afternoon at the end of the meeting he found himself leaving the auditorium with a small crowd surging into the hallway where Miles would pass. Clawing and stretching in the frantic throng like a maddened pilgrim invading some religious edifice to touch the likeness of a saint, he fought his way close to the front. But while the others cried out their emotions, he remained silent, cannily hoping for special recognition; and when Miles stopped in front of him at last, tranquilly calling him Brother and asking what his problem was, to his absolute surprise he briskly replied that he'd come only to volunteer.

Immediately a tall broad man, one of the Fung, took him by the arm and led the way upstairs to an office. Soon Miles came and strangely James suspected at once that they shared a weariness and dissatisfaction with the course of their lives. During their first brief talk, James was asked to describe his background, and he noticed a hungry gleam come into the eyes watching him as he stated the roll of his education and the boring jobs he'd held.

A long time afterward he discovered that because of his

febrile appearance and halting speech at their initial encounter, Miles actually believed he was somewhat mentally unstable and merely reciting the disillusionments of a ruined life. Behind his back a few of the Brothers still maintained he was a little crazy; but very quickly Miles grasped that an intelligent, trained, and capable man had come into his ranks, someone a bit like himself who possessed many thwarted yearnings he would not tamper with.

In an unstated, somewhat affectionate turn of mood Miles quietly accepted James, almost as if he believed his new convert would be marred by too much scrutiny. He put James on the payroll without fanfare. And he took a silent careful pride in his able apprentice that verged on being smugly clinical. James was aware of this peculiar vanity and wondered ominously at times what depths of spirituality Miles thought he was looking into. But the issue remained mute. There was never any emotional confrontation, never any real show of nerves or temper between them. Miles respected James too much for that; he always tried to pay some kind of homage to outstanding intelligence. And he liked people with training. It pleased him to have them under his tutelage. By cagey manipulation he brought James along, briefly making him a messenger; then a chauffer-bodyguard and superficial confidant. Soon he was slipped into administration as an assistant secretary, where he reorganized everything and saved the Brotherhood nearly seven hundred dollars a week. Not long after the elderly secretary of the Brotherhood, a retired high-school teacher of accounting, resigned in a fit of bitter jealousy. James was given his office a few days later in a dignified private ceremony.

As James began to direct the Brotherhood's transactions with the occult universe of formal business, Miles felt more secure. He observed there was a tough serenity about James now. He was rarely tense. The torment had gone from his eyes. Miles was sure his secretary cherished at least some nominal allegiance to Allah. But inwardly James was still wary. He feared the faculty for self-examination Miles tried to develop in people, because ultimately it never seemed to help him enough. As he lay on his leather sofa James understood wearily that when he really needed confidence it was almost impossible to muster. What little assurance he owned always evaporated as it had now, when he suspected that Miles was about to drop the guise of benevolence and direct at him for the first time a cultivated mistrust and enmity no one in the Brotherhood had ever endured.

Still he might be alarming himself unduly. Miles did accept him as a mysterious and near kindred equal. Under a relationship of those indefinite and engaging terms, mere suspicion was just another emotion, a stray quantum, which could mean nothing without an excess of proof. Even the harsh and bitter side of Miles would not violate that stricture, James decided, quickly turning his thoughts to the upcoming meetings with reporters from the national press. If there was anything James Fitzgerald dared to enjoy openly, it was his reputation as a rude and badgering outrider of the press. Whenever possible Miles kept him nearby to frighten and condemn the large pack of reporters who followed him around most of the time, taking down his life in their spiral notebooks as if it were being lived out as chapters in the most grotesque novel of the century. The mere sight of James, with his coolly flickering, ambiguous eyes dominating a strong, stocky frame bent slightly forward in an aggressive and threatening stance as he advanced upon them sometimes spouting caustic and contemptuous remarks, antagonized reporters and softened them up for Miles's heavy blows on the American conscience. In retaliation James was publicly cast as somewhat of a villain, the unworthy second in command who scrambled for the dirty assignments. This caricature greatly amused Miles and he liked to tease James about it, saying this was just a way the press had of keeping him down, christening him a lout so the country could have fun thinking only one demon was loose in paradise.

Yet James knew the press never really succeeded in intimidating him, and he continued to use his anger against the reporters contemptuously, as if he were a champion weight lifter involuntarily rippling his muscles. Once or twice he'd surprised them and spoken for Miles at public rallies. But somehow he was always a failure on the rostrum, because in spite of his quick, trained intellect, an evil uncontrolled flair for demagoguery leapt into his speeches and people complained to Miles about it afterward. Some of the Brothers even feared him. Most everyone found him too detached. They swore he was disdainful of them, and James was branded a snotty educated opportunist. Still it was hard to disregard Brother James. He was extremely capable. If anything should happen to Miles, he would be needed, but only after he had dueled it out with the popular favorite, Charles De Young.

One week later on a pleasant sunny afternoon, an incident occurred at Brotherhood Hall that alarmed Miles more than he would ever quite admit. Toward the end of the day an apologetic and rotund gentleman carrying an overburdened briefcase presented himself at the reception desk and stated his business as magazine writer. He was shown in and bustled across the immense oriental carpet in Miles's office to greet him with a bubbly, too false enthusiasm which escaped no one and set up wavelengths of animosity throughout the room. Right away his spoiled mouth hidden in a rich red beard aroused James's keen hostility to decadence. This man was too florid and oiled not to be aided by an excess of brandy and who knows, perhaps a creamy soft fifteen-year-old girl for his leisure evenings. The three men sat down rather tentatively around a large brass Tunisian coffee table and the writer introduced himself as Sam Burrell, Jr.

While the ground rules for the interview were being made up, coffee was served by a gracious young Sister wearing a white headdress whose presence, at once spiritual and ridiculous, set off a wild curiosity in the guest. Visions of the tales she must know clicked off in his mind like projected slides. The whole time she was in the room Burrell watched her guardedly; glimpsing as she moved about them her tender, uplifted breasts protruding from beneath a saucy youthful wool knit sweater. Two browned delicate hands served him coffee as he dared to look up at her directly. And surreptitiously she smiled for him, a sweet quick furtive gesture of a smile, a beckoning kiss really; instantly the bizarre and perhaps immoral character of the Brotherhood came through to him in that smile, and he felt a keen surge of outrage at the whole thing. He was certain it was all lewd, an obscene fraud, but he wanted to keep this to himself because he fancied an aura of implacable hostility about his hosts. A suggestion of something wickedly fraudulent was in their richly patterned oriental carpets and expensive Arabian decor, something not apparent at the moment, a sort of occult state of thinking, a danger. Burrell was sure the girl, who hastened out of the room, wanted to escape before some kind of trick or flash of black magic took place. Ominously his eyes traveled from James's petulant silent face to Brother Miles King, who seemed friendly enough but remote and tense. Strangely for an important man confronting a mere reporter, Miles wore an expression of anxiety, as if he were fearful about closing a business deal he didn't completely understand. But there was truly nothing sinister about him. In fact at close range the man seemed possessed of a softness and poignancy that was alarming. No lines of hatred were etched into those rather serious features. Could this be an illusion? Burrell suddenly did not know. Miles confused him. He swore he could actually feel an undefined touch of silliness creep all over his body and play with the yet unsaid words on his tongue. These feelings rose uncontrollably to the mottled surface of his flushed skin and radiated all over the room. Hurriedly he extracted a pair of gold spectacles from his breast pocket and put them on his round face. He threw one leg over the other with too much cockiness and then spoke.

"Sir, you are the subject of growing national debate and concern. And yet for all your fire the public has not been privileged to hear of any practical programs from you. Will you announce such a program soon? If so, what will it contain?"

Miles cleared his throat and began awkwardly, without any of his usual assurance. He eyed the fat pink reporter very evenly, taking solace in his tendency to perspire. "It seems to me you've asked two questions in one," he heard his voice saying. "Now about our program, you must realize that because this is a religious brotherhood we cannot spring a practical program on people just like that." He snapped his fingers, wishing immediately he hadn't. "I have not brought out this type of program because frankly the committee is still working on it. But you can be assured a time will come when I will present it for every man, woman, and child in this country to understand."

It sounded childish and feeble, a poor junior high-school recitation. Miles never learned to handle long-winded formal questions. He was best at stating what he believed to mobs of people. An instinct for safety told him to turn to James, to let James make it all sound smooth and intelligent and reasonable. But determinedly he stumbled on, unaware that James was angrily stirring in his seat to indicate he wanted to interrupt.

"As to what my program will contain, well, that's a tricky question. As an experienced reporter you know policies can change at the drop of a hat, but objectives never change. And the objectives of this Brotherhood are freedom, equality, and justice for the black man, with the good grace of Allah."

"Brother Miles, you mentioned a committee. Where does this committee sit and how well is it handling your ideas?" Burrell asked with a touch of mischief and the hope of whipping this silly recital into a satire that might someday be anthologized.

Here James nervously leaned forward in his chair. He was getting very tense. Miles never ignored him during interviews, but today he felt a subtle edge of reproach between them. Placing his fingertips on his temples, he exhaled heavily and stared at the carpet. As he sat back Burrell glanced his way contemptuously. Then Miles looked at him sharply, making it clear he wanted to go on for once without help. James was distracting him in a difficult situation. Already he could feel the initiative slipping away from him. He needed to say something important, to put this smug, little bastard back in his cage.

"Well, the committee I mentioned meets right here so I can

keep track of it. I think its findings are what you would call competently arrived at."

"Competently arrived at," Burrell said as he jotted it all down with a smile.

It went on that way, with Miles emerging as some kind of crude hill bandit who tugged at the ring on a fair lady's finger a couple of times before reaching for his knife, and then afterward tried to use medical language to explain what he had done. Burrell was posing another question, insisting this time Miles call him Sam, when abruptly James bounded to his feet, almost upsetting the coffee table. He looked straight down into Burrell's face, as if peering through a plate glass window, and the frustration and heated confusion distorting his features was terrible to see.

"You're trying to humiliate this man because you know he stands for something better than you," James cried aloud.

"No," Burrell said, rising from his chair very slowly. "No," he said roundly, shaking his large head. "You don't understand. I'm responsible to editors. I get the stories they want, that's all I do, my friend," Burrell pleaded, his reddish face discolored with stark amazement and horror at what might come next.

"Shut up, James," Miles snapped, jumping up astounded. "Shut your goddamn stupid mouth and get out of my office now."

"You lying son-of-a-bitch," James went on, completely disregarding Miles. "I've been watching you. You came in here looking for a minstrel show," he yelled at the short, stout man whose chubby arms quivered up about his face as James stepped up to him and slammed a muscular knee into his groin with such force the pain flashed up his spine in an instant and exploded in his brain as he screamed hysterically and was clubbed down by a vicious forearm while the sound still left his mouth. Swooning in a wash of agony, Burrell was spared the full force of a kick that snapped his head sideways. He never saw Miles leap at James and actually ride his massive back for a few seconds as James swerved like a madman to throw off the load and return to stomp all the life out of him.

Immediately two of the Fung crashed into the room with drawn pistols and rushed for James, hurtling into him high and low, spilling him violently back on top of Miles, who rolled over and got up quickly, his eyes widened with exertion and shock.

While James was guarded over on the floor in the center of the room, half a dozen Brothers came in and carefully removed Sam Burrell, who had slipped from consciousness, and carried him off to another office. Then Miles waved to his bodyguards and they retreated from the room, sullenly glancing back at the huddled figure still down on the carpet. As the door closed respectfully, James rolled easily to his feet and looked at the trembling and anxious form of Miles King standing by the window. His feelings were a congealed mixture of pity, scorn, and fluttering uncertainty. For a moment or two they stared at each other in silent, absolutely amazed wonder. Then James spoke. His voice was haughty and contained a new, savage authority that forced Miles to reach back with an unsure hand and touch the windowsill behind him. "The world is gaining on you," James told him hotly, "coming up on you fast. And you're tired, Brother, you're very tired. So am I."

Twenty minutes later, after Burrell had been hastily examined by a Brotherhood doctor and helped into a taxicab for the long moroseful ride to a downtown hospital, Miles returned to his office still quaking slightly and absorbed in apprehension. Burrell and his news magazine would tear at him now with the demented fury of a shrike, and the more conservative journals would surely croak their agreement in heavy unison. Soon the curious issue of his legitimacy would again be raised and this time Miles was not confident he could fight off attacks, especially if they came along a broad front. He was depressed. Quietly he sank into his leather chair and stared out into his office with hollow unfocused eyes. Toward James he felt only a vague sensation of dread and disgust. As time wasted away in the long silence all around him, Miles remembered for no traceable reason that James had been very taut and snappish lately. Immediately his mind strained for a little bit of evidence, some undisguised fact to build his observations on. But he was too spent and on edge to think. James was right. He was very tired, perhaps weary with self-deception, chasing impossible goals, and the labor of flogging a whole people to awareness when, who knows, maybe they just loved the taste of the whip. Any idea of analyzing James faded from his grasp to mingle with a hundred favorable tableaux of his loyal assistant working himself to the verge of a stupor, probably just to be smothered by futility in the end. Yet Miles sensed there were subtle alterations in James Fitzgerald's manner, outcroppings of petulance and dismay he hadn't seen since they first met. An amorphous strain of lazy pleasure and trepidation made him wonder exactly what baroque fears and chilling reverberations of madness he'd rescued James from. How little of James was truth and how much choice fiction? With a touching ironic delight Miles realized it was impossible to gauge. He'd never really wanted to know anyway. That was the lonely personal bond between him and James. Asking for explanations now could only be an act of censure. Still it was eerie to grasp only a few strands of an individual's life, a few wisps of character and hope, and try to weave them back into a design it was impossible to know.

But there was dangerous violence in James. And it had to be stopped. Miles would not permit violence around him. He detested ignorant confusion and force because he'd never really escaped from it. Tomorrow morning James would have to be cursed out for what he did, Miles thought, driving himself to the edge of a silent fury. He'd have to bend his neck and ask for forgiveness. He'd have to beg Sam Burrell to accept his apologies or it was back into the streets again, back to wherever the hell he'd fled from. But if he knuckled down as he was sure to do, then they could be friends again in their circumspect, efficient way. It was not such a bad arrangement. And this whole thing might work out to be a good lesson for James. Yes, it might. James was too damn aloof anyway. He drew out suspicion in people and that was a bad trait. He'd have to dispose of it though. And then quite abruptly Miles saw that through all of his meanderings he was really badly alarmed about James. Vague doubts, about himself, about everything in general circulated in his head. Irritably he got up from the desk. Outside the purple twilight had colored to darkness. The marquee lights were on. Up on the wall an electric clock marked two hours gone, never to be recaptured.

After leaving Miles confounded and shaken in his office, James stalked out of the hall, overcome by the insane temerity of what he had just done and said. His body began to quiver with an ominous remorse that only made him angrier. Brusquely he darted along the sidewalk, staring furiously at perfect strangers. Along the avenue he went, slowing his pace after a time as the great superblocks of brownstone slum houses etched into religious sadness by the fading sun fell behind his hard, alert step, separating him from Brotherhood Hall and the attack of madness that had seized his mind. But a fluttering turbulence still pulled at him with the swift power of a fatal undertow and the silky lightness of an evening cloak. His whole face was overheated and for a moment James was afraid he might pass out in the street. At last he arrived home, descending the hill very slowly, as if he expected to go sprawling backward with a sudden loss of gravity. Cautiously he opened the door to his apartment and went in, stopping to examine himself in the hall mirror. Around those light brown uncertain eyes and his churlish mouth there was a flush of excitement that added a harsh beefiness to his slightly boyish face. With ten less pounds on a frame that was swelling into chubbiness, James had a chance to be handsome. His complexion was neither very light nor dark and the tasteful conservative clothes he wore set off his usual businesslike manner nicely. James always dressed well because he knew it helped to conceal the hint of a bewildered genteel strain few people ever got to notice in him. He looked like a perfect middle-management nonentity. And standing there before his image, James was drawn to ponder why he was not what he seemed to be. For one of the few moments in his life he concentrated seriously on trying to grasp all of what made him so strange, so quietly pathetic and tortured. Slowly his thoughts uncoiled, but in their motions he detected something halting and ineffectual. Suddenly he was stricken with a pang of confusion and fear. He turned away from the mirror as his face warped into an expression of fiendish disgust. Going down the hall, he made his way into the living room, struggling to be calm, to forget he really had no life of his own to contemplate, struggling to understand why the ministry had ordered him to arrange for the destruction of the only person who ever believed in his complexities.

Sitting in a large chair by the window, he brooded over the assassination once again. In a familiar mood of oppression he attempted, and failed through sheer stupidity he told himself, to comprehend why the ministry wanted Miles dead. The future rested on strong authoritative figures like Miles; they had taught him that at Bern. Therefore the order had to be a bureaucratic or policy blunder. Someone in the structure had worked out the wrong problem and arrived at a disastrous mistake. Momentarily James was fired with the dramatic idea of a hideous enigmatic error, but just as quickly he let it drop, knowing this could not possibly be true. The cool punctiliousness of his orders dashed the whole false conception into a million splinters. And even if it were true, even if the directive were a mistake of some kind, there was no hope for a reversal anyway; the system made no provision for personal inquiry. It was intrinsically cold, Manichaean, and always fatal to those who deviated. In fact it searched for deviants with efficient glee. That was why Mahanti had questioned him so closely; he was probing for signals of total reliability as scrupulously as a technician might test a television circuit.

On the weekend Charlie De Young blew into town, giving off the vain, light scent of expensive toilet water and trailing irony and laughter, distorted bitterness and angry wit. In California he'd enjoyed his status as a minister without portfolio. Everywhere he displayed a humorous gravity as important matters were explained to him, but when he arrived in New York, the pose of a cheerful gray eminence was discarded. Immediately he found a cab and went to Brotherhood Hall to brief Miles on the California situation. "It's very bad out there. We need a whole new strategy. New mosques, new members, and some Brothers in the city councils to protect our interests. You have to go out and give our people some hope, but that's only the beginning, Miles. Our adversaries are already mobilized. They're up on the firing line. The police forces out there recruit their hands in the South. They go right into the front yards without asking. I bet they take the hoe right away from those boys and measure them up for battle fatigues before leaving town. I couldn't stand to live out there with all that tension. And if someone doesn't step in, war is going to break out in the streets. I'm not sure we can prevent it. Our people are frightened and angry. They're set to lunge at anything. Meanwhile the cops strut around like an armed militia and the rich people pretend nothing is wrong."

De Young rambled on for forty-five minutes, giving all the dreary details no one thought he'd absorbed. He was a tall, trim, fair-skinned black man who wore expensive suits and moved with the pleasant grace of a retired sprinter. As he talked Miles leaned back in his leather chair and listened attentively. At times De Young surprised him with abrupt revelations of a stubborn intelligence, which he roguishly cataloged, for it added to the stream of paradoxes mingling in their relationship. On a superficial plane they were almost winsome comrades in bawdiness, staging laughs, wild silly jokes, and occasional drinking escapades together with a masculine familiarity neither could establish with James, who was very serious and disinterested. At the Afro-Asian Peoples Conference in Djakarta they had drifted away to a private feast given by Indonesian diplomats and drank delicate rare wines, and eaten choice game birds and sweetmeats, and downed beautiful women until dawn burst, and they were discreetly driven back to their hotel in a black-curtained limousine. During the two-week stay James remained in his room every night and studied mimeographed summaries of the conference. He was terrified of foreign cities at that point; fear told him that moving through the unknown streets was another kindly ominous stranger waiting to wrest away his soul. He never knew they'd ventured into the delicious mysteries of Djakarta—the sex cults, the buzzing varieties of women, the underground rites—traveling along like two portly epicures stumbling up to a fabulous buffet. James didn't seem to care about anything except returning to New York and the safe routine of Brotherhood Hall. Never did he understand the intense jealous admiration in De Young's eyes when he watched Miles move among the diplomats and international journalists; and so it escaped him that Charles De Young revered the superior style of authority.

But to De Young, Miles King's powerful style and the allegiance it generated mattered more than almost anything. The careful subtleness in Miles, the precious nuances of his message did not touch him at all. He was interested only in power, in the sleek exhilaration of mass compliance. He fancied Miles's language, the scholarly and exact street talk that he could easily turn into good firm English. The percolating excitement of large crowds under Miles's hand tormented him with envy. He craved the same kind of admiration. But in the midst of rich times and staunch comradeship, De Young was never reluctant to praise the eminence of his fine friend. Many times in a half-drunken whisper he confided to the ear beside him that the splendid idea of Miles King was his true reason for being in the Brotherhood. And always Miles accepted this fawning with the stately benignity of a cardinal confronting an impoverished parish priest.

Essentially Miles was very contemptuous of De Young, even as he maintained him in an artificial and useful companionship. Instinctively he comprehended that in their manly coexistence, intermixed with good bouts of cleansing self-indulgence, one personality had to be dominant. Automatically he took himself to be the better man, the wise senior partner casting a shadow over a somewhat unworthy but talented associate. But secretly this conceited stance made him defensive until he noticed more and more that Charles De Young tried to assert an insidious and cool superiority over everyone around him. Casually he ordered Brothers to park his car, get his morning coffee, and carry out his whimsy of the day. Yet his commands were never harsh, and this worried Miles, for De Young seemed to put forth a manner that was ingratiating and soothing, as if he were always on his best behavior. People felt making him comfortable was a pleasure happily incumbent upon them.

And at times De Young's presumptions would spill over into their dealings. Miles observed now and then a strain of condescension would rise in his voice as one of his overbearingly clever suggestions was summarily dismissed. Then he would go away incensed, positive in his bitter convictions that Miles was lost to the vagaries of childish naïvete. Sometimes he whined to a few of the Brothers that Miles was power mad and didn't see his real qualities. But always he returned quietly and contritely to do what Miles had decided. He was never insubordinate. He never allowed suspicion or hostility to drift in his direction, yet Miles always found him too skeptical and worldly to be really trusted. For one thing he talked about political theories a lot, sometimes with surprising sharpness. And his mind seemed to contain a hundred schemes for gaining power. He urged Miles to run for Congress, insisting he'd slide into office on a gleeful avalanche of black votes. ("Why not turn some of this glory into politics? You can't hold power by warming it with your ass.") Constantly he harped on the idea of infiltrating political clubs in black districts and assaulting the structure of local governments. Then there was his favorite ploy: the conversion of the Brotherhood into a robust political party, a clear and definite fiefdom the country would have to respect. ("What leverage is there in being a religious folk hero? In the end who really cares? Listen, you can be more than a curiosity, Miles. You can be history.") But always Miles declined. Occasionally with an indulgent beefy laugh, but often in clandestine fury, for he hated any suggestion of practical manipulations. Miles didn't want to be merged into the smooth, clever machinery of American life. He feared the thought because it would obliterate him as a spiritual presence; it would transmute him into something destitute and mechanical—a prominent institutional version of flashy Brother Charles De Young.

When the briefing had ended with a handshake and the promise of a steak dinner some evening soon, Miles went to the window and opened it to let out the sweetish, lingering scent of toilet water. He loved the fragrance of a delicate perfume when it was coming off a woman, but in a man he took it as a sign of excessive preening and wicked self-gratification. But De Young was like that. He enjoyed thinking too highly of himself. The fat zircon pinkie ring, which lay heavily against the tan flesh of his hand, was a talisman for him. No one had ever been bold enough to tell him zircon was a stone favored by pimps, the ultimate sign of superficiality, pathos, and futility.

Biting down on his lower lip thoughtfully, Miles remembered zircon was also interpreted as a harbinger of ambition. A slow pang of concern went through him. De Young impinged on his life too much, Miles decided. He had a horrible way of attempting to cramp his importance when they were together that came back to Miles now in a flash of contempt; for he despised men who wanted to be valued for more than they were possibly worth. Underneath, men of that type always seethed with frustration. Their lives reverberated with a terrifying jingle and glared in the mind like the brittle intense light of a zircon.

It was too bad about De Young. In a narrow, selfish way he was a smart boy. But he possessed no real intellectual qualities, no trace of humane convictions. His knowledge of the world came from figuring up percentages. Compassion was an exotic feeling to him. He didn't really care about the fate of the black man. He indulged in sensuality as if it were a luxurious convenience, like a hot bath in the tropics. Without ever wavering, his mind spun around a well-tuned sense of artful skill. Charles De Young was a highly enterprising technician of life. But he was also dangerous. Miles was certain that in their jocularity a silent momentum existed that could do him harm. During his whole time in the Brotherhood, De Young never once admitted Miles's approach to life was correct. Always he suggested his ideas were superior and intrinsically mature. A certain implacability in De Young strove to blot out Miles's innocence. And in the intricate tracings of his meditations, a threatening sensation came through to Miles. He could only be relieved that he hadn't made the mistake of trusting Brother Charles more.

After delivering his little summary of the California crisis, Charles De Young sauntered out into the hall, deliberately leaving the office door wide open so passersby could see Miles pondering the intelligence they would soon learn Brother Charles had just brought. He was looking for his admirers now, the group of Brothers he called the Constituency. People going by in the hall smiled brightly at him. Once or twice he peeked into an office, flashing a big devilish smile at some startled face or flipping off a tickling witticism. Within half an hour everyone in the building would know he was back and the thought amused him. Moving along in the warm bliss of his immaculate vanity, De Young could not know a piece of interesting and revelatory data had been exorcised from the sheltering milieu around him. Silenced by orders from Miles, who feared the start of rumor and scandal, every person with knowledge of the disturbing incident with the magazine reporter was pledged to secrecy. Miles and James had met with the owner of the magazine and apologized in his offices. The owner had said the incident would be mentioned only in passing because Burrell had gathered enough material for a fine story anyway. Then James left and the pact was sealed over dry sherry. Later Miles took a vague pleasure in the whole business. He'd protected his name, his Brotherhood, and a valuable assistant by plagiarizing from the worldly theories of Charles De Young. What better revenge was there for a smart pupil?

In spite of the ripples of adulation he inspired, not everyone believed in Charles De Young. People enjoyed calling him the Next Man, Charles Nkrumah, and the secretary of state because he was funny and clever. Still there was something remote and studied about him. Essentially he seemed permanently removed from the improvisational style of the streets. Somewhere his life had taken a different route. He claimed to have grown up in New Orleans, but no one in the mosque there knew him. Once he had even refused to go to New Orleans on a special assignment. Around the country a number of Brothers had curious stories to tell about him. Some claimed to have run into him before he began using a name like De Young. Maybe it was De Jean or De Jong, they could never really be sure. A group of Brothers in California said he'd been seen many years ago interrogating black prisoners at the federal penitentiary in Atlanta. Others claimed he was a paratrooper under a different name. Every now and then a Brother would confront De Young with one of these anecdotes, but he never failed to turn it into an elusive joke. ("Sure, I've been around. That's how I picked up my schooling. I'm always right behind you and when you look around I'm in front. So be good, Brother.") The first time James heard one of these stories he cowered. There was a detachment in De Young that crisscrossed with his own, he was certain of this much. And so when De Young joked with the Brothers ("I was the best child pickpocket in Louisiana"), James never even tried to laugh. Over a period of time an unspoken animosity developed between the two men. Miles never succeeded in bringing them together. Brother Charles found it difficult not to ridicule Brother James. And in return James loathed De Young with the intensity and steadiness of current passing through an electric wire.

CHAPTER FIVE

AS AN EMPLOYEE of the Research and Intelligence Agency attached to a provisional unit dealing in internal security affairs, one of the ten secret teams operating within the country, Charles Warren De Young had risen to the station of GS-11 through a series of brilliant individual assignments. Within his purview (what he called the range of his guns) he was a unique individual equipped with the sure qualities of bravery, steady courage, and deadly style, especially style, which belong only to the choicest of men. The great American legend of the truly unshackled male, the challenger, the kid, the stud, the shooter, was so strong within him that no conscious effort, even psychoanalytic, could free him from it for long. De Young lived with violent fantasy as other men exist trapped by mortgages, inadequate salaries, and the good-natured boredom of suburbia.

Born in Council Bluffs, Iowa, forty-one years before, into the union of a Pullman porter and an arthritic domestic, who feared his coming would break her health and spirit, he fought against terrible odds through his childhood (stoned badly one day at school, he was then savagely beaten by his father for letting it happen) and blossomed into a handsome swaggering youth. After three exhilarating years as a halfback on the high-school football team he scorned a dozen college offers and took to the road, looking for excitement and perhaps a trace of his father, who had swung aboard the Kansas City Limited one sunset and never returned. In New Orleans he drove the get-away car during a gas station holdup where the attendant was beaten into permanent blindness. After his share was gone, he drifted into a segregated airborne unit and made thirty jumps before the war in Europe was over. The army told him he had a future and he believed it. Military police spy work on the German black market became his specialty. In the American Zone forty-seven successful prosecutions resulted from his arrests. And his numbered Swiss bank account held nearly sixty thousand dollars when he returned to Washington for training as an interrogator. A special office of the War Department borrowed him from the army to head a unique survey project in which black draft evaders in federal prisons were probed for the psychological motives shoring up their recalcitrance. Later that same year De Young left the army and entered a university in Washington, D.C., to get a degree in history. ("Life has taught me to look only for the facts," he told one professor.) His army money and the GI Bill allowed him to live and dress in ostentatious splendor on a campus where half the men wore odd pieces of tattered service clothing. But after two years he was bored. The light chatter of righteous and inexperienced college girls fatigued him into anger and disgust. It pleased him when a letter came one day offering a job with the newly established Research and Intelligence Agency. Still when indoctrination was over, all they did was put him at a desk in the political section to analyze magazine articles and books by black intellectuals suspected of favoring communism. He requested a transfer, and when he had almost forgotten about it, abruptly the order came down. (You are hereby made operative. Your job will be to apprehend subversive persons employed at factories engaged in contract work for the Department of Defense, et al. Special attention should be devoted to non-Caucasian workers.) Eight years later De Young's score was a round one hundred convictions, seventy of them involving black people. His favorite tactic was to use women informers who came into court and testified to large cash expenditures so the Bureau of Internal Revenue could be brought in to support his cool pressures for an explicit confession. During this time Charles De Young killed five men. In private judicial sessions the killings were invariably called self-defense or justifiable homicide. The agency avoided public trials and De Young was grateful. He didn't mind being unknown. It made no difference that his successes weren't recorded outside of agency files, for he relished his association with secret power.

Rarely did it occur to him that he worked at a job. He didn't understand that as an employee in a giant but largely clandestine bureaucracy, he shared knowledge with, and even stared directly in the face, those forces of relentless conformity manipulating the sensibilities of his age, the very same forces, unmistakably totalitarian in origin, which controlled a progressive view of the future and had not one modicum of feeling for the past. The world Charles de Young so badly accepted resulted in classified plans for chemical warfare in Asia, modishly sterile architecture, and well-programmed leisure-time fantasies—a synthetic man-enforced world where people found it difficult to ever be happy. De Young was allied in a conspiracy to make the human brain modern.

Never did he acknowledge this fact. There was never any need to think about the consequences of what he'd done. Besides he didn't like to delve too deeply into himself. Introspection cut into his act, ruined his timing, and possibly played havoc with the chemistry of his juices, that vital essence he could never know had dried up years before. And once or twice when he had wandered back over his career, what he turned up frightened him. He was perceptive enough to know a vengeful serpentine passion intertwined with his life. Uneasily he felt its roots were deep and strong in an unfathomable fear and despair. He suspected the same passion edged forward in him that had driven his father away from home and into a wandering anonymous death.

Case review was the part of intelligence work Charles De Young really hated. All day Monday he contemplated his appointment that evening with dread and irritation. And at the end of the day he deliberately left his office late, knowing they would be annoyed. His car was being serviced (one of the many tiny disturbances in a fitful day) so reluctantly he took the bus down to Union Square, where he decided to get off and walk. Turning into University Place, De Young strode briskly along for two blocks returning the admiring smiles of women who noticed his excellently cut gray-striped double-breasted suit. Then abruptly he veered off the sidewalk and up the steps of a cluttered dank secondhand bookstore. The proprietor, an elderly man who was seated in the dim light at a rolltop desk in the rear, didn't bother to look up as he passed and disappeared into the back of the store. Unhappily he rang a concealed buzzer and Sergeant Zito released the door catch and let him in.

Zito was the only security person on night duty. The two blasé, middle-aged secretaries with years of disinterested and efficient service behind them had gone home along with three young analysts who seemed to do nothing but read tracts from the Foreign Language Publishing House in Peking and compare the contents with editorials in black newspapers. But Lake was there, neatly dressed and clean as a cat, sitting behind a metal, government-issue desk along with a man named Riggs.

"Join us, Charlie," Austin Lake said pleasantly.

De Young sat down with mock sullenness. Lake and Riggs watched his well-tailored form ease onto a hard chair. They knew he disliked review, but considered it a totally absurd attitude, somewhat like a baseball player not wanting to show up at the park. Besides it was very clear, to the point of being a common joke, that Charlie De Young wanted badly an outlandish respect and approval from his superiors. Distractedly Riggs looked at the creamy brown Negro face with its faint splash of freckles. De Young was handsome. There was no doubt about that. The thick sandy moustache bushing out above his well-formed nearly beautiful mouth gave him a devilish insolent air. But the pinkie ring spoiled it, Riggs thought. The ring was big and too vulgar, probably an indication of the coarseness beneath all this finery.

"How is Brother Miles?" Lake began briskly.

"Miles is fine. He'll be in town for another week. Then he plans a speaking tour of California beginning in San Diego and working his way up the coast."

Lake nodded and wrote it all down on a large pad before him. Riggs did not speak.

"What about James? What is he doing?" Lake asked.

"As far as I can see, not a thing," De Young replied coolly.

"As usual," Lake said very slowly, as if it caused him embarrassment.

Within the agency a debate about James Fitzgerald, known humorously in the *Daily Intelligence Bulletin* as the Oxford-Cambridge Special, had continued on and off for years. Who was he? What was his mission? (Malicious mischief!) When was it to begin? No one knew. No one seemed to know anything really substantial about James. Every six months since 1958 the director had ordered a complete review of this baffling person. Yet the facts yielded nothing of value. He was still simply

> Fitzgerald, James Stewart, born November 10, 1928, in New York City (Harlem Hospital). Attended public schools and Amherst College on a partial scholarship. Served with distinction (see photostat service record back page) in U.S. Army Korea 1951–1953. Note crossreference to CIC file No. 27192F attached, detailing contact with Communist student club at Tokyo University. Worked at various jobs unsuccessfully U.S. 1953–1955. Departed for Bern, Switzerland, 1956. Employed by Bank of China, a cover occupation for training as subversive agent by Chinese Ministry of Foreign Affairs 1956–1958. 1959 to the present date part-time surveillance and observation three

years (see attached ref. to file no.), followed by full-time surveillance, resulting in failure to detect suspicious activity.

De Young watched Brian Riggs carefully, noting his clear, almost translucent English skin beneath which very fair blue veins could be seen if one looked hard enough. The line of his jaw was stern but not experienced, somewhat like a cadet's, and in his pure, untroubled eyes there lurked a formality strange in a young man.

Riggs was a commuter from Washington. He had been a college instructor in government and attended divinity school for a time before coming into the intelligence business five years ago. His job was to head a watchdog committee keeping track of provisional units and reporting their activities to the director, who was a social friend of his father. De Young had learned from one of the secretaries that Riggs came from a family whose activities in government went back to the War of 1812, and he assumed right away the younger man's aloof bearing came from being taken seriously, perhaps out of fear, during an uncounted number of confidential discussions in the agency and elsewhere. The secretary also said Brian Riggs would be the next director and De Young was mulling this information over in his mind when Riggs turned his way, addressing him for the first time.

"Charlie," he said a little stiffly, "the director has asked me to review the Fitzgerald situation with you once again in the light of certain national imperatives. At a meeting of the National Security Council last week, several of the members brought up disturbing news they had received about Chinese attempts to cultivate the Negro minority. This is now a matter of some concern in Washington. The president fears that perhaps all the recent advances in civil rights could be jeopardized by Communist-instigated disorders and the like. We know the Chinese interest in the American Negro is growing." De Young nodded sagely but he wasn't really listening. Educated talk bored him. Riggs sensed this indifference and raised his

79

voice just a little. "You will recall that the Chinese leaders have sent telegrams to various Negro leaders on important occasions, before marches on Washington, after serious riots, and so forth. They have been reasonably silent about the new civil rights laws and other measures. However, just the other day Radio Peking launched a series of one-hour propaganda broadcasts on the racial question here. Our policy people think this may be the start of a serious attempt to stir up trouble. The director and I believe"—he aimed a deprecating look at De Young—"that it is now time to go over some of the alternatives open to Fitzgerald."

De Young pursed his lips in disgust. He was tired of James. He was weary of this assignment. The agency had made him into a baby-sitter and he resented it. But at the same time he knew he'd grown a little careless in his observations and he didn't want Riggs to suspect inefficiency.

"Let's go back to his days in Bern," Lake suggested. There was a tinge of humorous mockery in his voice.

"All right," Riggs snapped. He didn't want to go over a file that was part of his memory, but he consented to make them more amenable to the decision already reached in Washington. "We know during fifty-seven and fifty-eight James would make occasional trips to Paris, presumably for operational training," he said turning back to De Young. "This is not a trivial fact. It means we have to assume he's well-drilled. But in that case why was he trained in Bern where they know we photograph everything that moves around the embassy?"

"Because he's not very important," De Young replied morosely as Riggs stared at him in sudden anger.

"A good point, Charlie," Lake put in good-naturedly. "I don't think this man is an operative at all. He couldn't be," Austin Lake continued, raising his well-modulated voice. "Possibly he never was. The Chinese may simply have used him as a decoy to make us apprehensive. After all these years, we should consider that theory," he added with a touch of whimsical finality.

The levity and indifference around him was beginning to

infuriate Riggs, but he addressed himself to it with just the right edge of malice and intimidation. "I'm here to review this case, Austin, not to demolish it. What you say has no validity. We can not, it would be amateur to assume, that Fitzgerald won't do something in the future. My feeling, and the director concurs, is that if anything surveillance on Fitzgerald should be increased."

"Why? Because of a few hostile radio broadcasts?" Lake retorted. "We don't have enough of a file on this man to justify increased surveillance. This man has been away from the Ministry of Foreign Affairs for some years. Undoubtedly he's just a fellow traveler now. It's my opinion that close contact with King may have helped to or completely changed his allegiance. He has a new faith to believe in now. And if he's intelligent at all, he must see that China is too poor and far away to help American Negroes."

De Young agreed with Lake but he remained quiet. There was no point in breaking in. He had nothing to add. It was safer to watch and be amused with Lake and Riggs, to secretly mock their facility for making everything abstract when you knew life was subtle, treacherous, and explosive, but never really theoretical. De Young strained to keep a droll expression off his face as he saw Brian Riggs turn on Lake and say evenly, "Somehow you don't understand that we are faced with a very unstable situation in this country regarding the racial question, and for this reason the existence of the Fitzgerald file is a matter of active security. Fitzgerald came to the attention of CIC many years ago. We can assume without contradiction that he is a trained provocateur. You do not possess evidence—factual, psychological, or otherwise—which leads the agency to assume he is not a potential danger to this country," Riggs said angrily. He hated to be challenged, and intuition told him control of the discussion was not in his hands. He was a little worried. What would the director say if he knew?

"I suppose you're correct," Lake said wryly. "However, using national security as our yardstick, everything we know about ministry operations diminishes his significance quite a bit. The ministry has neither the time or the resources for long-term operations. Their pattern of activity shows desperation, recklessness, and a willingness to write off people. You mentioned social instability, but does this really pertain to Fitzgerald? What provocative act has he actually committed? None. He's never done anything suspicious. Besides I would point out to you, Brian, that the source of instability and rioting is simple discontent. These upheavals are fairly predictable. There is nothing conspiratorial in sporadic seasonal disorders. And in any event one isolated individual, without an active following and substantial funds, could not have the value you assign to Fitzgerald."

"Oh, you don't know what you're talking about, Austin," Riggs cried, throwing up an arm in disgust. Lake smiled at him with just a whisper of condescension, and right aways Riggs was surprised and furious. But he controlled himself. His position demanded prudence. "I don't see what you're getting at," he said, shaking his head contemptuously.

"Look, what I think we must do is protect against Chinese influence among the Negroes and disruptive elements wherever they appear," Lake continued smoothly. "I don't think we can afford to waste time pursuing melodramatic alternatives. The agency is supposed to help maintain a stable orderly balance in society, not dash around in trench coats, Brian. What do you think, Charles?" Lake added quickly.

"I think we're spending too much time talking about James," De Young came back brightly.

Calculation suggested to De Young that now was the time to support Austin Lake fully. He knew Lake better and was sure he was the easier man to handle. Riggs was too distant and self-contained. And besides there was always the remote possibility that Lake's arguments would create enough confusion and uncertainty in Washington to precipitate a closing of the Fitzgerald file and free him for another assignment, possibly in a foreign country. With a serious face he turned to Brian Riggs and said, "Training or not, Fitzgerald is no more dangerous than college students who read Mao in paperback. I see him every day and his behavior is always the same, business-like and subservient."

Riggs looked away with loathing in his eyes. He didn't reply. He told himself he didn't need to. But he was incensed. His own assumptions had been used against him and he would not forget the insult. He understood what Lake was thinking. Lake wanted to try to control Miles King rather than concentrate on Fitzgerald, who was an established threat. For months Austin Lake had been telling friends in the agency that it was a serious policy mistake to grant the Fitzgerald file so much importance. Now he was obviously ready to put forth his own plan. And his plan would probably find backers in Washington. It would be sound and orderly and not cost too much. Lake was clever at presenting his ideas, but Riggs had heard enough of them. He could not comprehend why Lake seemed so drawn to Miles King. King was an annoyance, but never a real danger. Lake was strange. He had an affinity for Negroes. That had to be why De Young came in on his side.

After a few minutes of silence, Lake began talking. He was not so whimsical now and Brian Riggs thought he detected a strain of entreaty in the voice addressing him. "I know you disagree with me, Brian, but I feel King is the important man in this business. A charismatic figure like King can do more to upset this country than Fitzgerald ever could. With one speech he could make Negroes raid the banks or descend on the White House with torches. He's quite a formidable man," Lake said thoughtfully. "And he doesn't leave us many options. We could take the risk of letting him run wild and perhaps burn out, or we can try to use his strength to placate the unrest we all fear. I've worked out a recommendation that may solve the problem of what to do with King. Essentially I want him to perform under our tent where we can keep a closer watch on him."

CHAPTER SIX

"YOU PEOPLE are really going whoop-de-do," Clarence Williams said to James. On the restaurant table between them lay a copy of *Time* magazine with Miles on the cover. Just above his head a message read, "Brother Miles: Most Dynamic U. S. Negro Leader?" Inside the lengthy report, though it mentioned angry Brother James prominently, focused on the Brotherhood and Miles, whom the magazine nominated, through the power of an exceptional style, as the one man likely to become a permanent force for responsible progress, a force "more dynamic and ego-centered than the sometimes pale and unexciting Christianity of Bible-directed Negro ministers and their volatile followers." To forever prove their affinity for the man, the editors ran the caption, "All bad and no good?" under an artistic photograph of Miles lecturing a news conference at his headquarters.

James enjoyed what for him was a lighthearted mood, although a strong and persistent and steady pulse of guilt mingled constantly with his thoughts. Now and again he appeared preoccupied and abstracted, but most of the pleasure in this sudden meeting stayed with him. It had been a long time since he'd run into anyone he really cared to see, but Clarence Williams was an exception. They had worked in the same bank years ago and refreshingly, Williams had not changed at all. He went on telling stories of the intervening time with the same winningly insecure patter that had always been part of his personality. James could not help laughing at the total, unabashed lack of change in the man. Probably this affability, because it contained no hint of great ambitions or suggestion of devious plans, had been the deciding point in securing a teller's job for Clarence.

James remembered their first meeting. He had come onto the banking floor with a group of trainees. Immediately Clarence stopped working and stared so intently that everything in the immense room came to a near stop and a fast moment of panic zipped through the scene as guards studied each face quickly to find the robber and his accomplices. Later Clarence was asked to explain, and with startling candor he told his supervisor that the sight of a fellow black man tiptoeing through the executive suite had left him flabbergasted. It became a company joke. For weeks afterward James refused to acknowledge him. Then, after a brief month of whimsical circumspection, they became good friends and broke all the unspecified rules by lunching together each day.

"What are you doing now, Clarence?" James asked, trying to hold back a smile he knew was too broad and mocking for Clarence to take with ease.

"Well, you can't read about me in the papers if that's what you mean, but I always keep a job of some kind. Right now it's insurance."

"What ever happened to the bank?"

"That bank was too much for me, James. After you left I couldn't stand it. Every day I'd fall in there and look at all that money and say to myself, Clarence, if you don't take some of that money home with you tonight, you belong in Brooklyn forever." James laughed softly as Clarence continued. "It got to be too much of a struggle inside my head and I honestly didn't know if I could fight it any longer so I quit. I sold pots and pans door to door until I heard them banging in my sleep, so I laid off that and went back to Georgia for a few years. What have you been doin'? Somebody said you left the country for a while."

James frowned. "Yes, I had a dinky job working in a foreign bank, in Switzerland."

Clarence studied his old friend with great interest in his eyes. "Is that so? You're what they call a regular world traveler, James," he said with a trace of awe in his voice. "What's it like over there?"

James gazed across the table at the expectant, annoyingly childish face watching him. He hesitated and hoped Clarence would not press him. And then he noticed Clarence's eyes. These same bright eyes must have nearly popped out of the heads of black children fixed on the figure of a carpetbagger coming down some Southern trail in the years after the Civil War. They were the incredible, naïve eyes one saw in government photographs of impoverished blacks during the Depression, eyes that always grew rheumy with malice at age twenty and merged perfectly with a determined, cheated, angry visage. Now James examined Clarence's clothes; sloppily cut clothes of not really first-rate material, lower middle-class, anonymous clothes. He realized poor Clarence would never understand Europe. Finally, with hesitation he spoke, "It's just like here only they speak different languages."

Clarence seemed genuinely disappointed to hear this. He had thought the European continent was a great place, but as it was not, he automatically shut it out of his mind and later spoke of it scornfully, as if he knew all about Europe and held nothing but contempt for it.

A pretty waitress brought their food—fried chicken, black-eyed peas cooked with rice, kale, hot corn bread on the side—and served them in the thoroughly solicitous style that made Bevel's Southern View Restaurant famous as the place where a famous New York gossip columnist reported an elderly senator from Alabama had finished his meal and wept for the salvation of the Southern Negro.

"Country food," Williams said with gusto. "I'll take it any time." They ate quickly and lustily, digging into the food with the exuberance of section hands.

"Say, James, tell me something about this Brotherhood you're in," Williams said when he had nearly finished.

"Better than telling you, why don't you come on out to a meeting and see for yourself? Miles speaks every Sunday at two o'clock at the Brotherhood Hall. He also teaches Islam and the Arabic language three nights a week, and if you should decide to join now, the dues are cheaper."

"I don't know about any joining now," Williams protested, "but I'll come around one of these Sundays and check you people out."

James laughed heartily at his old friend. It was an unguarded, robust laugh and Williams, recognizing the long-forgotten merriment in it, laughed loudly too. He was a little presumptuous and he knew it, but it couldn't be helped. There was much deprivation in his background and things had started to go well so fast no time was left over to learn all the right manners.

In the middle of the week Clarence Williams picked James up after an evening class. He was driving a big, ostentatious, polished-down car and when James got in the back seat he found himself nearly smothered by two long-legged, good-looking girls who were all smiles and curves and titillating eagerness. They looked James over friskily, suggesting too obviously, he believed, that they were about to undress him right then and there. "Hi, sugar," one of them said brightly. "Do you want to know me?"

"You can bet top dollar I want to know you," James said, realizing suddenly how strangely fresh it sounded coming from him.

"Are you the serious one or the bad one?" the other girl asked. She was not as sexy.

"I'm the real bad one," said James with a crooked smile, daring her to go on.

"How bad?" she asked with a grin.

"As bad as you like it," he said casually, looking straight at her.

All three of them laughed very loudly and James slipped way back in his seat. Something told him there would be fun and no little mystery to this evening and he gave himself over to the suggestion. His arms came up around the girls and they rested their heads on his large shoulders. "My, you're a big man," said the sexy girl.

Clarence at the wheel, clutching a fifth of whiskey in one fist, turned around in surprise and delight. "Say, James, what is this? I let you in the yard and you develop a taste for chickens."

"You just drive and leave the playing to us," the girls protested. "And watch where you're going. This ain't no country road in Georgia you know."

The car zoomed up Seventh Avenue and turned into 139th Street where it pulled up in front of a place called the Club 48. Two short-range spotlights reached feebly for the sky, playfully mocking the big Hollywood-style arrival. Inside it was dark and very smoky: the huge dance floor, bordered by rows of miniature tables, was filled with couples. Round blue-and-white lights moved lazily over the whole scene while waiters in short red jackets hurried from the bar to the tables where men and women, wearied from dancing and too many drinks, laughed raucously and bantered with the scurrying waiters. On the stand a group of ten musicians dressed in formal attire eased into a rich and very sweet Ellington tune; the melody, poignant with nostalgia, drifted out over the room and many of the seated couples ceased talking abruptly to remember wistfully that Depression year so long ago when it had first been played. James floated over the dance floor holding one of the girls romantically in his arms. "What's your name?" he asked her with tenderness.

"Beverly," she answered softly.

They said no more but danced on for what must have been an hour. At first she was friendly, yet tense, and he could feel it in her body, but as they drifted over the floor she relaxed and moved closer. He could feel the wild curves of her sensuous form very close to him now and as they continued that way a warm and dreamy rapport laden with ripe but too earnest desire spread over both of them. James decided to make no moves until she did and his caution was rewarded when Beverly pressed firmly into his arms. She was dancing in a carefully lewd open-legged stance and her heat went up into his groin. On her back his fingertips tingled. He wanted nothing but to bend her backward over one strong knee and slake his lust right there. Her moist eyes met his and shone with pleasure. She had read his thoughts. He was completely excited all over, and once when he brushed her ear ever so slightly, he heard what sounded like a faint gasp, a permissive, free, and sexual little moan for his ears only. Then he kissed her on the neck with a warm delicacy that caused a tremor of agitation within her. Beverly's fingers spread over his back, fluttering madly, rubbing, searching, yearning; their mouths melted into each other; the wicked, deliciously insane gyrations of her reptilian tongue spun crazily through his brain, warming the whole of his existence. His groin was bathed in the sweetest and warmest of milk. They kissed hotly again. His heart, joyously suffused, floated up and unaccountably he felt alone with her, very far away and miles above the squalid world of irrational orders and demented grandeur he had sojourned in for so many years now.

The next morning Beverly fixed breakfast in her large, sunny apartment for all four of them. Clarence and Claire had to be called three times. Claire was the sexy one. Breakfast was an elaborate feast of omelets, tangerine juice, mounds of sausages, delicious coffee cake and imported tea. In its midst they talked freely, as though the breakfast had first happened on another quiet morning many years before. Claire pouted clownishly about not having enough money for new clothes and made loving eyes at Clarence, while Beverly talked seriously but excitedly of the great French dishes she loved to prepare. Before it was time to go, James had slipped into the kitchen and shyly asked her for a dinner date. She gave him the telephone number on a tiny slip of paper. In the hall they kissed politely with Claire looking on and he left with Clarence, who drove him to Brotherhood Hall for a ten o'clock press conference.

"What do you think of Bev?"

"I like her. She's sweet," James said.

"She sure is." Clarence let him out in front of the hall. "I'll call you on Monday," he said jovially.

"Sure thing," replied James. "And thanks for everything." He said it with a sincerity that almost embarrassed his old friend.

Clarence turned fully around, and what he saw was a contented face. For some reason he flinched and came back with an answer that did not quite fit. "Don't give it another little thought," he said as he pulled away.

In the hall several reporters from downtown papers stood around sullenly in a tight, apprehensive group. Miles was late. They had stories to write and were glad an official had shown up, but James only murmured something apologetic as he brushed past them and went straight to his office, thinking all the while about the pretty evening, about Beverly's soft, nude, pliant body outlined against the softer rays of dawn creeping into the bedroom. He knew it had been a very long time since he had felt such warmth and wonder in another human being. The whole experience seemed overladen with a thick and erotic mystery that gratefully freed him from the constraint always closing in to choke off his tenuous contact with humanity. Like a very young man just aware of a manly tenderness in himself, James began to relax and take delight in simple things. That day for the first time he showed a charming courtesy to the classes he taught. The somberness that was an inseparable part of his outlook quietly lifted. Right away the Sisters in the Brotherhood said he had a woman somewhere. Even the Brothers, who never cared much for him, admitted a woman with her thighs parted was maybe the only thing on earth to get him to smile a little and improve his disposition.

In the days that followed James handled the new feeling of having a woman to think about as though it were an exhilarating responsibility. His attention drifted to Beverly a lot. He found himself speculating dreamily after every date if it were not at all possible she might someday care enough to love him. If she did, he owed it all to that old fox Clarence. Clarence knew how to pick them. He always had, even though he overplayed his importance as a matchmaker and friend. It was necessary to see him fairly often or his feelings were hurt. Occasionally he pried. And now and again, when he talked about himself, an unpleasant spirit of very genial smugness appeared in him that couldn't be passed off as just clumsiness. Still Clarence was careful never to intrude too far into the territory of their affection, but this was annoying also, because he acted out his hesitancy, and James wondered intermittently if he could not find a polite way to end their friendship completely.

CHAPTER SEVEN

As HE ROSE into national prominence Miles King, like all famous leaders, accepted a certain regimen of personal security. The Fung was enlarged from six to twelve men, each of them masters of karate and deadly shots within the range covered by a .38 revolver. But this made no difference to the people in Harlem who believed in the power of omens. By their calculations, Miles was doomed. They said many times, even in Brotherhood Hall, that no matter how Miles tried there was no way in creation for him to avoid a violent death. It was ordained, a condition of his pervasive identity as a rebel leader, the natural and easy resolution to the unkind truths he presented with such desperate vigor. Miles had heard all these projections and dismissed them. Vaguely he understood death might come at any time. And secretly the very fact warmed him, for if he were murdered not even his fiercest enemies would be able to deny that his honesty had summoned the darkest and most repressive hatreds crouching in the human psyche to smash the life out of him.

But Miles wanted to die a great man if possible. And unknown to everyone he pursued an education in the lives of men who'd attained the stature he was still grasping for hungrily. Twice a month he sent Nicholas out to the library to get the books he wanted—popular histories and biographies dealing exclusively with the dramatic high points great men had reached. Their private musings titillated his passion for lucidity, and when he sat down to write his speeches in the evenings, a neat paraphrase or two Miles never intended invariably came off his pen. He cataloged important ideas on index cards, coined mottos by the dozen, and dictated long memos into the expensive recording machine given to him by the Fung on his last birthday. But above everything else Miles loved his speeches, which he assembled in the solitude of his office, working late into the night with the delicate scrupulousness of a bank examiner, working until his eyes were blurred with fatigue.

Lately he'd begun to extol Africa because it was large and worthy of his notice. Skillfully he described the place, its legendary and imposing mass, its green sunlit perfectly still plains, the incredible excess of natural riches covered by the lush soil. And lastly, almost as a cunning afterthought, the profusion of colorful and active black peoples spread throughout the continent in chaste, ideal splendor. Like a statesman he mingled the insidious prejudice of blood ties and the hysteria of current history. "The quest for freedom in Africa is linked with our struggle," he would cry out. "We are brothers. We must unite with them because they are the new revolutionaries. And we want to be part of that revolution too."

Miles was determined to get away from the simple militancy he sometimes practiced with appalling ease. He did not feel it was worthy of him, and the thought of becoming a mere radical sent him spiraling into depressions that sometimes lasted for hours. Yet beyond his fierce desire for nobility, Miles sensed that it might be impossible for him to ever accomplish anything of irreversible merit for black people. And this always filled him with a terrifying forewarning of doom.

Then not two days later something happened that summoned all of Miles's remotest fears to the surface where he could examine them through the distorting prism of reality.

One of the Brothers told him the strange news first. The Brother had heard it from an old black man in Brooklyn who called himself Abderahaman. For more than a week an odd story, part of the gloomy tapestry of suspicion and malice woven into the bleak life of the ghetto, had been repeated around. Numerologists, pimps, bartenders, and spiritualists had passed it along, sometimes in dread, often with glee. When Miles heard it, his heart quailed helplessly for a full half minute. Immediately he called the Fung into his office and had his limousine brought around to the marquee. After a quick briefing the car pulled away from Brotherhood Hall with Brother Nicholas and two bodyguards inside. Twenty minutes later it raced the setting sun across the Brooklyn Bridge and moved down into the narrow, squalid streets of the ghetto, which heaved in every direction, encompassing the withered dreams of half a million people who no longer cared to gaze upon themselves. Nicholas directed the driver as the big car crept through the stinking crowded streets where pedestrians waddled sullenly just ahead of it and small boys walked along curiously in its elegant wake. In a few minutes they stopped almost silently in front of a beauty parlor. All three men got out wearing black suits and sunglasses, the bulge from their revolvers pushing out the folded handkerchiefs in their breast pockets. Inside it was steamy and sweaty. The heavy air was filled with traces of acrid chemical smells. Miss Bernice, the proprietor, was not at her white appointments desk out front so the three men glided into the maze of booths and shampoo stalls where dark hands busily worked on bent soapy heads that never moved. Nadine, the woman they'd come to question, was not in her booth. Nicholas found her in the back. She was a small wizened dark woman who looked slightly ludicrous in her pink plastic smock. "What you want with me?" she cried with a fearful edge in her voice. She swore she'd never started any rumors about anybody, but she knew who did. Within the hour Nicholas had located the man, a surly West Indian super who was eating a bowl of soup and watching television in his dank and grimy basement apartment. At first he was incensed

("I got my dog in the bedroom; I put him on you for coming in here without knocking"), until he realized his visitors carried pistols. Then his voice became strained and wheedling. He claimed his information came from a numbers runner who picked up his selection every morning. When the runner was found, loitering in front of an outdoor telephone booth, he demanded ten dollars and then directed them to a barbershop on the far side of the ghetto. Here the owner was compliant but evasive. Sitting in one of his chairs, he gazed at his nervous image in the mirrors and explained politely that he'd heard the story from a customer, a black man wearing a red fez who had never come in before. Nicholas thanked him and left perplexed. All around him this insidious story bloomed like an evil flower in the night. His questions seemed to intensify its presence. He wanted to pursue it into the warren of sects and gospels that constituted the intellect of the ghetto. But it was pointless; and so, heartsick at having failed Miles, he went to the South Brooklyn mosque and phoned Brotherhood Hall to say that he had no lead to the origin of the rumor that said Miles would be killed publicly and within a week either in Los Angeles or San Francisco.

Miles took the news with equanimity. It was only a rumor that had reached him, not a traceable fact yielding evidence of a conspiracy. He couldn't remember the number of hearsay stories people told about him. Every week there were half a dozen fresh bits of gossip playing on his name. In a few days there would be a new story. He was positive of it. Besides he was not prepared to die. He wanted to live, to flourish. The thought of his corpse, gray and shrinking imperceptibly onto its dead bones in a satin-lined coffin deep underground, flung him into a mood of violent anguish. When he recalled how fitting and just martyrdom had seemed a few days before, a hideous laugh burst from his lips.

Over the next three days the rumor thickened and began to take on grand proportions, as if to prepare all who loved Miles for his horrendous exit from this world. The newspapers heard it ("Miles King to meet death on coast?") and one television station sent a mobile unit to Harlem to try for an interview in time for the eleven o'clock news. And at that hour Miles appeared on the blue screen, his dour face painfully concealing a hundred small irritations. Behind him on the sidewalk in front of Brotherhood Hall, the mysterious street life of Harlem went by. Those who had seen him on television before, studiously bludgeoning the guilt feelings of all white people within range, noticed this time Miles was just a touch deferential. His tall frame had a new slouch to it. The rich magical voice was low, almost tense; and people took petty satisfaction from these small deviations. The troublemaker himself was finally showing a little apprehension and it was sweet to savor. "The whole thing is a fabrication," Miles was saying slowly. "I'll be protected every step of the way. Any unauthorized person who attempts a physical attack on me will run into a wall of resistance." The interviewer wanted to know if he'd have men covering the rooftops. "Let me assure you," he said, affecting just the wrong touch of indifference, "that protection will be forthcoming from several organizations allied with the Brotherhood. No one can lay a hand on me."

None of it was true. Miles had planned to take his twelve-man bodyguard detail with him to California, but that was all the protection he had. Anything else required logistics beyond his command. Miles had no idea police chiefs in California, acting on an angry memo from the governor ("Under no circumstances will I tolerate the death of this man in our state") would make it impossible for an assassin to succeed.

On the eve of his trip Miles remained in his office and tried to sleep on a canvas folding cot Nicholas had set up for him. He'd been busy all day completing dozens of small arrangements James could have easily handled, and now when he welcomed sleep hungrily, his mind was alive and vivid. The immense and labyrinthine silence of the hall all around him only increased the lucidity in his brain. Alone in the building he loved with a perverse secret joy, Miles toyed with the idea of never seeing it again. And very briefly thoughts of treachery came to him like visitations out of the dark. Throughout his career the essence of treachery had always eluded him. When death came to one of the historical figures he emulated in the familiar form of treachery, his mind was never agile enough to grasp its import. The whole diabolically weak spirit required to betray another human being withered Miles's comprehension. He hated the necessity of knowing anything about it.

Unfortunately it was impossible to get away that easily. On many occasions intimations of treachery entered through the rear door of his subconscious and took the form of a slowed and violent dream in which a skillful team of assassins moved eerily forward, bowled over his guards, and theatrically riddled him with bullets. When he awoke the nightmare always evaporated, but tonight Miles felt it was horribly close. And at three o'clock in the morning he arose from his shallow bed and went to his desk in bare feet intent on thinking out a scheme to neutralize any incipient treachery in the people around him.

The next morning a crowd grudgingly estimated by the police as three hundred people watched tensely as Miles came through the front door of Brotherhood Hall and quickly strode past the double row of guards lining the way to his car. He looked quite regal in a black silk Italian-cut suit, and as he reached the curb he removed his sunglasses and waved confidently to the anxious faces all around. There was a little hand clapping and cheering as he got into the polished black limousine that had once belonged to the president of a gigantic life insurance company in Hartford, Connecticut. Brother Nicholas was at the wheel, flanked by a heavily armed guard who constantly glanced through the glass partition at Miles and Brother James, who had slid in beside him. In the follow-up car Charles De Young, armed with a huge .357 magnum pistol, rode silently along with three well-dressed bodyguards lightly holding their shotguns just below window level. De Young had instructed the men to jump out and cover the limousine if anyone rushed it at a traffic stop. A New York City police car lazily pulled up the rear of this strange little caravan. The driver dawdled along, sometimes separating from De Young's car at a traffic light. Next to him another man talked steadily into a hand microphone. A third policeman sat on the rear seat with a riot gun across his knees; he was a stout nonchalant man with cruel, languid eyes. His cap was arrogantly tilted back on his head, and only now and then did he reluctantly scan the sidewalks as the procession made its way down Seventh Avenue and cut across Harlem at 125th Street.

Miles sat in perfect isolation and stillness, the way a child does when it is concentrating against fear. He didn't say a word until they had crossed the Triborough Bridge and left Harlem far behind. Only after the car turned onto a parkway in Queens and picked up speed did Miles relax a bit, perhaps in the belief that he was now in neutral territory and no one would think of spattering his blood out here, among all these pretty little semidetached dream houses. Just then James broke into his reverie and said harshly, "Why are you carrying a pistol? You know it's trouble."

"I may need it," Miles replied, shooting his elegant cuffs just a bit and glancing at James with a touch of derision.

"You won't need it," James insisted. "Don't you understand, this whole threat is a simple rumor. People don't have anything to talk about so they make up stories about you."

"I wish you were right," Miles answered without turning his head.

"Of course, I'm right," James said more sharply than he intended to, for the rumor had shocked and infuriated him until he found the courage to ignore it. But even now he couldn't be sure this hadn't been an act of ridiculous self-deception.

"I don't think you're right about anything," Miles said with a sudden flash of irritation. "There is a lot you don't see, Brother. I'm probably a marked man. The rich, powerful white people in this country can't do a thing with me so they want me dead. They despise me and you know it. Just try and deny it," he said raising his voice to a slightly anguished key.

Anxiously James stared straight ahead. He felt inexplicably stunned and powerless just as he had been when one of the Fung first told him about the assassination story. Beside him Miles put on his sunglasses again and looked out the window idly, like a first-class passenger reclining in his deck chair on an ocean liner. Then quite suddenly they turned toward each other and James gazed unsteadily at his swollen and distorted image in the convex darkness of the glasses. Miles looked his best this morning and he felt shabby in his bulky brown overcoat. Beneath his controlled demeanor countless small currents of distress flowed rapidly. He recalled the abortive congressional investigation of the Brotherhood and the distant vagaries of Miles's relationship with the American people. But James didn't want to think. He was slightly confused. His eyes searched Miles's face for an expression of hungry, honest communion that strangely was barely discernible. Very carefully Miles began to speak again, his words overloaded with the peculiar dread of a man who has calculated his fate endlessly. "This country does not want a formidable Afro-American community, James. Unfortunately I'm the prophet of this type of community. And because of my prophecy I will have to go down the road all prophets must follow. The rich people, the government"—he moved his hand as if to brush them aside—"they all want to stop this talk before it goes too far. If I rally the black man behind me and threaten to link up with the African, white people will go crazy with fear. Why I'll automatically be on a par with them. These rich men don't ever want that," Miles said in a strained, dejected voice. "They'll see me burn head first in hell before they allow that. They'll smash the Brotherhood and start a period of murder and violence, and it will all mean nothing. When the killing stops, Brother, which people do you think will be stretched out dead all over the floor?"

James nodded wisely and turned away. Whenever Miles slid backward into this mood of sickening pessimism he tried to ignore it, but today all of it touched upon his nerves strangely. Nothing Miles had just said had quite the acute edge of tumultuous bitterness he'd expected. In a diffuse way James was suddenly vigilant. It occurred to him that for some involuted reason Miles was giving a very canny performance. Rather deliberately his eyes turned to meet the troubled face awaiting him.

99

Again the voice was melancholy, but it lacked gloom. "Brother, believe me when I tell you that if I am killed, I won't be the first black man to die for his principles. Look at Africa. Leaders die there every month and no questions are asked."

James quietly agreed and Miles lapsed momentarily into a calculated silence. "What an incredible fool I've been," he finally said. "Only a fool would take the role of prophet." The words came hesitantly and with a terrible sadness Miles couldn't control. Abruptly he faced James again, his eyes flashing, and said imploringly, "Brother James, no matter what happens to me I want you to remember one thing always, there never was a prophet on this earth who was any good, never."

"What are you talking about, Miles?" James said quickly in a strained emotional whisper. He was angry now and a little shocked. This eerie display of emotion embarrassed him. Miles was flinging all the sedate terms of their relationship into will-ful chaos. He was showing too much of himself. The heat of this unnecessary confrontation threatened James with panic. "I don't understand what the hell you're talking about today, Miles. You've lost me," he said with the beginning of a nasty snarl.

"I know," Miles answered slowly. "You don't understand me, Brother, because you think I'm a hero. I'm no hero. I never was," Miles went on, finding himself giving in to an odd compulsion for utter candor, a craving to divest himself of the childish plans he had thought out during the night. "What have I accomplished that is really heroic? Not much. Not for the people who really need it. Look at the shape our people are in. Life has squeezed them into pulp. They have high blood pressure at forty, suppressed rage, heart attacks, a whole range of nervous diseases. Why our average life span is only fifty-five, Brother. We die ten years sooner than everyone else," Miles almost shouted, astonished at the grievous truth in everything he said, for this was not the way he'd visualized this moment. Miles intended only to play the part of a desperate, frightened, wary leader, not to career into desolate bitterness. He only wanted to disorient James, to force a more active vigilance on him, but now Miles found himself drawn into the vertiginous horror of everything he wanted to control. He felt as if fear had betrayed him to the enigma of treachery.

James looked at Miles in amazement. He tried to see Miles from afar, as a figure against the horizon, in a place where the broken truths of Miles's private dreams could not challenge or contaminate him. Still the sensation of being manipulated by a supple intelligence remained with James. He remembered the morning Miles was in his office going through the files and it merged with the suspicions swirling about him. What was Miles looking for, even subconsciously? How much did he really know about his past and the baffling instructions that had come through George Mahanti?

Here the bodyguard on the front seat opened the glass partition and said, "I'm not sure we can make that plane, Miles. Traffic is getting pretty bad."

"Try and make it. I've got to be in L.A. tonight," Miles snapped, glad to be momentarily released from the tension he had so assiduously generated.

"We'll do our best," the capable voice replied briskly.

A switch was flicked down on the dashboard and the partition closed. As the car gained speed, Miles took a piece of folded paper out of his pocket and handed it over to James. "These are the secret telephone numbers at all my stops. Call me every night at eleven thirty local time."

"Yes, sir," James answered, relieved that Miles seemed in better humor.

"Remember now, you're assigned to preach this Sunday. I expect to hear you really rocked the house." James permitted himself a little smile as Miles continued. "Also, don't forget no one is to enter my office. I want a twenty-four-hour guard in front of the door. Clear the building by ten o'clock. No one is to sleep over except the guard."

"Yes, sir, Miles," James said respectfully.

"And one thing more. Keep an eye on Brother Charles for me."

James looked at Miles with terrifying hesitancy. The name

Charles De Young mingled with a cold tinge of probing anxiety traveling dumbly up from somewhere deep in his stomach. "Charles?" he said, as if the name had been punched out of him.

"Listen, James," Miles whispered, seizing his forearm very tightly. "Do as I tell you. You watch his movements around the hall. See how he conducts himself and listen for rumors. Watch Charles carefully," he demanded, lifting a finger and with a ludicrous gesture tracing a circle around an imaginary person. James looked on, trapped in complete bafflement. The energy to speak had drained from him. For a moment both men were unaware the car had left the parkway and nosed into the airport parking lot.

The policemen jumped out of their car first and watched with contempt and amusement as the guard detail formed a cordon around Miles and marched off in comic-opera fashion to the terminal building. Inside a horde of photographers and newsmen rushed across the marble floor and flowed around them. One reporter was knocked to the floor and kicked away for trying to breach the wall of security. The police had moved in to stop the shoving when an airline official ran up excitedly and said the plane was being held, as simultaneously a therapeutic female voice materialized throughout the building and hastened Miles to gate 21. With a dozen questioning reporters running alongside and a man holding a portable TV camera stalking backward in front of him, Miles answered their queries with a charming decisiveness missing from him only minutes before. The normal flux of passengers through the terminal began to congeal around him. People stood gaping wondrously at Miles. He was the stunning centerpiece of a colorful improvised tableau, the champion boxer who worships the crowds and the lights and has no life beyond the squared circle of adoration. Miles felt very wise and strong just then.

"What are your prospects in California, Miles?" one reporter asked curiously.

"The prospects are excellent. This Brotherhood intends to

bring every black man out there into parity with the white people."

"Has this talk of attempted murder bothered you?"

"Not a bit," he snapped back.

"What are your plans when you return?" a new voice inquired.

"That's the biggest secret in the United States right now."

The reporters laughed discreetly. Miles was one of their personalities. At the networks they took credit for creating him and he respected their perspicacity.

When he arrived at the gate, a final question came. "Sir, one last thing." He spied the interloper, a blond youngish man, perhaps Ivy League, with a voice full of handsome impertinence, as if he were about to raise the one unfair question at a presidential press conference, a pushover. "Have you considered the possibility of sabotage on your plane?" There was silence, but not out of shock; it was part of the sense of drama newsmen are taught to respect. Everyone knew the plane had been double-checked for explosives. But they stood tensely waiting for the answer.

The portable television camera had Miles in its eye, and he winked blatantly as he said in a disarming way, "Gentlemen, that's what I'm here to find out." And with that he vanished through the swinging doors leading to the boarding area.

Briskly Miles walked across the expanse of runway toward the great glistening plane. The prospect of a long relaxing flight made him wistful. His mind returned to the conversation with James in the car and he wondered if he hadn't been too obvious and dramatic about his weaknesses. He felt a pang of shame at badgering poor devoted James so viciously. Still Miles was certain he'd been successful in frightening James into a studied, effective state of alert, and that was all that mattered. He mounted the aluminum boarding steps zestfully, longing for the safety of a deep comfortable chair suspended beside a fleecy bank of clouds.

From the observation deck Charles De Young watched as

the graceful aircraft revolved in a perfect circle and taxied, with engines idling, to the takeoff zone where it was cleared for departure and smoothly moved forward, rolled at tremendous speed, and finally lifted off effortlessly and flew into the chilly sky beyond. Immediately De Young went to a telephone booth. He knew Lake wanted to be notified as soon as Miles got off safely. For thirty seconds there was a loud busy signal on to protect against wrong numbers, and as he waited it amused De Young that among his minor administrative duties Miles had stipulated he observe James Fitzgerald very closely.

CHAPTER EIGHT

MILES KING enjoyed a triumphant tour of California. In San Diego thick lines of curious, rejoicing black people strung out along the dusty boulevards to watch him pass. But in Los Angeles things were very different. Thirty thousand Angelenos, an elegantly dressed, sporting crowd, turned out to see him assassinated in the Hollywood Bowl. ("The first time he opens his mouth about white people, he's a dead Indian.") To spoil their pleasure he gave one of the most diabolically rousing addresses of his career and sent them away speechless with fury. His performance bewildered the implacably hostile Southern California press, but they granted him rave headlines for the style if not the content of his message. Outside the state Capitol in Sacramento traffic was held up for forty-five minutes while he called for an impromptu exchange of views with one hundred enthusiastic high-school newspaper editors. However it was in that peevish and isolated domain of provincial American sophistication, the city of San Francisco, that his greatest single day unfolded. Rumors of impending death preceded him with every whisper, and yet to the astonishment of a whole city Miles boldly led his caravan through the downtown section in an open car, waving to the crowds with the presumptuous and aristocratic airs of an official state visitor. San Francisco lovingly hailed his show of daring. Miles was everything they'd expected, valorous but dumb, obstreperous yet possessed of a cunning charm, a not unpleasant stranger in the Bay Area. He dined at the Top of the Mark with emirs from the Western states, spoke to immense crowds in the ghettos (people drove all night from as far away as Oregon to taste his wisdom), made three television appearances, angrily debated Negro rights with the mayor, and for five days was the most exciting show to reach San Francisco since the last World Series.

During this same period in Washington, D.C., Austin Lake's proposal was still under consideration in the scattered offices and suites of the Research and Intelligence Agency. (The director was firmly against a new building. This would mean congressional action, some newspaper publicity, and the chance of outside interference. He wanted everything to remain amorphous.) From the director's office word came that the florid and tough former Air Force chief of staff favored the recommendation. It possessed the appealing elements of simple brilliance and total subterfuge, but it would be a little more expensive than everyone thought, and within the agency there was organized opposition. At the first hearing Lake's plan was attacked as excessively clever and foolhardy by almost everyone present. One faction headed by Brian Riggs wanted nothing to do with Miles. Angrily they insisted that Fitzgerald alone was the operator, the central figure. At the second hearing another group, made up chiefly of younger policy analysts, brought in statistical data to prove Miles had no significant following with people between twenty-five and sixty-five, the bulk of the adult Negro population, and so could safely be written off. Near the end of this same meeting, half a dozen men in the back of the room seriously put forth the idea that King be assassinated. At the third and final hearing, which lasted seven hours, the lines of argument began to break up when the director called down and said no one could leave the building until a satisfactory agreement was reached. One deputy director, a former college dean who enjoyed fabulous prestige with the younger men, then came out for Lake, stating cogently in his memo that Miles King represented emotions that could explode in all directions with unforeseeable force if left unchecked. Two hours later the insurgents directed by Riggs, his assistants, three older men, and some statisticians, began to waver and the director, who later commended them on the intelligence of their reasoning, came in and took over the meeting. Brusquely he gave a short lecture on the dangers of impersonal thinking and unnecessary bureaucratic infighting. Then the Lake recommendation was voted on and passed.

For the better part of a week two accountants and a researcher worked overtime drawing up a will, copious records, papers and documents of incorporation, which the director immediately forwarded to the vice-president for international banking at the headquarters of the American Trust Company, an old and prestigious commercial bank in Wall Street. This man was Justin Blair, aloof, good-looking, and distinguished in a secretive and rarefied way most people can never comprehend. At fifty-five he was still young enough to be feared by older men and silently worshiped by the ambitious. He had been in the Office of Strategic Services during World War II and was a secretary of state for political affairs in the Truman Administration. Washington columnists, suspecting a glamorous enigma about the man, delineated him as "an important marginal figure and friend of the Washington intelligence set." His connections in finance were hardly ever mentioned, but *Poor's Registry of Executives and Directors* listed him on the boards of eight major corporations.

Once inside the bank the papers of incorporation and five accompanying checks were placed in a specially opened account under the carefully worded terms in the will, made out in the name of a recently deceased philanthropist who fervently wished to remain anonymous. The title of this account was the Federation of World Religions. It contained six hundred and fifty thousand dollars to be used by "responsible religious leaders of the Negro race pursuing the path of understanding and racial amity." When everything was ready, Blair enlisted the skills of an old friend and presidential confidant, Claiborne Cox, to serve as executor of the will. After a friendly briefing, Cox agreed and sent out letters on the impressive stationery of Satherwaite and Cox, Investment Bankers, summoning three prominent Harlem ministers to attend the first informal meeting of the federation.

One week later Claiborne Cox addressed the group in a regal hotel suite overlooking the lush hilly rectangle of Central Park stretching far to the north. Rising from his chair he went to the center of the large room with its background of gilded mirrors and impeccable Italian Provincial furnishings, slightly amused with the solemn and intense black men who were his guests. Rather sternly he began in his high nasal voice, "Gentlemen, American history has shown us that the federal idea is a path to salvation." For half an hour he went on, firmly lecturing about the need for a unity of purpose and objectives among black religious leaders.

The ministers stared at him curiously and nodded very politely now and then, waiting for him to finish the lengthy preamble and when at last he did the first question was, "Will the funds available from the federation be substantial enough for us to carry out our interfaith programs on a continuing basis?"

"Yes, gentlemen, by all means," Cox answered pleasantly. "But I want to stress the idea of religious federation to you. This is the real purpose of our venture together. Now as executor I am empowered to present each of your churches with initial aid totaling two hundred thousand dollars. However, it will be necessary under the terms of incorporation to include in our midst at least one member not of the Christian persuasion. Of course in time I would like to see more."

They were all silent for a minute, pretending shabbily to labor over an honest choice, yet it was apparent to each of them with almost telepathic quickness that Miles King was the only substantial figure outside of the Christian church worth approaching and thereby, for some fortunately unknown reason, the center of this whole inviting offer. They recognized too that this was pretty big stuff, auguring nice tax-free incomes, additional prestige, bigger staffs, and new cars for something no more dangerous than spending a little time with a ridiculous eccentric. Each of them eyed Cox hungrily for confirmation of these dreams, but the elderly well-dressed lawyer revealed nothing but the snobbish benignity that comes only after years of surviving the continuing ordeal of big money law, murderous proxy disputes, and the servicing of clients who demand total discretion and silence.

After a few moments of uneasy quiet, the Reverend John T. Lawrence, a young, earnest, well-known preacher said to Cox, "We would like to go to another room and deliberate on the name of the non-Christian member to join us in the federation. Are you willing to wait now for our answer?"

Cox smiled and nodded his consent. There was mutual understanding between them. He liked that. "Of course. You may take all the time you need."

When they left, he settled down on the luxurious satin couch extending across one end of the room and read some work from the office, confidently aware that the hasty and tumultuous rules of easy money were being fought over two rooms away.

In forty-five minutes the ministers trooped back into the room smiling sheepishly like a group of small mischievous boys. The Reverend Mr. Lawrence, the thoughtful one, had assumed the stature of leader. He spoke now, slowly and distinctly, with a bit more gentility than Cox expected. "Mr. Cox, we have decided that no meaningful religious federation is possible without the inclusion of Brother Miles King. We don't know your feelings about Brother King, but everyone in our community has an immense respect for him as a true leader of his faith. We are convinced"—the others nodded on signal— "Brother Miles and his movement are necessary for the strengthening of our goals as a federation. With your consent we hereby submit his name for consideration."

"That is fine, gentlemen," Cox replied with a suggestion of

joviality, "but what does Mr. King feel about this?"

"Our plan is to meet with him in a few days to discuss the matter," Lawrence said promptly.

Cox lowered his head as if vaguely disturbed. "Suppose King refuses to join you?" he said, looking up slowly. "Are you ready to submit another name?"

"We believe that will not be necessary," Lawrence replied. There was a strain of petulance in his manner. He sensed Cox didn't really trust any of them.

"Yes," Cox answered with half a smile. "I am ready to leave everything in your capable hands, sir. I think we've had a good beginning here this afternoon. And I find it interesting that you will be starting with an impressive non-Christian among you," he went on in a conversational tone.

The ministers smiled great toothy relaxed smiles full of the exaggerated coyness a group of extra bright grade-school students might show while having their picture taken. They shuffled their feet on the heavy rug like a troupe of dancers warming up for the main number. Someone cleared his throat very loudly three times. Cox took in all this animation with pure amazement. He expected them to break into song, but they refused. They just stood there and brazenly smiled their big ironic smiles as Cox's eyes widened with hostile, offended surprise. He was startled, angered, and even slightly hurt by their cheap back-alley manners. Pressing his lips together in prudent disgust, he examined each of them as they stood before him with the most casual indifference, not bothering to conceal their amusement at this doddering, old, self-important guardian of the rich. "If this meeting is adjourned, gentlemen, all you need to do is say so," he snapped. On the ride down in the wood-paneled elevator, Claiborne Cox refused to acknowledge their presence.

The following morning shortly after ten, the phone in James Fitzgerald's office rang. The secretary to the Reverend John T. Lawrence asked for Miles King. She was connected to his office, then Lawrence's voice came on the line.

"Good morning, Miles, this is John Lawrence speaking."

"Good morning to you, sir," Miles replied mischievously. He'd always enjoyed a whimsical rivalry with Lawrence, but at a great distance. They'd only met twice very briefly and he was roguishly curious about this businesslike call.

"Miles, I'll come straight to the point. I'm representing two other men besides myself and, to be frank, we have something of a very important ecumenical nature to discuss with you."

"How important, Reverend?" Miles asked, allowing his voice to sound cool and disinterested.

"I can't tell you how important over the phone, Miles," Lawrence said testily. "But it's vital enough to concern all those working to help our people."

"Don't turn your piety on me," Miles said a little angrily. "You proper church people have never been interested in anything but a pat on the head for a job well done."

"We're serious, Miles," Lawrence said sternly. "The people are demanding a breakthrough. They're tired of parades," he said slowly and with malice. "We were counting on you for a little common sense, but if you won't cooperate, you must realize eventually it will have to get back to the people in the streets."

"Don't you dare threaten me," Miles replied.

"Who is threatening?" Lawrence said with genteel exasperation. "You know I've never asked you for a damn thing before."

"They say you're a prudent man, John," Miles said cuttingly.

"Oh, Miles, for god's sake, I'm asking you to act like an adult for once. I'm asking you now, even begging you to join me at a serious ecumenical meeting. I think it's terribly important for the future."

"That important?" Miles asked mockingly, trying to conceal the tantalizing curiosity dashing through his mind. "All right. I'll see what I can do for you, but I'm telling you now, John Lawrence, if this is just another terribly intellectual discussion group with the tray passed around at the end for a playground fund, I'm going to denounce you and your bunch in every borough in this city. I'll show you how terribly hard it is to eat without that fancy money you pick up out of the collection plates."

"Miles, I'm not going to argue with you," Lawrence said admonishingly. "You have got to learn to control your temper and your acting ability and work with other people. It's the only reasonable way, Miles. The church has known that for decades."

"You certainly have," Miles retorted bitterly.

"The meeting will take place in the basement of my church at eight tomorrow evening. Please be on time and come alone, without the forty thieves."

John Lawrence's Second Baptist Church enjoyed a large and stable congregation. Every Sunday morning an overdressed, gay, festive crowd flooded into its Gothic Revival sanctuary to hear Lawrence deliver an elegant, devilishly prim and exhausting sermon on the evils lurking just outside for those who did not support the demanding cause of Christ with all their hearts and pocketbooks. The congregation adored it. They had a flair for spectacle and even though everyone knew John Lawrence was hardly the perfect messenger of heaven, it didn't matter. He was the embodiment of a style they wanted for him. His two-hundred-dollar suits and polished religious patter gave him the aura of show business, of money, and an ease they found it necessary to have an investment in. And so they believed, with all the naïvete of a mother whose only son has gone over to crime, that their pastor was not right or wrong but special, a rare, complex, and fabulous personality needing help in his work. At the end of his weekly oration a squad of ushers, elderly, sympathetic ladies in white, crept up the carpeted aisles on hobbled feet to collect the day's take as the organist ripped off an inspiring hymn to Calvary.

Lawrence, a clever, somewhat princely figure in his middle forties with two honorary degrees, was widely respected and had no difficulty in persuading his fellow ministers, the Reverends Messrs. Anderson and Harper, to let him open the discussion. The meeting was held in the church study, a long, narrow, well-scrubbed room lined with glass-enclosed custom-made bookcases, which towered up on both sides and occasionally reflected the noonday sun onto the mahogany conference table filling up most of the room. At eight o'clock the four men came in and sat down in richly upholstered high-backed chairs. There was nothing on the table and Miles could see his suspicious and petulant countenance very clearly in its lacquered depths.

"Gentlemen," John Lawrence began slyly, "this is a secret session. No records will be kept and I want your pledges that not a word of what is said here tonight will ever be repeated. This is of overriding importance. Miles," Lawrence said, looking briskly at him with a conceited smile, "have you ever heard of the Federation of World Religions?" He pronounced the words with pomp and pride.

"You know damn well I haven't. What the hell is this, Lawrence, a game of Twenty Questions?"

Lawrence then told him all about the federation, about how the money for it was left by a wealthy, self-made black businessman in Los Angeles (hair products, wigs, beauty salons) who turned devoutly religious in his final years and took up the advancement of ecumenical unity. He went on like a skilled and subtle actor sliding into an arduous and complicated role. Lawrence cajoled Miles, then praised him. He touched all the lodestones of popular black sentiment, showing a slip of cynicism, mixing emotion and practicality, civil rights and brotherhood better than any classic American politician of the center. His voice wavered with indignation as he discussed past feuds and bitterness, the legacy of deliberately conceived spite etched partly in callous intolerance, partly in expediency. ("Let's be candid. Without that Sunday pledge money, we'd all be teaching school somewhere or doing social work. There'd no big homes for us, no cars, nothing!")

And Miles listened to this incredible exposition, first with contemptuous amusement, and presently with a creeping restless fury. His resentment was founded on years of snide abuse by these very pious men, years during which his struggling Brotherhood was dismissed as a pathetic fantasy or held up to a concerned nation as the embryo of a fiendish conspiracy designed to split the country and destroy the true Christian ethic.

As Lawrence finished, he sat quietly with his arms folded, trying to suppress the expression of ugly scorn tightening the corners of his mouth. A minute went by without anyone speaking. Lawrence stared at Miles quizzically and then rested his head on the plush red-velvet backing of his chair, hoping he appeared unconcerned. The Reverend Mr. Harper, an elderly rotund man in a good brown gabardine suit, cleared his throat portentously. Marcus Anderson, a dark intense little man who presided over an insolvent church in central Harlem, just looked at his hands folded before him on the table. He sensed the meeting was about to end.

"Whose bank account are we going to raid?" Miles finally asked with strained disinterest.

Lawrence sat up in his chair promptly. "Unfortunately I can not disclose that information," he said agreeably. "Under the terms of the will, the donor asked to remain anonymous. But there are legal documents to buttress what I say, Miles. We are not conducting a raid," he added dryly.

"Then what are you conducting?" Miles asked contentiously. "Nothing you've said so far sounds right to me."

Suddenly Anderson and Harper shot looks of cautious hostility at Miles in a vain effort to shame him and curb his suspicions. A quick trace of panic had run through them. They wanted to get on with the business details and close out the meeting before Miles started ranting. Lawrence picked up their scent. He gazed at Miles with the kind, superior smile of a father treating his son as a man for the first time. "Does a forty-thousand-dollar check to the Brotherhood for initial administrative expenses sound right?"

"Forty thousand?" Miles asked querulously in an attempt to hide his surprise. He was certain now a joke was being played. He glanced at the others for confirmation, but they only smiled back very knowingly, as if it had once been a surprise to them too.

"Who asked you to do this?" he demanded, not knowing what else to say.

"No one," Lawrence said suavely. "A lawyer friend downtown, the executor of the will contacted us about the federation."

Miles nodded his head in disbelief and snorted angrily.

"Miles," Lawrence said, leaning across the table imploringly, "I'm asking you not to go off into a rage. Please. For just a moment give this opportunity some thought. Consider what this means. Every man in this room recognizes the fact we all have great differences of philosophy, but our basis of support is the same. Black people believe in us in some way. Now we have a chance to strengthen our position in the community and make some real advances together. Why don't you join us? Do you hate the Christian church that much?"

His appeal had penetrated to a sensitive depth and Lawrence knew it. He paused, waiting for a look of mortification to come over Miles's face. An urgent silence rolled through the room. Wearily Miles eyed the rows of leather-bound volumes sitting unused on their glass-enclosed shelves. He felt numb and strangely sad. "What you people won't do for money," he said a minute later, his lips curled with disgust as he dramatically stared straight at John Lawrence.

"Don't you understand, Miles," Lawrence retorted angrily, knowing he had to prick the other man's pride. "We're leaders, like it or not. We must make decisions for our people and get help wherever it comes from. All you understand is making eyes on television. They could squeeze you from a toothpaste tube and you'd come out grinning. People tickle their ass with your miseries and you love it. Why shouldn't you? When the hell have you ever been a leader?"

"I don't want any part of your goddamn federation," Miles said stubbornly and in a low voice, indicating he understood the conversation on another level.

"You talk like a child," Lawrence came back viciously.

"Just like the spoiled child you are. No one is asking you to abandon your precious following and go into the desert on foot." One of the others laughed derisively but Miles didn't look up. He never gave any solace to people he despised. "All you have to do is send a couple of coordinators to an office we'll set up. Perhaps four times a year, if you can stand it, we'll meet to decide on programs and oversee the thing. Is this too much of a challenge for you, Miles?"

"Of course, it's not," a weighty voice put in. "Miles has been doing everything his own way for a long time now, and I think he's right to be leery of strange entanglements."

Lawrence sat back in his chair as the Reverend Clyde Harper, a distinguished old preacher, stood up. Miles had heard about Harper for years and had met him a few times before. Harper was an African scholar and a pioneer graduate of a patrician school of divinity at a famous Eastern university. Occasionally he wrote for one of the middle-class monthly magazines on the role of the church in some controversy of the moment. The Harlem community respected his stature inordinately. Through his veins flowed a Presbyterian spirit of reason and expediency. Miles found his resounding basso voice a soothing relief from the idiotic taunts Lawrence flung at him.

"You have greatness in you, young man. I don't want to embarrass you, but it is true," Harper said with the trace of a proud smile. "I can honestly say I've never seen a younger man with so much ability. I think every man in this room has genuine admiration for the way you handle yourself but, Miles, you can't do it alone. It's too big a job. If you come into this federation, you can help all of us. We will all profit, and I suspect it may give you the kind of maturity and backing you will need to fulfill your destiny."

"Sir," Miles said evenly, struggling to hold down the loathing that had stealthily invaded all his feelings, "with all due respect you can go to hell before I let this half-assed cabal of pretentious little psalm singers become the backers of my destiny."

"You just wait a minute, Miles. That's not the way we

116

address our elders in the Christian church." The Reverend Marcus Anderson, a short, dark, spry man wearing horn-rimmed glasses was up like a bantamweight. "You can't come in here talking like that."

"How should I address you?" Miles asked angrily, glaring at Harper who looked back at him with a faint air of resignation and disgust. "Should I commend you for what you're doing? Should I allow myself to be used and soiled by hands I'll never see? You people don't leave me any room, Harper." There was just a modicum of sorrow in this last remark and Harper picked it up quickly.

"You don't see what's in store for you, Miles," he said smoothly and with concern. "Can't you see, young man, you have gotten too far ahead of yourself. The white man doesn't like it. You are getting to be a danger, that's what people say all over the country. They don't know what they mean by danger, but if they fear you, it doesn't matter. Now personally I like many of your ideas," Harper continued. "They are basically very sensible and I'm sure the other men here respect your thinking too. But let me remind you of one thing. There have been others with similar visions. Many of our scholars and thinkers have stressed our affinity with the Afro-Asian world. Still they didn't go into the streets and push it before the time was right. Why, Miles, you are in a great tradition. Why go off on your own when we need you here? Won't you please consider coming back to us?" It was a pretty speech he had made and Harper knew it. He sensed now that Miles would give in to them.

"The trouble with this whole business," Miles said heavily and so evenly they could not anticipate him, "is that too many of us believe we own a piece of the truth. Reverend Harper, a lot of what you said is true. We both know that." Miles knew this was a lie. He had gone too far by himself to believe in greedy old men now, but this lie gave him room to breathe and regroup his thoughts. "Believe me, sir, if you had come to me alone and talked that way without any offer of money, I'd be damnably tempted to join forces with you. But it is the company you keep which leads me to disregard you and take your advice as the last mouthings of a sanctimonious old fool who's been frightened away from the truth like a dog driven away from his dinner plate by a man with a stick," he shouted furiously through the room. There was no reply, nothing. The weight of certainty in his words prohibited it. Yet Miles wanted to continue on. He wanted to explain his convoluted fears, his fatalism, and the terror that smothered him each time he thought his great will and dynamism had begun to wane. Urgently he felt the pull of a compulsion to tell these worn-out men how afraid he was to lose his innocence and the ambiguous charisma that had emancipated him from servile obscurity. Miles wanted to reveal himself in order to diminish them, but pride held him back. And he understood that any show of superiority would only enrage them more. After a few interminable seconds, Harper's words reached his brain.

"I feel sorry for you," the elderly minister blurted out contemptuously. "You don't know how to make life work for you."

"Miles, I frankly don't understand what you mean," Anderson said with genuine puzzlement. "Are you telling us you think you can carry a whole people on your back without any help?" He looked over at Miles with the vicious tenacity of an embittered petty thief.

"I'm only saying," Miles replied disgustedly, "that if you are really serious with this talk about progress, then it would be best for each of us to prove it individually."

"Goddamn you, Miles," Anderson cried out abruptly, slamming his palm on the table. "Goddamn your conceited ass. You're taking us for fools," he screamed. Behind his flat lenses Anderson stared out with murderous eyes. Mayhem was loose in the room now. "You're pissing in our faces."

"Hold on there, Mark," Lawrence shouted futilely. "Not here. Not in my church."

"You stupid smug bastard," Harper suddenly yelled at Miles in his heavy voice. "You played us along. You had humiliation in your mind all along. You wanted to ridicule us because we're not as famous as you. You want to see us down just like the white man and the Arabs you follow, the Arabs who've perpetuated slavery to this very day," Harper thundered vengefully, his voice sputtering with fury. "I wouldn't be surprised if you had some Communist connections too because it's sabotage you're advocating, Miles. You're out to destroy the aspirations of a people and deliver them to something inhuman. And I don't want you to walk out of here without thinking you've made an enemy for life, because you have," Harper cried, leaning across the table. His eyes glistened with hate.

The smell of hostility and exertion braced the air. The meeting was almost out of control. Harper stood massively in his place, both of his huge fists at his side, as if he were ready to batter Miles unconscious. At the head of the table Lawrence rose authoritatively but Anderson moved menacingly on him. "Son-of-a-bitch, who are you with now?" he hissed.

"Get out of here," Lawrence demanded more in fright than bravery. "I will not have fighting in my church. All right, Clyde," he shouted. "OK, you can stop this," he said nervously without looking at Harper, who held his ground. "Please be seated. Everybody, please sit down."

After a long sullen pause the three ministers took their chairs again. Everyone around the table glared at Miles with bleak, unrestrained hatred. He had cheated them out of money and made them sweat like longshoremen and they badly wanted him dead.

"Perhaps in the future, two or three weeks from now," Lawrence said to no one in particular, "we can meet again to reconsider our relationship and discuss things some more. Maybe then we can hit on some new idea for unity in peace. How do you feel about this, Miles?" There was no answer and for a moment Lawrence gazed around the little room helplessly. Forlornly he shrugged his shoulders. The money was gone. "This meeting is adjourned," he said in a voice that was much too loud.

CHAPTER NINE

ON THE SAME EVENING Miles made his way to John Lawrence's church, James sat in his office at Brotherhood Hall and tried to work. He didn't want to go home right away because there was no telling what mysteries the darkened streets might hoard. Ever since Miles returned from California and heard about the pathetic wavering speech he gave at the Sunday meeting, James was sure he was being followed. But even though he'd darted breathlessly around a dozen corners to await his pursuer and confront him, the man never came and James began to wonder about hallucinations. Every evening as he neared his door, the rational saving mechanism within his mind went to work pressing assurances on him for the long night ahead. Sometimes he would lie in bed and meditate on all the incredibly fatalistic things Miles said as they rode out to the airport. But he still didn't know what the conversation had meant, if anything, and he did not want to know. He had watched De Young as Miles demanded, and Charles had done nothing suspicious. Yet he found his attitude toward De Young was more intensely aloof and hostile than ever. He avoided meeting Charles whenever possible. He dismissed De Young from his mind and loathed thinking of him at all, because in his present uncertainty James knew any attempt at sagacity would be stupid and deceitful.

He'd heard nothing from Mahanti, and it was almost five weeks since their first meeting. Again and again this led him into the tempting assumption that the ministry did not really want Miles dead. At worst they'd always sought to quietly subvert outstanding figures like Miles. It was absurd that they would murder him. The ministry had no motive for such an irrational crime, and as the days went by, James again allowed himself to savor the idea of a mistake. Yet he was not relieved. The ministry had located him in a faraway country after many years and that was proof of their purpose. As he had in combat, James felt death very close to him. He remembered that the ministry had published a monograph on assassination. This document outlined the mental processes of a potential assassin, observing cheerfully that professional killers were not romantic outcasts, but peculiarly parasitical entities functioning as murderers for the sole purpose of maintaining themselves in an exiled and solitary land of negation. If he obeyed the ministry, James understood he would inevitably enter that land also. With a sickening spasm of woe, he comprehended that the ministry's Red Star of optimism never blazed fiercely enough for him. But he couldn't be the first man to hold this knowledge; others must have abandoned their allegiance when it asked too much of them. Where were they now? He searched his mind wildly and turned back a hundred answers, all pinpoints of light in the dark. He even toyed with the notion of surrendering himself to government authorities. This might be his safest move after Mahanti discovered he'd done nothing to develop the assassination plot. But here a crazed voice told him the government was as deadly as the ministry. They would surely exchange his soul for someone the Chinese held, and that would be his end.

Only Beverly offered him some relief. Although she didn't understand his complexities and had never heard of the Ministry of Foreign Affairs, Beverly knew how to make him relax, at least superficially. She never permitted him to discuss perplexing subjects, and if he did, she would laugh coyly and extend one long, elegant, sensual hand over his shirt front to soothe everything that troubled him within. And she was girlishly discreet. James never had to answer the obscure probing little questions women use to assemble the quality of a man's past. In return James didn't ask what she did before they met, and he didn't care. She helped to equalize the tumult of his life, and he found himself craving her affection. In the late evenings they would lie together nude in her huge darkened bedroom consumed by the endless and graceful rhythms of sexuality and indescribable closeness. Under him her strong, lithe body flowed outward and back effortlessly. Occasionally she would jiggle very hard and throw her head back in a beautiful hoarse laugh that drove him wild as he plunged into the diffuse muted exhilaration of pursuing her movement for movement until a nervous spark grew between them and they rose up, and then sank down into pure bliss. With a sheet over them, they slept this way many nights.

James never told Beverly how much she'd done to shore up his life, because he wanted her sweetness to stay fresh and unaware. He suspected this period of intense devotion merely helped to stave off the day when he would go mad. Unwittingly he was beginning to accept madness even as he fought it with the horrible desperation of one battling the onset of a coma. The ministry seemed so ethereal to him that he couldn't be sure it ever really existed. At times he could not remember if he'd actually been in Europe. He tended to believe the ministry was a contortion of his mind, a blotch of terror in his brain cells, a Gothic manifestation of his inadequacies never to be discarded.

A week later an interim report from the United Nations Economic Committee on Asia and the Far East came in the mail. Enclosed was the card of Dr. George Mahanti, chairman.

Boldly James decided to call Mahanti immediately and appear totally unconcerned and disoriented, as if he hadn't understood the directive. Mahanti was at a meeting so he spent an anxious two hours in his office at the hall reading Miles's correspondence before going out to the drugstore to call again. This time he reached Mahanti.

"How are you, Brother James?" the sophisticated voice said.

"Fine," James replied nervously, not sure if he should hang up and flee from the booth.

"Are you ready?" It was said very casually.

"No." James tried to say it politely but without emotion, like a man declining hors d'oeuvres at a party.

There was a long pause.

"Oh, I see," Mahanti finally said in a tone of honest regret.

James didn't answer. He didn't know what in the world to say next.

"James," the voice was serious now, more commanding, "there is a small park at the foot of East Seventy-Seventh Street, right by the river. You can not miss it. Please, meet me there tomorrow afternoon at four."

"I don't know if I can be there," James replied stupidly. "Miles . . ."

"Good-bye," Mahanti said after listening carefully for a moment.

The meeting place turned out to be a large, fancifully equipped playground maintained by the city of New York for the convenience of wealthy young mothers not inclined to trek eight long blocks to the public meadows of Central Park. On one of the many benches, near a gaily colored carrousel sat George Mahanti, dressed in an elegant black walking coat. James went up to him clumsily, like a waiter carrying an overloaded tray. When he sat down, Mahanti turned a completely cold, taut, but weary face to him and asked gravely, "What has happened? Why haven't you followed the orders?"

"I thought I would have more time," James answered lamely. It was a pitiful excuse, but he'd spent half the night thinking of what to say to Mahanti and his mind would not function.

"The orders said immediately," Mahanti cried out almost reproachfully. James wondered how he knew this.

"I understand," he pleaded desperately, "but there hasn't been enough time. I can't work under pressure this way." Irresolution had now taken complete control of James. He was almost chattering as he waited for Mahanti to acidly remind him of all the time he'd been allowed.

"Stop cringing like an idiot," Mahanti said contemptuously. "Do you want to attract attention to me?"

James stared at his feet mournfully, expecting to be insulted, possibly threatened, and surely brushed aside forever.

"The ministry assumed you could do this job because you were trained at great expense. I see now it was a mistake to rely on you. Apparently you are nothing more than the witless incompetent you appear to be," Mahanti said scornfully. "My first impression of you was correct. I truly regret it is now too late to remove you, but you have my assurance"—he formed the words bitterly, as if he loathed and detested James—"that if I could arrange it, you would be summarily dismissed."

A pang of anticipation rose in James. He wanted to provoke Mahanti with his obtuseness. "I'm sorry," he said very softly.

"Sorry?" Mahanti cried incredulously. "Sorry for what?"

"I'm sorry I messed things up. I know they'll blame you," James continued, tensed for the vicious slap of Mahanti's gloved hand across his face. Suddenly he'd realized Mahanti was in direct contact with Bern and almost certainly had the power to write him off as a failure.

"Let's forget that for the moment," the Pakistani said with less anger. "I've arranged for you to have some help. I will explain everything to you later. I want you to come to my apartment this Wednesday evening at seven. You know where it is." James nodded more in shock than obedience. "Good. Do not be late. My car is here," Mahanti said, looking up. "Wait right on this bench for five minutes before you leave. Don't do anything to make anyone remember you. Do you understand?"

James watched him walk jauntily across the playground to the big, luxurious car. He smiled sweetly at a group of children playing dodge ball, and a strikingly beautiful woman sitting near them sort of dipped her head in a patrician gesture of recognition for the richly outfitted foreign visitor. As Mahanti's chauffeured English car disappeared up the block in little puffs of exhaust, James got up and walked briskly to the ornate railing overlooking the filthy oiled water of the East River. Madly he wanted to jump, to obliterate himself, but his hands froze as soon as they touched the metal.

CHAPTER TEN

EARLY THE NEXT AFTERNOON, Austin Lake took the air shuttle down to Washington and was picked up by an unmarked agency car at National Airport. He popped into the back seat and stretched out his lean, athletic frame for the relaxing ride into the city. Lake was a conservatively dressed, nearly handsome man of thirty-five with six and one-half years of service in the agency. His face was chiseled American and pleasantly worn at the corners like a hunter's face. He owned the amiable, even personality prized in intelligence work because it made few mistakes. His superiors tended to trust him. But today he felt this advantage was about to get away from him. The director had phoned that morning and asked him to come down for a consultation and he was frankly worried; this wasn't known procedure, recalling an operator from his post to confer privately.

The director favored a small, neat, and austere penthouse office situated atop an old records building run by the Bureau of the Budget. The large casement windows behind his desk overlooked the perfectly still inner courtyard of a new government building facing the next street. The lacquered model of a B-17 on the director's desk was the only concession to sentiment in the room. He took Lake's coat with the graciousness of a man welcoming a new friend to his country club for the first time.

"Can I buy you some coffee, Austin?"

Lake said he could and the director touched a button on his intercom twice.

"Austin," he said presently, "I asked you down here because I want your appraisal of the situation now."

For a moment Lake gazed out of the window behind the director's chair and tried to make out the form of a secretary moving about in a tiny glass-fronted office across the way. "Well, sir," he said heavily, "I think our posture has been very sound, very intelligent. No one could possibly have suspected the source of the money. And there was never any reason to anticipate failure of the project. It just happened that way."

"I know that, Austin," the director said, raising his eyebrows in irritation. Lake noticed his hands were folded prudishly on the desk. "To be frank with you, I was very disappointed. But I'm not blaming anyone and I want you to know that your stock in this company has never been higher."

"Thank you, sir," Lake said, knowing the director had told a lie, for the only criterion for praise in intelligence work was success and he had failed to meet it.

"Now tell me, Austin, what do you think happened between King and his cohorts? Should we have sweetened the pot some more?"

Lake smiled faintly, as if he had just heard something slightly ridiculous. "I don't believe so, sir. It seems to me we were not faced with a money problem at all. What confounded us was the stature of this man. He must be something of an egomaniac in addition to other things, the kind of a man who automatically keeps his distance from people he feels might diminish his appeal. It was our mistake not to weigh these nebulous human factors surrounding King more carefully. But I see no reason not to try a new approach."

While Lake spoke, the director reached across his desk and picked up a large, gold-and-porcelain table lighter. He lit his cigarette carefully, taking in small mincing puffs of smoke.

Lake suppressed a sneaky smile. The director was spoiled and a bit of an actor. His family had been socially prominent in Washington and Virginia for decades; during World War II his handsome face, framed by a leather flying helmet, appeared in the newsreels quite often. His appetite for beautiful women was almost legendary, yet few people knew how much he relished success in the clandestine universe of intelligence combat. Now he leaned across the perfectly clean desk top holding the cigarette cocked elegantly in one fist. His face was a bit florid but still pleasant to look at even though he would be sixty in a few months. "Austin, I would like very much to go along with you," he said slowly. "I think you understand that. But we have a little trouble on our hands down here. It seems one of the people contacted through the federation, a Negro minister named Anderson, got on an all-night radio program in New York and said he'd been offered a huge sum of money to help suppress Negro rights. He revealed everything he knew about the federation and claimed the backing for it came out of some government agency. Now personally I think the man is just guessing. He's probably just grabbing for headlines or hoping Cox will get in touch with some hush money. However, a smart-aleck columnist down here picked up this little item and handed it over to one of our more staunch critics in the Senate and now there's a whole clique of runny-nosed liberals on Capitol Hill who want to know what the flap is all about. And to be candid, I don't know there is one." He stopped here to let his words rest upon Lake with their full impact. "It is possible, Austin, that we've made a drastic mistake in shifting our attention from Fitzgerald to King. This changed the whole nature of the assignment, accomplished nothing, and has left us with an exposed flank. The shift was based on nothing but a lot of intellectual talk."

Lake gazed down at the desk top absently. A sensation of vertiginous personal failure and sheer embarrassment made him want to vanish from the earth. He didn't dare confront the director's face as the voice directed at him said very evenly,

"All I hear around this goddamn city is loose talk, Austin. The air is full of it, but you rarely see one damn piece of information to substantiate anything. I think this whole asinine Washington talk syndrome has filtered into our work and hurt our efforts very much. It's reached the point where, at least in this instance, we can not substantiate what we're doing."

At this moment a good-looking secretary came in with a tray and noiselessly went out again. Lake watched her go feeling terribly deflated, like a schoolboy who has let his favorite teacher down. Silently he waited for the blow he knew had to be coming, reassignment to Washington with a new reputation for vacuous schemes that produced nothing but reverses for everyone.

The director looked him straight in the face. "Austin, I want you to do me a big favor," he said in a less edgy voice. "Go out and get me some hard information on this entire subject of King, his Brotherhood, Fitzgerald, and this peculiar Negro milieu. I want to study something fresh and penetrating for a change. We need to know a hell of a lot more about these people, because they may not be important to our jurisdiction at all. They may be immune to everything we've theorized about them. You have good instincts for this kind of thing. Do what you can. And don't forget to try and update the Fitzgerald file."

"I'll do everything I can, sir," Lake said respectfully.

"I know you will. I'm sure of it, and don't worry about your ideas. We'll get back to the fancy stuff later."

"Yes, sir," Lake said quietly.

"Call me in a week and let me know how you're doing," the director said, lifting his coat wearily from the rack and ushering him out of the office. Leaving the building, Lake remembered he had not been given the chance to touch his coffee.

The storeroom-office behind the old bookshop was in complete darkness as De Young's disembodied voice boomed out from the rear, from behind the table with the projector on it.

"These shots aren't too good. They were taken at night from a fast-moving car, but they give an idea of the fun he's been having."

On the screen in front of Lake and Brian Riggs, who had just arrived from Washington, a murky little movie of two couples riding in a car through a blacked-out world flickered hopefully for a few minutes and died. Riggs turned away in disgust and lit a cigarette. He recalled his angry chagrin when the director told him to return to New York. De Young and Lake were incompetents who probably would be out of the agency in another year, and Riggs did not want to be around them. He felt superior and at the same time slightly embarrassed.

"We're having a little trouble getting footage," De Young explained. "Our man only goes out at night and he likes places where it's dark."

"Run the first one again, Charlie," Lake said petulantly. "And keep that chatter down."

A brief tableau with the same people in it came to life before them, and then without warning the film raced wildly ahead before steadying into a slight jerking movement. "It can't be helped," De Young said casually. "This is all hand-held footage taken from the back seat of a car."

On the screen Clarence Williams and James were out for a walk with their girl friends. They strolled down Fifth Avenue at a leisurely pace, frequently leaving camera range to window-shop or vanish completely behind large trucks mired in the heavy traffic. Finally there materialized a crude but unobstructed head-on shot of the group wending its way through the thin gray light and dreamy atmosphere of tumultuous rush-hour crowds half paralyzed in slow-motion photography.

"Who is the other man?" Riggs asked snappishly.

"Clarence Williams, an insurance salesman," De Young answered confidently. "He's had almost a dozen jobs in the last fifteen years. He and Fitzgerald worked in the same bank in nineteen fifty-four."

"Any record?"

"No, he's pretty much of a nonentity," De Young replied with the curious lilt of a man keeping something to himself.

"What kind of a check have you run?" Riggs demanded abruptly. He'd caught De Young's tone and didn't like it. Something in it told him De Young was deceiving him.

"FBI fingerprint, bonding houses, armed services." The answer was quick, blasé, and very sly. "We checked the records of the clerk of the court for both civil and criminal cases in the twenty largest metropolitan areas. He's never had any contact with the law."

"All right." Riggs sounded annoyed. "Give me a rundown on the girl with him."

"That is Miss Claire Edwards, girl about town."

"A prostitute then?" Riggs asked searchingly, seeking a way to pierce De Young's enthusiastic smugness, the attitude of utterly foolish prerogative he wore like an imperial cloak. Brian Riggs knew with a queasy certainty from what he had heard and seen of De Young that his whimsical egotism was not a sign of brilliance, but a harbinger of disloyalty in a yet unidentified form. He made a mental note to have De Young run through psychological tests when this assignment was completed.

"No, I don't believe she is a prostitute, Mr. Riggs," De Young said hotly, after pausing for a moment. "Edwards is just a good-looking and frisky young girl."

"Oh, I see," was the curt answer. "You can testify to that I suppose."

This remark caught De Young unprepared. Its hint of suspicious malice shot through him like a sliver of steel. In the way it was delivered he detected the ominous power of a man who had penetrated a particularly annoying riddle. Riggs was sharp, De Young knew. He had a reputation for undermining his superiors and fingering his enemies as security risks. Probably Riggs had the knife out for him because he supported Austin Lake, not that it really mattered. People like Riggs never needed valid reasons.

131

"Put on the next reel, Charlie," Lake said politely, trying to soothe the antagonism around him.

A sharp, clear five-minute sequence came on the screen.

"Who is this girl Fitzgerald goes with?" Riggs asked coolly.

"She's cute, isn't she?" De Young said. "Her name is Beverly Carter."

"How long is her record?"

"Shorter than you think. Five years ago she was picked up for prostitution and acquitted. Probably some cop looking for it free. Ever since she's been working the big time for a nice, respectable house on West Fifty-fifth Street."

"Is she still there?" Riggs asked sharply.

"No. She retired undefeated a month ago."

"Reason?" There was behind this question the cold unrelenting insistence of an exasperated detective browbeating a suspect in the back room of a police station.

"Unknown," De Young replied simply.

"How old was she?" Riggs would not let up. Through the darkness, he stared back at De Young with the cold eyes of a mugger measuring his victim's skull for the blackjack. And De Young quickly realized for some unknown reason he was actually defending these girls.

"Beverly Carter is now twenty-eight," he answered with all the confidence drained from his voice.

"Let's have the lights," Lake said suddenly, easing his voice between the two men. Secretly Lake felt guilty; he blamed the failure of his plan for generating much of the tension in the room. Rather familiarly he called out to De Young, "Charlie, to your knowledge is it common procedure for a girl to quit at such an early age?"

"Not unless she hasn't got any kick left," De Young said quietly, thanking Austin Lake for momentarily keeping Riggs away from him.

"What is it, Austin?" Riggs asked smugly. "What sliver of daylight do you see in the universe now?"

"I think it an interesting possibility that this girl could be

132

romantically attached to Fitzgerald," Lake said, speaking almost to himself.

Immediately Riggs snorted with amusement and De Young let out a ludicrous chuckle that echoed across the room.

CHAPTER ELEVEN

SPRING WAS APPROACHING. The president, a shrewd and vague-looking, middle-aged man from Nebraska who boasted he was once a soda jerk, proclaimed its imminent arrival as he crowned a gorgeous South Carolina college girl Cherry Blossom Queen in the Rose Garden of the White House. But while the nation smiled on the season of rebirth, a familiar voice, almost foreign in accent and riddled by dark humor, broadcast an irksome bulletin across the land. Another of those prominent civil rights leaders, mincing in tone, threatening in gesture, warned America again to do the right thing for black people or the springtime idyll might explode into the most tumultuous and violent summer the country had ever witnessed.

Partly this was true. In recent weeks some determined ambuscades had taken place in various cities between frenzied blacks and sharpshooters on the police force. Homeowners in these cities vehemently demanded a return to law and order. They marched on city halls, circulated petitions, harassed timid public officials, and threatened congressmen, gleefully searching through democracy's little bag of tricks for the one small item needed to restore sanity. When it couldn't be located, they turned sour. One man in Rochester, New York, set up a remote-control Gatling gun on his lawn. ("I've got nothing against the colored you understand," he told neighbors, "but they're getting tricky like the Commies. We give them a slice but, no, they want to snatch the whole pie.") Intellectuals around the country, who angered all sides with their prolonged holdout for official boards of inquiry, increasingly viewed the disturbances as episodes in an undeclared guerrilla war.

There was merit in this observation, but it was indistinct, like a clarion call fading in the hills. Syndicated political columnists and other social observers dismissed the idea brusquely. Still many people were troubled. Anarchy and communism seemed to be growing in the world, expanding into Asia, splitting off new cells in the viscera of South America, propounding a lunatic doctrine of suffocating doom. True all of this remained a vague sort of threat, confined to the drinking water some said, but there were lots of strange signs around. People like Miles King seemed to prosper with an unnatural ease. And China, that seat of enigmas, red on the map and heavy in the heart, was a real woe. One could see in the faces of Chinese leaders, those puffy, impenetrable, yellow Oriental masks, an intimation of cackling jealousies and possessive hatreds. They wanted everything Americans had. They harbored grasping demands on all American rights—property rights, trading rights, even the sacrosanct right to turn your back on any man, the honest privilege civil rights troublemakers were trying to outlaw in Washington. No phony government or diplomatic gentility could shield their enmity. And the horrible thing, some people claimed, was that you could often see this very same naked rancor in black faces. Maids had it now, and so did all the delivery boys. The teen-agers were impossible and frightening. They were all beginning to sound like Miles King.

The storm of imminent crisis around the country did not escape Miles. Reports came into Brotherhood Hall daily about the surge of unrest. Emirs from Chicago, Detroit, and Philadelphia discreetly inquired if it might not be time for him to make an extended lecture tour abroad. One evening a messenger arrived from the Los Angeles mosque with a sealed package containing a detailed strategy for operating the Brotherhood underground. But Miles would not change his energetic routine. On Sundays he addressed huge audiences of the faithful and flailed away at the pernicious system that had driven them to him. He continued to praise Africa and ridicule capitalism. His remarks were sharper and more dramatic than ever, yet Miles was apprehensive. The assassination rumor and Lawrence's strange offer still preyed upon his imagination. Frequently he found himself trying to discern what unexplainable occurrence would happen next. At night an extra man sat outside his door and he slept with a pistol nearby. Pills were prescribed for a series of blinding headaches he managed to keep secret. Then one afternoon as he played basketball with the Fung on the small, deeply cracked parking lot behind the hall, Brother Nicholas came racing from the building and blurted out the incredible news that had just interrupted regularly scheduled programming on all stations. The announcement (it was more than a year overdue, the Pentagon said) stated simply that China, the Peoples Republic, had earlier that day successfully tested its first military weapon employing nuclear fusion, a hydrogen bomb of some thirty megatons. The explosion had taken place barely five hours before at Lop Nor in the remote western province of Sinkiang. Instantaneously its effect diffused out from there to cover the whole world, and in the first few hours provoke the outraged beginnings of extreme consternation and hostility in Western capitals.

Immediately Miles dressed and went home to the large suite he maintained in a shabby, genteel hotel on the West Side. He paced from room to room, excited and terrified, worried and elated by this bizarre news. After a while James arrived with the late papers and shot him a long, poignant, questioning look before leaving. As the hours passed and he sipped from a large snifter of brandy (his doctors had ordered liqueurs in moderation to help his circulation), Miles began to experience some of the lilting merriment a small bettor feels when his horse shows up two lengths ahead of the favorite in the clubhouse turn. Beneath all his misgivings Miles sensed the presence of wild good fortune. Why here he hadn't even blown hard and the sevens were flying; for in the Chinese mushroom cloud Miles saw the dramatization of all his virile fantasies, the culmination of his prophecies, the vindication of his pleas. Here was the event his crusade had always needed: raw destructive power in the hands of a nonwhite people he could easily claim friendship with. Now every black man in America would follow him, twenty-two million people, an aggregation larger than most countries. Miles sat back in a shoddy wing chair and savored it all. Like someone newly rich he faintly disdained his former condition. He chuckled softly at the anxiety that had clung to him. The following day Brotherhood Hall issued an order for the printing of one hundred thousand handbills announcing a mammoth rally to "explain the meaning of the bomb to all black people."

The rally was scheduled for Sunday afternoon at two o'clock. A wooden speaker's platform about ten feet high had been erected by six Brotherhood workmen at the corner of 125th Street and Seventh Avenue. The thoroughfare was closed to traffic for four blocks in either direction, but at twelve thirty the crowd had already overflowed the blockaded area and a squad of Brothers went out to set up portable loudspeakers in the side streets. One-half hour later the crowd was immense. It teemed very far in all directions and even from the speaker's platform it was not possible to glimpse its perimeters. Gay banners and white-and-crimson Brotherhood flags were everywhere, for the Sunday congregation had settled in the middle of Seventh Avenue to form the nucleus around which thousands of blacks in their bright holiday clothes swirled and rotated as they waited to hear the significance of an event everyone agreed was already epic. After a while a slight wind came up and this seemed to agitate the crowd. People looked back anxiously at the imposing line of faded and decayed tenements, the only objects rising over a field of dark heads that appeared to run in all directions to the horizons. At one-thirty word reached the speaker's platform that side streets eight blocks away were filled up. Whole families had arrived from Brooklyn or the Bronx and been forced to return to their homes to see the rally on television. Many green-and-white New York police cars were now mired in the throng and soon teen-agers began to stand on them. Slowly the crowd became a little tense, a little worried.

At quarter of two the television crews arrived with a police escort, and the multitude of blacks parted courteously and stared with taut, quizzical faces as the technicians struggled forward with their equipment. Ten minutes later they were ensconced on a rickety platform hastily put up facing the rostrum from which Miles would speak. The turrets and long lenses jutting out from the bulky black boxes of the television and newsreel cameras made it look as if Miles would be bombarded with death-dealing rays the minute he appeared. More than one angry spectator made obscene gestures at the platform. Some small boys shouted curses and threats; a group of mean-looking youths in black berets and leather jackets materialized and began to shake the flimsy stilts holding it up as people nearby shouted encouragement. ("Do it to them good, Brothers.") Finally two black policemen fought their way to the scene to find nothing but a ring of dark hostile faces harboring contemptuous eyes they didn't want to challenge.

The day grew warmer, and as two o'clock came and went the crowd stirred restively. Folding chairs had been placed on the speaker's platform, and De Young and James surrounded by six of the Fung began to suffer in their heavy winter suits. But then at about twenty after two the crowd began to shift and roll with excitement as Miles was spotted mounting the steps to the platform. As his name rippled through the light afternoon air, a wild spontaneous shout crackled against the windows across the huge boulevard filled with indistinguishable faces. Now the entire multitude seemed to take one giant step forward and contract around the speaker's platform like some shapeless microscopic animal responding to stimulus. Quickly James walked to the rostrum and stood before the thicket of microphones sprouting up at him. He was recognized; a knot of Sisters directly below him clapped joyously, and as they did Miles loomed suddenly from behind him, a trim muscular figure in a well-cut gray suit. He was wearing heavy, dark glasses and on his head sat a thickly embroidered and colorful wool cap. "Now it is my great pleasure to give you," James began eloquently.

"Brother Miles. Brother Miles," insistent voices from below chanted. A rustling sound came through the microphones followed by the familiar voice, strong, brisk, and very clear. "Brothers and Sisters, isn't this a fabulous day," Miles cried dramatically. The throngs responded with a tumultuous frenzy of shouting, whistling, and screaming that reverberated down through the avenue like the distant roll of cannon fire. Almost two minutes went by before the cheering and clapping subsided enough for Miles to speak again.

"Let's not deceive ourselves though," he shouted, raising both arms high in the air. "The only reason we are here today, the only reason we know anything about this bomb at all is that they couldn't possibly keep it from us. It's just too big," he said happily.

"Now let me tell you a little secret," Miles whispered mischievously into the microphones. "Tonight when you go home those people up there"—he pointed directly at the camera platform—"are going to tell you I'm a bad fellow." A rowdy chorus of sustained booing immediately descended on the newsmen. "Don't believe it for a minute," he added with a sly laugh. "They want you to go out and beat up the Chinese laundryman on your block. Then you'll be a patriot. That's not the same thing as understanding though. I'm here today because I want you to understand what is happening in the world and how it affects you. I want you to listen and think," Miles said with dignity.

"The first thing I want to say is that this is no puny, run-of-the-mill bomb our Chinese friends have built. No! This is a hydrogen bomb, a hundred times stronger and badder than the atomic bomb they dropped on those Japanese," Miles cried with a sudden thrust of emotion. "It can dissolve cities in a pillar of fire and seed the winds with radioactive dust. It can cool down the earth and bring on a new ice age. It is a very great weapon." He shook a clenched fist. "It is an equalizer." There were loud barking shouts of agreement, a profound murmur of deep interest. They could tell Miles was going to be good.

"Everything has changed," he continued in a theatrical but subdued voice that added mystery to each phrase. "For the first time in history a nation of nonwhites has a definite share in the fate of the world. They can bargain. They can demand and the world must listen. It cannot afford to ignore these people any longer. They can never be ridiculed again. Now this new power can be a force for good or evil, and as a religious man I want to remind you all that the Muslim God Allah always asks for peace."

"You are the prophet," a Brother near the rostrum shouted. "You are the man."

"I am an earthly prophet," Miles shot back, pointing a wary finger at the man. "I am a temporal leader, nothing more. The significance of what I'm discussing today is much larger than I can ever be," he said, gazing out to the far corners of his rapt audience.

"Now we must ask ourselves how all of this came about," Miles went on with assurance. "As every schoolboy knows China was until recently a lowly, backward, miserable place, a country without courage or hope. But after nearly one hundred and fifty years of constant troubles, wars, revolutions, exploitation, and hunger, the Chinese found themselves. How? By what process did this come about, Brothers and Sisters?" Miles asked, raising a finger in the air. "I'll tell you. It came about because China finally rejected everything alien to itself. It rejected the false promises of the Western world. The Chinese flung out the commercial concessions making millions of dollars for white foreigners, and with this abolition something else went too—the Western idea of the Chinese as a people of no consequence."

A great surging restlessness seized the crowd for a moment. Miles had reached very deeply into its imagination and he knew it.

"A people of no consequence, is that familiar to you?" he yelled harshly. "That is what they think of us in this country we are told is our home! And as I understand it, at the same time we are supposed to be free. But what exactly is this freedom they press on us? To me, it seems pretty much the freedom to be poor all your days. The freedom to be servile. Or is it the freedom to return to a rathole at night? All right, I'll tell you what it really is. It is the unrestricted license to be ignorant and be enslaved by that ignorance. We must save ourselves from this fate because it means chaos and degradation when what we need is clarity. What we need is purpose!" These words rose out of Miles in bitter explosive bursts.

And the colorful and boisterous throng cheered wildly. In the soft spring heat its mass, spotted with bright dancing yellows, shimmering greens, tangerines, grays, oranges, and blues set against a field of startling white shirts, swayed like the slinky configurations in a mirage. Miles, flushed with exhilaration, took in everything before him as confirmation of a new, more exalted status. Never did it occur to him that for most of his listeners the whole thing was a good Sunday outing tinged with a few histrionic truths that could never help them. For a moment Miles stood with both arms in the air, smiling and waving as the cheers swelled around him and then subsided respectfully. Behind him Brother Nicholas came up and opened a large black umbrella over his head.

"I am aware, as most of you are, that certain people in this country resent this triumph," Miles shouted cockily, his tone haughty and sarcastic. "But it so happens that there is nothing they can do. I'll bet down in the Pentagon Building a few generals have already commited suicide. They weren't ready for this bomb, not this year or next year or ever. You see, our Chinese friends have set an example of strength, an example we'd do well to follow." He was interrupted by steady purposeful applause. "And I believe it is our destiny now to match this fine example by making a reciprocal gesture of strength. I'm not talking about something long-range either. And I don't mean a Mau Mau or anything like that, although god knows we may need one before our struggle is over. What I have in mind, Brothers and Sisters, is a declaration of solidarity with China in recognition of her historic feat. A message from the united black people of this country. I promise you here and now that I will draw up such a declaration in your name."

James bolted forward in his chair in utter disbelief. De Young frowned at Brother Nicholas, who looked quite sad and worried. All through the crowd people quieted suddenly, for they understood Miles was again exceeding their imaginations and stealing the edge from their joy, and this always rankled a bit. "My declaration will be from you to people just like yourselves over in China who now see change coming," Miles continued. "Not piddling change, not token change, not a cup of coffee and a dried-out ham sandwich, but total irreversible historic change!"

Miles expected a riotous salute and it came. He was surrounded by noise so loud it hurt his ears, but strangely there was no really unrestrained jubilation in the sound washing over the speaker's platform. The crowd seemed to be merely preying on his oratory and commending his words, grasping only rhetoric, only that part of him appealing to its senses. This knowledge irritated and depressed Miles. He felt a driving urge to go on, to rant until he had made each of them understand what he thought and felt. But a pang of failure widened alarmingly in his stomach. Miles didn't really want to preach anymore. He told himself this Sunday was partly a festival and long lectures might spoil its tone. Besides, poised elegantly before the tangle of microphones, all the power and magic summed up in the joyous panorama reflected in his dark glasses passed up suddenly into Miles's consciousness and there blossomed to heroic magnitude. At once Miles became Lenin addressing the people in Saint Petersburg, or the great and benevolent Mao of China reviewing rank upon rank of freedom fighters. He witnessed himself as the letter and spirit of a new undeclared black order, an American historical personage with unprecedented international prestige. And as the rally dipped to its climax three-quarters of an hour later, Miles King had made more enemies in the United States than he could placate in a whole lifetime.

CHAPTER TWELVE

ANY GENUINE SUPPORT Miles King enjoyed from the mass media dried up like some esoteric chemical poured out in the light of day. Now he had to be attacked and pitied because the official sensibilities of the nation had been violated. Like the barely tolerated guest at a fancy dinner party, Miles had told the dirt everyone knew was coming. It was time for him to accept penance. And as the reporters and cameramen crowded into the majestic lobby of Brotherhood Hall after the rally had ended in a small riot, with four cars overturned and a few shopwindows smashed, they dared to shout antagonistic and bitter questions at him through the crush. Later it was discovered a militant street gang in black berets planned the disturbances, but this made no difference. The gang was secretly linked to Miles in the morning papers, which printed a host of emotional and conflicting stories about what had really taken place. Alongside dense columns of outraged opinion, there appeared an array of striking photographs revealing Miles in his sinister dark glasses, chin thrust forward bravely, as he seemed to berate and flail at an endless multitude of transfixed black faces, with one forearm raised in a gesture of defiance, but suspended, as the whole scene emerged in American eyes, at a fixed and immutable point, a turning point the newspapers rushed to explain, down the road to ruin and death.

Miles had lost his quality as a star, the magical temerity that had been his strongest asset. Now all of America was primly curious to know why this insidious interloper was crying allegiance to a band of stinking primitive Chinese coolies on the other side of the world. It was surely a demented act, touched with an obscene and unknowable conviction. And as in any strange event, there were bad omens. What if this all too bizarre black man should pierce the nation's prideful conscience and open a dark closet of horrors. All the numbing insanity, congenital fears, pathological lusts, and bitter greed in America might rise to the surface like a bloated body sunk in a riverbed. And the ultimate unforgivable terror in all of this was that Miles just might possess a larger grace of some kind. He might be royalty in rags, an angel of vengeance heading a strong black race in adversity. During the next two days a thousand palpitations of fear raced through the country, throbbing with a bitter desire to see Miles killed.

Out in the streets of Harlem most people were uneasy and thought Miles had gone too far. (One shabby-looking man leaning against a mailbox said to a reporter, "He speaks for the crazy hand-clapping ones that follow him. Rest of us love this here country.") Within the Brotherhood everyone seemed to support the China speech and the declaration, although privately many groups of Brothers and Sisters met in dismay and voiced furious objections. Finally they went to see Miles and came away reassured by a promise that on the following Sunday he would issue a partial retraction, and then outline a revolutionary program designed to make the Brotherhood the only effective organization in the country black people could turn to.

That night Miles hardly slept, and in the morning his body ached with tension, The once barely visible lines under his eyes tightened into new scars of distress. He gave out no statements, showed no panic, but Miles was appalled. Confronting that disappointed little delegation in his office the night before had intimidated him. He was frightened to death of waning as a personality, of never being heard from again. Around the hall they sensed his mood and stayed well clear. When he passed De Young in the hall at noontime the other man looked at him quizzically, as if he were greatly embarrassed. Miles would never know De Young partly blamed himself for the histrionic extremity of the China speech. He'd encouraged Miles to think in political terms, and the result was a dangerous fiasco. The intensity of his egotism stopped De Young from seeing the rally was Miles's idea alone. Cockily he agreed Miles had always been right about the source of his identity: If he wasn't a religious figure, he wasn't anything at all.

As the day went on Miles acted on a decision he sensed he'd made many hours ago, in the turmoil of his sleepless desperation. He determined to make a public withdrawal of his declaration of solidarity. His private secretary placed a call to an old friend, the host of a late-night TV show dealing in controversial opinion. After three attempts he was put through and a pall of woe came over him quickly when he heard the familiar voice, now smoothly apologetic and tinged with sullenness. "Miles, I know you want to come on the show and I can't help. You were crazy to say those things. How can you declare solidarity with Communists? It's not even funny. Look, if I gave you so much as one second of time, my producer would tar my ass black and ship me to Hong Kong in a barrel."

"Can't you let me on even to retract?" This came out automatically, but without force. The exciting tension of other days was no longer operating between them. He would almost have to beg.

"Ah, I'm afraid not, old buddy. The advertisers wouldn't hear of it. Besides no one would believe you anyway. You've confirmed the worst things whispered about you."

"What do I do?" Miles asked in the strongest voice he could manufacture. Fear of permanent eclipse was on him like the first prickly symptoms of a fever.

"Get out of the country while you still have a passport," was the quick answer. "Move. Fly pal. Go to Haiti. Think it all over and then come back on your hands and knees. Turn on the tears at the airport. Kiss the goddamn runway. That's the only way to get back in solid again. Repent! And they'll love you like yesterday." As a spasm of shock recoiled through his mind, Miles heard, "After all, old buddy, nature abhors a vacuum and so do I."

James left home at five Wednesday afternoon and took the Broadway local uptown to 168th Street where he made a free transfer to the Independent subway system. A light-headedness that had come and gone all day toyed with him once more and then vanished. His thoughts flowed back to the evening before when Miles had addressed a handful of tired and uninterested reporters in the auditorium of the hall and withdrawn his declaration of solidarity with the Chinese Communists. A few flashbulbs went off; one man asked curtly if mimeographed press releases would be handed out; Miles posed for the Brotherhood photographer; and the meeting ended with the fractured echoes of reporters' voices rattling against the gloomy ceiling as they drifted up the aisles.

James had gone home stung with a peculiar disappointment. Although nothing about the declaration had been said between them, James tried to convey to Miles in his elliptical fashion that he supported the idea. With a surging, grasping hope, he'd prayed Miles would not collapse under the emotions storming in from every side. It was in his mind that the ministry could not assassinate Miles once he declared himself an ally. The declaration might save his life, save both their lives, but now it was gone.

James let five trains go by before he boarded a southbound local. He felt weary, but strangely alert. He knew he was running on body chemicals and little else. Twenty minutes later the train arrived in the huge neon-lit Columbus Circle station. Several policemen were on the platform, and their hard faces and bulky blue silhouettes seemed to demand he remain underground, where it was safe. Deep in his mind the mechanism of reason turned over like a small, powerful generator. James moved down the platform quickly, but with new purpose. He was looking for the one policeman possessing the right face, an open, tough, forgiving stranger who would accept the incredible true story coming from his lips with nothing but the ease of someone indoctrinated in the mad logic of urban life. This, James realized lucidly, was the sole means of saving Miles. But it was not to be. One policeman, sensing distress or even quackery in the man veering close to him, turned away and suddenly James was by him and sailing up the iron steps like a frightened junior clerk two hours late for work. In the rich twilight he crossed the circle rapidly, and at the last possible moment climbed aboard a crosstown bus. He sat in the rear, and as the bus nosed across Fifth Avenue some impulse told him to get off. A cab took him to the East Side Airlines Terminal. He strolled through the waiting room, not totally certain a ticket wasn't already typed out for him at one of the service desks. When he came out at Second Avenue and 37th Street, it was quite dark. The remaining seven blocks were easy. He arrived promptly on the hour.

Mahanti opened the door and let him in. He had no inkling of what his feelings were, but somehow James expected to hear soft voices conversing in the sibilant fluency of the Chinese language. He expected to come upon a roomful of grave Chinese faces, but in place of this severe reality he was ushered into the pompous fantasy of Mahanti's marvelous living room, that chamber of gentility where an air of aristocratic prerogative sat like a sheen on every opulent stick of furniture. The whole history of England was there if you looked for it. Chippendale predominated but some artifact from every period was to be seen. This time James was not intimidated though. The sight of all these riches filled him with an odd surge of pathos.

"Do sit down," Mahanti said politely. "You're right on time, my friend. I'm glad to see that. It indicates seriousness."

James sat down timidly, with a sense of awful trepidation.

"Brother Miles," Mahanti said in a voice touched with an English lilt, "has created quite a controversy."

This was the first time Mahanti had ever mentioned Miles and to James his tone sounded detached and neatly marked by the limits of sociological curiosity.

"Miles has always been controversial," James replied a little defensively, knowing it would be a struggle to keep a clear picture of Miles before him.

"What he says about China is true," Mahanti said quickly, as though James had not spoken. "Your Brother Miles, along with the American generals, realizes the true meaning of Chinese achievement."

James sat uneasily on an antique chair. The protruding scrollwork on the back forced him to lean forward for comfort. Mahanti was seated opposite him in a chair elaborate with rococo foliation designed at the Chippendale workshop in the middle of the eighteenth century. His voice was pleasant and discursive with the little trill in it common to English-speaking people from the Indian subcontinent. He might have been talking about anything.

"The detonation of this bomb is an historic event. It divides us irrevocably from Russia, which is just as well. Their polluted brand of socialism could never have succeeded in China."

Against his will James smiled very faintly, like a student recognizing the major themes of his favorite lecturer. Mahanti saw what the smile contained and went on.

"The strongest phenomenon in the world today is the illusion of a better society for the Afro-Asian world. Most countries never admit this. China does. She is honest because she can not afford to be anything else. Under the old regime the weight of false tradition and other people's illusions sat upon the country like a coat of armor on an undernourished peasant. Now China seeks to exist without illusions and so practical problems have finally been solved. The usurer class was liquidated, drastically curtailing the people's suffering. They have never enjoyed a better life. In fact we do not allow people to exist in misery or privation. This in itself is a revolutionary idea. It intrudes on one's free will"—he said it sarcastically—

"but revolutions inevitably make demands of this kind on people. I think you know what I mean. You are part of a revolution yourself, James. In your own way you are heroic. I admire you. I do. You adhere to the intense demands inherent in any revolutionary situation, though I suppose you sometimes have doubts."

These last words made James shudder with anxiety. He felt drawn out between his tenuous determination never to harm Miles and the grotesque attraction deep within him for grand ideas and messianic personalities, the powerful urge that had driven him to the ministry and later the Brotherhood. A swell of nausea overflowed in his stomach, not from disgust but out of pure cold terror. James found himself unable to answer Mahanti. The dark face opposite him tightened just a bit. Mahanti stared at his averted eyes with a hint of panic, but he continued on suavely. "Doubts are the result of so-called free random choices, usually the worst choices. If we allowed this process of choice to go on, everything would fall apart. You see revolutions must be insulated against ideas, especially reactionary ideas. Then they can gather strength and generate an energy of their own. China would have collapsed years ago if widespread doubts had appeared."

Mahanti got up and went to the sideboard to fix a drink, and in that moment James felt strangely drawn toward him because he sensed they were both captives of the ministry and its workings. His eyes followed Mahanti impatiently, searching for any little sign of verification. He wanted desperately to glimpse some sign of turmoil and resignation behind Mahanti's screen of gentlemanly manners. A powerful craving to expose George Mahanti as a weak, grasping, pretentious little functionary focused in his mind like the rays of the sun drawn through a strong magnifying glass. In a thoroughly childish way, he overlooked the pain of his own vacillation. When Mahanti came back and handed him a goblet of club soda, he didn't acknowledge the insult.

"Great discipline is the heart of a revolution," Mahanti said, openly studying his companion. Abruptly an intense feeling of suspicion and resentment flickered in James. Again Mahanti was masking his real predicament and retreating behind the falsity of Anglo-Indian gentility. James felt rage was slowly coalescing in him. Once more Mahanti was setting him up for a round of clever repartee and part of the outraged anger he experienced when they first met returned. Then suddenly the Pakistani leaned forward and said tautly, "Brother James, revolutionaries can not ask the people to do what they are incapable of themselves. I offer China as an example. There, through stoicism and bravery, a small group of men escaped an army of occupation and returned stronger than ever to lead the people out of a hopeless morass. Now every citizen of China accepts party discipline. Your people in this country must be made to accept discipline too. They are weak." This pricked James but he suppressed the urge to lash back. "They need a hardened leader. This must be a man who has subordinated his will to the larger purposes of revolution, because only revolutionary steps can alleviate their plight. Brother Miles, for all his recently acquired merit, is not this man. Already he has rescinded his declaration of solidarity with China. Already, after a mere two days of adverse reaction, he has collapsed. He is nothing but a contrived personality, the product of television and the radio. Therefore the Ministry of Foreign Affairs has directed me to instruct you"—he spoke with some formality—"to assume total control of the New Brotherhood of Islam after the death of Brother Miles. You are to use and develop the Brotherhood as a means of disseminating Communist party discipline."

A weird inquiring look came from Mahanti but it did not have any keenness in it. James watched the Pakistani very closely and what he saw was a touch of pathos and subservience in that cocksure face. The sweetish aroma of Scotch lay in the air, and behind Mahanti a floor lamp cast a soft glow over the rest of the room, leaving them in a subtle shadow and granting Mahanti a somewhat ecclesiastical air as he continued speaking. "You will be a leader. However, your position, especially during the first week after the assassination will not be easy. After Brother Miles is killed, we have planned a surge of chaos. The following evening a prominent church in Harlem will burn to the ground. Then a rumor charging un-identified persons with an attempt to destroy Negro leadership will spring up. After that major riots will erupt in several ghetto sections of New York, and also possibly in other cities. Someone may try to assassinate you in all this tumult. You must be very wary. Through it all, you are to remain silent. Hold back and let the confusion build around you," Mahanti said harshly, like an officer giving an order in combat. "Even-tually the press, needing a villain, will seize on you, the second in command, and demand you be brought to justice. But at the same time, they will try to court you," the Pakistani said with an ironic smirk. "Reporters will crowd around you with cam-eras and microphones asking, even pleading, for a statement, any statement. They'll try to make you an electronic specter like Miles King. When this happens, I want you to explode." Mahanti was sitting on the edge of his chair now, gesticulating emotionally but carefully. "Use everything we've taught you," he said smoothly. "Attack the United States as it has never been attacked before, not by King or anyone else. Directly ac-cuse the government of murdering Miles King because of his Chinese sympathies. Accuse it of silencing a great dissenter. Cite this as a major crime against the Negro people. Demand Washington end its undeclared policy of racial extermination around the world. Cite Asia as your evidence, using Korea, Japan, and Indochina. Cite Africa. Dramatically point out the reasons for the carnage at your feet, and never let up until you have aroused this country and rallied every single living Negro to your banner. Never let them forget the memory of Miles King, the latest in a trail of black martyrs stretching through American history. Claim it was the high priests of Christian morality who stabbed him in the back with their horrible as-sumptions." With this phrase Mahanti's voice began to rise and quicken. For the first time James noticed Mahanti's ridicu-lously small childlike fists. "The ministry will support you with a barrage of propaganda messages. We will flood the world with support for your charges. In Asia and Africa there will be street demonstrations. The world will be indignant, outraged. Slowly, very gradually your position will become impregnable. You will head a separate hostile nation lodged in the side of America like a dangerous infection. No one would ever dare touch you because they could never be sure of the repercussions. The result can only be that the Negro people in this country will look to you alone for leadership."

Mahanti pulled his chair closer now and continued to speak in an impassioned but businesslike way. "Listen carefully now, Brother James. Miles King will be assassinated this coming Sunday at his regular meeting. Your immediate part in this is small, very small. First you must draw ten thousand dollars from the bank, using identification I will give you. You will do this tomorrow. When you have the money, put it in a brown paper parcel along with the key to your second apartment. Check this parcel at the Port Authority Bus Terminal. Then put the claim check in an envelope and send it to a post office box number you will find with your identification papers. On Sunday one hour before the meeting begins, you are to unlock two doors in Brotherhood Hall. The first is the fire exit in the rear of the orchestra floor on the left-hand side. The second is the door leading to the top balcony. The assassin will do the rest. Do not contact me for any reason. I will be in touch with you in time."

Contemptuously James examined the smug face before him and saw its assurance vanish almost magically. A wicked lucidity had come into his thinking. Mahanti gazed at him with the terrified alertness of someone who is about to be shot. He turned uncomfortably in his chair but his eyes stayed fixed on the hostile Negro face confronting him. Finally James spoke with extreme bitterness and choked anger. "Where the hell are you going to be when they kill Miles?" he shouted.

Mahanti fought to remain poised. Ever since James had arrived, he'd noticed something menacing in his behavior. "I will be here in New York lobbying for you at the United Nations, of course," he answered quietly.

James leaned forward malevolently, as if to pull him off his chair, and Mahanti sat back very nervously. "You think it's a dreadful thing we've asked you to do," he said quickly. "In your heart of hearts, you believe this. We know, Brother James. The ministry knows everything about the people it selects."

"What does it know about you?" James asked angrily.

"That I'm reliable," Mahanti retorted desperately. He didn't want an argument. Shouting might bring house detectives or even the police.

"At what, running messages?" James yelled. He was about to bound up and fling Mahanti through the living-room window. It drove him wild that the Pakistani would not admit he was just a lackey. "You lecture me about revolutionary bravery when you're nothing but a goddamn messenger boy. I know your kind well. Harlem is full of them."

"I'm not an activist," Mahanti maintained in a loud, excited voice. "I'm only here to give orders from the ministry."

"You're a goddamn messenger!" James screamed. "Admit it. That's all you are, a frilly black messenger boy in English suits."

"No," Mahanti cried, leaping to his feet. "No, I am not," he cried in a precise jumble of words. "I am important to this movement. I am as important as you are," he shouted, moving about the room with great agitation. Suddenly he stopped and faced James, pointing a wavering finger. A few locks of his sleek black hair hung over his forehead and he looked oddly drained. "Let me tell you something, my black friend," he cried in his exact plaintive voice, "no matter what I am, no matter what you have discovered me to be, you and everyone close to you will die if you disregard what I've told you this evening."

"Is that how they told you to threaten me?" James yelled, bursting from his chair and stalking Mahanti evilly into a corner by the window. "Is it?" he cried, raising a powerful fist high over his head. For a moment all Mahanti could do was make a low plaintive sound. James panted over him. The rest of the room appeared far away and small, like one floor in a doll's house. Then out of nowhere an incredibly vicious punch ripped into Mahanti's stomach. He crashed head first onto the carpet screaming in agony, trying to hold in the swiftly ruminating hot pain, a pain so intense it made him feel his mouth would be torn apart as he gasped all of it up in a quick series of horrible convulsions. He'd rolled over three or four times before his eyes began to focus on the husky figure of James Fitzgerald stalking across his magnificent living room and out of the apartment.

CHAPTER THIRTEEN

THE NEXT EVENING Miles worked late in his office at Brotherhood Hall. Night classes had ended hours ago and the building was silent with the dense sheltering quiet Miles enjoyed. For three hours he had been at his desk dictating memos into the handsome machine at his elbow and inserting message belts into special mailing envelopes to be sent to emirs in Phoenix, Chicago, and Seattle. He worked slowly and laboriously, frequently erasing words and starting the instructions all over again. The effort was infuriating and taxing, for Miles was telling his subchiefs they were to abide by his strict orders and never again mention his declaration of solidarity to their congregations. The fatalism and weakness in every word stung and embarrassed him. But Miles continued to work steadily, driven on by a mechanical and businesslike absorption that would not slacken.

Still he could not escape the suspicion that his career and his movement seemed a little sickly and were perhaps about to shrivel under the insidious strength of some devastating organic disease he might not be able to contain. Ironically the power in his fierce renown was recoiling on him, and Miles shuddered before it. The violent reaction to his street rally had at first made him gasp with amazement. Then the distasteful memory of John Lawrence's enigmatic offer welled up at him. All the tormented hatred spewed at him when he refused to enhance Lawrence's mysterious federation came upon Miles again with the quickness of a lance flung out of the darkness. Even now, when he thought the whole incident had dissipated, ominous reverberations remained to plague him. The night before the Reverends Messrs. Anderson and Harper had gone on television and for the standard fifty-dollar guest fee called him a resourceful agent of the Chinese Communists. Lawyers for the Brotherhood assured him there were ample grounds for a suit, but Miles refused to hear of it. Intuition told him it would be disastrous to challenge these men with their propensity for fanciful lies and elaborate tales of secret funds. If half of what they might say was reported as fact, the Brotherhood could crumble with dissension, flinging him back into the numbness of obscurity. And in a sense he alone would lose everything, for Miles knew how much he needed his power and prominence. With a controlled desperation he fully understood his craving for the immense strength leadership granted him. Greedily he remembered those moments of rapture when the audience roared with adulation. And he found himself frightened at how badly he'd abused his appetite for affection at the street rally.

An uneasiness at these revelations touched Miles, but he was calmer now. He allowed himself a tight little smile. Things were going to fall into their natural order again. They had to, Miles thought, turning out the big fluorescent lamp on his desk and going to the window. His office was situated in the front of the old theater building on the right side of the marquee. After the Brotherhood bought the building, he ordered the marquee left up when many of the Brothers and Sisters wanted it removed. It amused him to think up messages for the people on the street. He realized it wasn't exactly dignified for a place of worship, but it was a fine place to advertise, good business sense all the way through.

A light rain had fallen. The fuzzy, dull glow of neon signs

colored the sidewalk in pastel light up and down the avenue. A soft look of benevolence came into Miles's face. He gazed into the street rather proudly and saw himself as the guardian and sacred protector of the diminutive tantalizingly vulnerable figures passing beneath his window. Above all, their interests, so long neglected and depleted of advocacy, had to be looked after.

Immediately the suspicion this was a pompous lie crept up on him. Not long ago he'd railed that these very same people enjoyed nothing better than spreading vicious stories about his impending death. Now he was patronizing them. For a long moment he wondered if these anonymous black folk living out their tattered and embittered existences really meant anything to him at all. At times he believed his own fate counted more than anything. He came first no matter what happened. Suddenly disgust at his mean petty streak of egotism worked on him. He didn't want to be a small-hearted man, but Miles feared life might still scale him down anyway. Frustration at his cruel selfishness mounted in him until he felt extremely nervous. A flash of obsessive hatred at everything overwhelmed him for an instant. He cursed the Brotherhood for making him famous. His mind thrashed wildly about with all the agony of a man who knows he will somehow fail to save himself.

Reluctantly Miles went back to his desk and snapped on the lamp. In the last few days he had come to feel it was imperative to make himself a bit more understandable to white people, even though he knew this effort was bound to be futile. The inane reaction to his essentially harmless declaration counted as evidence with him. He was angry and disappointed with himself for retreating so quickly, so easily, under a surge of disapproval that probably wouldn't have lasted. Now he stared down at the papers before him, wondering if this was not another mistake, something else white people would use to strip him of character and soul and reduce him to the status of a fading oddity. He'd gone through a number of outlines for the Brotherhood's new program and none of it sounded right. His handling of words was still too clumsy and unsure. A bitterness at his lack of an ordinary passable education stirred within him. He couldn't even write a fair sentence, he told himself tauntingly. If all the fancy television people knew that, they'd never stop laughing at him, not that it really mattered. Turning the papers over ruefully he surveyed the remnants of his ideas and pristine hopes. The grasp of futility knotted in his stomach. Then he broke free, telling himself it was foolish for him to try to write speeches. They only deteriorated into an almost hallucinatory mélange of slogans and half-formulated ideas. He fed on the nervous excitement of crowds. How many men could dare to say that? Only a few, invariably the good men with nothing to hide.

Several minutes went by as Miles suffered in turmoil, struggling to give himself some dignity without guilt and bombast. To his alarm the emotions racking him continued to build wildly. He fought to calm down, but the effort only cut into his will to battle the robust tensions taking him over. A spark of reason told him to get out of the office, take a walk, wear down his virulent energies, and think everything into place. But at this juncture, seemingly out of his thoughts, Miles heard a mysterious, light, yet continuous knocking at his door. The sound reverberated through his skull with an irritation beyond description. In a fury he remembered the bodyguard who'd relieved Nicholas at ten o'clock had gone out to an all-night drugstore for coffee and sandwiches. He swore loudly, hoping to discourage the knocking that had ceased momentarily. In perfect silence he unlocked a desk drawer, removed a .38 revolver, and placed it on his desk. As he resumed working the knock came again and it riled him. He suspected a prowler (or perhaps even an assassin) and hoped it wasn't a Brother or Sister with a problem. The last thing Miles wanted was to be seen in a state of confusion.

"Who the hell is it?" he called out abruptly in a controlled frenzy, gripping the pistol in one hand.

"It's Charles," a voice from the corridor replied heavily.

An unpleasant sensation of surprise went through Miles. He

took the safety off his pistol and turned out the desk lamp. De Young would make a perfect target against the light from the hall and Miles was assured by this knowledge, for he was now subconsciously aware that there was something hesitant in De Young's behavior and he was probably not alone.

Slowly the door opened and Charles De Young entered the room, unsure and confused in the dark. He didn't see Miles's shadowed form behind the desk until he'd located a table lamp in the corner and snapped it on. For a quick moment he sensed danger as Miles closed a drawer somewhere in the gloom. "I wasn't sure it was you," he said to Miles rather slowly and without his usual gaiety. "Why is it so dark in here, Miles?"

"I was just leaving. I've been going over some important work all evening and I didn't want to be disturbed, Charles," Miles replied evenly. A cold deliberation was in his voice and it thrilled him a little. He would pick on De Young now and find out who was with him. The fluorescent lamp on his desk flickered to life.

"May I speak with you a minute, Miles?" De Young asked abruptly. There was an undercurrent of gravity in his voice, and Miles looked across the room to where De Young was standing with a sharp expression. Obviously De Young was under some kind of pressure.

"What's it all about, Brother?" he said automatically, with the curt tone of a man absorbed in vastly more important matters. Already Miles sensed De Young was going to heap more bad news on him.

"I think you'd better sit down to hear this," De Young replied evasively.

"I'm fine where I am," Miles shot back in a flash of anger. All of this equivocation galled him. "What's the mystery about?" he demanded.

De Young wet his lips furtively. Miles thought he noticed dark circles, always the residue of corrupt living, smeared under De Young's eyes. His mouth set into a firm haughty line.

"Miles, do you remember the discussion we had just before

you flew to California? We talked right here in this office for a few minutes."

"Of course, I remember," Miles retorted irritably.

"You asked me to watch James, to check and see if any of his movements were suspicious or unaccountable and I did. Nothing came up then." Miles stood perfectly still and listened. He was wildly alert and set to buck at whatever was coming. A tingling sensation, the palpable presence of danger, fondled him and then retreated. Miles was prepared to hit De Young in the mouth. "But now I have very disturbing news." De Young said this wearily but his voice sounded false and devious.

"What the hell are you talking about, Brother?" Miles said menacingly.

De Young wavered, questioning his next words. A subtle intimation of folly played back and forth in him. He was badly worried. "James is mixed up with Communists," he said finally, trying to give it some impact.

The suggestion of a very wicked smile came into Miles's face. He was relieved. The suspense was over and he was pleasingly puzzled at what De Young had said. Anger and cunning combined to make him comfortably wary. For some reason De Young had been quite brash, and Miles decided to master him right away.

"So what," he snapped contemptuously. "That's what they say about me, or didn't you know? It's the easiest thing to say about anybody, Charles," Miles said patronizingly, with an idle shrug of the shoulders.

Outwardly De Young retained his composure, but a severe oppressive feeling tore at him. This whole assignment was too deep. It contained too many complex subtleties he couldn't quite get at. The pressure was on the back of his brain at all times. He couldn't quite elude or tear away from it, and even worse lately he'd become more and more aware of a strain in his character mingling immense fear and a horrible passive despair. The temptation to blame Austin Lake for all his troubles offered itself up to De Young but he turned it aside, temporarily. He spoke to Miles again, indecision hanging on every word.

"Miles, you don't seem to understand what I'm telling you. Brother James, our trusty secretary, is a Communist. He only joined the Brotherhood to begin taking it over. Your life is probably in danger." The stupidity of his pleas stared Charles De Young in the face. James was completely harmless and he knew it. This confrontation was quickly becoming a fiasco. On his own he would never have approached Miles this way, holding out such an obvious insipid story. All of it was Lake's stupid lame idea. A surge of bitterness toward Austin Lake cut through him, but immediately it was slowed by regrets. Lake was in trouble with the agency and De Young gave him the benefit of sympathy. Yet he hated to be pushed into foolish situations. He hated to look inept, especially in front of Miles.

From across the room Miles studied Charles De Young distastefully and decided he was a very bad liar. He could only reply to such antics with contempt.

"What made you come here with this weird story, Brother?" he asked wickedly.

"Well, first of all I kept following James after you came back from California," De Young said quietly, attempting to sound earnest and loyal at the same time. "I always knew something about James wasn't right. Don't ask me why but I always suspected him," he said eagerly.

"What happened then?" Miles asked slyly. He knew De Young's story was about to expand away from him like a child's balloon filled with helium.

"I ran into another man interested in James," De Young said quickly, "and this man was from the government." Now it would be up to Lake to give this fantasy credence, De Young thought angrily.

"And is this man with us tonight?" Miles asked derisively, sliding his hand into the drawer where the pistol lay and artfully glancing at the door.

De Young nodded wearily. His part was finished and he was glad. Miles was making him feel like an imbecile.

"Then show the gentleman in, Charles," Miles said in a clipped commanding voice. His anger was rising swiftly once more.

Without another word being exchanged, Austin Lake pushed aside the half-opened door and came into Miles's darkened office. The effortless way he materialized unnerved Miles a bit. He couldn't believe any white man would ever walk into his domain so confidently.

"Who the hell are you?" Miles asked incredulously, as if the visitor were thoughtlessly trespassing on the grounds of a private estate.

Without saying anything, Lake eyed De Young and came straight up to Miles. There was a faint ironic smile on his face as he took out his folding plastic wallet with the identification cards in it.

"This means nothing to me," Miles said coldly as he handed it back after noting the title and address of the agency. He smarted with resentment against De Young for arranging this scene, which became more incomprehensible by the minute.

"Now that I've told you what I know," De Young called hesitantly from the far corner where he sat by a huge table lamp, "I'd like to go, Miles. It's my turn to open in the morning and supervise the electricians working on the stage."

Suddenly Miles was consumed with rage. The urge to dart across the room and smash De Young senseless tore at him. Yet he wanted to answer with restraint because the presence of this stranger made him wary and uncertain. But all at once it was impossible. "Goddamn you, Charles," he shouted bitterly, "stay where the hell you are. You brought this white man in here and you'll stay where I want you until he leaves."

De Young settled deeply into his chair, steeled by anger, undermined by embarrassment, and protected by the semi-darkness. He couldn't remember when he'd been as miserable.

"Sir," Lake began politely, stepping into the soft purple glare of Miles's desk lamp like an actor going before the camera, "I want to make it clear right now that there is not the slightest element of personal hostility in my visit. I am here because the security agency I represent has strong reason to believe your movement is in real danger of subversion from within. If you were an ordinary man and yours an ordinary movement, none of this would really matter. We know Communist groups exist in this country, but they have no strength or significance. However, Mr. King, the implications of communism touching your great movement are enormous. It is a matter of some urgency and import."

"Sit down," Miles said to Lake as he eased himself into the big leather chair behind his desk. Quickly he checked to see if De Young had moved and then assessed the rather pleasant and straightforward young white man in front of him. He was a bit flattered by what Lake had said and he liked the reasonable, manly way everything was explained. Still there was something peculiar in this meeting, something false Miles couldn't define. "What's all this talk about Brother James?" he asked, fluttering his hands impatiently.

A certain familiar pressure exerted itself in Lake's mind. He recalled his strained and somewhat enigmatic conference with the director. Ever since that day he'd experienced a constant and inexplicable mixture of exhilarating freedom and peril. He was on his own the director had said, but was it merely to prove his incompetence? The thought toyed with him as he replied to King. "Sir, we have incontrovertible proof that James Fitzgerald, secretary of your organization, is in the employ of the Chinese Ministry of Foreign Affairs."

The whisper of a smile then touched upon Miles's keen features, alerting Austin Lake to trouble. "And who trained, Charlie?" Miles asked. A biting look of clever mockery was all over his face. Lake was startled. He envisioned penetrating questions being shot at him. How long had he known about James? (Would Miles ever believe it had been years?) Why hadn't the agency approached him before if the matter was so important? His plan to flush James by planting nothing but uncertainty, doubt, and suspicion around him now seemed puerile and amateurish, just as De Young had warned him. But Lake yearned to do more than just stuff a file. He wanted to terrorize James and triumph over him; yet as he tried to return Miles King's condescending smile Lake knew the whole elaborate ruse was collapsing on him. At first he didn't actually realize what was happening as Charles De Young spoke up suddenly from the other side of the room.

"Miles, will you listen to what the man is saying and stop acting like a damn fool," his voice cried out from the soft darkness where he was seated.

Immediately the urge to recall these words took hold of De Young. He sensed his own fear of what was coming. He could feel the mood of sullen, revengeful power in Miles closing in on the point of showy vulnerability he always tried to conceal from himself. A tiny pleading look appeared in his eyes, but Miles couldn't see it and didn't want to although he knew it was there. Miles didn't care if De Young wanted mercy from the truth. He was completely incensed.

"Don't you speak to me that way. Don't you give me orders, you humpback flunky," Miles yelled at him violently as he bounded to his feet. "You're scum, Charles. And you know it. Look at you cringe and cower. I've seen Pullman porters with more self-respect than you'll ever have. I pity your miserable ass, boy. You're the kind of black man I really hate and pity because you have no pride. Anyone can use you, Charles. And anyone can discard you," Miles shouted with disgust and contempt. "You're the kind that has sold us out for generations."

De Young began to protest but he couldn't. Like a man in a dream, invisible forces bound him up. He was helpless and stricken with shame. Miles was forcing a wedge into every fissure in his personality, every flaw in his stance.

"Oh, I've seen it in you, Brother, all that deceit and vanity. Believe me, I have. You're evilly vain, that's point number one." The words were sharp and merciless. "You want everything played your way. But you're confused and that's how the white man has manipulated you. He's played on your confusion, played on the things in you that are weakest. Given you clothes, hasn't he, Charles? Money, clothes, an occasional woman he's through with, an apartment you could never get

165

for yourself. Tell me about it, flunky! I want to hear what they gave you for selling me out. What was it, a new sports car with no key in it?"

Austin Lake was startled and then intensely fascinated by the way Miles worked on poor De Young. It was a beastly, inhuman attack driven by the perverse ferocity of a wild animal turning on one of its own pack. And all of it was bitterly couched in a snarling articulateness common to shrewish wives and gutter-smart men who always unconsciously store up signs of weakness in their associates. The subtle hatreds and rivalries that must exist between these two men amazed Lake, but he wasn't embarrassed to see them worked out in front of him. By intuition Lake was sure he was learning something valuable here, even though the whole scene was going by very fast. Carefully he shifted in his seat and glanced at the exasperated and saddened figure of De Young. He'd never seen De Young appear so subservient and helpless. Of course, De Young was through on the assignment. Then out of some superior generosity Lake decided to let De Young tell him that. Perhaps more valuable nuances in what Miles was saying might be made clear to him if it were done that way, for this astonishing occurrence only made King more of a mystery to him because he couldn't have anticipated it. He saw his naïvete and quickly resolved never to suggest it in De Young's presence.

Miles continued to shout curses and insults at De Young. Savagely he ridiculed his manhood and lifted the lid on a contempt and uneasiness he claimed always to have felt in his presence. ("You played the stud too much, Charles. It made me question you, boy. Where are all your women? I mean the ones I didn't help you get.") But then his voice began to rise and fall with a slight dramatic sadness, which did not escape De Young. He knew secretly Miles suffered for him because Miles viewed him as a stray soul, a genuinely empty man without real abilities or a stable identity. The thought stirred him acutely. Something outrageously smug was in the kernel of this attitude. Only a slave could stand it for long, De Young sensed with progressive indignation. What right did Miles have to feel sorry for him, to patronize him into an abstraction? De Young's resentment had a clear, sharp, meaningful edge and upon it he built confidence. Humiliation spread away into a violent loathing of Miles. Yet De Young understood the contradictions in his life revealed tonight would never disappear from his thoughts altogether, and for exposing them he hated Miles with an odd distant anger. Now even if Miles took it all back, and probably he would in some devious way, never again could they ever pretend to be really at ease together. Too much had passed between them this evening for that kind of deception to flourish.

All at once it was quiet in the room. Miles had finished his tirade. ("You were never much, Charles. Why don't you do me a favor now and get out of my sight.") He was weary with the nagging guilt a parent feels after beating a child. Only a look of questionable pity remained on his face. In the confusion of this hellish evening, the tight caressing atmosphere of psychological control and inurement he wanted to establish had drained away. Miles was more frightened than ever and he half trusted De Young even as he abused him. De Young could be telling the truth, but his relationship with this white man was still murky and unexplained.

Miles felt the rush of untutored fear and suspicion in him speeding toward collision like two brightly colored billiard balls traversing the green felt table. He grimaced and then stared down at his papers before glancing at Austin Lake, who sat across from him. Very apologetically he nodded in the direction of Charles De Young and as he turned away a dramatic crash splintered the ominous quiet surrounding all three men. De Young had leapt from his chair muttering inaudibly and knocked over the table lamp next to him viciously, smashing it to the floor as he bolted from the office and vanished as enigmatically as he'd come.

Arched forward in his seat Austin Lake watched Miles carefully. For a while they contemplated each other through the fluorescent haze without speaking. Lake could see Miles was very tired and he was prompted to leave as soon as possible. A curious little hungry smile formed on his lips as he gazed sympathetically at the famous black face so close to him and yet so abstract and unattainable. "Sir, would it be possible for us to meet again?" Lake asked respectfully.

Miles stood perfectly still behind the desk. As always his mind was working for an angle. Perhaps this pleasant young man really knew something damaging about James. If not, he might be of some valuable use in another way. Still Miles felt a little vulnerable and betrayed. But a delectable curiosity was beginning to work on him. "We'll see what you have to say for yourself Sunday after my meeting," Miles replied with the practiced arrogance that always best concealed his true feelings.

CHAPTER FOURTEEN

BEVERLY CARTER lived on upper Riverside Drive, just below the George Washington Bridge, in a neighborhood that was not part of Harlem, but not clear of it either. The tenants in her building, a reluctant mixture of foreign students, bourgeois blacks, and Jews left behind in the great migrations to green Westchester County, never ventured onto the broad avenues to the west where ragged improverished black people stood around all day waiting for numbers runners, drug couriers, and thieves with their booty to sell. Like contented grazing animals, her neighbors moved up and down their strip of well-policed Riverside Park and dashed headlong to the subway on weekday mornings because it was on the fringe of enemy territory. The apartment house Beverly lived in stood in an impressive row that formed a massive barrier to the scenic but polluted Hudson River slipping by beyond the park. It was done in the château style, a monument to the art of some magnificent fabricator who had gone on to do his best work in the Bronx and Queens. As he got out of his car a few blocks away sometime the next afternoon, Austin Lake was vaguely surprised to find himself in such a genteel setting.

Lake set out purposefully along the wide, empty sidewalk.

Anyone passing him would have been sure he was nothing more innocuous or interesting than a semi-prosperous insurance salesman moving on to an appointment. What drives were operating his mind Austin Lake could not say, but every one of his trained impulses demanded he continue on the present bearing. Yet Lake knew what he was doing was a little too provocative, a little too clever and unrealistic. The director would probably sneer and say it was top heavy with thinking. But it promised big dividends, for once again Lake found himself obsessed with the singular elusive notion of triumph over James Fitzgerald. He reasoned that if James heard from a number of reliable friends that the federal government was investigating his life intensively he might fall apart under the nervous pressure of waiting to be arrested. He might split from within like an overripe tropical fruit. If not, he might seek to contact the person monitoring him and ask for instructions. Total inaction after all these years could only indicate a pathologically strong will, or that no worthwhile case existed anymore. Either way there was a definite consolation and Lake was glad of it, for like most intelligence people he really hated mysteries.

He remembered at times he wished he'd gone into the State Department. At his university, government service meant either State or Intelligence. Good clever people never went into Commerce, and Interior was for cowboys and hitchhikers. But there was something peculiar about State. It was a fortress of mannered snobbery and archaic procedures, like the British House of Lords. He disliked the pervasive gossip and the pointless social distinctions. (People with Irish names had a way of making sure you knew their forebears were Protestant.) And the ineffectual sons of the rich on top exerted all kinds of petty bureaucratic pressures. Below the level of assistant secretary you were pretty helpless, almost as helpless as he was now.

He went into the building, opening one huge, elaborately decorated black steel door handily and stepping into the sundappled quiet of an enormous reception hall faced with huge cold blocks of stone. The door swung shut behind him portentously. The hall, with its carved medieval table, was ludicrous but genuinely intimidating and Lake walked softly to escape the grating reverberations of his footsteps on the paved floor.

Unexpectedly a few stray images of Miles King drifted into his mind and a swift depression came over Lake. King was capable of running his career in a dozen ways, but he was a fascinating, seductive person and Lake was a little proud of admiring him so freely. For one thing King had a lot of raw emotional power and embittered perseverance. Heading a mad cult with outlets all over the country was an oppressive job, but Miles did it easily. He could probably run General Motors if called upon. The man was a magnificent archetype of strength and cunning, Lake thought, yet his task was impossible and his enemies were omnipresent. In Washington he was merely a case now, a homosexual case perhaps (he did live alone unmarried), a rude cocktail party joke, a nasty freak, a vicious delinquent for sure. Experts in every field—sociology, psychotherapy, spiritualism—sought to use him. Two or three newspaper columnists specializing in the decline of prominent personalities remained at his side, but only to gather material for their clever obituaries.

In the elevator on the way up, Lake smiled tolerantly at the extent of his sympathy. And suddenly the stunning conceit and falsity underlying his absurd compassion rushed back at him mockingly. Abruptly he realized he had no way of knowing what King really wanted in any sense. King was a public enigma who focused attention only on his detractors. Uncomfortably Lake spied his blurred visage in the shiny wood paneling of the elevator. From the beginning he had been fooled by his own spurious, self-important motives, his own liberal incoherence, and crackpot intelligence theories while Miles King escaped him, shrouded in lively ambiguities he could not penetrate. King and Fitzgerald were linked in that way; both possessed subtle energies completely unlike his own. Thinking about them made Austin Lake feel naked and overextended. He was not his own man after all. Is this what the director had been trying to tell him? Lake wasn't sure. He didn't want to be sure. He understood clearly that what had started out as simple arithmetic was quietly evolving into calculus.

The elevator clicked to a stop on Beverly's floor. He got off and walked down the hall searching for the apartment number next to the name Carter on the badly lighted directory downstairs. When he found it, Lake rang the buzzer anxiously. Beverly put the chain across the door and then opened it just a crack. Automatically her face registered surprise at seeing a strange white man. He was obviously not a peddler.

"May I come in?" Lake asked abruptly and without thinking. He knew it was a stupid way to open. Regulations said you were always supposed to show them the credentials first.

"Who are you, mister?" Beverly said, suppressing the lilt of apprehension in her voice. For a moment she feared he might be a former client, and if he was, he had to know the deal was always no private appointments.

"I want to talk to you about James Fitzgerald."

"Are you with the police?" she asked timidly.

Austin Lake held up his plastic wallet and Beverly looked at it. Without reading a word, she took down the chain. "Where are you from, sir? I don't want any trouble," she said fearfully as Lake stepped into the foyer.

"I'm sorry if I frightened you," Lake said politely, not really wanting to give her the name of the agency. He looked at her softly and then smiled with a touch of embarrassment, feeling like a voyeur for having seen her in so many back-room movies. She was not breathtaking, he thought, but she was beautifully brown, sultry, and suggestive, a quality missing in the films. He tried not to gaze at her gorgeously pugnacious breasts, which stood out under a white cashmere sweater and saluted him. She smiled back at his earnest good manners and they went down a carpeted hallway into the big living room, which was all French Provincial with white wall-to-wall carpeting. Beverly was frantically nervous. Her piled-up Cleopatra hairdo seemed unsteady on her head.

"Has anything happened to James?" she inquired tentatively.

"That is what I'm here to find out," Lake replied.

"Where did you say you were from?" she said, trying to sound at ease.

He took out the wallet again and held it up briefly. "I represent an agency of the United States government. We want to talk with James, but we haven't been able to find him for the last two days. Miss Carter, have you seen him in that period?" Beverly looked at him for a long second and said haltingly she hadn't seen James in a few weeks. Immediately she sensed Lake knew she was lying. She watched him take out a little notebook and begin courteously, "I want to ask a few questions of you. I hope you won't mind. Please try and be as accurate with your answers as possible."

There was something cute in the way he spoke and Beverly slowly said she would cooperate. Gently she placed a nervous and almost trembling hand on the silken arm of the sofa. She wanted no part of the government.

As he began Austin Lake remembered his appointment with Miles on Sunday afternoon. He decided to push Beverly a little for some tidbits of obscure knowledge Miles might not know about.

"How long have you known James Fitzgerald?"

"Let's see, I guess it's been about three months now. I'm never sure of dates." She smiled weakly. In her voice there was a silly little tingle.

"How did you meet?" Lake said not looking up. He could not deny it, something about this girl (maybe the heavy scent of her erotic perfume or the thick rustle of her opulent costume jewelry) excited and titillated him eagerly. Her tight pants made her look ripe and willing. A sensation of desire spread in his groin.

"Oh, a mutual friend you might say"—all sorts of sensuous implications came into this—"a fella who was an old buddy of James introduced us."

"Name?"

"Clarence Williams," she said quite slowly and reluctantly, watching Lake write it down as if it had tremendous portent.

173

"Address, please. I'll need an address for this man."

"I don't know," Beverly snapped. Suddenly she was wrestling with tempestuous anger, for the bland insidiousness contained in the question had a probing expectant quality to it she had heard many times from happily exhausted clients wanting to indulge in discussions on professional prostitution. She hated the way Lake was taking everything for granted. "Clarence lived someplace in Brooklyn. I had it written down once but I threw it away. He moved out of town you see," she added with a flourish of imagination. Lake shot her a questioning stare and she blinked defensively. He eyed her tight pants with something like obvious hunger as she battled back the exasperation and fury and spreading helplessness taking her. He wasn't getting anything, she told herself weakly. Let him get it at home. Let him go out and buy it. She decided not to lie again.

The interview continued. It went on for half an hour, Lake seriously putting forth queries as Beverly fed him small twisted bits of the truth. He asked a great deal about Clarence and after a while she suspected he had all the real answers anyway, but Lake did not. He was discouraged as he envisioned another dreary scene like this with Williams and whomever he might lead to. The disgusted urge to forget hounding James moved him powerfully. The clarity of the morning had been marred by a thousand tiny mistakes and apprehensions about King and the director and now he wanted to lie down with this girl so badly it almost made him swoon. He realized it was all adolescent madness, but the impulse didn't slacken and Lake saw he might have to take himself out of the assignment because his perspective was no longer there, his will had drained down into his scrotum to continue the battle with a devilish familiarity vanished from his mind. No longer did he really give a damn who Williams was. In the maw of his anxieties and flounderings Williams could be a transvestite if only he gave Beverly the word. It had become that longingly simple. But Lake knew better. Williams presented him for the first time with the outlines of a genuine clue combined with retreating overtones of mystery. He was an unknown, obscure person visibly affecting the prime suspect, a link with what? Probably nothing, probably one more ruined life kept smoldering by the tenacious desire of an ardent black woman to see him be a man, somehow. And Lake knew all of it would imprison and disgust him. His meager hope was that surely along the way there would be many more temptations and hopefully a sexual side trip or two. Once again he examined the smooth muscularity of Beverly's strong velvety thighs, imagining himself to be caught up in their luscious grip. The girl was an inspiration, he thought more humorously, aware now of her extreme discomfort, for Beverly had begun to squirm a little. Her legs were tightly crossed. These strange proceedings, without real words or discernible emotions frightened her almost into speechlessness.

Finally and to her immense relief Mr. Lake, he had asked her to call him that instead of officer, got up to leave.

"If you see James, if he comes around here, will you let us know?" he asked in his sincere boyish way.

"Oh, yes, of course, sir," she replied, looking up at him with her large brown eyes. "But how do I get in touch with you?" This was the one piece of information she badly needed. James had to get help. He had to get a lawyer and avoid these people before they inserted his life into the hopeless complexities of the courts.

Lake extracted from his pocket one of those large leather wallets with notepaper in it and jotted down a phone number. "This is the New York City Police Department Bureau of Special Operations. Ask for Sergeant Zito and leave your information with him." Then a strange moment passed. Subtly it came to Beverly that if she took the note a very large commitment was involved. She might become enmeshed in the fate that awaited James. Lake saw her ambiguity and extended the folded piece of paper promptingly to her. She held back and after a second or two reached for it unwillingly, as though it were somehow contaminated with a horrible slime. "Don't lose it," he warned.

Lake had reached the door when he heard her coming up behind him rapidly. "Officer Lake, what is this about?" she asked in a thick and bewildered voice. He turned. She was trembling. "Honestly I've only been in trouble once in my life. I don't want anymore."

"It's a very serious matter," he said in the sober voice that had become so strangely menacing to her. "Just contact me if you see James and you'll be all right. I promise you that."

She let him out, put up the chain again, and drifted into the sunny living room where fears of her vulnerability overwhelmed her. Unsteadily, to the rustle of her fancy golden jewelry, Beverly sat down and began to cry softly.

CHAPTER FIFTEEN

CLOSE TO MIDNIGHT that evening Clarence Williams returned to his home in Brooklyn. For an hour and a half he had traveled the subways riding down his own dread. With a route map in one hand, cramped into a tiny corner seat, he tried to smuggle himself away from the other passengers. He was convinced with a crazy singular intensity that a faint odor of gasoline still lingered in his clothes. Earlier in the evening, now a dozen dreamy years ago, he stole into the basement of a church in Harlem and set a fire, which almost consumed him, and there began his troubles. Quickly the police appeared on the spot, leaving him to choke and stumble alone in the burning cellar. The dense smoke almost crowded the life out of him before they went around front and he had time to slip away, sickened by the encounter with his own hysterical, unheard screams.

Clarence let himself into the apartment and immediately took comfort in the order and familiarity around him. Every room was a little gem of housekeeping, neat as a breast-pocket handkerchief, decorous as a shoeshine, a delight to the proprietary instincts he cherished. Few people suspected he was at all inspired by good taste and it pleased him to show off his apartment and watch surprise brighten in the faces of his guests. Later they realized it was a small, clever game Clarence played and their respect for him was enlarged. Clarence liked it that way because he thought of himself as exceedingly clever. The sport of making other people see this enchanted him, for it bestowed to him an air of artifice not otherwise apparent. But his home was more than just a setting for Clarence, he held a strong protective feeling for it and was riled by the thought of burglary. Each object in the place, every prissy clue to his thirst for acquisition brought him joy. Clarence believed in arty lamps, nightclub piano music, and kitchen gadgets the way other people believed in the Scriptures. His greatest need was to have material things. If you had to do without them, it was a dog.

He knew it was chiefly due to luck that he was able to afford so much. There was no other way for him to account for the appearance of Mr. Mahanti in his life. One day this careful-talking, little foreign man had rung the bell. On first sight he figured him for the slickest of con men and the impression always lingered, even after Mahanti said he had good-paying work for him. Right away he started talking about James and how he owed James a debt he wanted fixed up. Clarence remembered James; but even as Mahanti spoke about him, he knew they had never been close, if they had known each other at all. But he couldn't turn his visitor down. What Mahanti wanted had been harmless enough, and the money was beautiful, it was a winning ticket in the largest of sweepstakes.

This evening though was too much, Clarence thought. A fright took him as he recalled how he'd shivered when the flames got close. It was stupid of him to be burning down churches like a common criminal. What was the meaning of it, he asked himself, but of course there was no answer. He was told to make it look like arson and that was all he knew. As an uncomfortable, passing thought, he wondered if he had done anything in setting this fire to hurt James and his Brotherhood, but purposely he made no connection. Then a horror crept over him. Had this night made him a murderer? Could it be someone was left trapped in the flames, smothered by smoke, bitten by the heat? Fear of this set him off on a new round of thinking, and Clarence sought to recreate the fire scene clearly, but a suspicion of something bigger and more menacing than the conflagration appeared to him. He named it guilt knowing it was not, and the deception failed to take hold. Like many of his deliberate lapses it carried no weight, the just reward, he always bitterly thought, of being an inconsequential man. All Clarence was left with was the reasonable assumption that no one would be in a church on a Friday night.

Still he was plagued. A desire to know what he had brought about ate at his caution. Quite abruptly he hoped the fire had done little damage, yet even as he turned on his television set for the news this idea became a sham. Clarence knew compulsively he was looking for clues in a scheme he didn't want to understand. A deliciously wicked fascination was egging him on. He was buoyed by sensual tremors.

The late news was spotlighting the fire, a seven-alarm blaze. Clarence listened to the commentary for a minute and then delicately turned down the sound. He watched the disaster with rapt energy and awe, as if he were able to see much more than the image in front of him.

The first sign of trouble had been spotted by a man passing the spacious, manicured grounds of the Reverend John Lawrence's Second Baptist Church. He noticed a curlicue of smoke escaping from a partially opened window and ran to a fire alarm box, but it was already too late. Moments later the beautiful church stood in a roaring fire. Every stained glass window in the nave was blown out by the force of expanding heat and combustion. The building had already burned wildly for three hours, giving off a searing heat that came out on television as disfiguring tongues of dissipated evil casting faint shadows in the corners of Clarence's living room. Huge fire department vehicles, arrayed on the perimeter of the blaze, shielded officials looking on in astonishment as long graceful columns of water played futilely over the scene. A thick gray smoke climbed into the sky. The police and fire commissioners arrived; but all efforts to put out the fire lapsed into failure. The church seemed to burn weirdly, with an energy of its own abetted by gasoline, a chemical powder, and magnesium strip fuses Clarence had sprinkled around the basement. Hundreds of people assembled behind police barricades to watch as the fire grew more intense and menacing. Finally the roof collapsed leaving dark, stately, Gothic arches to stand alone in the midst of the conflagration. Then the cameras switched to the Reverend Mr. Lawrence, who had arrived from his home on Long Island, and as they did one wall disintegrated in the flames. Lawrence bowed his head and Clarence guessed he was sobbing. He watched the preacher being led away by a uniformed fireman while the police pushed back their wooden horses and relocated the spectators twenty yards away for fear the whole block might start to go up. Eventually two other walls fell down and the fire subsided. It was eight hours after the first alarm when specialists in white asbestos suits at last moved in to finish the job. By morning nothing at all was left of the Second Baptist Church except part of a charred wall in the middle of a broken, still smoldering landscape bordered by dried-out brown grass gone sour at the roots.

Clarence went into the kitchen in a mood of aggressive foreboding. A painful uneasiness flexed and coiled through his stomach. He remembered the preacher Lawrence had stirred up a lot of attention a few weeks before with public charges of a conspiracy to defeat the drive for Negro rights. This evening he had set fire to the preacher's church and he felt clammy with sin. His wall of deceptions, the flimsy cleverness he prided himself on was beginning to collapse. He was part of some plot as he had known darkly all along, but he didn't know if his side was good or bad, and suddenly with this knowledge all of his limitations roused inside him. He recalled that first meeting with Mahanti and how the stranger had talked in the vaguest of terms about James, while repeating blandly his amazing offer of big money. Mahanti had worked hard on him, probing his depths of honest weakness and fraud until he was sure he had bought a good little workman, and this hurt Clarence because it forced him to look at the extent of his dishonesty. The range of things he hid from himself was indeed very big, and Mahanti had seen that with the reflexes of a psychoanalyst. In fact the people behind this whole thing must have contempt for him, Clarence understood that finally, and his emotions lashed out at Mahanti, the suave seducer smart enough to hide his own vulnerability behind the hedgerows of English gentility. A spasm of rage and jealousy worked up into Clarence's chest and he hated Mahanti with a hot flame of resentment because his employer could vanish into limousines, and quite possibly talk his way by the police; a man with such powers never really needed the hired hands.

The empty feeling of someone waiting on a hard bench to be interrogated sat upon Clarence, but like an innocent suspect he was buttressed by hope and a quick identification with all the forces of right. After all he had gotten away. He had plenty of money. No one might ever know of his part. There was consolation in being a small gear in the machinery, yet again his recurring curiosity seized him. If he was strong and safe, who was he hurting? Did Lawrence have the kind of enemies who sent foreigners to set up the revenge, or was Mahanti small fish too? Clarence puzzled at this but came to no conclusion. He was not in the mood for conclusions anyway. He wanted hard not to think of anything, for when he did his mind went full circle back to James, who must be the center of all this activity. There he decided to prepare for bed comforted temporarily by his proven ability to draw out the laughter in his old buddy James.

CHAPTER SIXTEEN

EARLY THE NEXT MORNING at about eight o'clock James mounted the steps of an old brownstone in West 140th Street. Half a block to the east, Eighth Avenue, a squalid garbage-and-glass-strewn thoroughfare stretched away to infinity like the sands of a secret desert within the city. Westward, Morningside Park came uneasily to rest on an elongated and verdant slope reaching ten blocks in either direction. Its terraces, shaded by leafy oaks, offered the prospect of tranquility and idyllic spring romance to the students of City College packed into a mélange of neo-Gothic and modern functional buildings just over the rise. James envisioned the scene here in a few days: brilliant spitting torches among the blooming trees, agitated wrathful shadows flung against the buildings, sporadic gunfire, and the flickering lights of police cars; smoke everywhere and violent, surging, inarticulate mobs racing through the streets to protest the death of a martyr.

An unusually bright morning sun made each brownstone in the block stand out as a bleak and drab sentinel against the hostile neighborhood. Once, many years before, this had been a middle-class block of good houses. A certain facade of shabby, genteel respectability persisted, but it was merely a facade, for anyone in the area could practically recite the names and crimes of those modern-day desperadoes hiding there in tiny furnished rooms, waiting for the inevitable day when two patrolmen would show up with drawn guns and ask them to take a ride over to the precinct.

James went into the cool, dark wood-paneled vestibule. Out of habit he peeked in the mailbox, which had never been used. He then took out a brand-new key, a copy of the one hidden away in a harmless-looking parcel at the bus station, and let himself into the building. A narrow hallway, heavy with gloom and the suffocating smell of dust-laden carpets opened to him. In the rear a gray light from an unseen source slanted against one peeling wall. The atmosphere was thick with stale smells—traces of cooking gas and furniture polish, perspiration and cold leaky toilets, all the leftover airs of tenement living—but no sign of life, not even a cat, was to be seen. James began to move forward on his tiptoes, afraid now of disturbing a houseful of faded and decrepit souls. He was halfway to the stairs when suddenly a large door on his right popped open noisily. An elderly black woman, quite dark and dressed in the daintiest of nighttime creations, thrust her head and shoulders out. She peered at him harshly through very thick glasses while assuming a demanding air of physical confrontation. James stopped where he was but didn't speak as the old woman made him out. His silence seemed to aggravate her and she made an ugly face.

"Who?" she inquired in a sharp accent full of West Indian hostility and tension.

James felt a string of foul curses were coming next. "It's Mr. Michaels, Mrs. Emerson," he said politely.

She waved a long, bony, muscular arm in disgust. "No Michaels in here," she said, looking him up and down with too obvious distaste. "You have the wrong house, mister."

"I'm Michaels."

"Oh, yes?" The answer hovered between a question and a condemnation. Mrs. Emerson was not sure. She stared at James with great concentration, looking for something in him to challenge. "I never see you here, so I don't know."

James was sure she had no clue to his identity, although she probably remembered with great exactitude that Mr. Michaels had two rooms on the top floor and always paid his rent by sending a money order. For the longest instant they examined each other carefully in the dim light of the hallway, then the old woman majestically raised her head high. "Pass," she said in a voice so haughty and cryptic it could have ushered gladiators into the arena.

The apartment was old and in bad condition. Half a dozen major replastering jobs swelled under the faded wallpaper. The first room, a miniature box without windows, was so cramped that one squat, heavy Victorian desk displaced all the volume like a large stone in a pail of water. In the other somewhat bigger chamber a brass bed, rocking chair, and a big cracked mirror covered with dust had finally come to rest. The only window in the place let in some feeble light from an airshaft. There was no kitchen. Mrs. Emerson made it clear to all her tenants that they were lucky to have any shelter at all, and cooking in the rooms was something she wouldn't stand for; the bathroom was situated at the end of the hall. James was glad he lived elsewhere.

He went to the window and peered down the grimy black airshaft, which was coated with heavy, delicate networks of accumulated soot and dust. An abstracted look of repugnance came over his face, but James continued to stare downward, trying to glimpse the bottom of the shaft hidden from the angle of his vision. A slice of sunlight cut across the dirty windowpane just above his head and dropped steeply into the room, making it appear more hopeless and forlorn than ever. For a long time James did not move at all. His mind roamed among random, unimportant thoughts, carefully avoiding the nexus of pain and anxiety throbbing in him unceasingly. It was only by degrees, by tortured minute accumulations of detail that James allowed himself to drift back to that heart-stopping moment Thursday morning when a cheerful postman rang his bell with a fat special delivery packet. Although it was only two days ago it seemed like years. Stupidly he accepted the packet with a weak smile. Its bulk was mostly made up of discarded reprints of United Nations proceedings wrapped carefully around a large sealed envelope containing a bank identification card complete with photograph. There was also an address: Economic Committee on Asia and the Far East, Post Office Box 1122, Grand Central Station. Under it someone had scrawled an order to return the card. Of course he'd done it. His exhausting fatalistic drive wouldn't allow him even that small deviation.

Once he'd taken the packet (intuitively he anticipated Mahanti would come back at him immediately) James perceived that whether its existence was a threat or a plea he had allowed himself once again to be drawn into the plan to destroy Miles. It was pointless to resist, even though he wanted nothing else. The only solace he could grasp was a false superiority over George Mahanti, for in reestablishing contact so quickly Mahanti had demonstrated his utter subservience to the ministry. He had confirmed the putrefying essence of his condition as a menial lackey. James was proven right, but in a perverse turn of logic his observations revealed him as no better than Mahanti. Neither of them harbored the courage of renunciation or the impulse to purify themselves. The ministry knew this, as Mahanti pointed out. They probably counted on it. The fight had been a mere overnight reprieve, a childish melodramatic incident the people in Bern could only have regarded with exaggerated glee. But James was glad he'd knocked Mahanti down. He relished the wild physical pleasure of sending his brutal fists smashing into Mahanti's soft unprotected belly. He only wished he'd gone further, gone berserk as he had often enough in the war. And as he entered the office of a Swiss bank in Rockefeller Center on Friday morning James wished with a sickening clarity that he'd killed Mahanti when he had the chance. Still he went through the procedures flawlessly. Using the coded identification card (a facsimile machine correlated his photograph, number, and thumbprint), he drew ten thousand dollars, money he knew had started out in Peking and traveled a circuitous international route from Hong Kong to Beirut and then to Bern. In Bern an executive of the Eastern Star Import-Export Company had lodged it in a reliable bank under the name electroprinted on his card. The bus station was easy. A red-faced attendant accepted the airlines bag containing the money and key without any questions. Fifteen minutes later he sent off the claim check and disappeared amid the crowds flooding into the subway even though he had no real destination.

Departing reluctantly from his meditations James moved away from the window and sat down in the old rocking chair. The arms felt gummy and unclean beneath his fingers, but James sat back in suspended pleasure. The tarnished brass bed glinted eerily in the waning sunlight as the chair swayed to and fro. James wished he could remain in this unknown timeless room forever. Slowly he rocked back and forth, not really thinking or caring about anything when startlingly, and with the oozy premonition of a fainting spell, he remembered the big church fire in Harlem the night before. A momentary nausea played over him, but he fought it down quickly and desperately. Wild intuitions told him the whole assassination plot was going to go wrong as surely as everything he'd done in his life had somehow been tainted and denigrated and twisted out of his hands by unnamed powers merely joking with his myriad weaknesses. Details of the lurid fire whirled up at him. He was horrified and intrigued. A large church fire, as Mahanti had outlined it, was to be one of many signals goading him into action after the assassination. Therefore nothing was really left to him but the tenuous hope that this was a separate tragedy, an occurrence no more related to him than it was to eight million others in the city.

He laughed nervously at this absurd reasoning, although what he actually wanted to do was to cry out in furious agony. He wanted to lose control, to scream himself into a sweating, frothy hysteria so that someone might hear his cries and rescue him from the deadening trauma of inescapableness and morbid fate. Diabolically James wanted to be saved from himself, even though he perceived this was not possible. He was penned up more savagely than an animal in a cage. His masters (whoever they were) never had to worry about him because he possessed no means to elude them. That he couldn't recall their faces, their clothing, the nuances of their manners anymore only increased their hold over him. He remembered it had been years since he had seen a Chinese face. And his senses now rejected the experience. Reason whispered to him that no ministry existed. But still its weight bore down on his life as relentlessly as the mechanism of the universe, as completely as the laws of nature or the unknowable principles of an arcane psycho-philosophical science. The ministry was brutal and universal while James was merely frail. This was the nature of his predicament and it would not be reversed. Resignation could be his only accomplishment.

Momentarily James understood this without any terror. He saw the tracings of his fate worked out in his actions of the last two days. Like a man preparing for a profound experience he had avoided everyone he knew for two full days, ever since the postman arrived on Thursday morning. No one at Brotherhood Hall had seen him. He'd even stayed away from Beverly for fear she might see the awful dread in his eyes, or sense it under her touch. The configuration in this infinite network of hours contained nothing but pitiful resignation. His presence in these abandoned rooms was deep proof of it, for Mahanti had ordered him to give up his key and assume his normal duties as if nothing were happening. Driven by instinct and perhaps fear of a breakdown, fear of the onset of insanity, he only half obeyed the order. An odd mingling of indolent energies had led him here to contemplate his life. His existence seemed to have circled in upon him, and James had no explanation for it. Fate carried him along.

After a long time he rose almost majestically from the chair and checked the place for any sign of his occupancy. Finding none he locked the battered door for the last time. Carefully he picked his way down the stairs as quietly as he had come, hoping now to cheat Mrs. Emerson of a last look at him. The vestibule door was almost within his grasp when suddenly the landlady's door sprang open again and she confronted him with hard, suspicious eyes. She wasn't wearing her glasses and her sight seemed improved as she examined James without pleasure, as if he were a mediocre piece of yard goods. Mrs. Emerson had on street clothes now, clothes twenty years out of date, but impeccable; they hinted at a stylish youth James would not have guessed at. He eyed the old woman pleasantly and then smiled a little, but her harsh expression did not change. She had been telling herself for the last two hours that Mr. Robert Michaels, top floor rear, was probably some kind of criminal. Why else would a man keep such strange and irregular hours?

CHAPTER SEVENTEEN

EARLY EVENING had come and gone when Charles De Young finally jockeyed his big Chevrolet into a parking lot near Union Square and walked to the bookstore. He knew Lake had probably been waiting over two hours for him, but like everything on this peculiar day it seemed annoyingly irrelevant, for De Young sensed with his fine instincts for vigilance that around him more important rendezvous were being kept. The devasting church fire in Harlem with its putrid atmospheric residue of charred wood and harsh, nauseating chemicals contributed to this strange mood. And he knew all afternoon a dozen currents of apprehension had swirled through his mind, alerting him in a subtle and familiar way he'd learned long ago to respect. Miles was speaking to him again, or at least nodding, so he dismissed their last bitter encounter as the nervous center of his tensions, but no relief came. Curiously De Young didn't expect any.

Lake was in the back room sitting at his metal desk in the corner. As De Young entered, he felt a crackling antagonism in the air and saw traces of nervousness plainly stand out in Lake's demeanor, in the way he looked at his watch and said, "Charles, for once you're right on the button." He was covered and glad of it, because in the next instant Brian Riggs, followed by a younger man in a tweed-vested suit came across the room without saying a word. They sat down but De Young could see it was only for a moment.

"Now that you've arrived, Charles," Riggs said shortly, "Austin can brief you on our meeting."

De Young was a bit startled, but he only nodded. He kept cool. The younger man, who had inserted his fingers into his lower vest pockets, peered at De Young with vaguely concealed disgust. In his querulous expression of extreme prudence De Young recognized the elaborate snobbery of the well-pressed, well-spoken agency desk jockeys, some of whom were said to be driven raving queer by all the wildly secret weaknesses they read about in otherwise strong men.

"Since you're still nominally part of this assignment," Riggs went on, "I want you to go over some of the possibilities Austin and I agree should be put to King." Although he had no idea of what they were talking about, De Young in a very calm voice—he was surprised at his composure—said he would. But Riggs was clearly amused at this. He stared into De Young with his clear blue peremptory eyes, whose icy vision De Young rapaciously feared and despised because, when it confronted him, some brittle mechanism of self-protection in his will flinched and broke. He would perspire in a minute, he knew that. He always began to sweat when he had to prove himself. And De Young knew sickeningly that Riggs was reminding him of the absurd visit to Miles and his humiliation in front of Austin Lake. He was calling him a lackey and a failure as Miles had. Surreptitiously he was asking for proof of his worth.

Suddenly Riggs was standing over him and De Young felt whipped. A sense of anxious anticipation told him calamitous troubles were ahead. He seethed with bitterness at Austin Lake. "I'm leaving now, gentlemen. We'll meet again next Tuesday at eight and review what King has to say," Riggs announced with a touch of hard joviality. To De Young he sounded like a landlord giving a busted gambler twenty-four hours to raise an enormous rent.

In the first few minutes after Riggs and his assistant left, De Young and Lake did not speak to each other. Both men retired quietly to their desks, which were at opposite ends of the room. A strained noiseless quiet prevailed. Between glances at a thick memo in front of him (Abstracts from Negro Nationalism in U.S. 1914–1930) Lake warily eyed Charles De Young, who appeared to be busily searching for something in the clutter on his desk. He guessed De Young was vaguely exasperated. For a while he considered leaving, but he stayed because it slowly occurred to him that De Young intended to ignore his presence completely. Almost fifteen minutes had gone by before he decided to address De Young and perhaps placate him.

"Charles, you are looking at the next agency liaison officer to the Senate Foreign Relations Committee," he said with a wry and beleaguered half smile.

De Young glanced over at him with the trace of a hard, twisted smile on his lightly freckled face. He nodded slowly and gravely. Institutional humor never amused him. He knew no such plum awaited him in failure. Somehow blacks were always fired outright with nasty orders never to speak of their involvement with intelligence work. "Is this one of the possibilities you're going to discuss with Miles?" he asked bitterly.

"Don't try to be amusing, Charles," Lake said with a clever smile. "If you'd been here on time, there would be no mystery. You're creating your own sense of paranoia. And I tried to shield you anyway. The least you can do is recognize that," Lake said in a voice that wavered with irritation. He always found it hard to admit to anything but personal decency in his motives, but Lake knew some of De Young's hostility was justified. After all the time he'd put in at the Brotherhood, his credibility there was now dangerously compromised. De Young was through in this assignment and it was mostly his fault.

Remnants of a moody explosive silence circulated between

them. They were on the verge of shouts, anger, a rancorous confrontation, but nothing happened. Lake's forefinger tapped the desk in relief. He glanced at his watch and went back to reading the memo, waiting for a few minutes to elapse so he could slip away without feeling routed by poor De Young's desperation. Exhaling a long sigh of disgust, De Young sat back with his hands thrust deeply into the pockets of his handsome worsted suit. A steeled fury pushed forward by frustration dug into him. He wondered when Lake would meet Miles and what they would discuss. They would have to start with James of course, but how long would it be before his name and identity came into the conversation? How long would it take for him to become completely expendable? De Young thought with a melancholy indignant shudder. He took out a cigarette and lighted it rather lazily as his mind dwelled fervently on the fiendish way Miles had humiliated him a few nights ago. A now familiar loathing for Austin Lake came and went. And right away he saw how completely his hobbled pride and a pang of self-pity prevented him from asking Lake anything about his meeting with Miles. He told himself he didn't want to know. De Young was half convinced he really didn't care.

Lake closed the memo he was reading and locked it in his middle drawer. Slowly he got up and straightened his tie in the shaving mirror near the door. He was all ready to leave when something made him stop, something made him turn to De Young and say apologetically, "We're all tired, aren't we, Charles? King is burning up our lives like cheap fuel."

De Young shrugged disinterestedly. He sensed Lake was about to begin some sort of sentimental exposition and he wanted no part of it even as Lake went on. "Charles, what do you make of Miles King? I mean truly as a man. To my way of thinking, he's almost too baffling not to be essentially quite simple."

De Young nodded. "That's fair," he replied, knowing Lake wanted him to start babbling and perhaps drop half a dozen psychological clues, points of reference he might use to navigate out of his confusion. He's been brooding over this ever since the other night, De Young realized secretly. And this realization, superficial as it was, disturbed him because he couldn't stand intellectual discussions of character or anything else that probed too deeply into personal ambiguities. He looked into Lake's disappointed face with pleasure and felt an old bullish strength returning to him.

"All right, Charles," Lake said as if he were too weary to go on if De Young would not. "We all have our little corners of vulnerability."

De Young pretended not to hear, yet his tongue seemed to move involuntarily. "What do you mean?" he blurted out quickly.

"Nothing, Charles," Lake answered so firmly De Young almost felt he was in the wrong. "I'll see you tomorrow at the Brotherhood meeting," he continued, as a ripple of surprise moved across De Young's face. "Sit as close to James as you can. I'm curious about his reactions when Miles speaks."

"I'll do that," De Young said, relieved now that he could see Lake was definitely leaving.

Then it came. By accident or malicious design or simple-minded duty Lake broached the one question that had disoriented Charles De Young all day and given his actions a tone of irreparable triviality. "By the way," Lake asked, "how is James? What is he doing?"

"Nothing much," De Young replied automatically, but with a sudden jolting awareness that he was telling lies as fast as his mind formed them. "He's been laying up with that babe of his."

"I'm not surprised," Lake said, as if he had just grasped an important certainty. "He spends a lot of time in the sack."

"You would too," De Young came back quickly, trying now with great mental exertion to hide the dismay spreading over him. He had not seen or heard of James Fitzgerald in three whole days.

Abruptly Lake said goodnight and departed, leaving Charles De Young to struggle with the network of worries that spread within him it seemed, like the thin hardy fibers of his nervous system. In one corner of his mind the apprehension that had plagued him with the insistence of a light nagging headache was still alive. He prayed he guessed right about James's whereabouts, but the grimly humorous image of his elusive and silent adversary slipping aboard a tramp steamer in the harbor sneaked up on De Young and gave him a rise of ambiguous pleasure. He liked that ending a lot because it contained all the wonderful elements of action and mystery missing from this assignment. Immediately he envisioned himself flying to some teeming foreign port to greet James as he came off the boat. His imagination erupted into full rhythm and he reveled in this mixture of fantasy and egotism, spite and very cool bravery. De Young understood mysteriously, as psychiatrists are said to intuitively fathom the arcane miseries of the human mind, that he'd managed to survive the boredom of intelligence work because in his wide, vivid, and powerful urge to order the world he always came off the winner. He remembered again Miles had expressed a certain elaborate sorrow for him and he laughed very softly. Pity was too somber an emotion for what was left of a gay Saturday night.

CHAPTER EIGHTEEN

SUNDAY MORNING DAWNED huge and bright outside Miles's living-room window as he stood before a large gilt-edged mirror and knotted his elegant white silk tie into place. He was very tired deep down, from the long night of hard work he had put in to fashion the last touches of his new program for the Brotherhood. But he let himself think the big breakfast he had called down for would bring him out of it, even though he knew his weariness resulted mainly from floundering too long in the deep pool of his tensions. When the meal came, he ate it quickly and sent for an extra pot of coffee while he picked up the thin sheaf of papers next to his typewriter and read avidly, as if it were all new and subtly stimulating, the program he believed he'd put his very survival into.

For a man with no high school or college on his record it did not read badly, he thought. The words were moderate, the temper sound, the outlook earnest, but in the long tradition of American documents that cheated Indians of choice lands, and turned blacks away from the polling places, decent schools, and drinking fountains, a surge of guilt warned Miles. He knew all this though, and it no longer troubled him excessively, because for days on end Miles had fought his principles in pitched battle until at times he saw nothing but the blank and terrible wall of injustice. And he understood, in the clamor of his nerves and a devastating cycle of headaches, that it was compromise for him, a responsible stance, a reasonable ethic, or death in the yellowing back papers of recent history.

Once more Miles went through his pages. And it was one time too many, for nothing got by the stifling ambiguous familiarity he felt for this work except a few key phrases he now seemed to dread. He was asking for legitimate foundation help to publicize the Brotherhood's role in contemporary black life, immediate government assistance for all indigent black people (this was surely an invitation to secret government investigation), the establishment of interfaith seminars on Black Islam at famous divinity schools, and kindness from the American heart. Every homily of the middle-class vernacular, each candy-sweet sentiment embedded in the popular taste was paid allegiance to; in a hilariously unintentional way Miles had fallen into a wild parody of American aspirations, spiced by his cultivated and bizarre genius for titanic resentment. He was dealing out fifty-two jokers, rolling away on a sociological hayride, tickling the ass of Miss Liberty, but none of this occurred to him as he made a few nervous and unnecessary corrections before slipping the program into a leather briefcase. Then rapidly his thoughts focused on James and the strange charges he desperately wanted to hear more about after the meeting. Out of nowhere the telephone rang. Brother Nicholas was in the lobby keeping his nine-thirty appointment to drive Miles uptown to the hall.

Shortly after ten on the same morning, a slim fair-skinned well-dressed Negro man carrying a large attaché case mounted the steps to the elevated subway station at Simpson Street in the middle of the vice-ridden and brutal slums of the East Bronx. He stood nonchalantly at the head of the platform and boarded a downtown local, which stopped every five or six blocks to let on crowds of black and Puerto Rican children going to church in Manhattan with their parents. He noticed the girls wore flared and starched white dresses and carried white plastic pocketbooks. The boys had suits on, and miniature fedoras, which gave them the hard, stubborn look of their fathers. Some of the passengers remembered the polite, almost prim young man with his attaché case. According to a subsequent police department reconstruction of his movements that morning, they thought he was a preacher headed downtown to meet with his following.

James arrived at Brotherhood Hall a little after twelve, almost two full hours before the start of the meeting. Under the marquee, three of the Brothers blocked his path and playfully asked him where he had been keeping himself. When he said he'd been away on Brotherhood business, they looked at each other merrily and then roared with sudden wild abrasive laughter. Caught up in the challenge of their humor, James stood among them for a minute and attempted to trade a few insinuating bits of devilish repartee before going up to his office. As the main door closed behind him to keep out the press and a few early arrivals standing petulantly about the sidewalk, James once again experienced the vibration of a constant nervous excitement that had allowed him only snatches of sleep during the night as he pondered what was about to happen this afternoon. But he was not tired, and as the tiny battered elevator took him upstairs James knew it would be many hours, perhaps days, before his body relaxed enough for him to feel exhaustion. On his desk he found seven or eight telephone messages, including a few from Beverly. Perfunctorily he swept the whole pile into the wastebasket and went off to see what Miles was doing.

Outside it was a clear quiet Sunday, unaccountably cool for that time of spring. A group of little boys stood forlornly on the corner holding tiny white-and-crimson Brotherhood flags that fluttered and died listlessly in the breeze. As James walked down the corridor, the bright sunlight slanting through the open classroom and office doors gave a solemn hospital air to the building. James found Miles in his office, in the middle of a boisterous and emotional interview with an African journalist. He stayed for fifteen minutes, glancing about the room blankly as he tried to suggest to Miles something important had to be dealt with. When no one spoke to him, he stared moodily at the dull spinning reels of the tape recorder, hoping to destroy the intensity of what was being said. But the two men continued on, hunched halfway out of their chairs and gesticulating carefully, as if appealing to the one person who dared to understand all they were ready to say.

Back in his office James put his feet up on the desk with the uneasy, vacantly rude air of a young executive about to deal with important thoughts. All around him in the hall he sensed the histrionic drama of a Sunday Brotherhood meeting drawing itself together. On Sunday everyone seemed to move with an alacrity and tension missing in other days. Everyone was afraid of mistakes, afraid of committing some specious little act that would mar the resounding tone Miles loved to feel around him. James knew in a half hour or so the Fung were going down in the elevator to the tiny room behind the stage. Soon Nicholas would take down a fresh box of cartridges. Later he would return with a leather-bound copy of the Koran and a half bottle of the effervescent water Miles sometimes drank before going onstage. In cramped dressing rooms below, the Brothers and Sisters who were to act as ushers would be energetically brushing off their clothes and wiping their highly polished shoes before putting on white gloves and lining up in the doorways to come out on the orchestra floor. Right now Miles was probably typing a few notes on an index card. De Young would be drifting around talking with cronies because he knew Miles didn't like that kind of behavior on a Sunday. An expectant quickness permeated every minute as time for the front doors to open neared. James remembered that the first few people entering the hall always felt subtly foolish and embarrassed, somewhat like a pack of naïve tourists who had invaded an elegant château moments before a grand ball was about to begin.

Shortly James knew he would feel the dutiful pressure that

drew him into the ritual enveloping his duties every Sunday. First there were the microphones to be checked, then all the lights. Visiting speakers had to be welcomed (Miles feared his Sunday intensity was too intimidating); and the press had to be penned up in a small reception room, while clipboard in hand, he drew up a list of who was in the building and issued special passes. Then he would finally go and see Miles and destroy forever the stifling presence of inconclusive doom that seemed to blur and distort nearly everything around him.

Ten or fifteen minutes went by, and to ease the stiffening of his nerves James wandered down the corridor and into the washroom. He felt cold and lost among the blank, clean white tiles and pathetic empty stalls. Slowly he bent over one of the large deep porcelain basins and delicately splashed icy water on his face until it seemed numb. As his head rose gingerly, he was abruptly confronted with his face in the stark mirror before him. His light brown eyes shimmered more opaquely than ever and were buried in a visage that was fiercely haunted and masked with a shocking grimness. A faint involuntary gasp came from him. Hurriedly he dried his face and fled, leaving the door swinging behind him as he found a staircase and went down it in a barely controlled headlong dash, which ended suddenly moments later as he realized he was about to come out behind the big stage sheltered in the immense gloomy quiet of the hall. Eerily he trod across the darkened boards pursued by the inane but omnipresent notion that with his next step every light in the place would wink on and blot out his sight while the police closed in from all sides shouting commands and threats. To his left, marked by a narrow swath of yellow light, James saw the door to the backstage room slightly ajar. He heard the familiar murmurings of the bodyguards and it comforted him.

Except for the hard precise footfalls echoing in his path, no sound broke the stillness. Bright red exit signs stood out beckoningly on all the walls. A large illuminated clock read ten to one. Quietly James sat down on the dusty steps leading to the stage and all at once numerous recollections of Miles swam into his consciousness. Some of the placid and vigorous awe he felt for Miles dawned on him once again. It plagued him, metamorphosing swiftly into a preposterous abstract guilt that diminished his intricate sufferings to nonsense. James did not believe Miles was going to die this afternoon. His brain could not accommodate the idea of Miles being slain. Curiously, through his obtuseness, minuscule fears, and ambiguities, James understood that if Miles was killed his own life was surely nearing its end because he and Miles shared many unspoken beliefs, many intuitions about existence, and fate would undoubtedly treat them evenly. It was something they always secretly recognized in each other, but something they never dwelled upon because it was pointless. What Mahanti said about taking over the Brotherhood was only a manifestation of their connected fate. James knew he could never rise above Miles. The whole idea was grotesque and touchingly impossible. Never could he duplicate the oblique warmth and respect of their friendship with another human being. Their singularity and strangeness had become a permanent bond. And so the timorous resolve, which had come into him with the beginnings of this unaccountable day, grew stronger. The vague dreadful resistance James had husbanded for the last six or seven hours fortified him. He allowed himself to believe he was prepared in some unstable but effective way to subvert the plot against Miles's life.

His first stroke (it seemed disastrous and unbelievable) was to trap the assassin in the hall. Then he would tell Miles where the man was hidden and watch while the Fung probably beat him to death. Destroying the assassin was the least he could do for a man who had given his life whatever stability it harbored. After that he didn't know what would happen. And he told himself it didn't matter, although he prayed that by the undefined terms of their friendship Miles would calculate the infinite value of his life against the probing questions that were sure to come to him and remain silent. James hoped uncertainly after today everything would revert to the turbulent but pleasing routine of the past. Frantically he wanted the com-

200

fortable life around him to weigh upon and crush whatever memories of the ministry he might retain. Yet it all seemed so hopeless.

Now without realizing it, he was on his feet. Agilely he cut through a row of seats and went up an aisle heading for the fire exit Mahanti had instructed him to open. There he stood and waited. On the other side of the door people were milling about, and to James it sounded like thousands were out there waiting to break in and pillage the Brotherhood. Quite a few busloads of college students had arrived. On campuses all over the country, Miles had been taken up as an example of the true modern rebel and recently black undergraduates from nearby schools had attended Brotherhood meetings in numbers large enough to irritate the faithful. The Brothers and Sisters did not really care for outsiders or intelligent questions being shouted from the audience. They knew only that Miles belonged to them. They did not understand this Sunday the students would be coming to hear what new wild things Miles had to say now that the establishment had brought him under concentrated fire for the first time.

It was one o'clock. Silently James unbolted the heavy door and waited for it to open. He measured the seconds with his trembling pulse; a minute passed, then two. Five minutes flew by and nothing happened. James retreated from the door in awe and confusion. Suddenly he remembered the church fire in Harlem two nights ago and an augury of disaster, a terrifying vision of Miles shot and dying in his own blood made James woozy. For a moment he was overcome with a pervasive and deadening helplessness. Fearfully he fled through the hall, stumbling and dodging among the seats, fighting to get to the unlit flight of stairs leading to the balconies. Nearly in a panic James hoped the assassin had come early and hidden himself upstairs. But at the same time he perceived everything was going against him. Dimly he saw he did not have the power to prevent Miles from being assassinated. The killer had probably eluded him once and would do it again. More slowly now he climbed over the velvet chain sealing off access to the upper balcony. At the landing he stood under the red bulb high above the door and fumbled noisily with his keys. His hands were actually wet with perspiration. His breathing was rather constricted and harsh. Then from behind him a cautious sound reached his ears, the velvety crunch of a light footfall on the carpeted stairs. He wheeled about in horror, dropping the bunch of keys, fearing somehow it would be Miles. Instead he faced a perfect stranger, a slim, elegant young man with an attaché case who seemed not to take notice of him as he reached the top of the stairs. The stranger's air, so confident and uncanny, forced James to shrink into a corner in bewilderment. The man grasped the doorknob and magically the huddled rows of unused seats appeared before them. Slowly he turned now to James. The red bulb above the door cut deep shadows over his face, which bore no expression at all until suddenly he smiled. James saw his large white teeth stand out in the semidarkness. It was a truly horrible smile, a clear demented sign of death.

At one twenty Brother Nicholas went downstairs and switched on all the main lights in the hall while two of the Fung threw open the front doors and watched the crowd trickle down the long corridor to the orchestra floor. Miles had concluded his interview. He rose and thanked the African and they made a dinner arrangement for later in the week. After a while he sat down in the large chair behind his desk and went through his opening remarks before going downstairs.

James returned to his office, relieved the assassin had come and plucked him from the maelstrom of uncertainty. He felt stronger and slightly courageous now that he knew the man was in the building and could not escape. All that remained was to tell Miles about him before the meeting began. That would be relatively easy, James decided. Slowly he poured out a glass of water and found himself drinking it down greedily. His watch notified him it was just about time to go downstairs and start his round of preparations, but some free instinct took him over to the window where he looked out for a few seconds. On the street below, people streamed toward the lighted marquee and James took heart, feeling the presence of so many souls would grant him the determination he needed to save Miles for them. As he locked his office door, a touch of heady confidence perked him up. For reasons he could never explain a comfortable self-assurance propelled him down the corridor. He was twenty long paces away from his office when an ominous sound overtook him: the hard sweet jangling of his telephone. He ignored it, keeping on for a few steps, damning himself for not having taken it off the hook, but the sound reached into him with the insistence of an alarm bell. James felt tension suddenly cling to his throat like a spider's web. He perspired a bit and walked more slowly, hoping to get to the elevator before someone noticed he was running away. The faint sounds of the meeting arranging itself downstairs floated up to him. The phone went off again in his ears, and he turned back almost in a run. He flung open the door with palpitating thwarted anger, praying this call was routine, an annoying and minor part of his work as Brotherhood secretary.

The receiver came up to his face like a strange object. James heard a surprised inarticulate gasp from the other end. Beverly spoke, her voice warped with anxiety.

"Please, I'd like to speak to James Fitzgerald. Can anyone tell me if he's there?"

For an instant James tensed horribly. He didn't want to give away his identity if it wasn't necessary, yet the words burst harshly from him. "What is it?" he nearly shouted. "What do you want?"

"James," Beverly cried out full of bewilderment, "James, I've been going crazy. I've called and called for three days and nobody knew where you were. I even called Mr. King. I called Clarence and he didn't know either." Here the strain in her voice snapped. The sounds of pitiful sobbing came over the telephone. The sudden wild urge to curse and abuse Beverly swept over James. He struggled to control himself, to come down to the level of affection and communication.

"What is it?" he said in a low, hard artificial voice. "Tell me exactly what has happened."

"There was a strange white man here looking for you." Again she was taut, uncertain, just a bit impersonal. "He acted very suspicious, like you were in some kind of serious trouble," Beverly went on, slightly calmer now that she had stated the main point so clearly. James kept silent, breathing harshly without complete comprehension of the moment. He could tell Beverly had been crying a lot. Surprisingly he was able to guess at the vacillation and terror she had probably lived with these last few days. But something in the way she unfolded the incident told James that Beverly had done nothing to hurt him.

"Who did this man represent?" he asked quietly and with great composure.

"He said he was a security man from the government and he asked all kinds of questions," Beverly replied in something like her normal voice, for she was drawing most of her strength from James's apparent steadiness and had no idea that with her answer he wanted to bolt and flee the room, but could not. A part of his intelligence assured him this news was not too bad, yet he was shaken and worried. Only his thin resolution to halt the assassination plot kept him from hanging up and walking away from everything Beverly was saying. Desperately he tried to minimize her words and distort their meaning. Ever since Miles's speech praising the Chinese Communists, most of the sophisticated Brothers had feared some kind of security investigation and this visit to Beverly was undoubtedly the first of many signs it was being undertaken. Even Miles had cautioned this could happen.

"What did you tell this man?" James asked after a long, wary pause. His voice was firm and nearly conversational now. James was half sure no jeopardy existed for him in this situation. Suddenly he felt a sheltering warmth for Beverly that came out in his words. "Did you tell him anything important?" he asked pleasantly.

"I didn't tell him a thing. I lied like a trouper," Beverly answered swiftly. James caught the whisper of a giggle in her voice and laughed softly. He was feeling more relieved by the second. Beverly came back chuckling. She sensed her own relaxation. Her words began to flow. "He had me scared because he was so serious, you know. But I sent him out of here as confused as a little boy looking for the bathroom."

There was a startled delighted pause and then they burst into ringing intimate laughter, which brought them as close to their private domain of blissful ease and fervent sexual obliteration as the distance between them would allow. They thought and functioned for a delicious instant as romping playmates, as a man and a woman who prized their silken hot intimate familiarity with an abandon too fleeting and powerful to describe. Beverly began to ask for James in the languid tone of her voice, in her laugh, in the very things she inspired him to imagine she was doing. He felt a momentary pang of guilt for not having called her when he spotted the messages on his desk. All of the involved and satisfying ways she pleased him welled up in his body and tantalized his nerves. He wanted to fondle and comfort her even though the very idea seemed whimsically insane. Smoothly, with intimations of secret fun later in the evening, James broke off the conversation.

"I'll be around tonight. I don't know exactly what time, but don't open the door or answer the phone until I come, understand?"

"Yes," she whispered sweetly, and then threw a soft kiss into the receiver. The phone clicked and she dropped it into its cradle softly and turned to face her sun-filled living room with all the excited grace of a princess in a meadow. Then briefly her delight contracted as she remembered forgetting to tell James her questioner had left a number where he could be reached. Probably it wasn't important though, and she decided to wait and tell him when he arrived that evening.

James hung up with a coolness that surprised him. Not a shadow of panic crossed his mind. This was going to be almost like an ordinary Sunday. James was almost sure of it. Rapidly he was out the door, moving briskly along the corridor, spurred by a quick tremor of anticipation.

Downstairs the hall was packed. Every seat was taken. Stragglers stood against the walls cooling themselves with flapping cardboard fans provided by a prominent black undertaker. A contingent of TV reporters and columnists who had covered Miles throughout his career clustered in front of the stage like a girls' basketball team before breaking up to take their seats in the first two rows. Austin Lake, sporting a large green press tag in his buttonhole, was with them. He glanced at the drab peeling walls and craned his neck to see the once elegant and gilded ceiling where clusters of powerful light bulbs had been cheaply rigged over opulent chandeliers covered now with ages of dust. Thirty or forty years ago black vaudeville had been played in this building for white audiences. When the talkies came in, all of that died. White people retreated in their powerful cars to the big show palaces downtown. A silver screen was thrown up to catch the dazzling spread of light projected from a tiny booth, which gave the nation more glamorous performers and most of its manners in the good times before television sprang up. The Brotherhood acquired the building after six months of haggling with the owners in southern California. Lake would never know what a struggle it had been for black people to purchase this building that he allowed to fascinate him for an afternoon. The deal was completed only after a huge payoff in the form of an unredeemable loan was made to a New York syndicate eagerly awaiting to convert the lot into a parking field.

The atmosphere in the theater was overbearingly warm and suffused with some rare manifestation of tingling heat. An undercurrent of suspense and terrible racing excitement rose from the audience, exerting a wet palpable pressure not unlike the weight of the sea at great depths. Lake inspected the voluble, almost raucous crowd, thinking how far away from his children's free world of green trees and pleasant homes these black people dwelled. He was certain in the voices and bustle around him the artful chaos of Africans pouring into a market town arose to mock him personally. But there was in all he imagined no threat, no lance flying strange colors stuck into his suburban lawn; instead Lake was taken with a rather joyous sensation of personal absurdity. A ripple of pleasure at being inside Brotherhood Hall during a Sunday meeting went right through him, and in its wake came a crazy vision. The future police state the intellectuals worried about was never going to happen, Lake realized. Never could it take hold because Miles King and people like those around him possessed exotic energies enough to defeat any system of mere calculation.

Abruptly all talk around him ceased. The echoes of many voices drifted sadly up into the rafters. Two bodyguards wearing shoulder holsters, which bulged ridiculously under their tight-fitting jackets, came out onto the brilliantly lit stage and took up positions at either end of the row of folding chairs. An East African with a great swollen head of thick black hair shyly appeared and was applauded respectfully as he took his seat. Soon another African in native dress followed him. After a short while an Indian in a Congress party suit came out and made a low bow. Lake leaned forward in fascination, wondering if there was not a wild beast yet to be seen. Suddenly, like a character in a play, Brother James walked across the stage and Lake's heart leapt with startled recognition.

In the offstage room, Miles sat pensively in a worn-out and collapsing armchair, his speech rolled up and clasped tightly in one hand. He could hear the Brothers and Sisters outside, the expectant buzzing and chattering of hundreds of idle voices, and it annoyed him. He was also irritated at Nicholas for not finding De Young and bringing him to the room immediately. Glancing about he noticed how deadly grim his surroundings actually were. The cubicle had originally been a jerry-built dressing room and a costume storeroom. Several years had gone by since anyone had thought of painting it. Miles fired off a quick imaginary order to have the place fixed up. He envisioned a few used leather armchairs, some tall handsome lamps, and soft brown knotty-pine paneling on the walls. Then anxiously he got up and began to pace about uneasily, his face filled with the shadows cast by the naked uncoated bulbs jutting awkwardly from wall sockets. The ordinary stage tension he felt before all Brotherhood meetings was extreme today. He found it impossible to concentrate.

A number of worries plagued him mercilessly. He feared what he had written, what he was about to say, even as he was subtly urged to go out and lay it before his congregation. Intuition told him he was a fool. He understood the sickening pathos that awaited any leader who ventured to parody his own majesty, but this insight reverberated through him strangely, causing the onset of more intense nervousness. In a quick doleful turn of mind he considered destroying the speech and talking extemporaneously. Briefly this notion took complete mastery of him, but he eluded it. Today Miles feared his audience. He sensed nothing but apprehension in what they might demand of him. He didn't trust himself to speak this afternoon without prepared words to limit his attention as he tight walked over the turbulence of his fantasies. He knew everything he was about to say would be exploited by his enemies as a sign of overreaction or perhaps even disintegration. White people were ready to burden him with minute analyses of his cowardice, while blacks would dismiss him as shallow and clownish. Yet Miles resolved to go ahead. At least he would now be discussed again. The country could not ignore this latest enigmatic turn in his career. It really didn't want to. He was always news, especially when he bedeviled the imagination.

Rather quietly now Miles sat down again. He had only begun to relax when abruptly a bitter uncertainty played over him. He remembered the aftermath of his address praising the Chinese, and the whole distorted muddle that sullied the lost days following it flooded into his mind with a haunting resonance. No one in the Brotherhood had come to him then except with criticisms. James was curiously involved in a hundred petty administrative idiocies that might have waited. De Young vacillated between pity and what had to be vicious scorn. As usual he was left alone to find his own way, and lifted now by a small stirring of his great pride Miles sensed he was probably doing the right thing. If not, he could always vary his opinion over a discreet period of time. He could always tango smoothly away from danger. He could call upon luck and superior perception to veer him away from the real horrors of life that attacked and crippled other men. Poor John Lawrence certainly didn't have any of this gift, Miles thought condescendingly. His pretty aristocratic church was gone now, and with it all his good fortune. Miles smiled patronizingly as he wondered again what that whole interfaith federation scheme had been all about anyway.

Just then the door opened and De Young came in, followed by Brother Nicholas who announced, "You told me to bring him to you, Miles, and I did. But I had to look all over hell to find him." Miles nodded, conveying an unspoken sign of approval, and the door closed softly leaving the two men together. Although he appeared quite aloof and even surly, Charles De Young openly scrutinized Miles, searching for little indications of what their relationship now was. All he received for his effort was a calm, meaningless smile.

"Sit down, Brother," Miles said, motioning De Young to a small wooden folding chair while he took the more comfortable seat.

De Young sat down obediently. He glanced at Miles and then looked away in obvious disgust. "I was up on the top floor with a few of the Brothers. That's why Nicholas couldn't find me," he muttered for no real reason.

"That's all right, Charles," Miles replied jovially, for a certain harsh assurance had come to him now that De Young was in the room. "I just wanted to get your expert advice on a few things because this could be a big afternoon for me."

De Young did not sit straight up or even look at Miles. But he was alert suddenly and waiting. He sensed a renewal of the haughty contest of wills between them, and this time he was determined to humiliate Miles. It had become a question of simple pride. Purposely he neglected to ask Miles why this particular afternoon was so important.

Miles gazed at him, radiating a mild insolent curiosity. He realized somewhere in his consciousness he was still furious at

De Young for bringing Austin Lake, a common government investigator, into his private office. Miles knew De Young was too smart to make a mistake like that, and an old familiar slithery abhorrence of deceit gathered itself together in him to bolster his controlled angry suspicion. He was ready to take a new tack, to challenge De Young again, to defend James against his snide willful accusation, but he curbed the instinct. After the meeting, when he saw Lake again, there would be time for that. Now he had to work on De Young. "I have with me a new program for the Brotherhood." He said it weightily, but not without a hint of bombast. "This program is going to help bring in all kinds of outside help from major American institutions to elevate the position of the black man. Not just my followers, Charles, but everyone. Do you see?"

De Young said he did quietly, although he noticed Miles glancing uncertainly at the unrolled sheaf of papers he had, as if he didn't know what to do with them.

"What I'm going to say out there today cuts me off from the past, Charles," Miles continued in a somewhat more confidential tone. "I'm looking for a broader base, what they call a coalition, a new block of strength to help my work, and I think I can get it." He stared into De Young's face without realizing he asked for approval or at least some indication of acceptance. But De Young seemed hostile and withdrawn so he continued. "The commotion over my declaration with China really shocked me, Charles. It made me think. It was only a trick of what I call rhetoric, but when everybody got mad, I saw it was an unnecessary trick, a frivolous trick. I saw I had to move in another direction. When a strong corporation needs a broader base, what does it do? It absorbs companies in businesses it covets. That's all I'm doing in a way. No one I'm asking to join with me can rise above my image anyway."

De Young nodded a little wearily, as if he had heard it all before. Sullenly his eyes traveled over Miles's clothing. He noticed Miles was wearing a pistol in an armpit holster.

"Now I expect some criticism," Miles said with a sigh of resignation mixed with churning anger at De Young's supercilious behavior. "People won't understand right away what I'm doing. They'll say I'm not the same old Miles anymore. They'll claim I've weakened. I know that. I expect it."

"Then what are you afraid of?" De Young asked briskly, but with a cold insidious finality.

"I'm not afraid of anything," Miles came back quickly. "I just wanted to know, since you fancy yourself a political expert, what you think of all this. That's all I want from you, Charles," he added with an amused suggestion of contempt.

"Why me?" De Young asked, his voice rising just a bit. He was violently determined now to ridicule Miles, to humble him.

"Why not you, Charles?" Miles retorted smoothly, innocently. "You've been my political aide for a long time now, whether I needed you or not. Don't tell me you've run out of bright ideas."

De Young smiled bitterly. Miles was sharp today, there was no doubt about it. "I don't want a pat on the head for telling you what you want to hear," he said savagely. He could not stand being patronized and he knew Miles had picked him to share these confidences because he was considered nothing more than a turncoat mercenary schooled in the slimy nuances of compromise.

"I'm not asking for anything from you but the truth as you see it, Charles," Miles answered in an oiled and righteous tone. "I know I have no right to expect anything more than that, friend."

A furious exasperation was rising in De Young, choking his inflamed will with triple strength. He felt all of his wiles, all of his innate brutish power and daring was being blanketed with a horrible false compassion for what he was not. He fought in turmoil to bring forth the correct words of shattering indignation needed to vindicate him and dramatically lift his personal banner high, as the skull and crossbones might crop up on the open seas. The swift contorted agitation in De Young's face came on Miles by surprise, and in the next instant he realized De Young had sprung up from the little wooden chair assigned

211

to him and was speaking with a snapping but controlled fury. "You make me laugh, Miles," the voice over him said with hot sarcasm. "For years now you've stumbled around this country like a blind beggar without a bell. You've preached, you've led people on and built yourself up real big and accomplished what? Not a goddamned thing!" The momentum of De Young's anger, the steam of his frustration, and the searing heat of pure wrath were propelling him now into a clearer atmosphere where he could speak more freely than ever. He was certain Miles had felt this way the night he humiliated him in front of Lake. "And you'll never accomplish anything. You're not capable of it, friend. All you care about is Miles. Good old Miles, the beast roaring in the jungle because that's all he can do. You love to roar, don't you, Miles? You love the sound you make. You love what other people have made you with their miseries and their pennies. You don't surprise me by begging now," De Young continued, slipping out of his role of underling as deftly as someone shucking off wet clothes. "You don't really mind crying, as long as you can do it in the spotlight. But I was never talking about that, Miles. No, my friend. I was never talking about showing up on your knees with a bowl stretched out in front of you. I was talking about being a man. You never understood that, so go on with your act," De Young said, drawing together the fingers of one hand as if to catch the simple grains of sorrow held there. "Go on, be expedient. Go out and sing for your supper. That's all you need to know from me."

Miles's eyes were almost dancing with amazement. He felt horribly exposed and saddened and guilty. He could not look at De Young. A silence blossomed in the room, which now seemed too small for both of them. Charles De Young sat perfectly still, contained by nervous energy and a pleasing coalescence of certainty and rage. After a while Miles spoke, and there was a wary astonished edge to his voice. "I owe you the courtesy of an apology, Charles," he said quite carefully. "I've taken you for less of a man than you show yourself to be. When you brought that white man in here the other night, I was on edge and embarrassed. I hope you'll overlook my rudeness to you."

De Young did not attempt to reply. Instead he brushed at his thick sand-colored moustache with an idle forefinger. He knew just how shallow and contemptuously insincere this conditional gesture of apology really was. And besides he did not forgive Miles. The concealed and fixed homicidal rage, whose source he did not know, stole from Charles De Young the grace to forgive. It was not in him to shake hands, to proffer part of a smile, to move through the ritual of reconciliation with the airs of an actor and the reluctance of a slighted child. De Young knew Miles would never see his true merits and he sulked quietly, determined that nothing was going to placate him.

Neither man had mentioned James although he dwelled somewhere in their minds with the gentle power of a saint and the cruelty of a primitive god. For a few seconds they stared at each other with the malevolent circumspection often seen in leaders of rival street gangs. All at once they heard the light thumping noise of people nearing the door and Brother Nicholas spoke from the other side, asking to come in. Permission was given and the door opened. Nicholas entered hesitantly, sniffing the aftertaste of personal confrontation like an experienced bird dog. His small hooded eyes swept from Miles to De Young's smirking face with a swiftness that was artistic. But he asked no questions because it wasn't his place, and also he was with a strange white man seeking a favor. Immediately the man knocked on the door foolishly before stepping daintily into the room. Looking up from his chair, Miles fixed him with a steady malicious gaze. He recognized the type if not the individual: sea blue shirt, youngish lined face, ironic smile, and on this one teased blond hair. Miles made a distasteful face. The intruder took one step backward, pointing to the green press tag in his lapel. Then he ventured to speak. What came out was pure sham gentility, an amalgam of distrust and entreaty. "Sir, my network has three hundred hours of unedited film on you. Every major event in your career is in our library. May we take some color newsfilm for an evening program? It will mean additional lights but I promise to keep the crew out of your way."

Miles listened precisely to the voice and decided he liked it. "You certainly may, sir," he replied with an excess of snide elegance.

In the topmost balcony the assassin crouched among the dusty unused seats and watched. To him the spectacle below possessed a boldly captivating, extravagantly festive air he'd never encountered in the reformatories of his youth or the state prisons in which most of his twenties had ebbed away. He looked on with the unalert innocence of a child. The two thousand or so people packed into the theater, lit by the searing whiteness of television lights that almost obliterated them and enlivened by a spirited, not quite controlled intensity, made him feel he'd stumbled wondrously on a hidden convention of trolls. The noise was almost deafening for a place of worship, he thought in a brief moment of confusion. Finally he forced himself to stop gazing at what happened below for fear it might trick him into a serious mistake. Carefully he looked around behind him and then peered at his watch in the darkness. It was time to begin work.

Drawing the attaché case closer he silently opened it and took from its molded plastic padding the beautiful precision weapon entrusted to him by the strange foreign man he was working for. With a tremor of excitement, he recalled how they'd sped along the West Side Highway in a fancy limousine that swept past all the great ships rising out of the water to tower above the elevated road. It was his first ride in a chauffer-driven automobile (not counting trips to numerous station houses squeezed between a couple of detectives on the rear seat of a squad car) and he was more awed than impressed. Right away he took a liking to his employer, who called himself Mr. Mahanti. The name was probably fake, but the supercilious elegance of the man, something he'd seen only in a few top gamblers, was as real to the assassin as a ten-carat diamond in the palm of his hand. And with class went money: a thousand in advance with two thousand coming after the job.

Working with tense expert fingers the assassin began to set up in the dark. He was very good and he knew it. His weapon was a Soviet Army Ak rifle similar to the one used by Allied troops in NATO. But this one was more thoroughly machined and it had a custom-made polished walnut stock finished off with a steel butt plate. Delicately he fitted on the smooth oiled barrel and screwed it very tight. Then he eased the thirty-round magazine up into its chamber until he heard an easy click. His skilled fingertips played over the weapon with all the vibrant delicacy of a piano tuner as he adjusted precisely the front and back sights. Rather deliberately he looked down into the audience again while he hefted the gun slightly, searching out just the right groove and balance for his sharpshooter's grip. Below, in the middle of the stage, Charles De Young, a man he'd never seen before, appeared to look straight up into his eyes. Panic nearly seized him as he inched away from the upturned face on the stage and saw that the man down there was merely hesitating before telling an absurd little story designed to warm up the audience. Every few seconds from then on De Young fell evenly into his sights. Yet the assassin could not conceal from himself that he was concerned about getting away. His best hope was that the enthralling scene spread before him would disintegrate into hideous chaos once he began to shoot.

Not ten minutes later James came out onto the stage and took his seat four chairs down from the rostrum on the left side. With an expression of studied concentration, his eyes avoided Charles De Young, who was speaking to the audience very casually with one hand inserted elegantly in his pocket. Slowly James let his troubled gaze move over the large, cheerful pulsating throng packed into the hall before finally settling on the speaker with a narrow tawny venomous uncertainty. His thoughts were an elusive melding of hate and sudden great worry. As he watched De Young, the man he now knew to be his chief adversary, his knees began to tremble involuntarily. James was trembling with a degree of fright and bafflement he could not judge. Through the heavy static of his confused brain he heard De Young go into his windup and deliver a couple of punch lines with the detached joviality and utter assurance of an old-time radio comedian. The audience, unsure of its reactions at first, tittered lightly and then let out a roar of convulsive laughter. A few people clapped tentatively. James made no move. He struggled to betray no expression, for his whirling imagination, his flabbergasted senses were still in the stuffy little offstage room where Miles had just laid before him the amazingly exact charges he was probably never to know about until they could be used to destroy him.

As he had entered the room, Miles was cool and a little distant. They went over the meeting preparations as usual before Miles turned to him with a distressed but amused look and said a hysterical woman had called several times in the last few days pleading to know where he was. James could see Miles was straining to maintain an aloof disinterest, and his mind wandered repeatedly to the few desperate words he was compelled to tell Miles quickly and forthrightly and without melodrama. The presence of the assassin in the top balcony seemed to control every nuance of his thought, every small gesture he was about to make. The urge to confess, to purify his motives consumed him. Everything they talked about seemed bitterly extraneous and stupid. But outwardly James remained calm. He allowed himself to go on as if nothing were happening. He did not hear the reflective and concerned tone in Miles's voice as he said, "You've been pretty scarce around here this week, Brother. Is everything all right?" They'd continued and finished their work just as they had for what seemed like every Sunday of their lives, and James had mustered total control of himself now. He felt both vaguely substantial and insanely pent up. Momentarily he thought of the day he left Siato in Japan never to see him again. And then as he was about to utter the tremulous phrases already formed in his mind, Miles suddenly addressed him so gravely and openly the words were smothered in his mouth. At first he could not believe what Miles was saying. He watched Miles labor to be fair and precise and this only enhanced the horror of what he heard; it only terrified James and drowned him in an immense frustration that, second by second, stole all of his weak determination. In an even, steely voice Miles went on with his story. There was not much to it but the details shattered James. De Young a few nights ago had come to the hall with an unknown white man, a government man, an investigator. Together they had claimed he was a trained Communist instigator, a danger to the Brotherhood. The government man said he was prepared to prove all the allegations.

"Nothing has been presented in evidence or yet been proven about you," Miles said dryly. "Obviously you have my complete confidence or you wouldn't be here. I believe in you and I don't like back-room charges, Brother. I just want you to carry on with your duties and leave this business to me." All of it sounded so hopeless, so hollow to James. He was sure now that fate willed they perish together, like unwanted kittens thrown into a pond. All the unspoken vagaries and metaphysical circumspection of their friendship seemed to circulate between them now like a heavy mist in a meadow. They were close and yet unalterably separated. James could feel only a curious weary attenuation. He tried, but it was impossible to speak. He could not communicate what he thought about anything. He could not know Miles took his look of horrified surprise as a sign of innocence. Vaguely he understood Miles, with his convoluted fear of treachery, had been driven to be honest about De Young's disclosure whether he wanted to be or not. Probably Miles was convinced the charges were untrue, for he feared the thought of deceit around him. But none of this mattered now, because in his fidelity to an amorphous ideal of friendship Miles had virtually taken his own life. In his terror of decline and betrayal Miles had silenced himself.

Abruptly it was all over. Miles said something encouraging again, clasped him on the shoulder, and then turned away, indicating he wanted to be alone as he always was for a few mo-

217

ments before appearing onstage. James was left staring into the huge audience of black faces, weighted down by his own impotence and malignant feelings of inevitability and doom. The people beyond the stage seemed to be smothering him with their density and perfumed sweat. Blurred figures moved across his vision as the visitors took their seats on the stage. The excitement around him rose like heated air in the desert. Miles was about to make his appearance and intuitively the crowd knew he was near. Brothers and Sisters in the front rows on one side had caught a glimpse of him behind the curtain and an electric sense of their discovery carried in a wave to the back of the hall. "Here's Miles. Here he is," Charles De Young cried into the microphone before stepping away with just that exact touch of deferential awe needed to spark the crowd and set off a combustion of grasping, clamoring emotion, which gave way suddenly to hushed reverence. Into the shimmering aura of the relentless white television lights Miles came. For a crystalline magic instant he seemed impregnable. His smile was stunning, his gait presidential. He radiated a polished glamour that could be hailed only by cheers, announced possibly by trumpets. A magnificent roar went up. The audience strained forward as if set to run amok. The tempo of passionate noise mounted. Miles came to the rostrum and raised both arms.

"*Salaam Aleikum,*" he cried lustily.

"*Aleikum Salaam,*" two thousand voices answered with joy.

Then for a fleeting half moment Miles turned amid the frenetic excitement and found James with his eyes and shot him a reassuring glance. Stupidly James managed a forlorn crumpled smile, but apprehension was closing his throat. He tried to cry out, to warn Miles of what was about to happen. He opened his mouth a bit, but no words came, and now Miles was looking straight ahead, into the avid dark faces of his followers. Simultaneously the assassin coolly lined Miles up in his sights, examining the striking figure far below him on the floodlit stage through a bead in a circle mounted on the front of the rifle, and a disc with a peephole in the rear. What he saw pleased him. All he wanted to do now was wait for a tense moment when all attention was gathered together in Miles. At the foot of the rostrum a tape recorder began to spin. Charles De Young took his seat to Miles's right and watched his leader dutifully. He wasn't as close to James as Lake wanted, but he could still see James, half slumped in his seat, apparently preoccupied with something else.

"Brothers and Sisters," Miles began, slowly addressing the intent mass of serious faces staring on from all sides. "Brothers and Sisters, in the name of Allah, the compassionate, the merciful, let us look for a minute at the continent of Africa. In the countries where Africans are in control, what do we see?"

"Freedom," a lone voice responded boldly.

"That is right," Miles said, shaking a finger warily. "We are witnessing a measure of freedom in those lands not open to us here," he shouted, pointing to the floor dramatically. From the audience Austin Lake gazed on raptly. He was certain Miles had just looked him deliberately in the eye and had no idea he would never know for sure.

"One of the reasons we lack freedom is because of the economic situation. Now the economy of Africa is partly tied up with the economy here. They are part of the same network. I'll bet many of you didn't know that. It is not advertised because that wouldn't be good business sense. It might make you stop and think a minute. And you'd be thinking dangerous thoughts. You might see the maze you're in. You might see how thoroughly you're controlled by the same system that reaches into Europe and Asia and Africa. And you might see the first crack of daylight in your lives."

The audience began to murmur loudly. Miles looked down at his papers. His face appeared bloated by the small reading light on the rostrum. De Young could see his hands were shaking slightly. He watched with snide curiosity as Miles sought out his listeners again. "Today I want to discuss with you a new program designed to bring some of these economic riches into our own lives where we need it."

Obedient, grumbling, isolated clapping and the heavy rustling sound of people tapping their cardboard fans on the palms of their hands escaped from the studious multitude, when out of nowhere, out of some inchoate and nearly flabbergasted intimation of horror, what sounded like the hard flat crackle of a rifle shot echoed throughout the hall. Instantly De Young grabbed for the holster inside his jacket and at the same time he wheeled and saw James leap from his chair and yell something at Miles that was lost in the gathering noise. Quickly but rather sweetly Miles put a hand to his forehead like a man casually scanning the horizon. De Young was now on his feet, waving his pistol helplessly while everyone around him seemed to move and speak with dreadful slowness. For a long moment nothing else happened. To those in the front rows, Miles appeared to waver where he stood. Blood trickled between his fingers. Someone screamed madly as if to signal his doom, for instantaneously death rained upon him. A ripping fusillade of bullets sought him out, five or six came down like a bolt of lightning and tore into Miles, smashing his chest and snapping his bones. A pitiful groan came from the riddled man still miraculously standing at the rostrum. Then another shot hit the stage. A man running by knocked De Young down and his pistol went slithering away. The audience fell and tumbled from its seats onto the floor. A frenzied woman began to whoop eerily. Children screamed and cried in hysteria and grown-ups cowered under their seats as if suddenly stricken by a tormenting paralysis. Only a handful of people actually saw Miles sag grotesquely and finally lurch backward over several chairs that immediately collapsed with an icy and distinct clatter.

Not one person subsequently agreed on what happened next. Sick with fear the audience lay prostrate waiting for the tragedy to end. Gradually three or four brave souls rose timorously to their feet. A fantastic scene came into view. Behind a pile of chairs the twisted, utterly still form of Miles King lay forsaken, issuing very faint diminishing groans, which stopped after a moment although Miles was not dead. But he had left the conscious world, which no longer even flickered in his blank retinas, to float in some protective state of near death lighted only by the most profound rays of sunset. As he began to sink into a coma, James rushed to him, wildly flinging aside chairs. Other men ran stupidly in circles around the stage, generating new pandemonium with their thundering feet and guttural bereaved shouts. While more heads appeared above the seats, a bizarre psychic urge to deny everything they saw seized hold of the spectators, who now saw Miles in his agony, his eyes wide and lost, his mouth bitterly askew. More kneeling, sobbing figures had gathered around him. Brother James and Brother Charles and five others looked down in disbelief at his white shirt, heavily soaked in dark red blood, which ran so freely it spilled over and stopped up the bullet holes in his chest.

Abruptly a tall white man who had been sitting in the press section ran forward and tried to mount the stage. He was kicked savagely away by one of the Fung, but five or six others came behind him and one man, a photographer, circled a bewildered guard and began taking pictures. The television crew started working again. Half the audience had stood up when dramatically the shooting started all over again. A huge spotlight rolled onto the stage went on with a surge of blinding energy. Four of the Fung knelt around the rostrum and began firing insanely, like little boys with new cap pistols. Every head turned and saw what they shot at: A young-looking man, a black man, was caught hideously in the beam of the overpowering light. He dodged back and forth, popping comically in and out of the curve of white light spread partly over the unused seats. Wild desperate shots failed to hit him. He possessed a vitality that was exciting and tantalizing. The shots continued to ring out with flat, sharp, terrible finality. Five Brothers waving drawn pistols sprinted murderously up the aisle almost trampling each other. Simultaneously a bunch of uniformed policemen came into the back of the theater and then dashed toward the stage. Within seconds a tremendous roar of guns, sounding like massed rifles, exploded from the door of the balcony. The assassin fell through the spotlight beam clumsily and hit the floor with a heavy sickening crash. James looked up and hoped to god he was dead.

Shattering screams and shouts broke out from every corner of the hall. Emergency doors sprang open and policemen ran in. One woman, crushed by her own fright, screamed over and over again until she was knocked down by an enraged and frustrated Brother. Austin Lake finally managed to get onto the stage where two men in white, presumably ambulance doctors, had materialized with sinister precision. They bent over Miles, working feverishly with a portable resuscitator. A plainclothes detective, shouting through a bullhorn, ordered an end to the confusion but no one listened. All over the hall there was a terrible moiling anxiety the police interpreted as an incipient riot. Men shook their heads attempting to rattle free the feeling of monumental helplessness turning over on itself in the hellish disorder of their emotions. Women simply wept as if life were at its end. They were neither Brothers nor Sisters now. They were the near hysterical family of the deceased.

Suddenly Charles De Young detached himself from the tableau of grave figures grouped around Miles and yelled to the audience without aid of a microphone, "He's hurt bad. But he's still alive. We can't help him by making noise. Brothers and Sisters, please." Uneasily a hopeful silence gradually filtered over everyone. Only the men standing nearby heard the chief of detectives tell his assistant, "These goddamn black fanatics will turn this city into a shooting gallery yet. I wish to hell I could lock them all up."

CHAPTER NINETEEN

ONE HOUR AFTER the shooting Manhattan General Hospital, where Miles had been taken, refused to confirm his death. Suspense and shock were molded into the faces of the witnesses as they stood apprehensively in long lines while police clerks sitting at big tables blocking the main exits from the hall took their names and addresses down on large ruled sheets of paper. After leaving the hall most of them slowly walked the five dreadful blocks to the hospital to join hundreds of other Brothers and Sisters waiting in dolorous silence for an initial bulletin. Shortly, a horde of curious, restive onlookers carrying blaring transistor radios converged on the area. They elbowed and shoved Miles's followers aside until whole sections of the crowd were dominated by their rapid chatter and the high-pitched, synthetic, and grating sounds of rock 'n roll music. Shoulder to shoulder with some of the newsmen present they exchanged idle bits of vicious gossip and morbid speculation. ("They say his camel's been shot. That's a good sign.") A few heads turned angrily, eyes brimming with hate and a suggestion of restrained pleading, but nothing was said. A tense half hour seeped into a long unbroken period of exacting quiet. Then, very abruptly, a fight broke out: two

223

short, stout, determined Brothers against a flock of Italian boys in black-leather suit jackets, who cursed and kicked and swung wildly as they broke off the battle quickly and scattered from the frayed edge of the crowd, retreating down the long, wide block shouting incoherent hatred for Miles and violent revenge on the Brotherhood. ("We'll round up all the stupid monkeys he let out of their cages.") Curiously the disturbance did nothing to penetrate a thick solemnity, which came into the air like the heavy discharge from a faraway solitary smoke-stack.

A number of well-dressed white people arrived, alighting gingerly and solemnly from cabs and private cars. Many appeared to be burdened by genuine grief. Newspaper reporters who saw them lapsed into a prurient condescending stillness and refused to approach them for stories. After a while more than a dozen intense-looking Arabs arrived and circulated through the crowd, staring at everyone suspiciously. Minutes later Austin Lake got out of a cab and pushed his way forward. His report was telephoned in. The agency had contacted the hospital and knew already of Miles's fate. It was personal tribute that had brought Lake. At first he understood he was sad and dismayed, as if a good colleague at the agency had died. But with one look at the silently agonized faces all around, a sudden upsurge of grief took him like a fierce wicked chill. Not long after Lake, James arrived from the hall. Lake watched eagerly as he moved soundlessly about with an expression of harrowed astonishment dominating his face. He attempted to close in and listen as James consoled people who came up to him by assuring them the entire Brotherhood had to carry Miles's great work forward.

Two hours went by and the crowd did not break ranks. An immense weariness seemed to hold it together like strongly bonded molecules. At first not everyone noticed the tall white-haired man wearing a conservative three-piece suit as he came through the massive doors closing off the main lobby. Only as he walked to the top of the steps did he draw complete attention. Everyone saw him now, larger than he really was, and he appeared an augur of terrible news. He took from his pocket a white piece of paper and read slowly and firmly into a microphone belonging to one of the radio stations covering the story. "Ladies and gentlemen," he said, looking out at the exhausted pitiful crowd, "the man you knew as Miles King is dead. He died at three o'clock this afternoon following emergency surgery." Then apparently the lost mournful faces at his feet demanded something more and he said with great feeling, "I'm very sorry."

Within a few minutes they had drifted away, spreading out over the vast sidewalk in front of the hospital like a tired throng leaving an empty reverberating stadium. Some wept, making the slow crinkled agonized faces young children make when crying. But most of them went away quietly, knowing they were no longer Brothers and Sisters, knowing it was all over. There would be no more excitement now, no more parades. It was time to be somber, time to reflect in the most private chambers of the mind, and in a humble way to be thankful Miles had appeared, at least for a while, to point out the invisible horizon only he saw.

Three and a half hours after it was known Miles definitely had passed away, in the dull dead mournful end of Sunday evening, the Chinese propaganda barrage started. The Ministry of Foreign Affairs broadcast through Radio Peking the most angry and violent stream of denunciation ever directed at the United States. The Japanese monitoring service receiving signals from Radio Peking expressed astonishment at the ferocity of these attacks. Cautiously they handed the news over to the local office of an international press agency. In less than an hour American television and radio were on the air with a major story: Communist China planned mammoth rallies in her largest cities to honor Miles King. ("We do not want the world to quickly forget our friend Brother King, the slain freedom fighter, who was the tip of the arrow aimed at the heart of racial imperialism.")

By ten o'clock in the evening there were intimations of a developing international crisis over the assassination, and the news media did nothing to spare the public fright. Shocked viewers heard the Islamic nation of Indonesia would follow China's example. From Moscow, Paris, and London came reports that African students would hold memorial parades and lead demonstrations around American embassies. Many summaries of Miles's career were broadcast and people began to remember, slowly and thickly, the giant street rally in Harlem not long ago when King had pledged solidarity with the Communists. Americans recalled with visceral uneasiness the utter frenzy and dramatic insolence of that day. Suddenly they felt a little harassed.

Yet a few hours later this spate of news stories began to provide relief of a fashion. Obviously this was all too much. The temptation existed to laugh at what seemed another of those blundering Communist attempts to embarrass the United States with simpleminded propaganda. Sensible people began passing the whole thing off as a damned circus while hoping a quick burial and the crush of bereavement would keep King's followers off the streets. But it was not to be that easy. Before going to bed the nation saw its television screens jammed with tumultuous films of placards and flowing banners bearing virulent foreign protests over a killing it now wanted with some desperation to forget. One station after another showing reruns of the assassination tape was beseeched with requests for immediate cancellation of this material along with an inordinate number of violent threats.

In black areas around the country the speed of international reaction came as a refreshing surprise. Those who had known and seen Miles were gratified because the new events proved Miles had immense stature even beyond the confines of his own country. But no one thought of demonstrating or sending recognition for these amazing gestures of solidarity. In a radio interview an important civil rights figure dismissed the idea as absurd. Instead he spoke of the deceased as a great American, giving life to the clever speculation that black leaders, like the Communists, would make the name of Miles King an equivalent of martyrdom for their own selfish schemes. Many people

226

realized at once how quickly an uncomfortable myth could be created around this dangerous rebel, but a larger, more furtive issue escaped examination. In the most convenient way the martyrdom of Miles King covered up an uneasy and unthinkable suggestion in the minds of blacks: the hint of massive complicity in driving Miles into successively spectacular acts of drama bound to end in his assassination.

Meanwhile James took upon himself the eerie task of burying Miles. Quietly (he wondered if he were not actually following Mahanti's order to say little and act inconspicuously) he had the body brought to a mortuary and began to oversee the sad initiation of the Islamic funerary rites. When he arrived home stupefied and drained, there were several callers, reporters asking desperately for interviews, which he politely declined but not without the unnerving sense of doing it in a void. He felt utterly and completely lost. A familiar sensation of fatalism had hollowed him out. Yet he was terribly weary of it. Somewhere James knew he was overcome with remorse and woe, but it seemed very far away. Thoughtlessly he toyed with the idea of going to see Mahanti. Only the knowledge he would collapse in the streets kept him from making the attempt. He did not know that all over New York known street-corner agitators found themselves trapped in a series of swift police raids. Under intensive all-night questioning many were to admit being paid to start trouble. ("It was a black man from one of the foreign embassies. We didn't know about Miles. He just gave us a date.")

The next morning newspapers were full of commentaries and picture spreads on the assassination, although there was no mention of a rumor in Harlem that said Miles was the first trial victim in a larger plot to kill off all American black leaders. Oddly few questions were asked about the motives for the murder ("It was a strange case of black revenge justice," one paper claimed) and little was made of the disturbing fact that the assassin's body revealed no identification at all. No one had come to the morgue to claim the riddled anonymous corpse and the killer remained a totally mysterious person without a wallet in his pockets or a label in his suit. He could not be linked with anyone. (Secrecy also surrounded the murder weapon, now described as a foreign-made rifle, which was in the possession of an agency "other than the city police.") Civil rights leaders, anxious to gain public favor with a show of initiative, proclaimed a period of peace and racial amity. But the nation's most prominent newspaper felt danger enough to warn its readers: "The life and death of Miles King illustrate a tragic theme of our era. This gifted, brilliant, and thoroughly twisted individual might have brought outstanding recognition on himself and a whole people. Unfortunately he never seemed able to bring himself to a genuine knowledge of his best qualities. There are many who suspect he never wanted to, but whatever his personal tortures he willingly turned his great powers to evil means. None who saw him on television will soon forget the fear he projected when he attempted, happily without any success at all, to link the Negro citizens of this country to the outlaw nation of Communist China." The tabloids, with barely restrained jubilation, described Miles as a man who changed doctrines the way other people changed shirts and expressed hope his funeral later in the day would not descend to the outrage of rioting and looting. At any rate, they continued cheerfully, the Brotherhood breathed its last when Miles took those four slugs of vengeance square in the chest.

Earlier James had arisen from a watchful sleep and gone up the hill to get the papers. He read the editorials with sullen disinterest. Now fear attached itself to him, a churning fear of what might happen next. He wondered what Mahanti was doing and if Mahanti still idiotically believed he could take over the Brotherhood. A sudden hostile curiosity about De Young's whereabouts came over him. Somehow he suspected they would never meet again. Then angrily and for no reason he dismissed the thought. He was becoming more tense by the minute. The brief walk had made him tired. It had depressed him. He went into the kitchen and fried two eggs, trying to concentrate on details of the funeral he felt it was his sole and terrible obligation to provide for Miles. Then only intermittently did his awful deficiencies and apprehensions touch him.

As he ate James perused the front pages. No rioting had occurred anywhere in the country. New York had a peaceful night except for an incident in Queens where a band of teen-agers smashed a supermarket window to "punish the people who silenced our only leader."

He snapped on the radio. The monotonous news from abroad cheered him somewhat. In every time zone it seemed there were demonstrations protesting the assassination. Islamic governments had submitted diplomatic notes expressing anger. Some American tourists had been beaten up by West Indian agitators in London. Four African governments issued state-ments at the United Nations demanding details of the investi-gation of Miles's death. ("A political killing pure and simple.") The official reply briskly noted this was a civil matter, but asked, with a rare hint of consternation, for pa-tience with the authorities handling the case. By the time this answer was released to the governments concerned, private diplomatic moves had already been made. An agitated Ameri-can ambassador let all interested parties know he would dis-cuss the matter at a special late-morning conference. More delegates came than he anticipated, and with great embarrass-ment he proceeded to explain what little he really knew.

It was not enough. All over the country an invisible dread at the harsh demons this peculiar assassination was letting loose began to grip people forcefully. They were glad Miles was dead, but the reaction seemed so immense and disproportion-ate. There was no relief, only a new sudden pressure. And given credence by the irresponsible statements of police chiefs, portent by the rhetoric of newspapers ("King was a Commu-nist hothead and the instigator of a witch-doctor mentality"), and subtle reality by the obvious confusion in communications and government circles, there began to grow a suspicion that Miles King in death had set a destructive plot to work against America. Only the King funeral later in the day gave hope the commotion and bewilderment would soon end.

At eleven o'clock in the morning James arrived at the funeral home where Miles had been taken shortly after a half-hour exploratory operation exposed his condition as appallingly hopeless. As secretary of the Brotherhood he was in charge of all funeral details and the task was overwhelming. At the same time none of it seemed even slightly real. Hard as he tried, James could not comprehend that Miles was actually gone, and this triggered not a few weird quirks in his behavior. It was impossible to leave him alone with the body for any length of time. Whenever he had a few minutes, he would sit very quietly and try to relive the assassination, try to insert his body between Miles and the deadly bullets streaking down on him, try to muster the idea that Miles was merely wounded and recovering in an anonymous private clinic somewhere. But none of this worked. Always he was left with the hard residue of what had happened. And the spooky, suffocating night scenes, which came after the public announcement of death, constantly returned to him, slipping into his consciousness like the richly hallucinatory visions of a man who is drowning far out at sea. He recalled two hours after the body arrived a small wrinkled black man wearing a soiled red fez had appeared from nowhere to recite the Koran, a symbolic act beginning the Islamic funerary rites. The man had materialized with the airs of a disciple out of the Bible, calm, reasonable, and utterly unreal. He read for hours in a droning hypnotic voice. James swore he could feel the cadence of that voice creep up on his back. He imagined he could even touch it with his fingertips. The stranger frightened him terribly; and late in the evening, with his palms touching in a fervent holy gesture, he asked him to leave so the body might be prepared for burial.

The Islamic funerary rites continued when the body was placed on a stretcher pointed in the direction of Mecca. Soon two Sisters came and carefully washed the corpse. Then the nostrils and orifices were stuffed with cotton and the women departed. Half an hour later the orthodox Arab burial director James had summoned from the Middle East Institute presented himself. On viewing the body, his eyes widened with shock and outrage. He began to jabber violently in broken, stuttering English, his words tumbling out half formed and singed with malice. The body had been fouled, he claimed loudly. Miles should not have been touched, he shouted in furious anguish. As it was now the angels Munkar and Nakir would never visit Miles in his grave because he had not been given the martyr's unwashed burial. Quickly his hands came together in a theatrical gesture of entreaty for the deceased. This was all he could do, he explained sharply, before retreating into an Arabic prayer where his voice calmed, almost purred with what sounded to James like deadly curses and contemptuous oaths. James watched the venomous eyes in the small, controlled head. Irritably he listened to the strange prayers. He felt excluded, disdained, and by quick turns his rage began to build. To contain himself he asked the visitor for reason and understanding, but a desolate pleading undertone was in his voice and it riled him. He was begging a perfect stranger, an obnoxious Arab who despised him as a heathen, a man he would have shot dead in the war by just raising his rifle to hip level, and all at once it was too much. Violence seethed in his head. His abused dazed senses erupted into the only emotion left to him. A swift partly closed powerful fist reached out, striking the Arab with a full stunning blow across the face. Down went the other man, nearly flying up on his backside. James moved for him, unsure whether to lash out a second time, but the Arab scrambled to his feet in fear, certain now he was faced by a madman. High, sharp, effeminate sounds came from him as he withdrew from the room pursued stiffly by James. Fearing a terrible beating, the Arab broke and fled headlong through the funeral parlor, yelling and cursing the place as a lair of crazy devils in a harsh repetitive prattle that James couldn't quite get out of his head even now as he carefully checked a long typed list of funeral arrangements for the third time in twenty minutes. Some of the unwarranted hysteria of that senseless quarrel still boiled up into a sour apprehension he'd tasted in his stomach the night before, when finally he calmed himself and ordered the body sprinkled with the ordained perfumed mixture of camphor and rosewater.

The crowds along the funeral routes gathered early. One full hour before the procession was to start its long terrible walk through the streets, people were jammed up three deep near the big intersections in Harlem. There was woe in the air, but much uncertainty too. The din of foreign reaction was baffling, and it cast a pall of nervous concern over the whole day. People were worried that somehow Miles would not be properly attended to with all the confusion. And a maudlin anxiety to inspect the funeral for themselves drove hundreds more to view the procession just before its scheduled start. Many of the early arrivals had brought battered orange crates, small stepladders, and folding chairs. Behind them ranks of tense, drawn spectators, with their arms folded seriously, stood in suspenseful silence. Rarely did anyone mention Miles by name, but there was conspiracy in this oversight. Read only in the eyes it said, Anyone who dishonors Miles today will be half dead before help can get to him.

This pact proclaiming peace for the dead champion succeeded. All was quiet. The police, moving by slowly in cruisers overloaded with riot gear, watched this strange solitude warily and decided it was merely an ominous calm preceding a disastrous hurricane. Then the first shimmering and discordant stirrings of the funeral parade floated over the crowds. Out of its tinny and disorganized ramble eventually throbbed a huge muffled drumbeat, final and immensely sad. They were coming from the direction of Brotherhood Hall and not until they turned onto 125th Street could anything be seen. Then quite abruptly the procession came into view. A bizarre alertness surrounded it, which was fascinating, odd, and very spooky. A large gasp of woeful alarm and surprise escaped from the crowd at what greeted it. In accordance with the ancient Islamic traditions, a group of Brothers and Sisters, all elderly, blind, and infirm led the way, chanting out a dismal prayer for the dead. They wandered and hobbled about in their ragged finery, dragging and separating out unevenly across the broad street, suggesting in their unsure movements something undeniably grotesque, a hint of the wicked helplessness a stroke victim must feel. The drum continued its heavy dramatic thumping, a big full annoying sound more frozen and louder now. To the rear of the sick and the blind walked a man bearing a small reading desk with an opened copy of the Koran on it. Now and again he broke into a long, quick, excited melody of bereavement, which startled everyone by its mechanical perfection and virtuosity. Finally the bier, supported by six men walking in lock step appeared, and moans of awe, mingled with fascination, issued from the spectators. Strangely the bier did not seem to be part of the parade. Nothing about it was odd, surprising, or foreign. It presented no dangers, put no one off; quickly many stripped themselves of other emotions and cried, weeping at what they knew, at what was final and irrevocable. With the sight of the bier, the funeral became a true symbol of mourning. Tears rolled down the faces of old women. Even some men turned away, their shoulders forming the unmistakable hunch that betrays shame at the onrush of uncontrolled emotion.

James was supporting the bier on the forward end, to the left of Brother Nicholas. He moved slowly, his gait a little jerky and not quite in step with the others. Within his clinched limited circle of emotions, he felt only an awe that Miles was going to be buried, mingled with a sort of timid schoolboy fear at the sight of all those passionate and distraught faces. Obediently, steadfastly he gazed ahead, fixing his eyes deliberately on the elderly Brothers and Sisters who set such a horribly slow pace. Soon it would be over, James consoled himself hurriedly. But on this day assurances were not enough. The spectators, walling him in with their grief, their woe, their density, and the minute terrors that plagued every second of their dreary bitter lives, seemed to reach out and claw at him. Their contorted emotions and twisted sentiments knifed through his skittish concentration and assaulted the wrecked fortress of his existence. And without warning James was grappling with hot slippery panic. A wave of pure mental agony surged over him. Out of some chamber in his mind escaped recollections of the hundred small kindnesses Miles had shown him. Intimations of the naïve faith and trust Miles bestowed upon him played up and down his nerves unpredictably. The envelope of warmth and manly intimacy existing between them was all gone now, James realized with a horrible start that jerked the procession to a halt momentarily. An infusion of crippling dismay both profound and immediate swarmed over him. He mourned Miles in an abrupt uncomprehending turmoil that weakened his knees and brought him very close to stumbling. "Keep it straight. Make it look like something, Brother," Charles De Young cried angrily from the other side of the bier.

They continued. The drum maintained its dirge. The procession, escorted by half a dozen police cars on the flanks, had traveled the length of 125th Street and turned up Broadway. There to his shock and mounting alarm James saw the crowds were bigger, heftier, more intense than those left behind. Something ominous was creeping into the day. The sidewalks overflowed people into the gutter. From the narrow windows of massive red brick housing projects that spread in every direction like forlorn, inexplicable monuments, thousands of eyes peered out, fixing on the procession with an awed intensity that seemed to diminish it. In a spasm of sharp futility, James felt impotent and betrayed, as he had at the moment Miles was shot down. He faltered again but picked up the pace somehow, perhaps because his mind was no longer directing his limbs. Slowly he scanned the host of brown and black faces lining each block they entered. He gazed up ahead and behind at the dense outpouring of people, thick at each corner and four rows deep in between. What did they want or expect? James thought. What could their hopes be now? And suddenly an anger and resentment at all of it, backed by a stiffening of fear, rose in James. He was incensed at the mute curious frightened faces peering on stupidly. A rage at their audacious silence worked over him. Their stolid immensity gave him chills that fed his belligerence. He was driven to yell out, to curse and abuse them. And he actually opened his mouth, but the vision of all those unpredictable faces as far as he could see up the avenue silenced him. He was intimidated and he felt it

234

in the stomach. Fear was gaining on his piddling anger. He realized how much of the totality of his folly and indecision was in the streets this day. James saw, for the first time perhaps, the legendary far ends of Miles's allegiance—what furious stifled crowds he commanded, what hostile legions of discontent he marshaled. And he knew quietly, with all the certainty of a skilled diagnostician, that he could never lead half a dozen of these people.

Out of a side street crept a television mobile unit and James turned away instantly. He closed his eyes. His head was swimming. Like a man in a car out of control, everything seemed alien and speeded up, but the result was just a vague heavy sadness, a sadness at personal sterility and a grieving, mournful emptiness at Miles's demise. Miles was being cheapened. His death was a vacuous political event surrounded by vulgar posturing. Even his funeral was an embittered parody of the tingling spectacle he loved. It was animated only by a grotesque dignity in the people lining the gutters, and used greedily by television to tickle the national prurience. Beyond that stood the vast government propaganda departments, ready to somehow use this event as an argument or defense in a larger contest of international bickering. A slithering of shame and disgust went right through James. All of it was his fault. He alone was to blame. Finally in his frustrated little rages and intrigues he'd done something really calamitous. He let the world use Miles, weep over him, spit on him, champion him, and in the end of course, discard him. That would come too; and James understood it would be another sign of his worthlessness. With eyes full of self-pity he looked over at Brother Nicholas supporting the front end of the bier with him. For just a moment he felt inanely superior, for Nicholas had been too devastated by the killing to see Miles was to have no real dignity even in death.

And the drum continued its measured, almost ludicrous beat as the funeral procession moved on up Broadway to the tip of Manhattan. The cemetery was still three-quarters of a mile away and Charles De Young was brutally tired. He was positioned on the side opposite James, supporting the bier in its middle, at the point of greatest load. His back and his legs throbbed and ached with fatigue. His mind was near exhaustion, but De Young didn't know if he cared or not. He understood his career was close to being terminated. Real disaster had finally come to him. The agency was furious, incensed, and foolishly implacable over the assassination. Miles had simply died, been mysteriously snuffed out, and no one assigned to him had even suggested in their reports that a plot against his life might exist. When the Chinese propaganda began to come in, the director had been summoned to the White House, there to be confronted by an enraged young presidential assistant and the attorney general. He'd been forced to admit the agency was investigating Miles thoroughly. Two capable men were assigned to the file. In return a suggestion was given that his resignation would be welcome if suitable answers were not quickly found. The reaction through agency channels was unbelievably swift, and now De Young felt the pressure like a swimmer stricken with cramps in deep water. He tormented himself with scenes of his humiliation and his downfall. What names were they calling him in their comfortable secret little offices in Washington? Which bitter ironic sobriquets had been dreamed up for him, De Young wondered.

Intermingled with these worries other emotions tugged at De Young. Much of the dreamy, hot confusion that welled up in his brain after the shots were fired still lingered in the sensation of abstract shock. In a silent reproachful way he was stunned at his own ineptitude, at the stark failure of his competence. Yet at the same time he denied his culpability. He tried to pretend he wasn't even surprised Miles was dead, but this falsehood was eroded by the troubling recollection that the night before the killing, when he met Lake, a suspicion of something dangerous and shattering evolving around him had played with his thoughts. Then he'd made the colossal error of ignoring his fine instincts for intrigue. On Sunday he hadn't prowled around the hall as he knew he should have. Instead he killed time with his friends. He hadn't even looked for James, although James had been missing for a number of days. The assassin had slipped right by him. The killing was set up while he slept, but still De Young refused to let feelings of guilt or remorse touch him. He was just thankful no one in the agency knew he had lost track of James.

Yet the murder itself remained sharp in his mind. Without trying, he could experience the bland moiling frenzy that swirled through him when he heard the first shot. He recalled everything slowly, minutely. He saw himself reaching down and collecting Miles's scattered speech from the stage. And later when he read it, De Young remembered how he shuddered. He loathed and hated the speech. The subtle begging, the backhanded pleading, the studied pompous reasonableness of it all insulted him, hurt him because he knew Miles, at least unconsciously, was trying to emulate many of the ideas he'd put forth in their tense brief quarrels over the years. De Young was afraid of the speech because Miles in attempting to copy him was headed straight for the wastes of mediocrity. It was unfortunate, De Young thought bitterly and not without a trace of obvious confusion. Miles was slipping fast, but there had been in his career a great deal that was impressive, if not strangely brilliant—private conversations with foreign statesmen, wild beautiful speeches, witty memorandums, a host of spontaneous insights, and even the establishment of the Brotherhood. And De Young wanted to claim all this as his own. He'd always coveted the prestige that clung to Miles. He realized all of this hungrily, longingly, as the Brothers and Sisters trooped to the hospital and he slipped into the backstage elevator and went up to Miles's office, beating a pack of clumsy detectives in search of evidence. Quickly, frantically, kneeling behind Miles's huge walnut desk like a deranged man, he'd collected all the papers, tape recordings, and notes he could find. These were hidden in his office at the hall, together with the bundles of material secreted away in Miles's private safe. (In their haste the detectives had never considered a large wall safe hidden behind an empty slot for one.) Enough was now preserved for scholars in some distant year (or a publisher willing to insure a large guarantee) to see what forces Miles represented in the history of his country.

De Young was a little proud of his coup. It proved he was not without dignity and some intellect. It showed he appreciated Miles, and this made him comfortable. An exciting feeling of superiority rose in him. He pitied Miles more than ever because he was safely dead. Now he personally controlled the Miles King legend, De Young reasoned smugly. A subtle contempt for Miles played over him. Like many an ambitious middleweight, Miles had challenged for the heavyweight crown and lost, his footwork and small feints brilliant in the gym but insubstantial under the lights. And worst of all he'd failed to pass the test of guile. He trusted people. He believed flattery. He humiliated anyone who tried to help him and De Young could never forgive that, especially since Miles had degraded him in front of Austin Lake and damaged his pride irreversibly.

Still on the deepest level of feeling he knew, De Young was concerned. If he couldn't save Miles, could he save himself? The question plagued him. Right now, in the midst of the funeral, he had no answer and he wasn't sure he ever would. Of course the agency would try to blame him. He remembered once he'd said James was harmless, and it was probably true at the time. Lake had upheld him too. Lake, the cool operator, the handsome incompetent, the charming bungler. Suddenly, vigilantly, De Young looked around. It came to him that Lake was surely having the funeral photographed. He felt a revulsion, knowing Lake, desperate because he had no inkling of the assassination, would grow careless now and perhaps inadvertently give away the agency's clandestine interest in Miles.

Lake was through, De Young decided. He wasn't clever enough to save himself once the bureaucracy went to work on his nerves. He would end up tied to a psychiatrist, crippled, maudlin, and despicable. And De Young knew he stood edge to edge with a similar fate if the assassination was not solved. But fortunately this catastrophe had brought him one clear dividend: James could conveniently be blamed for all of it whether he was innocent or not. It would be fairly simple to do. His inactivity all these years could be twisted into bland subversion. His odd friendship with Miles could be called arcane treachery. Without too much trouble, James could be made to sound like the first Chinese-trained interloper into the vast barrenness of American Negro resentment. His unveiling would save De Young's head and the labor of his best years.

Looking for some stray, seemingly irrelevant sign or clue to the future, De Young's mind focused on the disorder that had come out of Miles's assassination like fruit tumbling out of a cornucopia. The Chinese continued their insults. In Moscow a mob of African students from Patrice Lumumba University had marched on the American Embassy flinging ink bottles and bricks. An official sent out to warn them was savagely clubbed and now the air was full of official protests and recriminations. Washington wanted action, so did Moscow; and blacks only casually interested in Miles began to suspect something very big and portentous was behind his death. In barbershops, poolrooms, and bars it was recalled white people had once plotted against his life in California, but here suspicion petered out into aimless theories and diffuse arguments. There were no street incidents, no public anger. Not yet. Blacks felt something more subtle was at work and the trend was to wait until more cards were dealt. But De Young was trying to think ahead, trying to discern the arcane motives of the Chinese Ministry of Foreign Affairs as it issued a statement through a friendly East German diplomat renewing its insidious charges of official collusion in obscuring the facts surrounding the King assassination. Fed by this driving pressure a fury of indignation was certain to build up in black people. It was only a matter of time.

Momentarily De Young broke from his absorption with disaster. His mind followed a new channel. He glanced around wearily. The sight of so many distressed people relieved him a bit and he realized he was obsessed with plotting. He'd been underground too long. He no longer comprehended simple realities or cared about obvious emotions. Until this moment it

239

had not occurred to him something contrived, false, and very eerie was motivating the Chinese propaganda barrage. Immediately he wildly guessed that it actually centered on James. But just as quickly he dismissed the idea. The mottled and confused sounds of the parade came through to him very clearly. De Young wished he could see James's face, even as he prayed no totally new enigmatic expression would greet him when he did. He could not allow himself to assign any real importance to James, yet the notion of doing it intrigued him. Still James seemed too small, self-contained, and insignificant to represent Chinese interests to the American Negro; but if by some grotesque and freakish circumstance he did, then his apprehension could bring great distinction. Here under intense strain De Young's mind refused to reason further and he was left grasping the vaguest of assurances and the simplest of hopes.

But it was something, a small barrier against his fears, a thin tenuous lead he had to follow, somehow. Against it stood darkness, dismissal, humiliation. A bitter-sweet desperation came over De Young. Underneath it, he experienced nothing but complex misgivings about James. His thoughts wandered back to the grim, quiet, gray scene in the mortuary driveway that morning. James was there, looking tired and badly dressed in a rumpled black suit and a dirty raincoat. After supervising the closing of Miles's extravagant African-mahogany coffin he stood talking to the mortician and a few drivers in a shed area behind the gravel driveway. Off to one side Nicholas walked around silently with two or three downcast Brothers. Just as they were all about to get into the line of polished black limousines, he'd turned the corner and everyone looked at him solicitously, almost warmly, except James whose eyes revealed what De Young thought was terrified surprise and hate. On the way to Brotherhood Hall they rode in separate cars; and as James assembled the Fung, numerous pallbearers, and elderly marchers on the small parking lot that had been Miles's basketball court, De Young began to suspect James was ignoring him because he was no longer supposed to exist. With a faint start, he was sure now that James never expected them to meet again.

A spasm of outrage worked itself into his brain. All of his energies and tensions were focused on James. He seethed with a quick fierce hatred for James, for his petty efficiency, for the whole perverse idea that he'd so far carried off the funeral with order and a gloss of religious dignity, the way Miles would have enjoyed it done. And out of all this turbulent concentration came the beginnings of a plan, dim in outline, but intuitively right. Begin with Clarence Williams, De Young told himself feverishly. Get Williams. Have the city police bring him in to a station house as a possible suspect. Keep him from the phone. Sweat him for five or six hours. Break him open until everything he knows about James spills out. Then bring in the girl and everyone in the Brotherhood working under James. Find the person controlling James if he exists and you're saved, De Young reasoned. Pleasantly De Young pictured himself as an honored guest at one of those silly-ass but tearful secret ceremonies in the cramped agency auditorium where they pin a medal on you no one must ever see. In his imagination he already had the medal. On his private stage he was already a hero and this heightened his determination to preserve his career, to fool people like the director and Riggs, to subvert this fiasco into a bland sensible triumph. The fantasy worked on him like a dose of heroin pulsating warmly through a junkie's veins. Dull elation combined with vigilance is what Charles De Young felt most keenly as the funeral procession neared the cemetery.

They had carried Miles over half of Manhattan, not believing he was in the elegant casket nearly crushing their shoulders. Up through the teeming desolation of Harlem and into strange Jewish neighborhoods they had come, moving past curious and vaguely sympathetic faces. Hundreds had spontaneously fallen in behind the bier and the procession stretched for seven or eight blocks before trailing off into a wake of playful youngsters relieved that a serious day was

241

over. Still they trudged on, marching under the intricate latticed shadows of the elevated tracks as strong and upright as if they bore a president on their shoulders. It was a dreadful compelling sight, this thick, long swath of blacks with police cars trapped on its edges; and on many streets good white middle-class mothers anxiously called in their children. Still the funeral train continued, cutting into an enclave of Irish where people trickled to the sidewalks, their faces sullen and tentative. At last they reached the huge baroque iron gates of the cemetery and turned into it smartly. Up ahead two wary gravediggers stood by their work. In accordance with ancient customs the body was removed from the coffin and placed in the deep grave on its right side, propped up by bricks. The pallbearers crowded around to view the face, turned toward Mecca. Brother Nicholas whimpered. Many people cried softly. A shawl was rent. Three handfuls of dust were cast into the grave by each of the bystanders. The sera 112 of the Koran was recited. Before the grave was filled the correct answers to the angelic examination on the catechism were prompted into the dead man's ear by two boys serving as tutors. "Who is your God? Who is your prophet?" they shouted.

CHAPTER TWENTY

JUST AS THE final prayers began James left. Purposely he'd positioned himself on the edge of the tightly packed mob flowing away from Miles's grave, and when the tambourines started to clatter and the onlookers went into a last stuttering spasm of sorrow, he slipped away. Coolly he walked down one of the paved branch paths to an adjacent road, which did not lead to the gate where the television mobile unit would be parked, waiting to get some good pictures of the stricken, huddled mourners leaving the cemetery. It was a huge vacant place, this cemetery, a vast manicured and landscaped field studded with thousands of anonymous tombstones reached by following beautiful forlorn access roads named after old English manor houses, James supposed. This at least was something to think about, a game to distract him from the genteel desolation all around. But unaccountably the refined sense of unreality lingering in his head grew and blossomed there like a wild tropical flower, rank and outrageous. He knew the ministry propaganda campaign was tormenting him in ways he could not yet feel. Combined with the evil elusive terrors of the assassination everything had come too swiftly, and James was practically anesthetized.

Yet one of his basic talents (perhaps the only rational skill he possessed), his ability to work through a problem slowly, thoroughly, with a fine degree of meticulousness, asserted itself tenuously. It dampened his instinct to panic and cooled his exhausted nerves. He felt strangely safe and warned himself against any kind of optimism because it always led him into the most hideous self-deception. Still he was glad to be alive, secretly glad to be able to walk away from Miles's grave with such outward composure. James was sure this was an achievement, but he could never explain it. He only knew it helped him to think in an oddly rational way and that gave him a hope too fragile for examination, but at the same time comfortingly significant. James understood that if psychic cowardice bound him to the ministry, if controlled hysterical indecision made him an accomplice in murder, if his pathetic ambiguity had propelled him to the precipice of insanity, if a foreign power was at his service, then he intended—no matter what was to happen—to survive. Now that Miles was gone, he intended to live and perhaps even reconstruct his life around the principle of self-knowledge and struggle.

As James got within a hundred yards of the gate, it began to rain. Buoyed by his thoughts he began to jog lightly. All the terrible inadequacies that had torn at him so constantly seemed tamed for the moment. He gave himself over to a giddy sheltering sensation. The physical act of running and moving his body purposefully lightened his remaining tensions. More lucidity returned to his thinking. Without fear or pain he remembered Beverly's phone call just before the assassination. A chill touched him but he didn't break his stride. Memories of the huge church fire in Harlem resembling the one he was to expect after Miles was dead returned to him unaccompanied by emotion. He dwelt studiously on these occurrences for a minute, feeling divested of the patent helplessness that had always bound him. Everything seemed to flinch weakly before the balanced lance of his reason. Yet he was not completely without worries. The immensity of that church fire, which yielded so little to scientific scrutiny, forced upon him an uncanny awareness he tried to shun. He realized many strange details had to be resolved before he could outlive his weaknesses and slip free from his predicament. But at least he had a clever idea of where to begin.

Three blocks away the terminal of the elevated subway line reared up black and rickety in the cold slanting rain. James headed for it quickly with his coat collar up. He thought again about the man who had questioned Beverly and spoken to Miles. And for a marginal instant the overmastering urge to flee took him completely. He went up the steps two at a time and walked stiffly to the toll booth. Through the bars an old red-faced man was fiddling with a radio and James heard snatches of opinion and commentary on the Chinese propaganda barrage, which sounded stupid and ridiculous, although he couldn't say why.

He ambled along the platform, intent but not really thinking. In the background the long bulky shapes of idle trains stretched down the unused express tracks. An engineer dressed in comical blue-striped overalls came by and told him the next train departed in three minutes. His heart jumped foolishly, but he was still calm. His thoughts drifted back to Beverly and her mysterious questioner. From long ago he recalled that the ministry often warned of situations like this, theatrical attempts to panic a suspect into irredeemable mistakes. He remembered you always had to find out from as many sources as possible how much potentially damaging information had been given and then assess the possible danger. Frequently there was none. James meditated on this for a minute. He could not be sure whether he was deceiving himself or not, whether his inadequacies were disintegrating or simply combining in an unfamiliar but poisonously subtle form. Thoughtfully he stepped into a phone booth partially hidden from a newsstand. In well-controlled haste he dialed Clarence Williams's number in Brooklyn.

It was a long ride from the end of Manhattan to the shabby residential section of Brooklyn where Williams lived. James sat alone in the empty end of a subway car and watched the blurred string of racing lights just beyond the window. For a time his stomach felt constricted and he pitched lightly on his seat. He really didn't want to see Clarence, for uneasily he sensed Clarence was more important to him than he should be. On the phone when they talked briefly about Miles, he had been inanely cordial and then anxious. A suspicious concern hovered over everything he said, especially when he attempted to sound casual. Several long silences made them both uneasy and James knew Clarence didn't want him to come out but could not muster the nerve to turn him away. As usual Clarence was solicitous and cleverly polite. He mentioned Beverly's frantic call and asked if he needed any money or anything like that. ("She called over here sometime last week with a crazyheaded story. You know how women get. I don't know yet what she was talking about, buddy.") When their conversation ended, he was almost certain Clarence would not be there when he arrived, and again part of his mind seized desperately on what Beverly might have said to him. Yet strangely he was hopeful that Clarence could help dispel his doubts because Clarence was so garrulous and full of shallow, silly fear. But he dreaded their meeting. Everything about Clarence, his sly awkwardness, his strained whimsicality and hunger for small tidbits of respect, nagged at James unpleasantly. Fortunately they were not close friends, but he still owed Clarence the favor of getting him a woman he adored; and this was not the kind of debt he could dismiss lightly. Over their distant and timorous relationship it cast a dramatic spell. James could remember more than once he'd sensed something fascinating and irrevocable existed between them. Clarence once introduced him as his best friend in the world. It was an outrageous ingratiating remark and he and Beverly laughed bitterly about it later, but it reminded him of the kind of beguiling and ironic claims Charles De Young made around the hall and he never really forgave Clarence for saying it. Still all of that really meant nothing now. After tonight their friendship would end, James decided. The ludicrous remnants of their false association would be swept away. Clarence was a distraction, a pointless annoyance. He introduced dozens of needless uncertainties into life, which didn't belong.

The train pulled into a station somewhere in Brooklyn and James peered out the window, fixing his eyes on the grimy white walls banded with blue tile bearing the name of the stop. He stared at the elaborate lettering but it carried no impression to his brain, for out of nowhere an immense and frightening weariness had taken control of his senses. He felt terribly dull. The funeral had depressed him more than he knew and now, left with nothing to do but sit, he heard the drums and wails and saw again the sad, swollen crowds and all of it came down on him brutally. His head seemed empty and buoyantly light. He convinced himself he was straining for consciousness. The suspicious and aquiline faces of numerous Arabs standing along the parade route offered themselves up to his fears. He was sure they had come to taunt him in some way, to grant talismanic significance to his impotence. James felt these Arabs knew or at least suspected (Miles always claimed he could feel Islam in a man; it was a great part of his vigilance) that he'd given no real commitment to Islam. He could hear their terrible sibilant voices hissing that he feared the principles of self-examination and submission to Allah. And as these thoughts rippled through his mind, the whole assassination scene materialized once more with all the sudden vividness and garish sensuality of a tormenting dream. He heard the initial shot, flat and hard sounding, before turning quickly, dumbly, to see the deadly hollow-nosed mercury-fulminate bullets strike Miles full in the chest and explode, spewing little showers of blood and flesh. Then he rushed to Miles in a dream state, mindless and choked with a complete inarticulate horror that shut out the noise in the hall and cramped his throat tightly in the flush of a thousand emotions. The damage was fantastic, worse than could ever be told. The bullets had ruptured and shredded Miles's lungs, now filled with thick blood and resembling potholes in the street on a rainy day. And the people at the hospital had been very shrewd. On orders from the police or somebody, they had kept the news from the

247

crowd outside. They had allowed the crowd to settle into its apprehension and grief. They had seen to it the agents of law established total domination before the ridiculous story of death in an emergency operation was given out to the world. All of it had worked beautifully. An important moment had passed outside the hospital and evaporated into the air, probably forever. The real possibility of great violence was dampened and nothing had happened since. James wondered if Mahanti understood that.

The train finally arrived at the obscure station where James got off. He felt released from the wild mélange of noises and stupefied faces in the subway car. A few people left the train with him and struggled down the long, dusty, poorly lit platform to the exit.

Clarence's neighborhood consisted mostly of two-family houses needing moderate to extensive repairs. Grass sprouted up boldly through huge cracks in the sidewalk. After the rain shower an evening warmth had settled and children played wildly in the damp streets, shouting and running under the thin artificial boulevard lamps. James walked more quickly than he wanted to, driven by a surreptitious urgency he couldn't define. He recollected that a man on the train had been reading a newspaper with facing photographs of Miles and Mao Tse-tung on the front page and this gave him a tingle of nervous excitement. It was a bombastic touch Miles would have appreciated. Miles loved drama and confrontation, especially when it was a little contrived. Not that he was just flashy and superficial. Never at any time in his career, even when he shouted his vague and histrionic message through a drafty storefront, had Miles been a mere demagogue. Many in the Brotherhood knew of his midnight struggles with the larger, more elusive questions of human meaning. More than once he'd been heard cursing his limited education in a voice shredding between hatred and tears. Many times he'd pathetically described his lowly, aimless beginnings to Nicholas, who pretended sadly not to understand. Everyone knew a cunning streak of irrational fear and suspicion claimed a good part of him, even on his most relaxed days. And this knowledge set up interesting repercussions. Emotionally it opened up the territory of his aspirations to many of the Brothers and Sisters. It gave Miles the stature of a tormented heroic quester. People idolized Miles because he dared to attack questions they couldn't even begin to suspect the answers to. Time after time he stole up on the question of what the fate of the black man would actually be. On some days there were intimations in the things he said of a very bright and hopeful answer. Then came moments when he wavered and collapsed into scalding rhetoric. His more idealistic followers—the younger, very earnest Brothers—sometimes accused him of faltering before certain truths, but older, more cynical people were both awed and terrified by his efforts and applauded him with the satisfied gusto usually accorded strong men in a circus.

Silently James applauded too. The spirit of Miles's career, his tumultuous naïve ramshackle expedition through the American psyche touched him again as it had daily when Miles was alive. He missed not seeing a group of reporters in the corridor today. He missed the Brotherhood; and he felt very brave and uplifted because he was part of it and had helped to administer it. Not that the Brotherhood ever approached perfection. It had never succeeded in defining the meaning of life or doping out a clever survival manual for black people. That was what black people expected and it was foolish. They had always expected too much while evading the responsibilities of new burdens. But Miles had told them there were no certainties, only struggles; Miles had told them that hundreds of times and James remembered it now with great emotion. Like many people close to a deceased person James felt he suddenly understood the workings of everything Miles had said. But with this understanding came depression. (Once late at night Miles had called him in and wearily said, "Brother, truth is only made up of what destroys itself most completely as time goes by. Never seek truth.") For if Miles was almost a great man, James was woefully small. If Miles possessed intricate bravery, he was a sickening coward. At this moment James missed Miles desperately.

He felt the weight of an unknown fate was on him even though he'd survived everything up till now. A sly inevitability appeared to guide his steps. Still he was determined to go on, to protect himself, to survive. He refused to worry about Mahanti or Charles De Young. His mind focused only on Clarence, and confidence flowed into him. He could handle Clarence as easily as he had enemy soldiers in the war. He would glean from Clarence whatever knowledge he had and then toss him aside. For a minute a lot of the peculiar strength and power he had lived with in the war returned to James and refreshed him. A tough agitated sense of control rose in him as it always did when he entered a situation where he could take charge.

At last he reached the right house. Mounting the steps he found the front door open and was about to go in when suddenly a pack of small children burst thunderously from an apartment on the ground floor and ran by him, shouting and yelling shrilly. Two young women pursued them closely, angrily calling them back. The women eyed James for a moment with startled but delighted curiosity before dashing off to corral the excited children on the sidewalk. At the head of a flight of stairs on James's left a door opened tentatively and Williams called down to him. He negotiated the long, steep staircase cluttered with several dozen empty soda and liquor bottles left over from many of Clarence's discreet little supper parties. "Come in," Clarence said, his voice sounding almost as distant as it had at the bottom of the landing. James looked into his very thin smile distastefully and saw something strange in the tight corners of Clarence's mouth, something that told him merely to nod, to preserve a certain formality.

He stood now in the kitchen, a large, glossy room done up in horrible pink and black speckled with gold. Gleaming appliances reflected the grotesque checkered linoleum. Clarence, courtly in an expensive polo shirt and matching cardigan of cobalt blue, coolly motioned him into the living room and gestured for him to sit down in a big gaudy imitation leather chair, which could, he boasted, recline into seven positions. James slipped into his seat obediently and then gazed around with alert surprise. On the walls hung framed prints he recognized as impressionist. Two or three masterpieces of the Venetian school were displayed in pretentious gold-painted frames. But it was the furniture that amazed him to the point of embarrassed dismay. All of it was outsized, gigantic, and styled in the sweeping grotesque opulence specially drawn up to grace the homes of Puerto Rican bodega proprietors, flashy door-to-door salesmen, and Pullman porters just arrived at their first shaky plateau of gentility. James was astounded. None of this really seemed to match Clarence, not even in his most vulgar fantasies. He eyed one of the massive lamps standing on an end table like a crude and mysterious piece of primitive sculpture put into a secret jungle clearing. Vigilance was carefully rising in him now. He strove to conceal what he hoped was not acute uneasiness. He avoided Clarence's somewhat cocky stare as it measured his reactions to the place. Like someone caught in an awkward social position he stammered a bit and his voice, oddly light and stupid, divulged the depths of his amazement. "This is all quite something, Clarence. I'm not accustomed to all this finery," he admitted, angry at himself for sounding more gauche than Clarence usually did.

Clarence lingered in the doorway, caught in a furtive sporting pose. A faint patronizing expression tightened his lips. Finally he smiled. Yet this only revealed a nervousness in him, which showed some more as he mumbled something about getting cigarettes and abruptly left the room. James witnessed all this with disgust. On the telephone Clarence had been hesitant, now he was distant.

James felt a nervous tension fire in his stomach. He was determined never to see Clarence again after tonight, never to come back to this pompous little apartment proudly hidden away in the endless black slums of Brooklyn. Once more he examined the fantastic furniture set up all around him and his loathing of Clarence deepened. It occurred to him he'd always suspected Clarence lived this boorishly and this was why he and Beverly had never come out to see his new apartment. ("It's in a better house next door. The landlord and a decorator friend are fixing it up real nice for me," Clarence had bragged.) Yet James was sorry they hadn't accepted the invitation. An elusive instinct told him it might have saved a trip tonight.

Finally Clarence returned, puffing secretively on a cigarette. James could see he was trying to affect a certain sophisticated ease and this unabashed play acting irritated him. He found Clarence obnoxious because he acted as if he were in the presence of someone who offended his ostentation. He watched Clarence take a chair on the other side of the room and cross his legs primly.

"Now what's all the fuss about, James?" he asked moodily, not looking directly at his visitor.

"No fuss at all, Clarence," James replied, more than ever on guard as he observed Clarence putting on a pair of heavy dark-rimmed glasses. "I just wondered what Beverly told you about that man who came to see her."

Clarence stiffened. He put one leg over the arm of his chair and sat back uncomfortably. When Beverly called and said a government man was looking for James, he'd gone out and roamed the streets all night to suppress his terror and now it was gurgling up in him uncontrollably. "I don't really know too much, James," he replied, attempting to sound calm and confidential. His eyes roved uneasily about the room although with all the power in him he wanted to look at James squarely and convince him. "I guess you know she claims he was some kind of security investigator," he added hastily. With this he unsteadily got up and reached for a large ashtray on a near table. From the corner of his vision he saw James hungrily watching his every movement across the expanse of avocado carpet between them.

"What did he say to her?" James demanded, coolly exerting a bit more pressure against the reluctance that seemed to mold

252

every answer Clarence gave him. "Have you got any idea what he said to her?"

Clarence shrugged his shoulders. It was difficult to think. Guilt and fear were twisting a fine screw in him. He knew he needed all his wits to survive this confrontation, but a cruel apprehension ruled him instead. He was terrified of saying anything, fearing he might say too much. Still he had to give an answer. James was looking straight into him.

"I understand the man said you're in a lot of trouble." Again it came out a trifle too recklessly, in a flat resentful voice, and at the moment he heard his answer Clarence knew he'd given part of himself away. He knew his words contained too much accusation and not enough sympathetic description. Distrust made his voice echo. Yet he groped forward, trying to correct the mistake, trying to paraphrase what Beverly had said. But anxiety betrayed him and suddenly he stopped. For the first time since he'd entered the room, he looked at James directly and the coldness staring back at him made Clarence quickly resolve never to tell what he knew.

"She didn't tell me any more than that," he said carefully. "Talk to her. Talk to Bev. Don't talk to me about it." But here the unrepressible force in his swelling sensation of guilt propelled him on, and like a madman Clarence spoke far more than he was ready to say. "I wish I'd never gotten into this at all," he blurted out in real agonized frustration.

"Into what, Clarence?" James asked quickly, leaning forward, his eyes shining in anticipation.

"I wish to god I'd never gotten into anything in relation to you and your crazy Brotherhood or the government either," Clarence said even more quickly in a wild effort to conceal and slide over his turmoil.

James stared at him fiercely. Clarence knew more. He was certain of it.

Clarence fidgeted in his seat primly, attempting to act dignified and outraged. His stomach was in a cold boil. His back trembled. He tried to remember what Mr. Mahanti had said to

253

him that must not be repeated here. By some obscure telepathy he strained to duplicate the cool reasonable tones of his employer, but the effort played tricks with his shaky concentration and he wasn't ready when James shot another question at him.

"How come you're doing so well these days?" James repeated from across the room.

Clarence lifted his head slowly, fighting against the feverish, nearly explosive intensity that came off James. A distant impulse in his brain warned him not to speak, not to dare take the chance of uttering a single word. He glanced at the eyes burning at him from across the room. The question hung between them like a challenge to the death. James was set to ask it again when Clarence spoke, his voice spinning out its last reserves of stability.

"James, I'm very upset," Clarence began in a quailing murmur. "You got me very upset, buddy," he complained. "I invited you out here to my home and you come in sniffing and howling like a crazy man. It's not fair to me. Can't we talk about this later on, after you've gotten over Miles's death?" he almost pleaded. "I know a thing like that must be driving you half out of your mind."

An involuntary shudder went right through Clarence. Bravely he rose as if to show James out, but his guest didn't move. James simply stared ahead raptly, as though drawn into a dreadful absorption. A sardonic, crooked, exasperated smile touched upon his lips.

Then abruptly, acting on impulses that had circled through his brain in curious and ever-deepening swirls of trembling heat and crystal-clear presentiment, James leaped out of his chair and charged at Clarence, whose eyes grew immense and terrified behind his large glasses. Like two football players they tumbled to the carpet in a heavy tangle. Clarence, with lightning balance, emerged on top. A crisp, cruel frustration now free to operate told him to knock the fight out of James fast, and he clubbed his opponent brutally across the throat with a heavy forearm. His knee shot viciously to the groin. Clarence felt everything give easily before it as he watched James howl madly in pain and saw his back arching up only to quiver down again in submission. He got up angrily as James rolled over on one side, his mouth gaping open and issuing sounds of disbelief and agony.

"I asked you, I almost begged you to go away real quietly," Clarence cried, heaving slightly with exertion. He noticed a pleasant self-righteousness flowed into his voice.

James groaned or nodded, Clarence couldn't tell which. He raised himself up on one knee, glaring at the man staring over him. There was a strained bewilderment in his brain, but once again his fury was building up on top of it and James felt a little stronger. He sensed more strength as his wrath mounted swiftly upward, obliterating all thought and carrying along elements of hatred and emotions too numerous, too varied and intense for him to pinpoint or even care about. Suddenly, with a flashing whiplike movement Clarence never saw, he snared the legs towering above him and snapped them together. Clarence spun and fell instantly like a heavy book dropped off a table, but he was ready for more fighting. In a rage his legs lashed out, kicking James full in the face. Both men jackknifed away and flipped to their feet. Bent low they circled each other menacingly, looking keenly for the small advantage, the small indication of what would happen next. Heavy coarse breathing was the only sound in the room.

Clarence studied James intently. What he saw in the hard embittered panting face opposite was unleashed animal frenzy and a fiery hatred, which rushed into glinting pinpoints of light deep in those strange pale brown eyes. This stymied him a little, for he had brawled in the streets more often than he could remember and never before had such unrestrained intensity come into the battle. Those possessed, nearly opaque eyes, leveled at him with all the eerie malevolence of a rank wild beast, seemed the most wicked embodiment of everything he wanted to forget about his association with Mr. Mahanti— that secret bewildering, profitable, and illegitimate little pact, which had put suspicion in his mouth and squirming guilt into

255

every thought that came to him this evening.

He continued to circle around the room, but for the first time since James leaped at him something mechanical had come into Clarence's movements. Was he less sure because he knew a huge part of the hatred facing him was justified? The thought danced in his wavering mind and for a second too long Clarence dwelt on it and James struck. A stupendous numbing blow crashed into his jaw. A sweet, thick, salty taste flowed into his paralyzed mouth as blood gushed up freely over his lower lip and spilled down the side of his chin. He wiped at the blood fearfully. He backed away. Confusion enveloped him and James, sensing he could now take Clarence, moved in with startling swiftness.

The second blow to his face did not hurt much more than the first, but it dazed Clarence and his arms came down and suddenly a fury was on him. James stepped up, punching with the brutal speed and power of a heavyweight boxer, hitting so easily Clarence thought it was one fist and not two working in rapid combination that battered him. The fist began to pound, smash hard, and pound. It got heavier with each blow. It seemed to shut out the air and the room. Clarence couldn't breathe. He panicked, jerking his head this way and that, trying to avoid the terrible leaden blows. But his head began to slow down. He realized he was being hit in the body too. And then weirdly it came to him that he was actually being beaten to death. One agonized cry escaped from his bloodied mouth. Vaguely he heard a frenzied voice above and around him yelling questions, but he could only feel that James, in the middle of a fit of stark lunacy, wanted him broken and dead. He struggled to hear the shouting voice. Then with his last bare strength he pushed out at James and went down on one knee. A hard kick sprawled him limply on the carpet and he gasped desperately for breath. In one clear second out of a dozen filled with blinding pain, he heard James cry out once more, "Who pays you to live big?" Out of nowhere James savagely kicked him in the stomach three or four times. He began to crawl away. He had now seized the idea that he had something to tell that might stop this inhuman beating, an article of good value to trade for a respite from this agony. But in the same process an irrational association went through his beleaguered mind. If James was used somehow, why not him too? Had Mahanti ever envisioned this scene? Clarence wondered, as a new horror closed in on him and he realized how much that was inconsequential about Mahanti he really knew. It was too much. Timorously he saw it was all too little and too much. He could identify the man down to his suede gloves, but possessed not a glimmering of his real origins. Uncannily everything Mahanti emphasized—his name, title, manners, foreignness—all these things went well in a confession. Even the money had been excessive. Mahanti had insisted on enriching him, had played soothingly on his vain need for large funds, for luxuries; and now Clarence saw wearily the whole experience was an amalgam of pathos, condescension, and arcane deceptions. He felt empty, as if he'd been badly fooled by a magician. His aching body and besieged senses informed him that only the mean art of cunning separated him from violent death.

James started to come for him again and Clarence spun awkwardly over the carpet away from his grasp. The sickening idea that James would smash him to death before he could say anything more sent a flash of horror through his quaking body. His mind was a little clearer now and Clarence wanted to get up, but the massive weight of dismay and fatigue pinned him to the thick carpet. With a bitter surge of anger he felt some weak, damaged strain in his imagination had already accepted at least total humiliation, and everything else in him rallied to battle this sensation furiously. Up out of the center of his taut anxiety and the numerous racking fears of the pain James could still inflict, Clarence was taken by an overpowering outrage at what was happening to him there in his own home, in the middle of everything he'd ever hoped for; and a stuttering rage at his embarrassment and helplessness whipped his thoughts on. The numbing mist of physical shock floated in and out of his brain once more before subsiding. In its place came the sharp urges of revenge. Hatred of James and a whimpering malignant rage at his own weakness worked in and among each other to give Clarence a new strength, the thin muscular persistent force to raise his exhausted body. Slowly he struggled to one knee and got unsteadily to his feet, believing not even another kick or violent onslaught would put him down again.

He stared moodily at James, backing away at the same time, searching behind him with extended fingers for something to pick up and fling at the sullen, anguished mute face whose vision, nearly tawny-eyed and beastly, commanded the entire room like the broad beam from a solitary lighthouse. A tremendous loathing skittered through Clarence. In his hideous desperation he detested James more than ever. Pure malice took over his reason. He would cripple James for this evening, maim his manhood, mutilate that powerful physical presence taking up the room, blotting out his safe little home. Clarence decided with the atomized berserk speed of true hatred to grasp James by the head and force him to look into his own despair until his brain erupted. But already his tongue was speaking these thoughts and it was terrible.

"So who do I work for, James? Who pays me, buddy? Is that what you want to know? Huh?" Clarence cried in a mocking, vindictive, nearly hysterical voice. "I'll tell you about it, friend, because I work for a man who has done you a big favor," Clarence shouted, shaking one trembling finger at James. "One tremendous favor. For the first time in your life, you've got a woman to call your own, right, James? Well, you owe it all to this man."

James blinked in amazement. His arms, which had been up in a sort of boxer's guard, dropped to his waist. His eyes closed, as if he were trying to erase a painful headache; and when they opened again, Clarence could see a terrifying blankness. James looked like a child with a premonition of tears and this inspired Clarence. His petty outrage was working wonders. And he went on about Beverly, telling how she was a paid professional prostitute set up richly in a red-and-black velvet jewel-box room in a whorehouse so expensive only the richest men in New York ever dared to show their faces at the unmarked door. But if they got inside, everything was paradise. There were no windows anywhere and the atmosphere was carnal. Each room was littered with expensive clothes like an animal cage. And the girls just closed the doors and took it off and played trick after trick most girls would never play until this house (set up by a society moneyman from Lebanon) was opened and publicized secretly in the high-class clubs and bars where big salaried executives went to drink. Almost every man who went to this house wanted Beverly, Clarence yelled at James through his darkened and blood-stained teeth. They loved her. They stood in line for her. She was big, a famous whore, the lowest thing on this earth. But she was good, a real acrobat, a hard hustler, a fiend for all of it. She rode men down to exhaustion. And now, without ever knowing or caring about the admirer who left her just enough money to get out on her own, she was completely his, Clarence screamed. She was his and the funny thing was he cherished her over all other women. He adored and cherished her, especially over her friend Claire who worked in a department store and slept alone on clean sheets every night. "She sold it, friend, couldn't you tell?" Clarence shouted in his frenzy. "Sold it for a lot of money. More money than you've ever had in one night." He no longer watched James. He was too sure for that, and like a skilled hunter he fired bigger and bigger charges at his quarry. He ranted, mixing imagination with maddened spite so fast he could not have seen James move like a shadow across the pale green carpet and with one mighty effortless blow swat him into a heap.

Everything in the room flew away from Clarence at varying speeds, sailing freely like objects seen from a merry-go-round. The big color television set appeared to be falling on him. The heavy brocade drapes descended on him with a roar. Briefly he drifted in and out of consciousness. He was in a chair with no idea how he got there. James was somewhere over him again, as he always seemed to be hovering above him this horrible evening. And Clarence heard his harsh tortured bewildered breathing. This time there were no questions, nothing. James simply looked down at the veiled, rather dazed face in the chair and felt nothing but rigid numbness. Clarence sensed death. He heard his fate overtaking him, moving to punish him for his smallness, his trifling, hideously self-important, and stupid little crimes. Something warned him James was just waiting for the moment, letting his strength flow back before he killed; and in all his terror of death Clarence wished for life. But in a humble secret way, for he could not dare to let James see any of this in his face or movements. Yet Clarence hoped against everything James would spare him. He didn't want to die like a cheap criminal. He didn't want to be discovered heaped melodramatically in his living room with all the life pummeled out of him. Clarence couldn't stand the idea of being a murder victim because it was wrong, indecorous and wrong, tawdry in a fashion that suggested he was always much less than what people took him for. Murder equaled impropriety, lowness, hustling, and Clarence despised those things so he began to speak to James again, rapidly as he had before, but without any sharpness or recrimination.

His tone was urgent, but he struggled not to plead. With some coolness and a faint dignity he sought to explain his minuscule part in a drama he possessed no real knowledge of. He began to relate everything about Mahanti, how Mahanti wanted both of them to stay in the house for at least an hour. But suddenly none of this made sense and Clarence scrambled to get back to the beginning of his story, to tell it right and straight through. Then his jabbering began. In his desperation Clarence pressed his memory too hard and got the sequence wrong. Confused by his stupidity he couldn't seem, no matter where he began, to tell James danger was near and about to take him, to suffocate what was left of his life. Clarence tried. He stopped for a moment. He went back to the evening before. Mahanti came, rang on the bell long and hard as he did the first time, and he was very nasty. He wanted a special job done. They argued because ever since the last job the fear had been almost too much to live with, but Mahanti cursed and demanded like a born aristocrat. He threatened to inform the police and said there would be other reprisals. Here Clarence noticed all during what he said James showed no reaction, but he kept at it, he blamed his own jumbled and agitated speech. He'd given in last night. Then Mahanti switched and became friendly. He paid for the job with a lot of money Clarence said he was afraid to accept. After that he acted like he didn't want to go. He sat down in the kitchen and told a tale that was so wild, so evil nobody could ever believe it. "He said you're a Communist fanatic and you plotted to kill Miles and take over the Brotherhood," Clarence shouted out of his despair. "I didn't believe it, but that's what he said," Clarence protested as James's face began to drain from impassivity into a bleak dreamy despondency. He watched amazed as James put his hands over his ears, fast. It was sad and disarmingly weird, like James now shouting at him was very weird because it all seemed far away, a tiny sound dim in his embattled brain. He feared not a word really got through his own jabbering and protests, not one of the important things he was telling James. And Clarence was going out of his mind talking and watching James not listening that way. He had no idea what made him continue. But his voice nearly ranted with all he would tell. There was proof to support Mahanti, he cried. In the apartment he thought no one knew about, documents were hidden —passports, photographs, identification papers, and the money for the assassin who was killed—all waiting to be found by government men and the police. Every bit of it added up right, Clarence shouted at James as he witnessed a bewilderment and terrible confusion mangle the somber face above him. Interminable seconds of swift time shot through him. His enervated body seemed to float miserably. He could not believe the whole insane whirl of what he'd told James in those morbid and clenched moments just passed. Yet he kept on. He desperately urged James to flee. Mahanti knew he was in the house right now because he'd called Mahanti and alerted him. That was to be the final job. That is what he was paid for. There would not be much time now. No one could tell what

261

Mahanti might do next. He never said which side he was on anyway, Clarence added hopefully before rambling on about his own plan to vanish from the city tonight. But Clarence was so far into his confession, so dazed and worn that he could not have grasped the change that came into James right then. The utter, pitiless frustration wrinkling James's face did not communicate itself to him fully and so his death was easy.

In the middle of his stammerings a karate fist swiftly came down on Clarence, landing with the absolute finality of a guillotine. The blow struck him in the neck, alongside the Adam's apple, causing a momentary convulsion. Then it fell again like deadweight and Clarence's head flopped over hopelessly to one side. His eyes opened wide and fluttered closed heavily. His breath streamed out in a low hiss. He had died.

Sullenly James contemplated Clarence's face, beady with sweat, puffy, savagely bruised, and as inert as a billiard ball, trying out of a vague curiosity to fathom why it would never again sustain another expression. He examined the thick trickle of blood coming from one corner of the dead man's mouth and saw identical masses of it congealed to the bright fabric of the chair, but it meant nothing. Unexpectedly he discovered his own fatigue. From within his whole body seemed to sag in exhaustion. There was pain shooting up both his arms and the fist he'd bludgeoned Clarence with was already swelling and bruised. He was sure there were broken bones in it cutting into the tissue, and in this acute awareness his head gradually cleared.

A freshness of vision came over his weary eyes. Colors appeared brighter, deeper, less muted. James found himself guessing how long he'd been standing there over Clarence's body. Could it be just minutes or had hours lapsed? He fought to remember but his mind cringed at the effort and quickly James looked away from Clarence. But it was too late, for a smoldering and vivid recollection of what Clarence said came up at him. And for five or ten fiery seconds the whole experience surrounded James again. The terrific urges and tensions and fine cold energies, which ripped and tore at every cell in his brain, swamped him once more. He wanted to scream. His head echoed with the hard full whack of his fist on Clarence's neck. He felt something slump forever in his victim. And as he remembered Beverly his head was full to bursting. Frantically he sought to get back into his hysteria and murder Clarence over and over again; but then in a surprising turn he was much too tired. A mood of agitated reflection had come over him.

Slowly James strode out of the living room, leaving Clarence twisted in his chair, attempting to fend off a blow that had already fallen. A giddy and ruthless clarity began to control him. Strangely he felt free and relaxed, as if he'd never known anxiety. He was sure a soothing, purifying spirit had come into him and exorcised his former inadequacies. The shadow of fate seemed to no longer fall on him. Clarence's death brought him gratification, but he could not really explain why. Momentarily he didn't want to. He wanted only to luxuriate in the vision of freedom that appeared to spread magically from his body to push back the four corners of the room. Aimlessly he wandered in and out of several rooms, touching objects to be certain he wasn't imagining them. His light-headedness grew more vivid and it began to trouble James. He was too at ease. His relaxation seemed indolent and excessive. He wondered indecisively if he were not just pleased because a witness against him was dead. This was more logical than personal inspiration and spiritual poignance. It was more substantial than purification and all the other misty feelings that played over him now and were beginning to wane.

He saw, not without a touch of softly obliterating anger, that Mahanti had given him Beverly. But the familiar surges of hatred and loathing did not seize him. He continued to move about the apartment, his thoughts divided between tears and a complex of undiscernible emotions. He wanted to feel murderous and titanic but the energy was not there. He worried about Beverly's safety and protection with a warm and new realization that she was just a victim. If he had openly disobeyed Mahanti, he would have threatened to have her killed. She was a hostage meant to please him but her innocence was a hook in his mouth. Still he was driven to recreate their succulent affection and her beautiful attempts to soothe and calm his life. James drove himself to find this mood, yet he was afraid something sickening and tawdry blemished her now. He was a little afraid of Beverly.

An empty terror closed in on James and he refused to think anymore. A revolting sensation of being violated nipped at his insides subtly. The unreal truth of everything Clarence told him made his nerves sag. He felt hollow and miserably alone, totally controlled and manned by huge impersonal workings far beyond him. The devious and arcane motives of the ministry, large secret reserves of money and seemingly contradictory orders from Peking, doctrines written out clumsily on a blackboard, all these things appeared to direct his existence. A wise contemplative sense of despair claimed him as James dredged up all the bitter twists of betrayal in each move he'd made, for at last he understood completely that he'd been groomed to be caught and exposed from the very beginning. His ulterior manifest function (a term favored by ministry lecturers) was to be pounced on like a wild and crazed jackrabbit; and once safely penned up, disclosed to the anxious American public, the television people who knew him, the slick pious reporters and newspaper prophets, as the central figure in a Chinese Communist plot to take over the Brotherhood, as the despicable and bastard heir to the tarnished and broken crown of Miles King.

Lucidly James saw he was now all of that. The ministry had won, triumphed with contemptuous ease over the unsure ravings of his will, against the fierce quicksilver turns and twists of his tumultuous vacillating spirit and all the unremembered yearnings that lay beyond it. They had used his failures and inadequacies to totally destroy him. They had allowed his own spiritual ineptitude and psychic cowardice to seduce him into the absurd role of perpetrating a shabby but notorious murder. Now he would have to bear the hysterical turmoil of knowing every nuance of his betrayal.

The shock of this discovery made him start a little. But his

264

thoughts did not labor through labyrinthine processes to escape this conclusion. James saw the opening of reality quite clearly. He saw himself before the ruthless television cameras: manacled, overdressed but unshaven, physically worn, pale under the stifling lights, essentially frightened, and telling the long sad familiar story of the deluded zealot, granting the whole fantastic episode the correct twitching little touches of madness, a weird involuntary roll of the eyeballs, a pathetic lurch in being guided away, a thick patina of human interest. This is what the ministry wanted. They planned for him to be apprehended in this apartment, jailed, left to thrash in his own agony until he collapsed under the strain and sought revenge against the ministry by telling every detail of the plot, by revealing how he was used, by whispering an exclusive in every ear. This subject will parade the arch complexities of his lost years among the Chinese, some official in Bern probably concluded. And he will give the assassination of Miles King a new withering reality and many twists, perhaps a television special, certainly a heightened madness it could never pretend to by itself. But the details must be right James saw, so perfect as to be cliché. The evidence in his unused apartment, the manner of his arrest and confession (double murder would now back his words), all of this should be tinged with recognizable melodrama, for here was an ingredient to start ordinary minds churning.

Hastily James realized most Americans would only half believe his story; and a wispy sadness touched him lightly until he grasped part of the meaning of this public doubt, until he envisioned what chaos his self-destructive confession might bring on. Liberals would attempt to defend him without understanding his predicament and that could be dangerous. Most everyone would be outraged that he existed without exposure for so many years. His confession could be seen as a prelude to something truly awful, perhaps a war or some kind of destructive black conspiracy. He and Miles would be linked hysterically and reviled throughout the country until their names became shibboleths for what could happen to white people without a period of repression. From then on half-instinctive atavistic re-actions would take over: night-riding cars bristling with rifles would careen through black areas; open bigotry would soar in the opinion polls. And all this would surely provoke devastating black reprisals, block long fires in shopping centers, systematized looting, solemn presidential appeals to reason followed by a new surge of chaos. Finally troops would intervene, crack units only, strolling menacingly through a bleak smoldering landscape. The ministry would cheerfully play upon this upheaval with fiery accusations, huge parades, and lengthy speeches, angry as never before. As blacks were shot down by soldiers the ministry would warn Africa and Asia against the white man.

But not least in all this activity would be the great contemptuous pity for him. In the Islamic world he would be despised for allowing the destruction of his leader and his brother to take place. Privately all Moslems would want to spit on his hands with scorn, but before the world they would drearily defend him because of his religion. Blacks would denounce him as a liar and a scapegoat and pity him. But now James was thinking about how the ministry would phrase its compassion for his plight. He imagined the sound of the message, its faintly derisive tone and its official slightly stilted timbre. ("This poor unfortunate black man has been selected to bear the collective guilt of white people. He deserves nothing less than a cry of support from every quarter of the globe.") Of course he would be described as the first in a long line of black scapegoats to follow the trail of Miles King. After that essential point the ministry would turn to melodrama again. Brother James would be pitied all over again as a victim of gangster tactics and physical torture, a sad little nonentity seized upon because he was close to a great man.

And all of this had the chary truth of suspicion to support it, for the story James had to tell was much too pat, much too smoothly improbable to be completely acceptable anywhere. James knew exactly how the ministry would exploit this, how they would then slyly point to the lack of motivation in his crime. He understood with cutting precision how they were all set to deride whatever pitiful excuse he gave for acquiescence in a Communist plot to kill his mentor. He saw and heard how they would maul and twist the confession they had broken him into. And James discerned each of these steps with an absolute premonition of horror because he was helpless to prevent them. He could not save himself or put down all the lurking impersonal race hatreds in America before they flared into a raging, explosive atmosphere of seething abhorrence, before they insinuated themselves into every conversation and even the most casual encounters, to rule the country with a stuttering vile tension it would take decades to break. His confession, James understood, was merely the beginning. He did not know what else the ministry planned.

Absently he drifted into the kitchen and stared up at the pink-and-black wall clock molded into the shape of a tea kettle. Twenty-five minutes had disappeared since he entered the apartment and it felt like a day. Still the noiseless electric clock moved on. James fixed his eyes on the hour hand and waited for it to move. The minute hand swept by once, then again, and James looked away. He sat down hulkingly at the glass-topped kitchen table and gazed into the garish pink-and-black linoleum floor. He was consumed with a sense of his own obliteration.

Like a paralyzed laboratory animal he dared not move because he was afraid of what the effort might do to him. But unexpectedly his mind was plunging ahead once more, surging in a current mixed with quiescent indignation and restrained lassitude. He did not feel less obliterated, yet every faculty in him that was highly bred, sensitive, nervous, and intensely personal began to ruminate for him, began to turn spiritually against the ministry. James realized quite slowly and painfully that the end to this obliterating experience, the end to his future was still unknown because nothing had really happened yet, nothing had occurred to give the ministry its ingeniously easy triumph. He was still in transition from his past to his fate even though each second now diminished him and made him more of a slave to other people's expectations. And all of this riled him in a dispassionate way he could not control. A quiet loathing forced him to shut out the suggestion that anyone knew him better than himself, that anyone had stolen or manipulated the qualities in him that were unique and irreplaceable. A surge of vague defiance passed through James. He despised what people were ready to make of him. He hated the ministry's presumptions in warping a man and then employing his defects to show he could not change. He wanted rather helplessly to change, to defy and thwart the ministry for what they planned to do with him. Imprecisely but strongly it came to James that rebellion against the ministry could make him a more authentic and purer individual than he'd ever been before.

Yet it seemed so foolish, so unattainable now. Everything had happened the precise way they'd planned it and James could not envision how it all could be overturned, but he was driven to make an attempt. He was subtly impelled to challenge and destroy the idea of what he'd become. He did not want to die confused, alone, and misunderstood. James could not accept the idea of becoming less human, and he swore in a feeble tormented moment that he would denounce the ministry and reveal the true meaning of everything that had happened. He would show the world how devious and ambitious the Chinese really were and at the same time avert all the agony they'd formulated.

He was determined to reshape his spirit meaningfully; although he was not completely sure of what this entailed James was unwavering in his conviction to do it. And this unlikely appearance of a cool, passionate resolve made him feel stronger and more alert than ever. A heightened awareness of confidence swirled through him because he grasped that his desire to thwart and baffle the ministry would grant him fresh knowledge of the best things in himself, all the qualities the ministry never believed he could use. Still he knew the ministry might succeed if he did not act quickly. Nominally, in spite of his yearning to obstruct the chaos the Chinese had assiduously calculated, James remained in their control. He had done nothing to show them their hold was broken, but he wanted a few more minutes of reflection. Mysteriously James knew it would be a very long time before he had any real privacy again. He felt all the portentousness of what he was about to try; without passion he understood the minute nuances of audacity in his rebellion and it frightened him a little through his courage, for there were so many detached and disheartening paradoxes still to be faced.

This strange offering of hope and salvation had only come to him out of two ghastly and needless deaths. Miles had been systematically and viciously riddled and just as his brain must have exploded with shock and agony he died. Now he was hidden away beneath the ground. Soon he might be forgotten. Poor Clarence sat up dead in a chair with cooling blood stopped in his veins. And even now in the freshness and clarity of this new, almost spiritual resolve, a stale feeling of corruption and decadence crept into James. He was convinced that everything he touched withered away and died. Any human contact he experienced seemed twisted and degraded. He blamed himself for accepting Beverly's affection and even felt a twinge of pity for Charles De Young, whose life must be swamped in such contradictions. They were victims like him.

But James refused to be a victim anymore. He knew there had been too many black victims in the world already. And the blacks who were to riot and pillage in his support were the most victimized of all. Because of the pervasive antipathy controlling their drab lives, a foreign power had appealed to their misery with a bright, clever trick and this sickened James. He understood the vile condescension behind this artifice, and this knowledge gave a sudden spurt to his passive but moiling indignation. A sensation of largeness and importance touched him. In the deepest recesses of his mind, James concluded that his life might contain a striking portent of some kind for black people and perhaps all humanity. It sounded fantastic but the notion soothed his icy malignant contempt for the ministry; it allowed him to see all over again the evilly bland absence of

Chinese interest or conviction in the plight of the black man. It made him vow to destroy anything this inhuman.

Suddenly, in a rush of contained bitterness, he thought of Siato far back on the other side of his life. Then Mahanti's sneering face appeared to him as elusively as it would in a vision and he could barely control his rage at the guileful skill Mahanti had exercised in using Clarence. Mahanti had thought out every contingency quite assiduously. Probably he was not even surprised when Clarence called and said he was coming to the apartment. All along, James perceived, Mahanti knew he didn't believe in the ministry, not that they would have spared him if he had. And Mahanti was right, as always. He'd artfully used everything the ministry had in its Fitzgerald dossier, his constant and inspired vacillation, his morbidity, even the brief and superficial violence of their fist fight, to coax him into a position where he could obliterate himself effectively.

Here rather quickly James got up and went into Clarence's bedroom where he stared about nervously. He felt driven now by a foreboding that his chances for vindication might vanish if he did not leave this house at once. Yet the impulse to rethink everything that had gone through his mind and steeled him in the last few minutes pulled at James, but he did not give into it. Without consciously forming the suggestion, he knew that a complete record of his life, his piddling intrigues and abysmal shortcomings had to be recorded. He wanted this with a sharp, fierce desperation that seethed in him. He wanted it for Miles and for the Brotherhood and for the excluded black people of the nation. Only such a record could forever confirm his rebellion and give it complete validity no matter what happened to him.

The overmastering urge to talk, explain and interpret himself, to reveal what the ministry hoped to gain in killing Miles held back his desire to flee. And James wondered what was happening to him. It flashed through his mind that Mahanti knew he was here, and like an animal he scented danger. He ran from window to window staring at strange innocent figures down in the street. Then in a scramble he headed for the front door, but a new fresh sense of peril made him walk very lightly and then stop short. What sounded like a police siren seemed to moan closer and closer, twisting evilly through the dilapidated neighborhood. Gripping the windowsill he looked out into the street again, but there were no cars anywhere. Still he was terribly afraid he would not survive to tell his story and the thought made him tremble.

The urgency of escaping rose dramatically in him once more, but James could not respond to it. He had to force himself to set off through the apartment searching for a back door or a window near a drainpipe he could climb down. He was more calm now, and much more confident of a decision that was implicit in his effort to thwart the ministry. He knew he would seek out the anonymous white man who had come to see Beverly and Miles. He was sure this man would understand his predicament and do everything to help. He was a link to hope and so many other things James dared not think about now. Probably he was the opposite of Mahanti. And yet a strong reluctance took hold of James. He could not have explained it even in his most lucid moments. His fear of entrapment in the ministry plan was intense, but clouding it was a swift sudden fear of the naked realization that he would have to approach Charles De Young to contact this man who must already know so much about the intricacies and depths of his experiences. All of his hatred and mistrust of De Young welled to the surface and confronted him hideously. He knew in some way De Young was probably a degraded soul like him, and there was no telling what if anything the assassination had done to him. He might be subtly righteous, perhaps vicious, maybe even violent. And he might refuse to help. James was stunned by the tormenting irony of having to face De Young at this attenuated and momentous instant in his life, but there was nothing else he could do. He had to make his way to the hall and begin looking for De Young before he vanished with the many Brothers who were certain to drift slyly away from the Brotherhood now that it was dead.

For the last time he went into the living room again and looked quietly at Clarence, whose cobalt blue polo shirt and cardigan were ripped and askew. The expensive suede loafers he wore were nowhere to be seen and his beautiful golf slacks were torn badly. His facial skin seemed to be getting darker and dimly ashen. All the joviality, subterfuge, witless charm, and laughable pretension Clarence indulged in so happily had sunk into the inflexible deadened muscles of his face. He had assumed the forlornness of the dead.

In a corner of the kitchen James discovered a door leading to a back porch where Clarence kept the garbage cans. Outside the air was light with a subtle trace of spring velvet. James looked over the huddled backyards overgrown with the sweeping green fronds of rampant weeds and wondered in a soft melancholy turn if he were not going to die soon. Almost immediately the thought was lost in the welter of things James knew he had to say before any fate took him. And with this assurance he made his way down a rickety flight of stairs to the dark yard below, slipped through an empty space in the weathered board fence, and disappeared in the lane between two blocks of houses.

CHAPTER TWENTY-ONE

IN HIGH GEAR Charles De Young's big brightly polished Chevrolet sports coupe sped up the West Side Highway with all the windows tightly rolled up and the air-conditioner running full blast. In the driver's seat De Young sat straight up and tense, his eyes glaring at the black asphalt road disappearing beneath the car so fast it looked rubbery and suspended, like a very swift conveyor belt. On the wheel his hands perspired and occasionally slipped a notch or two despite the tight, almost frantic grip he maintained. Never once did he turn to Austin Lake, who was sitting quietly beside him.

The car raced on, traveling ten and sometimes fifteen miles over the speed limit, changing lanes abruptly in the sluggish early morning traffic that had just begun to thicken; always pressing on for the clear stretch of road, the extra length of running room. Inside the only sound was the pleasant deep-pitched radio voice coming through stereo speakers with a morning roundup of important news. The cool, nearly imperious voice in the car with the two men was reviewing some of the racial violence resulting from the death of Miles King and the worldwide leftist attempt to make him a significant martyr. In southern Indiana the Ku Klux Klan had mobilized and fought an all-night set-piece battle with black residents in an isolated small town. Black youths in Milwaukee went on a brief looting and burning spree before twenty-five were arrested. Alert police forces in three cities just managed to prevent rioting, but in Birmingham, Alabama, a young white boy was found with the back of his head blown off and the talk in that city was of cold mass vengeance at nightfall. In New York, at the United Nations a flock of querulous African delegates were planning a filibuster in the General Assembly to be followed by a three-day strike of all Afro-Asian representatives and their staffs. Abroad the news was no better. Rain in London prevented a torchlight memorial parade now rescheduled with thousands of jobless Indians and Pakistanis to join the agitated West Indian community. Over this tumult the shrill invective of Chinese propaganda urged the protests on in the harsh clever relentless language of violent retribution. Most Americans were apprehensive, suspicious and overtly hostile to the baffling and repugnant news seeping in from all over the world. Monstrously the death of Miles King had swollen into something pervasive and revolting, something most people could not bring themselves to discuss or even describe. The only thing to do was wait for an end to the crisis, and most national political observers said this would happen in about three days. Until then time seemed to pass unnaturally for most people, the languid turnover of hours seemed to induce a touch of angry despondency, an irritable yearning for rest and the safety of a calm routine.

Directing his gaze out onto the road, De Young tried to forget how tired he was, tried to dismiss his longing for sleep and a clear untroubled mind. His attention preyed on the stray wisps of early morning fog blowing in off the sullen, choppy Hudson River, and suddenly he felt light-headed and blank with weariness. Also he was frightened and filled with timid disgust. Since the assassination a nameless but acute aversion for everything around him had worked through his body acidly and thickly like pus escaping from a huge internal abscess. Any thought of James released an overpowering fury in him.

274

But he felt an almost equal abhorrence for the agency, and his job, and for Austin Lake.

With a practiced sideways glance he spied on Lake who sat on the front seat loosely, as if hopelessly weakened by the onset of total exhaustion. He noticed the cutting lines of fatigue in the other man's tanned neck and face, and this pleased him, but not enough. No shared difficulties, no sense of desperation or common fear of the agency were enough to placate De Young. He was bitterly weary of Austin Lake, fatigued by the sight of the man.

The sources of his antipathy were peculiarly clear to De Young. He knew they had failed together. He could trace every nuance of their pointless relationship, each and every shallow smart-ass conversation they'd had about Miles and James. All of their amateur stratagems were fresh in his mind, yet recalling these incidents only pushed De Young deeper into furious despair, only made him want to open the car door and shove Lake into the head-snapping ripping brutal grip of centrifugal forces that would carry him a few yards and then splay his stricken body against the unyielding asphalt with a casual momentum forceful enough to split all his bones. De Young knew the oppressive secrecy of this assignment, the need always to play a careful covert part in circumstances that became increasingly ludicrous, was driving him mad. For the first time in his life he'd become reticent and consistently anxious. He felt like a convict assigned to a cell with a man he loathed.

He started to say something to Lake, but he realized it would be just another inane remark and he remained silent. He was rattled and worn-out. He glanced at Lake again, at the absorbed and tired form beside him on the seat, and wondered if Lake really cared at all what he had to say, if Lake had ever cared. He reduced his speed, following the needle carefully as it fell back. Up ahead more cars were pouring onto the highway from a clogged side entrance. The slowness of their maneuvers infuriated him. And his mind played indignantly over the long, deadening night they'd both just gone through. Warily he was certain this night had ushered in a period of finality for them, but he did not know what conclusion to expect. It was all so precipitous and omnipresent, so vague and oily that it came apart in his mind. He cursed himself for answering the phone when it awakened him a little after midnight, ringing loudly, irritably, through his small yet luxurious bachelor apartment as he tried to lose himself in a swoon of deep sleep. Only an hour before he'd arrived home with the shock and exhaustion of the funeral standing out in the harsh strain masking his face. After a long bath and three double drinks he was still fumbling with the realization that he was close to ruin and Miles was gone forever. No attempt at cerebral or intellectual control could hide the fact from him. De Young could not stave off his apprehensions. Painfully he recalled the heavy, mournful way they lowered Miles into his grave. The overtones of unrestrained emotion and willing primitiveness frightened him. And the final scene of the Brothers and Sisters streaming away in tears over the lawns and hillocks of the big green cemetery would not fade from his mind. Now quite suddenly he had to contend with Lake and all his childish uncertainties. Over the phone Lake's voice was clear, intelligent, and reasonable as always, but he was unmistakably tired. He apologized twice for the call at the outset. It was not his fault. The director, phoning from his home in Washington, had roused him with some disturbing news. Clarence Williams was dead. His body was discovered by the police. They were to proceed to police headquarters and contact a liaison man with a section called the Bureau of Special Operations. Neighbors had identified half a dozen photographs of James as the last person in the apartment before the homicide. James must be apprehended and questioned under optimum conditions, the director said. He did not have to add this was a demand.

Astonished, De Young put down the receiver, dressed himself hurriedly, and went out into the night unsure he would ever return. Lake waited outside the baroque headquarters building, and bravely they went in and asked for BSO. After a five-minute wait, Lieutenant Hegan, the night liaison officer appeared. Without saying a word, he motioned for them to follow. They went down to an office on the basement level paneled in heavy dark wood and Hegan sullenly closed the door, as if he were both angry and totally in charge. De Young noticed he was a youngish stout man with small petulant dainty features. His shapeless sport jacket was cheap and soiled. As he listened to the man, Lake felt uncomfortable. He could tell Hegan had taken police science and sociology, and fancied himself an enlightened cop; but this observation only increased Lake's agitation and scorn.

For ten minutes Hegan talked on in his sonorous runaway Irish lilt, knowing even before he got into his briefing that it was superficial, a fascinating but meaningless set of facts only the taut men in front of him could put together. What he was doing was like passing someone a code. But he presented his deceptively simple story quite well. After the assassination of Miles King, BSO was contacted by a security agency in Washington whose name the department withheld from him. This agency requested BSO put Beverly Carter and Clarence Williams under twenty-four hour surveillance to insure they did not leave the city of New York. When the name Clarence Williams came in on the Brooklyn homicide sheet, BSO was notified and someone high up in the department called Washington, where they made the request that some photographs of a male Negro sent up by telecopier be shown to the neighbors. Fifteen minutes after that, an anonymous tip was phoned in saying one James Fitzgerald, who was now at the Williams's address, was the man who plotted the assassination of Miles King. The caller gave a Harlem address where evidence to this effect had been hidden by the suspect. This additional information was relayed to the people in Washington, who said two gentlemen from its agency would be over.

"Mysterious, the whole thing is," Hegan said to them with obvious curiosity. "I mean the way that boy Miles King was shot down while he was speaking to his own buddies. And this boy they found dead tonight had no record. Homicide checked it out. He was clean. No stealing, nothing on the books, although you can bet he was up to something. They always are, these boys with the fancy apartments, and he lived like a dandy they tell me. Posh. It doesn't matter though. We bring them in every day, on dope, numbers, and especially prostitution, these fancy boys. They lean to crime, the elegant ones. Enjoy all of it. The prisons are filled with boys who had fancy apartments."

At the Harlem address, a worn-out brownstone shabby even in the dark, they drifted into an elusory brilliant calm, which tantalizingly seemed to contain the taut energy of a pulsating intermittent suspense about to shatter horribly. Every light in the house was on, but there was no noise, there were no sounds that betrayed even the most secretive human activity, just an enigmatic breath of tension without a real source. As they entered the vestibule, a uniformed policeman appeared from the brightly lit parlor room near the door and pointed up into the stairs, into a tangle of weird shadows and glaring light. "The top floor rear, sir. They're waiting for you." Passing the opened parlor door both men briefly studied the gray-haired old black woman sitting primly in a straight-back chair, her dark withered hands somewhere in her lap and indistinguishable from the blackness of the genteel suit she wore. Opposite her two burly policemen shared a small, tufted Victorian couch like a brace of bulldogs holding a frightened pheasant at bay.

The carpeting on the stairs was worn down to a tangle of threads and matting. And under each door on the second and third floors, Lake and De Young noticed strong light slanting out onto the splintered boards of the hallway. But the people on the other side of those doors were utterly silent, cautious and tensely silent with anxiety until the mysterious movement of feet could be heard moving up to another landing. In the top floor apartment they found three detectives, all large men with crew cuts, thick through the shoulders in their dark suits and iridescent raincoats. Two of them came forward, while the third man remained back, standing under the naked ceiling bulb where his expansive white shirt made him resemble an enormous penguin.

"We've got some pretty strange stuff here," one of the detectives said after stiffly introducing all three. "It's very strange. We don't know yet what it means," he added a little plaintively.

Lake and De Young went over to the big Victorian desk pushed against the wall, close to where the third detective was standing. On top of it was a very large battered leather suitcase with frayed straps. The evidence against James was inside and it was very complete. With a mounting sensation of dismay and embarrassed pity, they went through all of it. Lake cataloged each item in a small pocket notebook as De Young pulled it out and identified it. Three passports were in the suitcase. The first was British, claiming James was a Jamaican. Another came from the Republic of the Sudan, and the last was from Portugese Angola; it contained the small pale green identification card carried by all black natives. The sight of it sickened De Young. There were at least two dozen photographs of James, most of them taken in the streets of Bern showing him in the company of Chinese. Lake quietly said some of them were stills taken from training films. A formal identification photograph of James was included with bold Chinese calligraphy running down the right side. In a fat unsealed envelope De Young found Chinese Foreign Ministry microfilms of their complete Fitzgerald file containing hundreds of brief reports on the state of clandestine Negro activities in America signed by James. When he showed it to Lake, their eyes met with unabashed alarm. Both men prayed these were forgeries. On the bottom of the suitcase, under a big opened brown paper parcel of United States currency, De Young came across a Polaroid snapshot of James coming out of the Swiss bank building in Rockefeller Center carrying an airlines bag. He handed it over to Austin Lake who nodded his head grimly and gave it back. De Young lifted the carelessly torn open package of money out of the suitcase and this seemed to be a signal because the three detectives suddenly crowded around him. Only the one who had introduced them spoke. This time there was hard distrust in his clipped voice. "We estimate it's ten thousand dollars you have there, all in fifties and hundreds," he said briskly. "If it had been anything else, the guy wouldn't have been able to get it up here," he went on, a little proud of his reasoning.

"What guy?" Lake asked sharply as they all looked at him. "What man are you talking about?"

The detectives were stunned and angrily befuddled. An expression of contempt and chagrin such as Hegan had displayed changed their features with its violent flush of hostility. Lake and De Young could see immediately they knew nothing at all about James or the assassination.

"I'm speaking of the individual who brought this here money up the stairs," the detective said hotly. "I didn't have any specific individual in mind."

Lake nodded slowly, absently, in apology but the detective continued on, determined not to be patronized. "Besides I don't see what difference it can make now," he snapped, glancing over at the empty suitcase. "This man probably left the country hours if not days ago."

On their way out Mrs. Emerson went berserk. For forty-five long tormenting minutes she had sat tightly and angrily in her straight chair while a pack of strange white policemen came and talked in low voices and went as they pleased without legal papers or any apparent justification, frightening her boarders and obliterating the calm of an ordinary night. But as De Young and Austin Lake wearily descended the narrow badly lit staircase, the strain of all this ominous activity boiled over in her and excitedly she leapt to her feet in a swift spasm of rage and sputtering hysteria. Like someone in a deranged fit she began to stagger toward the two policemen sharing the little couch opposite her, shrieking and holding her head in hysterical agony while she seized a table lamp in one hand and held it high. Her harsh shrill singsong West Indian voice dealt out scorn so rapidly the two men were completely shocked, then suddenly overwhelmed by her hatred. Quickly they got up and retreated behind the couch.

As fiery rampant bitterness glinted in each eye she screamed and orated through the house with evil clarity. "Because you are white, you goddamn people think you can come in here and do what you want with an old black woman. I know. I *know*. You think she is nothing, nothing, just a thing, but you are wrong and crazy too, let me tell you, plain crazy. I'm old enough to be your own mother and by law you must let me see what is going on in my own house because this is my property you are tampering with. You are playing with Emerson property now. You don't know that, do you. You goddamn bullying donkeys. Now this man you are searching for so vainly in my house, he was no good I can tell you that now once and for all. No good. Hear me? I could see with my own eyes what he was. All you had to do was to come to me instead of doing things your stupid dumb cop way. And he never paid his rent on time. I was about to throw him out. The police department didn't know that," she cried sarcastically. "In fact I had so much trouble with him I started to call the police many times. I wish to god in high heaven I had now to keep you evil-smelling fathers and sons of bastards out of my house I paid for. All you want to do is trample this old black woman, trample her under your boots. And may God damn that man on the top floor. Damn his black ass into the fires of the hottest hell for wrecking my place like this," Mrs. Emerson shouted frenetically before the two policemen finally came at her. Like a shadow she darted from their grasping arms and rushed headlong at Charles De Young, still holding the lamp aloft as if it were an extinguished but hopeful beacon. Bellowing and sobbing she cried out to him plaintively, "My son, you are the only one of us here. You must not leave me now. You must protect an old black woman. It is your duty."

Then they were at Bellevue Hospital, hurrying along through one dank long dim ancient underground corridor to the point where it swerved off from the main passage and dipped into a bumpy concrete ramp leading to the city mortuary. Inside swinging doors they discovered themselves in an immense room lined from floor to ceiling with giant file drawers. Everything was dazzling white, even the highly polished floors, and there was no noise, no suggestion of the myriad tensions that had lingered at Mrs. Emerson's house, nothing but over-powering whiteness too glaring for the eye to penetrate. De Young thought he could detect an unsettling hum from the air-conditioners and brilliant soft white fluorescent lights, but he couldn't be sure.

The attendant on duty, a very tall strong-looking white-suited black man with a completely bald head and thick tinted glasses, got up from his white desk; and moving quickly through the harsh brightness he cocked his head quizzically but made no attempt to speak.

"We are with the police," Lake said uncertainly as he approached eerily, like the shadow of a cloud floating across the desert.

"Don't make no difference to me who you are, baby. I only work here," the attendant replied blithely.

"Yes," Lake said politely. He was now aware that the attendant walked very gingerly, putting one foot in front of the other in tiny mincing steps and it made him uneasy. He had always despised homosexuals.

"The man we want to see is named Clarence Williams," Lake went on in a more firm tolerant voice.

"They called down and told me," the attendant replied impertinently. "Follow me."

With this he set out across the white floor assuredly, bounding ahead with all the swiftness and stealth of an Indian scout tracking a deer. In a few seconds he was at the right drawer, yanking it open with easy strength until it rolled all the way out and sagged from the wall. Lake and De Young peered forward. The attendant grasped the sheet covering the body, and haughtily, like a saleswoman in an expensive shop, he drew it off. "Is this your man?" he inquired in a mocking superior voice, knowing of course it was.

There was no answer. Both men gazed at the violently battered inert body in hushed sickening surprise and fear. Blood was still heavily caked around the broken mouth and chin. The top of Clarence's blue polo shirt was stiff and dirty brown with it. And as he viewed these horrible remains with revolting fascination De Young wondered in a quick convulsion of bottom-less desperate apprehension if Clarence would not be disposed of in the public crematorium the city kept roaring twenty-four hours a day. He grabbed the tag on Clarence's big toe but it contained only the corpse's name and some cryptic computer numbering.

"What kind of funeral is planned?" he asked the attendant with a trace of prim emotional hesitation in his voice.

The attendant looked a little surprised. He raised his eyebrows in amusement, but then he assumed his studied nonchalance again. "Well, they're not going to *burn* him, baby, if that's what you mean. A nice colored funeral director from uptown is taking care of him and his relatives are coming up from Georgia or some such place to see him off right."

De Young nodded petulantly and glanced at Austin Lake's brooding and disturbed face. Lake waved his hand imperiously and the attendant closed the drawer slowly, as if he were quite bored. They still remembered Clarence's smashed face sliding by them on smooth rollers and disappearing into the icy darkness.

Now, behind the wheel of his car as it moved in an orderly drifting line up the highway, Charles De Young was filled with boundless trepidation. He thought of the director who was probably just arriving at that cold spare office in Washington where he had been invited only once, very briefly, later to find out that he was not scheduled to be there at all. And he resented the director's prudish and abstract assumption that James would be apprehended simply because he wanted it done. He also resented over and over again his own failure and frustration. De Young was afraid of what awaited him.

His gloom forced him to believe a betrayal of some kind was near. Why else would the director have used the city police for surveillance when that was never done with agency men in the field? And what sardonic threat was intended by having James positively identified as the probable killer by the time they'd reached the liaison man? What was the director trying so hard not to say to their faces, De Young wondered despondently.

The director and Riggs (he could see them at lunch together in one of the fancier Washington clubs) were exerting an extravagant disproportionate pressure. And angrily De Young found himself hoping a smart police reporter would uncover just a small part of the story and break it in his paper. But there was one prominent detail he wanted to hoard for himself because even now he could hardly believe it was in his possession. Its vertiginous power seemed to haunt him since the moment three hours ago when Hegan had told it to him; and now and again he would repeat to himself the foreign musical name of the man controlling James, the name of a man whose existence he'd almost refused to believe in up to the sickening instant a stenographic pad bearing the name and telephone number of this man was put into his trembling, reluctant hands. He was fascinated and mystified by the name of this person who'd reached out so deliberately and enigmatically to contact him with evidence that only added a subtle terror to his swimming perplexity.

A relentless confusion seemed to dominate his swirling imagination, and at its center loomed the bland and unemotional face of James. He was forced to admit to himself that he'd never really understood James, never had the detachment to grant James any significance, even now when his life was attached to James in so many ways he could not acknowledge. He knew James was complex somehow. He conceded James a certain measure of profound confusion and a deep touching sociological pathos. But De Young could not temper his hatred for all the apparent weaknesses in James. He would not believe a man so foolishly humble had any power over him. Yet the denial of this power increased all the mysteries connected with James. It left him wondering who James was and what he wanted from life, if anything. And the more he considered James, the more De Young was chilled by the enigmas this man released. Suggestions of everything inscrutable about James had seeped into him while he stood in that dusty tight little abandoned room at Mrs. Emerson's and went through all those ghastly unnerving papers left there for him to read, examine, and ponder. He perceived as he went through the evidence that it was not about the man he despised. The face in the false passports, in the photographs, the anxious stilted phrases in the reports, none of these things seemed to have any connection with James. They existed only within the hard strictures of Communist thought and the meticulous planning of a ministry bureaucrat. Here James appeared as merely another vengeful black man, a useful turncoat, an unstable personality to be trained and discarded. The very abundance of evidence given away so easily indicated that much. Too many pieces were available and they were too clumsily planted for it not to be obvious James had been abandoned. But De Young was not absolutely sure. He did not want to believe it was that simple; yet the idea of more complexities exhausted him. Once more James was baffling him.

He tried to let his mind relax and wander back over the silent and invisible vicissitudes of a friendship he had never quite grasped, the strange trustful relationship between Miles and James. He could not forget them together, James grave and absorbed while Miles appeared always to hover above him benevolently. Had Miles really understood James? The question stabbed at him and forced De Young to blink. Instantly he wanted to scorn and mock their mutual dedication and efficiency, but this seemed ridiculous and beside the point. His contempt told him nothing and De Young found this intolerable. Whatever held them together in intimate suspension, whatever curious obscure terms they lived by threatened De Young profoundly. He'd decided when he saw them becoming friends that it was all happening at his expense, as a kind of easy joking conspiracy against him. Even now his recollections filled him with furious jealousy. And abruptly he concluded Miles had never actually known James because James was too diffuse and clever to be known. All James had done was make himself indispensable. From the very beginning he was afraid this would be enough to deceive Miles.

It enraged him to remember that once or twice when he tried to explain his feelings to Miles he was immediately accused of stupid petty jealousy, and then with artful derision laughed right out of the room. He wished Miles had taken him more seriously, had given him more dignity. Now those good old times when he and Miles were comrades seemed never to have existed.

It was getting more difficult to concentrate on driving. Beside him Austin Lake seemed to be dozing, and De Young grew angry when he remembered Lake had not bothered to ask where they were going. It didn't matter though, De Young told himself. Lake had scant connection with anything he did, and probably had no idea he was riding with the only man who would authoritatively be able to champion the memory of Miles King. Lake knew nothing about the dozens of tape recordings and voluminous bundles of papers and notes he'd appropriated from Miles's office, and De Young was greatly pleased. He'd already decided that in a few years, when he was through with intelligence work, he would publish this material in several volumes and explain in a long introduction what it all meant. This was better than giving it to timid scholars who would never understand the burgeoning hope and heroic pride Miles had aroused in the impoverished minds of black people. Besides, De Young did not want to share intellectual recognition with anyone. It was not his style.

The papers were strange. De Young had only glanced through some of them, but he was amazed by their volume and all the complexities Miles tried to deal with. It amused him to see how desperately Miles wanted the fate of the black man to be settled equitably. He noticed a lot of stuff about Africa in the material: short intensely personal biographies of famous Africans, and endless pages in a broad schoolboy script on African attitudes toward the American black man. Hidden deep in one pack of early writings, De Young found a mass of vague genealogical tables and charts, what he believed was a hasty maddened attempt to establish unknowable ties with a vanished ancestry. Much of it was too foreign and exotic for De Young to understand fully. He had never thought too much about being descended from Africans.

286

Suddenly his thoughts turned to James again. James was the only person alive who could possibly prevent him from grasping the success he craved. He was determined feverishly to strip the mysteries from James if they ever met again because James alone violated his notion of personal savage freedom. And in spite of weariness and anxiety, Charles De Young still believed he was free in a way. He knew his freedom was constricted only by what he could not account for, and therefore James possessed an intriguing hold on him. He represented a challenge that had to be destroyed.

Next to De Young on the front seat Austin Lake was not asleep although his eyes were almost closed. Lake felt a strong urge to sleep, a purely physical demand to slip far down into the hermetic oblivion of total rest, but tension kept him awake in a drowsy and weakened stupor he couldn't shake off. Lake didn't mind too much. He enjoyed the sensation of being drugged because he didn't want to be fully aware of what was happening around him any more. All of the abrupt violence of the last few days had unleashed a tremendous wearying turbulence and confusion in him. Bitterly he remembered how naïvely he'd assumed this assignment would go smoothly, without upheavals or serious conflicts, and now there was latent terror in everything. Miles King gasping in the soft bleary-eyed agony of his miserable death, trying with an instinctive biological reflex to move limbs already growing weak, was the most appalling sight he'd ever seen. And Clarence Williams' utterly mute and almost unrecognizable pulpy face had made his stomach writhe with uncontrollable nausea. He had never seen a human face so smashed and mutilated. Clarence Williams' features had just receded away into a mass of swollen dead flesh Lake could not believe had been pounded with just two human fists.

Not that he was oversensitive to violence. He had seen pain and death many times before, in the army and a few times in intelligence work. But in these two deaths, which had broken into his life so melodramatically, Austin Lake sensed an unrestrained random depravity he had never realized was all around him. And he had never realized until now how much of his essentially routine life was committed to the principles of terror and death. Like most middle-echelon intelligence people, Lake had fled into the safety of clever abstract ideas and interesting euphemisms. Now this shelter was threatened. Under the peculiar and subtle strains in this assignment all the familiar things, the easy classifications, the predictable behavior of one's superiors, the secure possibilities of success, and the easygoing amenities, all these things were disappearing. No one was pretending any more, especially the director. Last night when they spoke, his voice had been very different. Its timbre had altered and what came through the phone was a nasty troubled voice, exceedingly harsh with a touch of dissolution to it. For the first time the director was openly rude, quite bitter and demanding. He repeated himself, which was unusual, demanding several times that James be apprehended. More than once he lapsed into the clichés of the intelligence world, which he hated and primly avoided in ordinary conversation. When he put down the telephone, Lake was sure his career was ending.

He knew when his biannual fitness report was reviewed it would show he had failed to anticipate the assassination. In a sullen mood of false detachment Lake steadied himself for the moment when Brian Riggs would call and ask him if he were available for lunch. After Riggs had him at lunch, the rest would be simple. Riggs would explain the situation as a friend and sympathetic associate. The critique of his work showed he was erratic (no one was ever confused or stupid). He had turned down repeated suggestions for increased surveillance on the primary figure in the assignment. His counterproposal (secretly graded senseless and unimaginative after it had failed) had easily been subverted by Miles King, who was not really that important to the agency. He was excessively influenced and protective toward Charles De Young, a man whose own fitness report revealed shocking incompetence. The assassination had bowled them both over like tenpins. Then Riggs would lean forward and ask, very pointedly and helplessly,

288

what he would do if handed a fitness report detailing such instability.

In an ironic and humorous twist Lake wondered what Miles King would have replied. What deprecating insidiously mocking answer would Miles have given to such a puerile attempt at bureaucratic viciousness? A few inane possibilities ran through his mind until it came upon him dismayingly that there would be no answer. Miles was too large, too arrogantly free for the whole situation. He could never be shackled and intimidated by such high-school melodramatics. Riggs hated this notion of course. He despised it as a dangerously childish theory, as a ridiculous example of pseudobohemian romanticism, but Austin Lake was beginning to treasure it. He was beginning to cling to his memories of Miles as if he were afraid they would fade and eventually disappear. At the same time he did not want to be sentimental or condescending about his admiration for Miles (people like Riggs cultivated condescension to an art as fine as the minuet). Miles was far too noble for such self-involved priggishness. This nobility had drawn him to the man because in his own linear middle-class life there wasn't any chance for nobility. Any stance that distinctive was hooted down right away. Even Charles De Young, who was a black man and a companion of Miles, feared the concept of nobility if it appeared in other people. Behind this fear, Lake suspected, was De Young's furious desire to overshadow Miles, to check Miles and bring him down to a more common level, to a plane of existence where he could be humbled.

Lake toyed with this interesting conjecture. Once he'd imagined controlling people and prudently undermining the enemies of an orderly society was a quietly heroic calling, like manning a Polaris submarine or watching a radar display for incoming enemy missiles. Now he sensed a complicated disillusionment settling in him, a kind of generalized dismay at what he had become. In a surprising violent spurt of bitterness he hated De Young. He despised him because De Young was the perfect servant of all the criminal righteousness the agency represented. Undoubtedly that was why they were assigned together, so that De Young, the cynical all too ambitious black man, would restrain his imagination and bully him with the petty challenge of accomplishment.

Caught in a mood of frustrated absorption Lake divined how perfect an explanation of their relationship he had uncovered. In a subtle arrogant diffuse way De Young had always led him even though he never really seemed to know where he was going. He was always off on a virile punitive quest moving toward an end nobody could see. And Lake felt suddenly lost in this quest. He knew De Young's strange powerful anxieties, his terrible sulfurous hates had spilled over into his own life and disoriented him. Now he wanted to withdraw, to put some space between his personal existence and Charles De Young. He wanted to flee from the ideas and emotions De Young represented to him. Lake wanted to get away from the agency.

But this was ridiculous and hopeless. The agency was his career. His wife and children prospered because he had wisely chosen this career in the intelligence bureaucracy. Momentarily he reflected on his secure life at home, in the sunny quiet verdant suburb of Washington where his house stood back thirty yards from the street sheltered by a dark stand of spruce and oak. All of it was genteel, a little lonely at times, but essentially a good life, especially for the children who had privileges and a certain amount of arrogant status without knowing it. Of course he didn't see them very much and his absence made it easier to be sentimental for their welfare. But they helped to define his existence and Lake needed that. His home, his polite ordinary wife, and two small bright children were the only things that always told him he still knew what he was.

De Young no longer understood or cared about this sort of question, if he ever had. Only revenge and destruction occupied his mind. Yet he could never really be pitied because he was so implacably vicious. Working for the agency must have strangled his meager capabilities for feeling, his shallow willingness to examine himself, Lake surmised. Slowly he was reaching the same point himself. He was entangled in a deadening helpless ambivalence. Like James and De Young, Austin Lake knew he was being controlled.

For some aimless reason this revelation amused him temporarily. Ten years ago he would have laughed heartily at the idea, but his feeling about it now was more subtle and realistic. Age was clearing out his illusions and demolishing his naïvete. The process was speeding up all the time. Last Sunday in Brotherhood Hall he was exuberantly certain that no matter what happened in the world the spontaneous crowd of blacks around him could never be controlled, not really. His charitable and romantic smugness had allowed him to believe black people were immune to manipulation. Now that events had guided him beyond the frontiers of complacency he saw this was absurd and new fears encroached on him. As hackneyed and illiberal as it sounded to him, Lake was afraid he was being carried down into the mysteries of black life. He was half convinced that abstruse and unknowable elements common to the lives of black people had invaded his psyche and caused him pain. The idea was absurd but it captivated him; it shielded him from failure and worry, and so he played with the childish notion of fleeing from the sight of even the most harmless black man and reconstituting himself in safety. But first he had to get away from De Young, because De Young diluted his thesis. He was not particularly black. He was not particularly anything. He was merely a contemporary, merely a person with dark skin and Negro features who indicated what was to become of those guileless Brothers and Sisters packed into the old movie house waiting for the final answer to their woes. In his shallow way De Young was more prophetic than Miles. His message was that blacks, like the rest of humanity, would never be free of the world created by the agency.

In the farthest centers of his intuition Lake knew they would never really escape. They had no genuine hope. The world was simply not going their way; instead it was moving rapidly away from their subjective natural responses to a gigantic circuit of programmed intellect. In this machinery there was no black problem, no confrontation over race, only a mechanical and administrative function (nonwhite reactions to productive group stimuli) to be dealt with by a dry middle-aged man (perhaps himself) in a vested suit working patiently before a console of knobs and output printers and video display terminals. Yes, this would be the solution because this was what the world would accept, even if blacks hated it.

Then annoyingly James sprang into his calculations and disordered them completely. With the humiliating fear of a man who is outclassed, Lake wanted nothing to do with James. Foolishly he imagined James as a skilled high-ranking officer (the most brilliant always seemed to be colonels) in the ministry intelligence system, whose true mission had been planned for years. This might give an indication of how the assassination was carried out so smoothly. But after that it faded into vague speculation and imprecise conjecture. Only James possessed the true answers and he had vanished, gone, leaving behind some unaccountable documents including many that were obvious forgeries. Lake could not believe the microfilm was genuine. He prayed it was not. He knew that particular kind of microfilm could be stored for years and be retrieved by alpha-numeric command, or by association with other topics and materials. This process of retrieval was called boundary conditions. Lake wondered in James's case what these conditions were. What associations did the ministry really make? What critical information not yet analyzed was in those long clear Celluloid strips on which the sharply photographed documents looked like tiny discrete flecks of soot on a beautiful white tablecloth.

Wisely Lake did not go on. He did not want to try to outguess James and the ministry for the moment. Impulsiveness had been his trouble before. The director was right. He was too rash and intellectual. What he believed was pure astuteness had undermined him. Yet rather absently he wondered if James had anything to do with Miles turning down the foundation money. Then half a dozen puzzling questions rippled through his mind.

Although they had never spoken or come within plain sight

of each other, Lake could not dampen his intense curiosity about what the ministry had seen or touched in this ethereal personality. But he grasped that his attraction to James was driven on by the disconcerting and alluring question of genuine personal freedom, a freedom he never came close to possessing. Lake realized he didn't want James to be free either. And right away he decided to be the one to debrief James if he was caught. He would see to it, by going to the director if necessary, that De Young did not get the assignment by default. In a circumspect way Lake sensed he was a voyeur. Lazily he pictured himself sitting across from James in one of those peaceful underground debriefing rooms. Everything was utterly silent down there, inducing a nice sensation of absolute safety; dozens of men, many of them important officials of foreign governments, had confessed each tangled nuance of their existences in those pristine abstract little rooms. James would be no different. Protected, hidden from the outside, far from recriminations of any kind, James would surely make all of his life available. He had to. It might be his only means of retaining sanity.

Lake saw himself deep in heavy conversation with James, the two of them huddled together like a doomed convict and his last visitor. Of course he would have to be patient with James and respect his reticence at first. After a few weeks when they knew each other somewhat better, the real questioning would begin. Lake planned to scheme to draw out the other man's woes. He planned to approach James like a psychiatrist, not a common interrogator, and when the relaxed discussion began to flow, force his prisoner (the agency would call him a client) to develop painful obscure twists in his character. After the second month, when the preliminary sessions were coming to an end (Lake recalled it sometimes took six months to get through this stage), he would approach one of the more imaginative systems analysts interested in human personality delineation and ask this man to draw up a language (its name had to be reduced to an acronym—perhaps BAP for black anger and personality distortion) and a computer program based on the behavior patterns extracted from James so far. This information would be stored in the agency's time-sharing computer; and using the teletypewriter terminal in his office, Lake could test and compare all subsequent data with the model already formulated. James would have to explain the discrepancies.

Lake loved the idea. It was neat and scientific. It fitted into a routine that would leave him unplagued by anxiety. In front of his computer terminal he could deal with almost any problem he could anticipate, and many that were unforeseen. The agency's computer contained all kinds of files, some he had never even thought of using. There were two and one-half million computer words in the system, including supervisory programs for operatives in the field—chiefly those attached to embassies—variables used in specific long-range intelligence predictions based on scientific knowledge, utility programs for advising the executive branch during foreign crises, all stored in and among an uncountable number of tiny integrated circuits he trusted more than the devious convolutions of the human brain. His program on James could be called into play only by a specific command word issued through the terminal, and already Lake was entertaining two possibilities: Deus Ex Machina (possibly too clever) and Alpha Compleat, which appealed to his affinity for mechanical seriousness. The password was particularly important. It guaranteed the privacy of each personal set of files and programs from accident or malicious alteration by another person, and around the agency this was a constant concern. A perverse and vicious strain of intellectual vandalism had appeared in the last few months. Many programs had been ruined by what everyone believed was an organized gang entering private offices at night with passkeys. All over discreet little signs were tacked up warning the time-sharers to disconnect their printers when the password was typed into the computer so that no record of it showed on the print-out. Two men had been transferred recently for breaking this rule and Lake wondered how many passwords people like Riggs and De Young had memorized.

They would never get his. Lake was too circumspect and covetous to ever let that happen. He never let himself be drawn into any of the flippant camaraderie surrounding use of the computer. Not once had he granted access to anyone who needed information in his files, no matter how roughly they cajoled him. And he'd never seen another file besides his own. He refused to leave messages with the computer and was furious when his terminal unnervingly printed out the words, YOU HAVE MAILBOX.

As he contemplated these routine agency experiences, so efficiently childish and conceited in their workings, Austin Lake was visited by a sudden visceral turn of frustrated outrage. He felt both evil and foolish. A nervous angry conviction told him that to obey the agency in this case, to put James's life into a computer would be incredibly pretentious and even monstrous. Mysteriously he felt as if he were acquiescing in the destruction of some unstated human principle. He guessed what Riggs and the director would say to this, yet he couldn't flee a clinging sense of guilt and disgusted worry. Lake understood he could never persecute James this way. At his most dispassionate he was barely capable of it, and now he perceived nothing but unsteadiness and incipient rebellion in himself. But he wasn't a genuine rebel. He didn't want to be a rebel. He knew what happened to people who fought the agency. He struggled to be content, to be normal, but underneath his efforts Lake came upon an odd strain of intuition in himself that suggested James might be fighting madly against the same host of evils and pernicious weaknesses ruling his existence. Of course he had no proof at all. Intuition in a tenuous and humane form was his only guide. Still the more he considered James, the less certain Lake was that he was dealing with a great criminal. He strained to believe James had been coerced in some way to join in the assassination, and then simply been betrayed.

The thought of another betrayed black man in this world depressed Lake. If James had undergone an important conflict with the writhing sources of his own hope, Lake wanted it to be known. He could not stand the idea of suppressing this knowledge and with it the horrendous complexities of yet another black life.

Stirring himself from the rigors of concentration Lake glanced at Charles De Young manning the wheel of his automobile with inordinate assurance. The smugness and brutality in the hard black face (it was not really black, but a warm brown with distinct freckles) disgusted him. He held nothing but contempt for De Young, but a wistful and tense apprehension drifted through him every time he thought of challenging that familiar face and putting De Young back into a subordinate role. He tried to rouse himself to a small pitch of anger, but all he experienced was strain and a moiling exhaustion. Abruptly he was prompted to ask where they were going before he remembered he already knew. Besides if he asked De Young, the answer might be condescending and derisive; an argument was sure to start and he would lose somehow so he kept to himself. He kept very quiet as the car left the highway, circled down a ramp, and then nosed up a side street until it found the entrance turning down into the underground garage in Beverly Carter's building. They slipped into a vacant parking space and De Young turned off the lights. Neither man spoke and after the first hour Lake felt all his confidence returning. James was certain not to come to this place.

CHAPTER TWENTY-TWO

SOMETIME LATER, in a sort of deliberate pre-meditated daze, James Fitzgerald discovered himself striding uncertainly along the wide and filthy sidewalks of upper Broadway near his apartment. He assured himself that in the next few steps he would turn and travel the short distance home and rest and think about what he was doing. But for many vague and demanding reasons he continued on. To his blurred mind the avenue he made his way along was endless and terrifying, an immense starkly gray plain bordered by the sheer forbidding cliffs of massive decayed apartment buildings either hidden in the cool morning shade or standing out grotesquely in the strong but muted sunlight.

Subliminally, as if his eyes were closed to it, the sunlight bored into his brain. Its soft rays seemed to glare unmercifully and he told himself this was why he changed over to the shady side of the avenue where he knew it would be harder to recognize him. In the shade it was surprisingly chilly. He was a little shocked, as if he'd fallen into a shallow pool of stingingly cold water. His pace accelerated and at the same time became more mechanical as he kept very close to the storefronts and rattled over their steel cellar doors embedded in the sidewalk like a series of vicious traps ready to be sprung. He wondered if Clarence had been found yet, if his smashed and suppurating body had not been discovered and rushed out in the middle of the night to a hospital where they forced drugs into it until miraculously it spoke from death and told everything. Such events were almost possible, James decided. Here a protective little instinct drew him across the street, back into the sun where it was warmer.

Carefully but unobtrusively he studied the tense, annoyed faces whipping past him in the fresh orange-yellow sunlight as people darted by and converged on the subway entrance until it was obscured by a small anxious crowd waiting irritably to flow down onto the jammed platform. With an intense frantic difficulty he pushed his mind to concentrate on what he now understood his next move had to be. And looking sullenly around the emptying streets for witnesses he glided into an outdoor telephone booth which stank of urine and dialed the number that had come up in his imagination these past few hours like the unfathomable inscription on a powerful talisman.

The careful familiar voice was there, straining now to conceal a hoarse undercurrent of emotion that hurt James. He hung up immediately without saying a word. A sensation of shabbiness and deterioration gripped him. Quickly he moved on, hoping no one would observe or recognize him, hoping no one from the Brotherhood lived between here and his destination. Desperately he wanted safety and time to think, time to save himself.

Measuring every step against the invisible instant when he might panic and run, James turned off Broadway and descended a steep side street angling down to the deserted roadway of Riverside Drive. On each side of him closely packed rows of severely genteel brownstones reared up together quite righteously, as a group of old women might before they were about to state a monstrous accusation. James tried to ignore the pervasive bleakness. Instead he peered out over the slimy blue-gray water into the miniaturized landscape of New Jer-

298

sey. His eyes carefully took in the desolate industrial area climbing up from the bank opposite him. Amid some thin trees, almost at his feet, lay a compound of factory buildings low and rectilinear in construction and James focused on them, imagining he could crush them with his next step. When he got to the bottom of the hill and gazed across the water again they looked immense and their stolid presence reflected brightly in the dull sluggish water.

Immediately James was depressed. The failure of his little game of optical illusion plunged him into a bottomless disproportionate misery. He had tricked himself into momentarily believing a worthless illusion and although it was on a ridiculously insignificant plane this time, he remained despondent within a circle of nameless frustrations. After a while he began to feel more calm. Very deliberately he sat down on a bench facing away from the water and tried to forget who he was and what was happening to him. And as his moroseness abated slowly, a reckless imperative drive kept his mind churning. Even though he knew it was time to get up and move on, a heavy residue of utter weariness and subtle dejection forced him to remain where he was.

All night he'd been walking, running, scrambling far down into the dreadful echoing end of insanity, and crawling up again. A hallucinatory fever had taken over his senses. Like a deranged man he couldn't explain how he got from one place to another. One moment he was racing down the alley in back of Clarence's house, ducking like a crazy man among the mountainous rotted bags of garbage and the silent ferocity of angry red-eyed rats, then in the next lurching, almost arrested step he was swimming in the blur of voices and shadows and strange bright lights in front of Brotherhood Hall where the marquee blazed the cabalistic message:

MILES KING TONIGHT

Clumps of people stood back in the dark doorways and peered upon each other with mad, cheated eyes. But everyone was respectful, abstracted and diffidently respectful in the faraway manner of figures carved into a cathedral doorway. Stupidly James was glad no one knew he was a murderer, and he went about resolving his fate. Only it was impossible. He tried and found it impossible. De Young wasn't in any of the rooms James searched three and four times over. One Brother said he'd been in earlier and left, but the empty blank corridors yielded no suggestion of his presence, no echo of his joyfully sneering laugh. Sit down and wait for Brother Charles, one of the faithful elderly Brothers said to James, and he did. Hour after hour he sat in his darkened office, now perfectly strange to him, and deliberated upon the permutations of his silence. Finally panic overpowered him. The full, confident voices of half a dozen interrogators seemed to throng the hallways and he wanted to scream he was not a murderer, that no way existed to connect him with the deaths of Miles or Clarence. Still he waited, refusing to divest himself of the possibilities of hope, refusing to believe the man who had spoken to Beverly and Miles would not soon be speaking to him. And as the minutes went on, his agitated patience melted into amorphous frustration and misery. After five hours he knew De Young was not returning that evening and possibly never again. James could not account for this judgment, but he couldn't escape it either. Yet he did not leave Brotherhood Hall. He remained in his office with a strange casualness as the dawn grandly materialized outside, sitting behind the large worn desk he'd used every day when Miles was alive. He sat and waited with the rapt hopeless fatalistic absorption of a man who believes he is making his last dramatic stand against life.

Inevitably he was disturbed. Dozens of Brothers and Sisters had seen him arrive, and somewhere in the tumult of his thoughts James understood they would revert to their old habits and come knocking at his office door. He was not surprised, but pure annoyance combined with an elusive anger went through him as the first discreet knock seeped into the stillness he was suspended in. Politely, but in a thin, tired voice he called out for the visitor to enter. The door opened by agonizing degrees and Brother Nicholas stuck his head into the room, looked around dumbly and then came in followed closely by a very sharp-featured man called Malik Abdul. They advanced to the center of the room warily, like messengers entering the presence of a monarch. James was suddenly horrified at how shrunken and tattered Nicholas had become in just three short days. For the first few seconds he ignored the other man, but then something in his bearing forced James to look up at him, something unarticulated between them drew his gaze to Malik Abdul's dark slanted head. In the face confronting him James saw a concentration of intense disgust and malignant arrogance. His eyes shifted to Nicholas but he could feel Malik's cold reproach playing on him. Gravely he nodded to both men and Nicholas took it as a signal to begin speaking. In a rapid, pleading voice that seemed to escape from him like a diffuse plaintive cry, he asked James to please contact the police immediately because all of Miles's papers and tape recordings had been stolen out of the hall. Clumsily, rapidly, he repeated it three or four times, nearly shrieking in his claustrophobic misery that everything Miles had said or written was gone and so was Miles now and James had to, please, do something this morning, today. He went on as his eyes rose strangely. He went on as if no one were listening at all and he was going mad. Nicholas continued until sobs broke up his voice and his chest heaved monstrously as he cried with a bitter, unchecked desperation. When he had stopped, James, only guessing at the state of his own composure, assured them he would act immediately. He told them private detectives would be hired. He said the Brotherhood lawyers would be contacted in the morning. He mentioned aid from a friend in the mayor's office, and suggested offering a reward. He said anything that would send them away half satisfied, vaguely placated for just a few hours; and then James ran away from the hall, ran out of Brotherhood Hall into the disintegrating night he'd escaped from, ran without any idea of how to begin putting his life into a pattern that was not chaotic.

Now hunched down on the bench and staring into the foul

water a few yards away, James did not think about anything but eventual failure and pain. His enthusiasm for rebellion appeared to be gone, leaving him aghast at the despair and wreckage of his short life. Just to contemplate what he'd survived overwhelmed him. Still he did not want to be a martyr to other people's deviousness and manipulations. All he really desired was grace of some kind and an end to his frustrations and woes. Sluggishly James realized he was still committed to reshaping his life. He was still a rebel in all his weariness and pathos. But even so the ethereal notion of achieving a successful, planned rebellion, of molding himself into a strong worthwhile person seemed utterly ludicrous. He was half convinced it was hopeless. All he wanted now was rest and food. Yet he could not throw off the haunting intimation that everything he was going through at this moment was just a gathering of his strengths, a subtle rallying or recharging of his tremendous energies, a prelude to resuming the quest for authenticity. One level of his exhausted mind battled this sentiment, and for a few long minutes James again felt his rebellion was so tenuous he would never even be able to explain it in words. Then abruptly he experienced nothing but wonder at the temerity of what he was attempting.

But James knew he would go on. There was too much self-knowledge in him now to turn back into anything but a total and obliterating derangement. The ministry desperately wanted him to lose his sanity, and so James sought to preserve it. Yet at the same time he doubted himself. He doubted if he could avoid the trap of self-pity and vacillation. The strain of attempting to give his life unity would be enormous. It appeared far beyond his elusive optimism.

Of course there were many challenges to goad him, including the challenge of establishing a record (even a clinical psychiatric record) of his life and its strange unfulfilled wanderings, for James did not want anyone to retrace his miseries. He couldn't stand the idea of more black victims and more black martyrs. He let himself think somehow a record of his life might destroy some undelineated psychic pattern in the lives of black people, might overturn a despotic idol and free millions from its curse. Surely there was a kind of grace in this. And it might be the only unadulterated thing he'd ever accomplish, because for all his yearnings and desires to rebel James was beginning to understand this was a highly complex decision. He could not really make it conclusive by himself. Too little was to be gained by just being an individual who had rebelled against what he was, who despised the blight of his former life. Only the active sympathy of other people could nurse the rebellion along, and in the end this made it a kind of transition, it placed many unknown values in the superficially pathetic human urge to change. Numbly James allowed his imagination to try to total up what his belated thrust for affirmation might be worth to someone else. But he couldn't really guess. It was hopeless and foolish and depressing, just as everything seemed to be.

Once more his thoughts swirled about the anonymous white man whose aid and trust he needed, and to a naïve and surprising degree even believed in. He wondered what conditions this man would demand when they finally met. But most of all he wondered if they would ever come together at any time; he wondered if the unsure mixtures of time and circumstance, character and strength ever intended for such a confrontation to come about. Fear and suspicion nagged at him. Logic dictated patience. Yet his intuition hinted at despair and briefly swamped him with all the attenuated pathos he struggled against as he fled from Brotherhood Hall. He wondered where De Young was and why he'd become so evasive. Curiosity at what changes Miles's death had worked in De Young nudged at him.

But through all of this the tenuousness of his present existence bore down on James like a heavily weighed net. He felt his rebellion had come too late. He tried to see it merely as an afterthought, an intellectual argument in his defense, but it was too personal and alive with a hope he couldn't quite seize to support such needless deceptions. And futility did not take James completely. He was not afraid of his attempt at regener-

303

ation. He refused to flee from it as he had run desperately from Miles's call for personal struggle and selfhood. Instead he went his own way, trudging along, a tiny figure following the enormous curved and gracious facade of mammoth apartment buildings whose sun-emblazoned windows sparkled high above his head like softly falling diamonds.

When James appeared in the garage, carefully lowering himself down the ramp like a small boy cautiously dropping into a swimming hole, De Young was the first to see him. Out of the deep, soft shadows where the car was parked, he watched James with faintly spiteful disinterest, as if he were following the motions of a fly in a bottle. An angry exhilaration stirred in him. The good firm sureness of other days returned to De Young and for one farcical instant he felt a touch of happiness. The suggestion of a curt smile formed on his slightly flushed face, and a current of intensity flashed through his body. With a sly movement of his arm, he nudged Austin Lake, who was staring out at some spot on the hood of the car.

"Look," De Young intoned quietly, motioning with his head toward the direction of the ramp.

Quickly, with all the hasty bewilderment and blurred antagonism of a sleeping man suddenly awakened on a train, Lake turned and gazed into De Young's piercing and alert eyes. Tiny fingers of panic eased up into him as he tried to think, tried to hastily assemble all the stray thoughts and yearnings floating through his mind. But De Young saw only indecision in the pale, strained face looking at him. He saw a small curious effort at appeal that amused him. And even before Lake answered, he knew what he would do next.

"All right, Charles," Lake said absently, without his usual boyish aplomb, "I'll go out and identify myself."

In the same instant De Young reached across him abruptly, opened the glove compartment and took out his compact powerful-looking .38 revolver. In one quick professional turn of the wrist, it disappeared into the shoulder holster under his jacket.

"I can get him over to the car without any trouble. He knows me, remember?" De Young said very sharply, as if he were assuming command in a battlefield situation.

For just a second Lake stared at De Young incredulously. He couldn't be absolutely sure if his own quaking voice was speaking or not, but finally he heard himself almost shout, "You brazen son of a bitch. You greedy goddamn black bastard." And then suddenly he was full of a shameful and imprecise disappointment with himself.

He hardly noticed De Young's exquisitely contemptuous smile. Something kept him from seeing the nasty twist of triumph on De Young's too perfectly formed mouth as his adversary replied, "I'll accept it if that's the way you see me, Austin."

Lake's eyes lifted strangely with a sort of stifled bewilderment and outrage. De Young rarely used his first name and it sounded so prim and strange, so contemptible the way it was handed to him that he wanted to pounce on De Young and smash that creamy freckled handsome face into discolored jelly. But that was impossible. He was too afraid of De Young. He couldn't attack De Young and didn't dare get out of the car because De Young might instinctively kill him if he interfered. Lake was left to swim in his own humiliation.

Immediately De Young was out of the car and gone. The horribly tense and febrile intimacy between the two men was broken and Lake felt small and stupid. Nervously he rolled down the window and let in the heavy industrial odors of the garage: the metallic smell of chromium polish, a strong whiff of canned waxes, irritating traces of old dried-out leather, gasoline drippings, and overheated air. Then slowly, with a kind of childish dread he glanced up and spotted James moving quietly against the long mysterious hulls of cars parked in the dim surroundings. Lake was astonished to see him. He appeared smaller and shabbier than he had on the day of the assassination when he crossed the stage with an air of preoccupation and unstated importance. Now there was a quality of unthinking stealth about him. He looked like a cheap burglar.

And Lake was glad. In a fearful way he was extremely

pleased to see James looking so worn and close to defeat. With James before his eyes, he realized the extent to which this man awakened in him a fear of his own significance. Lake understood how powerfully the idea of James's inscrutability had played over his mind and nearly warped him to the point of considering treason against the agency. Quite suddenly he wanted to see James destroyed, but to his dismay this sentiment opened up a host of confused feelings he couldn't identify or define. Far down in his imagination, far removed from the superficial lust for revenge, he quailed with nervous excitement. He wanted to talk with James, to at least approach him, even as he realized the courage to do it had unaccountably ebbed away from him. But more than anything he didn't want to be pulled down into any more miseries, into any more of his own ambiguities. Intuition told him anything James had to say would ultimately be too shocking and brutal and curiously similar to the core of his own life and depleted spirit for him to ever accept; so in torment and violent shame he abandoned the idea for good. Instead he looked around for De Young, who seemed to have vanished, and troubled himself with the alarming thought that a car might come down the ramp before they had James and were gone.

As far as James could see, everything looked fairly safe. There was no one around. The warm stuffy garage appeared to be completely empty. No attendant was on duty and James dimly guessed the automobile commuters in the building had probably departed for their jobs at least half an hour ago. All around him a dark protective calm seemed to have fastidiously settled. Through all the degrees of his attenuated weariness James felt a bit more keen and vigilant, just a bit more assured. He knew he was nearing the best refuge there was for him right now. Beverly was upstairs. Probably she had sensed he was nearby and was busy preparing a big breakfast. After eating he would sleep, change clothes, get some money, and set out again, but not before explaining something of himself to her, enough to let her see the anguished circles his life had drifted into. And tearfully she would administer to his pains the intoxicating potion of her adoring pity and the shelter of her warm hopeful affection before allowing him to leave her for perhaps the last time. Quickly now he made his way to the elevator vacated on the basement level where its small window released a neat yellow square of light into the gloomy aisle dividing the garage into a stifling abysmal murkiness. James was about ten feet from the elevator when he initially sensed someone had darted up behind him.

"Hey, Brother." Unbelievably the voice coming over his shoulder was quite familiar, especially the easy, almost solicitous way it irritated him. "Hey, Brother," it called again, as if coyly attempting to fetch an animal. In an instant that tortured him with regret even as it elapsed, James slowed his rapid pace and then turned very anxiously and looked at the trim well-dressed form of Charles De Young with timorous eyes.

De Young stood stylishly and quite motionless in the middle of the sticky greasy concrete floor. He appeared completely at ease. The beautifully cut sharkskin suit he wore made him look like a man waiting to be picked up by his limousine. A surprised whimsical smile lit his face imperceptibly. James could not have guessed De Young had no idea of what would happen next between them.

For what seemed like an interminably long time neither man spoke, neither man dared to make a move. They merely contemplated each other across the blurring boundaries of old jealousies and submerged rivalries, kinetic states of mind that appeared to have no meaning here. A subtle urging warned James to leave De Young and go upstairs. Apprehension drained blood into his nervous stomach. Suddenly he didn't want to speak to De Young at all because there seemed to be in this strange meeting a weird and portentous air. It was all wrong. When he'd needed De Young he couldn't be found. Now oddly and suspiciously he was here and for some reason this made James recall the latent distrust between De Young and Miles. He remembered the devilish persistent way De Young argued with Miles until he was shouted down in fury. And in those few seconds a horrible suffocating intensity seemed to come off De Young like steam drifting from a work horse on a very cold day.

"I've been looking all over for you, Brother," De Young finally said in a friendly offhand way. This time James noticed his speech lacked its customary insistent verve. De Young sounded tired and unsure. James stood very still and peered at him not knowing what to think. His heart was thumping crazily.

And De Young's mind was racing. He felt a kind of unarticulated edge over James, but simultaneously uncertainty latched onto him. Why was James so quiet? He seemed contemptuously silent. And for the first time he looked truly formidable. Instantly De Young was worried, for he could not be sure James had not lured him here; he could not be completely sure of superiority. Panic laid a quivering hand on him. He felt foolish and a little exposed, but in the amiable controlled voice it was so easy for him to produce De Young went on; he made his first move.

"Listen," he said, extending one hand graciously. "Listen here, Brother, I think you'll want to talk to me. As you probably have known for a long time I'm not just a simple Brother."

All the gratuitous egotism in De Young's manner riled James. But he refused to show any surprise as De Young flipped a little wallet-sized identification card at him, although it seemed incredible De Young could ever willingly have masked so much petty prestige. "I looked for you at the hall," he said, throwing the card back. "I was there waiting half the night."

De Young nodded suavely and noted the tremor in James's voice. He inspected James with his lusterless brown eyes. "Where are you headed now?" he asked in his bored and mocking way.

"You know goddamn well," James answered hotly, trying to restrain an astonished anger rising in him.

De Young smirked very knowingly, as if he expected to be left where he was standing.

James stared upon him with helpless indignation. As usual De Young was overplaying his part and pretending to be more than he really was; but this time he was doing it with such sinister conviction that James briefly imagined they were the last two people in the world. Yet they couldn't be alone; De Young's partner, the only person he really needed to link up the tantalizing circle of his rebellion, had to be somewhere in the garage. They couldn't have sent De Young by himself. His case was too important for that, too portentous and intellectually demanding for someone like De Young. And using the last dry reserves of his cunning, James decided to make De Young see this and force a consultation with his partner.

"Let's go upstairs together," James said more amiably. "I have a few important things to get and then we can leave. I understand I'm in your custody."

Something in James's tone, a suggestion of firm but justified pleading, a hint of personal vindication and self-possession infuriated Charles De Young. In his glibness James sounded as if he were proud of a secret ideal he was about to reveal and this drove De Young mad with resentment and apprehension. He didn't want James to be able to explain himself. The idea terrified him. Angrily he bit down on his bottom lip. "Why do you want to go up there?" he asked roughly. "What can she mean to you?" he almost shouted in a nasty offended voice. "What?" And then evilly it came out. "Does she mean as much as Miles did to you?"

James didn't answer because he didn't know what to say and understood he never would. He looked down at the oily floor to hide the dismay he could feel delineating his face. All of his emotions yearned for Beverly. He desired nothing but to disappear into the enveloping nuances of her erotic and tender concern for him. He wanted the safety of her caresses even though he feared her a little now. He wanted to go upstairs because De Young was spreading fear through him. Suddenly his head came up, eyes shining with emotion. Quietly he faced De Young although he felt baffled and tense. He looked straight at De Young but could not guess at the hatred emanating from the other man, could not conceive of the fear and contempt that filled De Young as he realized his adversary somehow expected to survive everything that had happened in the last few days. Timorously James took a fast step backward. His whole body seemed to burn with a sudden heat. What De Young wanted eluded him and he experienced a strange loss of lucidity, like a person about to have a fit. "I demand to be allowed to make my confession," he shouted as his light brown eyes flickered up spasmodically. "I demand to give all the information in my possession to the right authorities," he bellowed at De Young, who now displayed a crafty and hideous smile.

"Of course," De Young said quite solemnly. "I understand your problem. You believe you have something to confess."

"You know I do," James said loudly but weakly.

"I'm not convinced of that at all, Brother," De Young replied archly, putting one hand delicately to his chest like someone righteously trying to defend himself.

"What do you mean?" There was dread in his throat as James asked this question.

"Let me put it this way, Brother. You're not up to giving a confession. I don't believe you're strong enough to go back through your life like that. What you do best is obey orders," De Young said, gritting his teeth a little and speaking rapidly so that James would not guess at his nervousness or see that he was merely sparring and probing recklessly. Above all he feared James would seize on his uncertainty and humiliate him; and in his urgency, in his frantic drive to outwit James now and forever he did not observe how seriously James had taken his charges. His mind was empty, blank, inchoate. All of his meticulous little observations, all the discrepant facts he'd hoped to confront James with someday were no longer in his brain. He could remember nothing but embarrassed feelings and irrelevant sensations. Bright but blurred images whirled through his memory and vanished, fled before he could extract any significance from them. His numerous and insidious fears of the mysteries enveloping James gathered around De Young once again and he lashed out at James while searching through the infinite and minuscule combinations of fact and alarm wandering through his head. "You obey orders very well," he hissed at James as he tried to gain control of himself. "Even when they tested your nerves by setting fire to Lawrence's church and upset everyone in Harlem, you managed to sneak away so we couldn't see how disturbed you were," De Young snarled to hide the uncertainty in his accusation. "You knew what was happening, didn't you, Brother? Deep in your mind you understood what they were doing to you," De Young cried. "Don't answer. You just go on and don't answer, Brother, because it's not necessary. You don't have to say anything because we've known all about you since the first day you came out of that embassy in Switzerland," he continued rapaciously. "Whatever made you think you had something to tell us?"

James could feel only gasp upon gasp of terror rolling over in him. Mahanti had said the fire was to take place after Miles was dead and he recalled struggling to suppress all of his most honest reactions to it. And now horribly it had emerged again, this time as an intricate factor in the pathology of his failure, a punctuation mark in the mournful chronicle of his years, a standard ministry reflex observation to make sure he was still disoriented.

"Whatever made you think you had something to tell us?" De Young continued in a calmer voice, for he could see James had been stunned by his mixture of fantasy and truth. "Your dossier is thicker than a telephone book," he said peering into James's dazed eyes. "And half of it has come from the ministry."

James nodded and glanced about with a blurred, startled look. He was waiting for a chance to speak, an opportunity to reveal his hatred of the ministry and all it represented. He avoided De Young's keen inquiring eyes and this prompted an angry accusation.

"Now you don't believe me, do you?" De Young said sarcastically. "Well, I can't blame you, Brother. In your place I wouldn't want to hear or believe anything. But the truth is someone in New York has told us all about you. He was very explicit about your orders," De Young said with debonair irony. "Of course, he never intends to see you again, except on television. Dr. Mahanti has gone to Switzerland on international business until things are quiet again in New York. But when he wants to come back, we'll let him. He'll get a visa without questions, just like any other important foreigner. We want the good doctor back in this country because, while we have nothing more to learn from you, Dr. Mahanti has just begun to show us his secrets."

"Mahanti hasn't shown you anything," James came back with surprising fierceness. "I know how he works. I spent years with people who trained him."

"I know all about it," De Young answered hotly, for he was worried because Mahanti's name, which had meant so much to him, had no visible effect on James. "But you know, Brother, unlike Mahanti you're not a free man," he began again with no real intention but to startle James.

"I'm not free," James said, staring at him with a terrible stubborn intensity, "but I want to be free."

"You don't know what you want," De Young said scornfully. James's appearance, almost saintly in its repose, disturbed him greatly.

Momentarily James was silent. Anger and chaos mingled with confusion swept through his mind. Fleetingly he looked at De Young. Words that seemed embarrassing but necessary formed on his tongue and died away. At last he spoke very slowly and seriously, as if he were pleading to be heard. "Brother, Charles, whatever your real name is, please, hear me out. Please, try to understand what I'm saying. I don't want to go free. I want to be free. I want to break away from the idea of what I've become. I want our people to learn from my wanderings and miseries. I want them to see what I've become so they can be different. The idea of what the ministry has made me into must be destroyed."

De Young's eyes widened with animosity and loathing. Now he saw why James was so calm. He trembled with anger and a deep sickening fear. He was ready to kill James for what he'd just said, for making him confront such uncontrolled emotion on such a deep and mysterious level. Only his fierce intuition shielded all the confusion heaving in him as he cried out bitterly, "You're trying to sound like Miles. You're trying to steal his ideas and get my sympathy but sounding like him won't work, Brother," he went on feverishly. "You're not even a miserable imitation."

"I'm not trying to be," James shot back. "Unlike you I never tried to be Miles. Of course, you can never understand that."

"What is there to understand," De Young shouted back in open rage. "Am I supposed to understand you're important because you think you are. Listen, you have nothing to say to me, Brother," De Young snarled. "And the black man out there," he said, pointing excitedly to no place in particular, "knows your story already. He knows all the details. He knows them even if he's never thought about them because your life is not that different from his. Only your pretensions are different. You're trapped in the bottom of a well like a runaway slave. You're confused, Brother. I pity you," De Young cried, relieved now that the extent of his hatred for James as a person and an unfathomable but pathetic extension of Miles had finally been articulated.

But James kept on talking. "If I'm as hopeless as you claim, and maybe I am, then what the hell are you?" he shouted into De Young's face. "What the hell are you?" he repeated viciously.

"A man who is not wanted for two murders," De Young replied with a little smile that was smug and overdramatic.

"I don't deny anything I've done. I can't," James said bravely through nervous lips. "I'm not hiding anything from myself anymore."

"What difference does it make?" De Young replied enigmatically. "No man could really face all the disaster you've created."

"I can," James said staunchly.

"Is that why you beat Clarence Williams to death with your

313

own hands, because you could face everything he told you about yourself and the girl?" De Young inquired, straining now to verify some of the endless conjecture that had streamed through his mind since Miles was killed and everything had turned into a boundless twilight.

"I was hysterical. I had only begun to confront myself," James explained in a voice rounded with emotion. "I was helpless."

"I see. And you're strong now," De Young said quietly, as he watched James for signs of desperation. Strangely he got no reply. James seemed to be drifting away from him, floating off into a calm protective realm he could not fathom and this bothered De Young. He almost believed James was performing some kind of psychological trick the ministry had taught him. Right now he might be drawing into a trained corner of his mind beyond the range of drugs and psychiatry. He'd heard something once about the ministry's experimenting with extreme mental concentration called counterstress principles, which made people into cunning zombies, and the idea ballooned outrageously in his memory. He wanted to turn away, to get help in dealing with the devilish passivity weighing upon James so terribly he appeared in the faded and thin light to nearly resemble one of the elderly Brothers who were kept alive only by the excitement of what Miles might say next. Lake would know what to do with James. He would know how to close down the subterranean metal circuits linking James to his refuge. But De Young could not bring himself to signal Lake even though he knew what transpired was easily visible from the car. Instead he stood there facing James and perspiring, his imagination racing between bafflement and fury, until in one vulgar crystalline instant he was persuaded that once more James was meditating on the peculiar faith he cherished. He believed James had retreated into an abnormal domain where his bizarre values left him insulated and safe.

Quickly he stepped forward and grasped James by the elbow clamping down hard on him with a stern policeman's grip. "You think you're better than everyone else," he said

314

tightly and furiously to James. "You don't know how sad you really are," he went on, speaking rapidly through his own heavy breathing. "But I know. I've seen all the documents Mahanti left for me to read and think about. And I've thought about them because they told me more about you than I ever want to know about any one person. They really frightened me, Brother," De Young said with utter disgust.

Eerily James looked at De Young with blank eyes. He tried to fire some emotion in himself, perhaps a semblance of pity or a trace of fear. But nothing De Young revealed so fervently seemed to touch him. All these stupefying complexities, all these dubious contradictions no longer had any meaning for him. Everything De Young told him was merely a corroboration of what Clarence had sworn to in his pain and confusion.

But De Young could not stop himself, he could not curb the curiosity and bewilderment and disgust flowing from him. He wanted to ask James how he had let himself reach such a state of degradation, but he couldn't do that either. "It was so cruel, so arbitrary the way they handled you," he said heatedly. "It was like seeing someone you know all cut up and dying after an operation that never should have been performed."

James remained still. Through his mind, so active until minutes ago with the hope of life, there now circulated the strong toxic chemicals of death. James doubted if he could escape the hideous conditions of his mangled life. He listened quietly as De Young continued to speak. "And it was all for nothing. We both know that," De Young said too emphatically, for he needed to conceal from James the fact that he did not know and had never known exactly what the ministry planned. "The ministry never could have succeeded because it misunderstood what the death of Miles would mean in this country. They saw chaos, but we know only sorrow, Brother. When a great spirit dies its worshipers are left in twilight," he said piously, striving to forget how much he'd been frightened by Miles's death, striving to keep hidden until the best possible moment the dramatic flourish he now wanted to execute. "Only you made their plans real. Only you gave them hope. You stole away the life of a

315

man better than you, took it away to feed your own weaknesses. I knew you would do it someday. I warned Miles to get rid of you because you were too strange. All you wanted to do was to hide in the work he gave you. But Miles liked you, Brother. Oh, he believed in you. He defended you against me. He never listened to me," De Young said as his voice rose to a pitch of bitterness. "He championed you. And you killed him for it."

James made no move to speak. He had no answer for De Young. Here in this garage, at the shrill end of his confused torment he did not have the will or desire to repudiate De Young. In the energetic coils of his arguments Charles De Young had strangled what was left of his existence. And with Miles dead, with all the oblique fatalistic unspoken beliefs between them dead, with the perverse but ominous bond of loneliness and chaotic individuality between them gone, James did not feel the will to go on. He experienced only a strange guiltless remorse. He listened to Charles De Young speaking very rapidly again in a voice edged with hate. "You killed Clarence Williams in the most savage way a man can die. And even now you're helping to destroy a whole people by your presence. All the people who stood behind Miles and millions more. Whatever you have to say will be used against Miles and all black people. This is all the ministry ever wanted from you," De Young whispered heatedly. "But you must never confess, Brother. Never. Miles would never confess in your place. He would never be that selfish," De Young said carefully as he observed James for subtle changes of gesture or expression that would abet the frenzied notion taking possession of him. He could not know James was thinking only of his rebellion for freedom and meaning, the rebellion he could now see had come too late. De Young had no way of knowing James thought that perhaps this was to be its real significance for other people. Then James felt two powerful hands on his slumped shoulders. Beyond him somewhere he even experienced the reverberation from De Young shaking him violently. And sadly he looked up into De Young's eyes, which to his vague amazement were extremely bright with desperation. De Young shook him again, mouthing words this time, words his mind did not care to interpret. But he could see there was genuine frenzy in the face pressed close to his; an inchoate elemental terror James would never realize came from deep uncertainty, for De Young was as frightened by the fiery emotion between them as he was exhilarated. He understood momentarily, in the midst of the crazed intensity between them, that essentially he might be no better than James. Both of them might as well be eels sealed in a tank and wired for their electric reactions. Or they might be two gladiators dueling for their lives against a background of distant chatter and astonished tittering. The only real difference in them was a test of commitment to different ideals. And De Young was drawn to believe that even if James saw him as despicable and venal, his commitment was stronger. Out of all he'd said to James he grasped that an existence that can be explained and defended, even with blatantly mercenary reasons, is still an existence that is familiar and somewhat safe, a condition far superior to groping for something else or having no existence at all.

And with these thoughts ringing in his head De Young began to attack James with renewed fury. "Don't try to be a greater man in life than Miles is in death," he shouted violently. "You have no hope, Brother. You could only have been a better man when Miles was alive. You're responsible for killing your own hope. And now I have all of Miles's papers, all of his notes, all of his ideas. I own them now. And no one is getting them. No one is going to tarnish them. In the future I will determine what Miles was in the past. Yes, I will," De Young cried, pointing a finger at his chest. "I'll interpret him because he never had enough sense to hear me out. If he had, every black in this country would be under his control, under my control."

Suddenly De Young stopped. His eyes lifted with a strange candid pleasure as he examined James. He spoke more quietly now into the shocked and devastated face opposite him, telling James rapaciously and brightly about the fate of Miles's legacy,

317

relating eagerly how he, as a practicing Brother, would be given the agency assignment to dispose of Brotherhood Hall. "With me in charge, there'll be no investigation, no interference from the outside. I'm a respected Brother.") First he planned to seal the building so there would be no communion with what went on there before. After a decent interval it would be razed and the land sold to developers. Here a slight giddiness played over him at the thought of what he was about to do next. But he understood that to truly prevail over Miles, James, who reminded him of nothing but his doubts and failings, would have to be eliminated.

Cautiously he reached into his jacket and withdrew his revolver from its worn and cracked holster. The lethal weight of the pistol pressed against his sweating palm. His thumb came down on the safety and it was off. He held the comfortingly brutal snub-nosed gun lightly against his trouser leg. James continued to look down repentantly, like a man who was no longer ready to go on suffering. The irrevocable loss of Miles's papers, especially after his brash and maudlin promises to Nicholas for their quick recovery, had hurt him more than anything he could ever remember. Next to him De Young perspired. Intuition warned him he was taking the chance of his life. Then rather deliberately he tapped James on the shoulder with his left hand while simultaneously offering up the pistol under the pair of weary eyes fixed upon it. "If you want to help Miles, if you want to get away from the ministry and everything they've done to you, I offer you this," De Young intoned in a barely audible voice.

"No," came a half-strangled cry. "No."

These words, the first from James in what seemed like hours, startled both men for a second. But somehow De Young kept his voice under control, somehow he continued to sound reasonable and coaxing. "What can you do now, Brother? What can you do now but go on to hurt Beverly and go on to hurt yourself some more. What is life, what is anything to you now?"

In that instant he placed the pistol in James's hand and

trembled with a curious excitement. Both men stared into the glistening depths of each other's eyes, unable to guess at the emotions that shunted between them now. A terrible hyper-stimulating fear told De Young, James was going to shoot him down for his boldness, yet he merely tensed a bit with exhilaration. He spoke to James again in the same vein of insidious dignity. "You have nothing to worry about, Brother. The agency will protect your story. And in doing so we will save you from everything the ministry planned. No one will ever know what your life has been. People will only remember your heroic grief."

During this exchange James fingered the pistol. Vague thoughts of preserving his rebellion here, of saving himself here with yet another murder coursed through him. But the dull metal, beautifully made gun seemed so heavy and useless in his hand. He was ready to throw it away, to send it skittering across the greasy floor and under a car where it could only be found after an arduous search. He didn't see the flush of curious anxiety in De Young's face. Still he knew it was impossible for him to kill again. And so did De Young. Gently and with great concern he took his gun from James as if to put it away. Neither man really knew what was going to happen next, neither man really expected to hear the flat sickeningly explosive sound of a shot; even as De Young viciously jammed the pistol against James's right temple and fired it with both hands, neither man was precisely conscious of what was happening, and so there was no struggle.

Rather casually Charles De Young bent down and fixed his smoking pistol carefully in James's warm and quivering right hand. Behind him he could hear Lake getting out of the car and he went over to the elevator and opened the door. He shouted something about going upstairs to report the suicide and in the shaky reverberation of his voice he saw Lake's hardened and outraged eyes from where he knelt near James; he saw them play scornfully over his elegant figure there in the elevator door and he tried to smile a little. As the small rattling elevator droned upward, De Young suddenly felt sick and envious of James lying down there in the garage with the beautiful calm of a drowned man descending eloquently to the ocean floor.

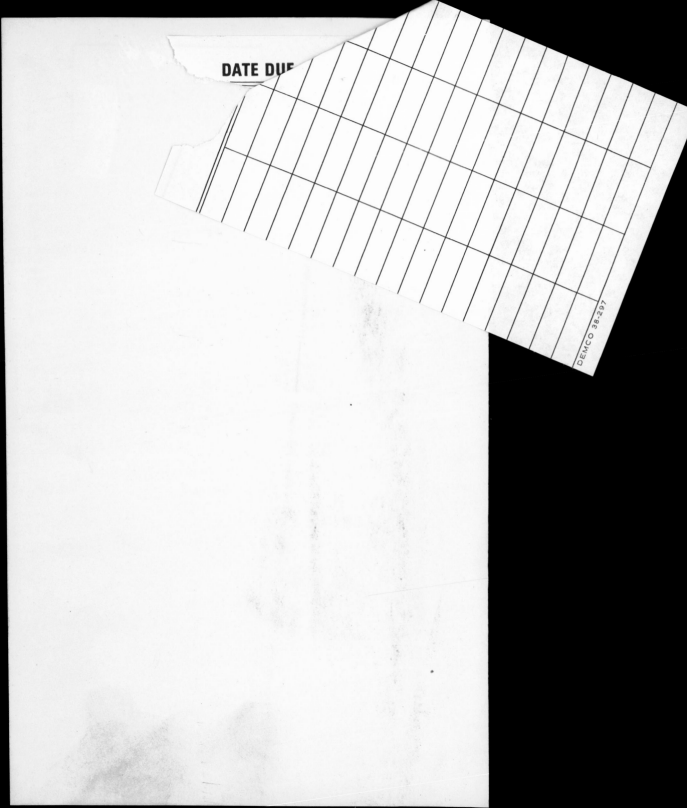